Spaced Out

SPACED OUT

Korissa Allen

ELM HILL

A Division of
HarperCollins Christian Publishing

www.elmhillbooks.com

Spaced Out

Published in Nashville, Tennessee, by Elm Hill, an imprint of Thomas Nelson. Elm Hill and Thomas Nelson are registered trademarks of HarperCollins Christian Publishing, Inc.

Elm Hill titles may be purchased in bulk for educational, business, fund-raising, or sales promotional use. For information, please e-mail SpecialMarkets@ ThomasNelson.com.

Publisher's Note: This novel is a work of fiction. Names, characters, places, and incidents are either products of the author's imagination or used fictitiously. All characters are fictional, and any similarity to people living or dead is purely coincidental.

Library of Congress Cataloging-in-Publication Data

Library of Congress Control Number: 2019953838

ISBN 978-1-400328147 (Paperback)
ISBN 978-1-400328154 (Hardbound)
ISBN 978-1-400328161 (eBook)

For Grandpa Norm and Uncle Barry,
Thank you so much for all of your support and helping me with this project. I couldn't have done it without you!

"You mean to tell me that I can only get half for this? You told me yesterday that I would be able to get full price," I tell the exchange clerk at the front desk. Trading is something I've learned to do over the years, and I've done many trades with him before. This trade, however, was very different from my previous trades. The object sitting in my hand was a one of a kind, Stoneard, very rare to this side of the galaxy.

"Sorry, but my price has gone down," the clerk says flatly. "Besides, I already have my gathering team out searching. I don't need any more, especially something that small. I mean, who would buy *that*?" He says it as if I should be up on the economic policy of Stoneards.

This is a huge setback. I have to pay off the debt I owe to so many people, and this would have paid for all of it, and I would still get to keep some for myself. I was holding up the line though, and I could tell the people behind me were getting restless.

"Fine, I'll just take my business elsewhere," I retort, turning up my chin and walking to the front of the store, with the Stoneard in my hand. I quickly stuff it in my satchel so no one would know I have it. Even though stealing is illegal here, people do it all the time, and usually they don't get caught. The government doesn't care enough to do anything about it. I look at the Stoneard one more time before closing my satchel and the front door of the trading post.

The story is, a long time ago, a diamond star exploded, sending tiny crystals all over the galaxy. A diamond star is one of the rarest stars in the entire galaxy, and they're huge, bigger than entire planets. There are only about 100 of them left in the universe. If you find an entire star, you would get endless fame and fortune. They would name the star after you, and you would control anything within a two thousand-mile radius. The trick is, they're hidden, and they explode often enough that finding one would be like finding a needle in a haystack. But once they explode, they aren't completely useless. The contents from the explosion, Stoneards, are actually very valuable, but I wasn't lucky enough to get a fortune from it. Instead of worrying about it though, I lift my head and trudge through the thick snow blanketing the city of Sacmuntas.

Sacmuntas is the city where I was born eighteen years ago. My father left us to find a Stoneard but never returned. Nobody knows what happened to him. He left when I was eight and my younger brother only three. My mother still lives in the house I was born in, but I left six years ago in search of a Stoneard, like my father did. My mother was very upset when I decided to leave. She cried in her room late at night when she thought no one was listening. I felt bad, but I knew it would be best for my family.

Sacmuntas is also the capital city of the planet Coreno. Coreno is one of the largest, most run-down planets on our side of the galaxy. The government here does nothing to help its citizens. I searched all over Coreno to find Stoneards, but I came up empty-handed, which I guess was no surprise. I traveled to the planet closest to us on the North side, Techario. Techario is known for its well-developed technology. It's a smaller planet, but a lot of people go there for work. It's not much of a living environment, due to a chemical breakout that occurred five years ago.

I finally found a Stoneard on the far side of Techario. I brought it back to Coreno and discovered a trading shop about three miles from my house where my father used to trade. I brought the Stoneard to the trading shop and thought I would get a sack full of Stoneians, which are coins made from Stoneards that we use as money. But I didn't get Stoneians, or anything for that matter, which isn't what I was expecting. Now I have a Stoneard in my satchel, my feet hurt from trudging through snow, and I'm freezing in my thin winter coat. Coreno and Techario have alternating seasons, and I went to Techario in the middle of summer. Looking back, maybe I should have brought a thicker jacket for when I came back here. I decide that maybe I should just go home, surprise my mother, and see my brother again. I make my way to the cleared streets so walking home won't be as treacherous.

Off in the snowy distance, my small country home glows with light from the kitchen, and the window on the second floor above the front door is slightly ajar. My father tried fixing it when I was younger, but it never shut properly. The front porch swing is littered with snow, and the steps seem too icy to walk on. I begin to walk faster and faster, until I'm practically running, which considering the circumstances is pretty much impossible. Before I realize it, I stand in front of the door to my childhood house, the doorknob just in reach, and the heavy snow covering me like a blanket. Finally, I ring the doorbell.

After a couple of seconds, I hear the shuffle of footsteps in the front entryway to the house. The doorknob slowly turns, and the door is being pulled away from me. My brother, who is taller and more muscular than the last time I saw him, appears in the doorway. He has a confused grin on his face that slowly disappears. We stand there, staring at each other for what seems like an eternity, until finally he utters the first words I've heard him say in six years.

"Who are you?" He asks me like this is the determining factor for what he is going to say next. I blink a few times, caught off guard by his question. "Mother, there's someone at the door." He sounds panicked, like he's afraid I might pull out a gun and start shooting. He twists his body but doesn't take his eyes off me.

I hear someone, probably my mother, start walking toward the door, the floorboards creaking with each step. She opens it a little farther, her glare stone-hard, and I almost scream. My father used to tell me that she could scare anyone off just by looking at them with something he liked to call "The Glare." The moment before she came to the door, I thought she would've come out and hugged me and brought me inside the warm house I grew up in and take care of me again, like she did when I was younger. But then reality hits me in the face or, to be more accurate, the door.

"What?" I ask myself out loud. She shut the door, and I'm still out here on the front porch, freezing. I press my ear against the door, to see if I can hear anything. The good thing about the houses in my neighborhood is that all of the walls are paper-thin, and most conversations can be heard by anyone passing by. I used to hate it, but now I don't mind it.

It's not hard to make out what they're saying, but their voices are low enough that I have to strain to hear them. "Mother, who was that? Why didn't you let her in? She's pretty," my brother was saying to my mother.

"She's nobody that concerns you. Just someone I used to know," my mother says sympathetically. She uses the same voice that she used when we were little, the voice that would make her seem less scary, even though she was mad at us. I long for that voice to invite me inside.

I can tell she has missed me and maybe didn't want to shut the door. I realize then that some things are meant to be kept secret. She wants to talk to me, but not in front of my brother. I pace the patio before deciding to sit on the porch swing that has been here since I was little. The wind rocks me slowly back and forth, and I find myself kicking snow to pass the time.

I wonder why my brother doesn't know who I am. He was seven when I left, and most kids have developed memory retention skills before then. He should know who I am, but the blank look on his face when he opened the door told me he doesn't.

I hear the door creak open minutes later and I look over at it but don't stand up. My mother walks out and turns her head to look at me.

She takes slow, careful steps toward me, careful of the snow, careful of me. I see the look of terror in her eyes as she lifts her gaze to mine. I start to stand up, but I'm worried about what she will say.

"I see you've returned," she says briefly to me. "I don't want your brother to know anything about you or why you've come back, understand? It would break his heart if he knew he had a sister but then she died, like your father." I look at the ground. I don't want to see the hurt in her eyes because I know I have caused her pain and loss in the past few years, and I feel guilty that I haven't come back sooner.

"I'm sorry I've been gone for so long," I start. "I wanted to help the family get out of debt. I didn't bring any Stoneians back, because they wouldn't trade for so little."

"Just promise me you will never leave us again," she says, her words rushed and tearful. She turns on her heel and rushes to the door.

"Just one question," I say before she can disappear forever. "Why doesn't he know who I am? He was seven when I left. He should remember me; I haven't been gone *that* long." She stops in the doorway, one arm on the frame as if that's the only thing keeping her from crumbling to the ground in pain and agony. And maybe it is.

She speaks so softly that I have to get closer to hear her. She doesn't want my brother to hear. "We… I didn't want him to know you, only to realize that he was going to lose you. I didn't want him to feel the loss that I felt when I lost your father. So we went to the medical center, and… and… got the Procedure done, the one that makes you forget whatever you need to forget in life. I told the nurses that I didn't want him to remember his father or sister. Normally, they don't let kids fourteen and under get the Procedure done, but I told them it had to be done. They warned me that something could go wrong. He has no memories of you, or your father."

I remember them telling us in school that the Procedure can be given to those who want to have certain memories erased. They inject a purple liquid into your brain and can see all of your memories. Then they delete the ones you tell them to. It's supposed to be for people who were in the war, but they use it pretty freely now.

She's crying now, the tears freezing to her cheeks. She doesn't even make an attempt to wipe them away. That's when I realize she *wants* me to see the pain she has had to suffer through. So I'll know that she's hurt. "Why didn't you do the Procedure too?" I ask in a soft voice.

"I wanted to be able to remember you, in case you came back. That's how much hope I had," she says without glancing back. "You should probably go. I don't want to bring you into your brother's life. It would be too confusing and…" Her voice trails off. I know why, she doesn't want him to hate her for going through with the Procedure.

I grab my satchel off of the swing. "I understand," I say, my tone as cold as the day, and walk down the steps of my old house. I hear the door shut with a squeak and I walk faster. No use in staying around a place I know I'm not wanted.

I walk down the road for what seems like miles. I'm getting nowhere, and my whole body is chilled to the bone. *I just want a cup of hot chocolate, and maybe a heavier coat or even a blanket,* I think. I don't have much money left (four Stoneians that put a frown on my face). I could have had more, if they would have traded with me. The snow is starting to fall quickly, covering the ground and erasing the roads that were clear only moments before. Somehow, it gets even colder, which surprises me. Four Stoneians would get me a meal, if I was lucky.

I lived in a quieter part of town. It was somewhat abandoned; our closest neighbor was one block away. There were houses around us that were once occupied, but everyone left when the houses became too expensive. Our house wasn't really close to anything, except for a tiny restaurant at the end of the street. It was called Rosario's and it always had warm food to eat. I start to head there until I see the light of the OPEN sign turned off. I sigh. Everything is closed, and it's getting darker. With no sun to warm me up, I start to get even colder, which I thought was impossible. I wrap the jacket around me even tighter than before and shiver even more than I already had.

All of a sudden, I hear footsteps behind me, soft but fast. I turn around on my heel, fast enough that I'm surprised I don't get whiplash. I had learned some self-defense moves while I was on my mission to find the Stoneard. I'm about to kick the person behind me when I realize it's my brother. He takes a step back, afraid that I'm going to hurt him. "Sorry, I thought you were someone else," I say in a gentle voice so I don't scare him away.

"It's okay, I'm sorry I scared you," he says back in a quiet voice.

"Scared me? Please, you couldn't hurt a fly," I say in a joking tone. He just looks down at the ground. "So, why are you out here in this weather?" I ask, trying to change the subject. "It's freezing out here. You should be inside."

He glances up at me. "I wanted to talk to you," he says. "I didn't get much of a chance. My mother says she used to know you. Who are you?" I don't know what I should tell him. The truth? But my mother said she didn't want to break his heart. I can tell he's waiting for an answer, but I can't bring myself to tell him the truth. I need to respect my mother's decision.

"I'm just a friend of your mother's. We haven't talked in awhile. You probably don't remember me. I've… been away… on business," I tell him, my voice shaking. I don't know why, but I can't lie to him. I haven't seen him in a long time, but I still remember all of the fun times we had together. I wish he could remember. Some of my favorite memories are from when he was little.

One time, I remember it was bath night. I had already taken my shower and was about to get in bed when my mother called home and told me she would be home late that night and won't be able to give my brother his bath. She told me that *I* needed to give it to him. Reluctantly, I searched the house, finding my brother downstairs playing with blocks and building a castle.

"Kyle, it's time for your bath," I called out to him in a singsongy voice. He looked up at me but kept playing.

"But mother isn't home yet, and I don't want to," he said in a stubborn tone. I walked over to him, and in one quick, smooth motion, I picked him up and carried him upstairs to the bathtub that I already filled with warm, soapy water. The whole time he was kicking and screaming in my ear. I dropped him into the bathtub and grabbed a washcloth and some soap. I started to wash his face while he was trying to break free. But he was really clever. "I want a toy to play with. I'll stop squirming when you get me a toy," he said to me.

"Okay," I said and stood up. I walked out of the bathroom and down the hall to his room to find his favorite toy car. I heard a splash noise and thought, *he's just having fun*, but when I got back to the bathroom, he was gone. *Great, I lost my brother. My mother will kill me!* I thought. Then I walked downstairs and found him in the living room, with soap in his hair. He looked over at me and grinned. I rolled my eyes and walked over to where he sat, playing with his blocks.

"Come on, we're almost done," I told him. He stood up and walked up the stairs. I followed him as he got back into the tub. "You are one silly little boy." He grinned at me with his toothy grin and went back to playing with his toy car.

"Okay. I just wanted you to tell me the truth," he says, now.

"I am telling you the truth. I'm just an old friend of your family," I say.

"My mother lies to me all the time. I think I can tell when someone is lying," he says back to me. *Wow*, I think. *This kid is good.*

"Look, I'm just finding a place to stay for the night. I'd like to get back on my way," I say sternly, my teeth chattering from the cold.

"You can stay with us," he tells me. "Under one condition, tell me the truth about who you are." I can tell he's taunting me. He's still really clever. But I made a silent promise to my mother that I would protect him from the truth.

"I am telling you the truth. But since you don't believe me, I'll just find my own place, on my own," I say with defiance. I know I've won. There's nothing he can say that will make me turn around and come back to my old home with him.

"Fine, I just wanted to get to know my *sister*," he says, and I know that he won. He knows it too. I stop, mid-step, and turn around.

"What did you just say?" I let too much astonishment in my voice.

He looks up at me. "I'm not as stupid as you must think I am. I just said I want to get to know my sister, but apparently she doesn't want to get to know me," he says with sadness in his voice. I don't want to hurt him. How does he know I'm his sister? Did I give it away? Did he always know? He couldn't have, he got the Procedure done. He couldn't remember anything about his past that was erased.

"What have you been told?" I ask him.

"I haven't been told anything. The Procedure didn't work on me." The Procedure didn't work on him? That explains a lot. But how? Then it hits me: people have said that if you're under a certain age, the effects don't work as well. My brother was younger than fourteen at the time. People have said if you're under fourteen, the effects are less strong or sometimes don't even work at all. That must be what happened.

"So, what's my name? What do you know about me?" I ask my brother.

"Your name is Zandrea. I know that you are my sister and you left us when you were twelve. I never knew exactly why you left, but I overheard mother say it was for a Stoneard to help pay off debt and to make us rich," he says confidently.

"You know a lot," I say, choking back a laugh. "Look, I'm sorry. Mother didn't want me to tell you the truth. She didn't want to hurt you. It almost destroyed her the day dad… disappeared. She didn't want it to destroy you if I never came back and you had great memories of me. I'm so sorry," I say, and I mean it.

"Well, it is what it is. I don't blame you for what happened. I know Mother was just trying to protect me," he says. "Come on. I'm cold and Mother is making hot chocolate. I'm so glad I finally found you!" He's so enthusiastic that I don't want to ruin the moment for him by telling him that our mother doesn't want me back at the house. I really don't feel like telling my mother that I told Kyle. He starts to walk away with a bounce in his step.

"I can't come. Mother doesn't want me in the house," I call out to him. He stops walking away from me, all of the happiness drained from his face. The grin that once occupied his face leaves but returns moments later.

"Oh well, once you're inside, she can't get rid of you. Come on, please," he pleads with me for a little while longer and then somehow convinces me to come back with him. As we walk down the slick road, where I almost slip more than once, I begin to realize how nice it would be to have a family again, to sleep in a warm bed and wake up with hot meals.

Kyle pulls me toward the front door, and I begin to feel nervous. My mother told me to leave, and now I'm back. *But it's against your will*, a voice inside my head says. *But it would be nice to be home again, and let's face it, you've wanted to come back. You never wanted to leave. You belong here, and your mother needs to take you back.*

"Are you coming?" my brother asks me. I realize I've been standing on the bottom step for more than enough time. I straighten my back and walk up the rest of the stairs.

My brother rings the doorbell, and I hear slow, concentrated steps, which I can only assume is my mother, coming to the door. For the second time today, I see the doorknob turn and then the door open up slightly, so not to let the wind and snow in. She glances at me, and then at my brother, and then back at me. She gives me a stern look that I can only translate into: *What is he doing outside of the house? Why are you back? I told you to go away and never come back.* I look away.

"Hi Mother! Look who I found, the girl that was on our porch this morning. I figured if you guys are friends, then you should talk," my brother says with fake enthusiasm. I can tell he's covering for me, trying not to get me into trouble.

"Honey, I really don't think it's necessary for her to come. I'll give her a call later," my mother says trying to hide the pain in her voice.

"I brought her all the way back here. And why call her when you can just talk to her now? She's really nice, and Mother, it's freezing outside! Are you just going to let her freeze? That's not what friends do to each other," Kyle says. He looks back at me and winks, so I know that he's making up a story to get me out of trouble. My mother sighs.

"Kyle, go inside and I will talk to her. Can we have a little privacy please?" my mother asks him. Kyle nods and goes into the house, but I know he still listens, until my mother closes the door. "I told you *not* to come back. Why was Kyle with you? What are you doing? I am so confused," she practically screams at me.

"Look, I'm sorry," I say. "I didn't want to come back, and I told him that. He came out and followed me down the street. He told me he wanted me to come back. If you want, I'll tell him. And I will explain that it's not your fault, and you just wanted to protect him. Something tells me he'll understand." I'm thinking back to our conversation a few minutes ago.

She puts her hand up, and I stop speaking. She's considering my argument. "I will think about it. In the meantime… come inside. It is really cold out here, and… I can't let my daughter suffer," she says, her voice quiet. She opens the door and allows me inside.

I take off my cold, wet shoes and leave them by the door. I take a deep breath, because at any moment, all of this could be taken away from me. I smell cookies in the oven and perfume that smells like spring. The house is cleaned, not a speck of dust anywhere, which is what I expected. She always had her house in top shape, no matter what.

I walk into the living room. and I'm immediately surrounded by bright colors that weren't here last time. The couch is new, and the TV is bigger. The biggest difference, though, is all of the pictures hung up around the room. My mother has never liked hanging up pictures. She says it makes the house look too filled up and cluttered. But now, there are pictures of my mother and Kyle all over. Everywhere you look, you can see pictures of them—hugging, smiling, having fun, and laughing.

All of a sudden, I get a sinking feeling. *I abandoned them. They moved on without me. It doesn't even look like they care that I left. But why would they care? I left them on my own terms, not because I had to. Mother doesn't want Kyle to know who I am, but he does anyway. The Procedure didn't work. And mother doesn't know that. And that's why I'm not in these pictures. Or Father. It's too painful.*

"Do you like it? I've been working on it for a while. Kyle has been a big help," she says, while lightly touching one of the picture frames.

"I do. But I thought you didn't like pictures hung up in rooms," I say. "You said it makes the room look cluttered."

She gives me a sad smile. "I've moved on," she says in a very sad and quiet voice, almost like she's ashamed of it now.

"I…" I start to say, but then the doorbell rings. My mother gets a happy smile on her face and walks really fast to the door. She opens the door, and standing there is a tall man. My knees start to shake, which is a sign that I'm scared. I walk around the corner so I don't have to see the man, but I can still hear him.

"Hi, come on in! Kyle, come on down. Chris is here," my mother says in a happy tone. *Chris? Where do I know that name from?* I hear footsteps, slow, coming down the stairs.

"Hi Chris," Kyle says in a small voice. He only gives Kyle a small nod in return.

"Kyle, stay here with… my friend. Chris and I will be back later," my mother says, and then I hear the door shut.

"Zandrea? Where are you?" my brother calls out softly. I step out from behind the corner and see my brother standing there with a small picture frame in his hand. He jumps back a little, scared. "I didn't see you there. Sorry."

"You have some explaining to do. Who is that? Why is he here? Where are they going? What is in your hand…" I have more questions, but my brother cuts me off.

"Whoa, slow down! I can't answer everything all at once." He takes a deep breath and tries again. "Look, all I know is his name is Chris and he's dating Mother. They've been going out for almost a year now. He comes over almost every night and takes Mother out somewhere, and he's super rich. But he doesn't exactly like kids, even though I'm pretty sure he has a son, and that's why I don't like him. He's rude and totally not Mother's type, but I can tell she likes him, so I don't complain. I just want to see her happy, and ever since Father left, it's been really hard for her to get out again. Since she has met him, she's been a lot happier. He said he lost one of his daughters, but something tells me that's not the case." He looks down at the picture in his hand. "This is a picture I found of all of us, before you and Father left. It makes me happy when I get sad and lonely. Mother doesn't know I have it, and I would like to keep it that way, otherwise she'll take it away, and I will have nothing left. I should go put it back."

So mother has a boyfriend now, she changed the color of the walls, she got new furniture, and she hung pictures up around the house like she said she was never going to do. What else has changed?

Mother comes home late, and since she didn't assign me a room or anything, I sit on the couch looking at pictures of my mother and Kyle. I look at one in particular, it's of my mother splashing Kyle with water. His hands rest in front of his face, probably trying to protect himself from the water, but underneath his hands, you can see his bright smile. They both look so happy, and it gives me a feeling that I don't belong. *This is not your home*, a voice inside me says. *You're nothing but a "friend" of your mother's who has missed out on a life you wish you had been a part of.*

After my mother tucks Kyle into bed and kisses him goodnight, she comes downstairs and sits next to me. "Your aunt took that picture. She's really into photography," my mother says to me. I know there is more she wants to talk about, but she's afraid Kyle will overhear. I don't care. I need answers only she can provide.

"Why did you let go of Father? Are we nothing to you anymore? Why has Chris invaded your life and you didn't even bother to tell me? I mean I know I only got here this afternoon, but you could have at least said something about going on a date tonight! I mean he just came without any warning, for me anyway. One second, we're talking, and the next, I'm watching Kyle without any advance! You can't just do that! I haven't been here in six years and you expect me to know everything about your lives." I'm so furious that I can't help yelling at her. I don't care if I wake Kyle. My mother turns from my face to the ground, and I can't help but wonder why no one can look me in the eye.

"It's not that simple," she says finally. "I would have told you, but I didn't know myself. He comes over so often that I have everything ready and I'm always dressed my best. It's tiring, but he's a really great guy. I know you haven't met him, and I didn't tell you I was seeing anyone, but give him a chance, for me. I think he would make a great father for you guys. And no, I haven't forgotten about your father. I think about him everyday, but it's time I get back into the world. It's time I meet new people." She uses her soothing voice I can only assume she uses with Kyle. But I'm not a baby, I'm not three years old. I don't need someone to always be protective and keep me safe.

The only person in my life is me and Kyle. I need to take him under my wing, considering I have lived with him half of the time mother has, and I still know more about his life than she does.

"You know what? I wanted to come back and live here again. I wanted to have somebody to hug me and love me and take care of me. When I was out exploring, I only thought of you and Kyle. I was determined to come back to you guys with a fortune, but I didn't. And Kyle doesn't know who I am or what I'm doing here. I am all alone. And as much as I would like to stay here and get taken care of, I have a life outside of here. And Kyle, I know he doesn't like it here either," I say.

My mother's expression goes from happy to upset. I can tell she was happy when I told her all I thought of was her and Kyle, but I have to tell her the truth. I'm not as happy as I thought I would be.

"I just don't feel welcome like I thought I would," I say quietly. "You didn't run to me with open arms like I imagined. I'm just going to leave, like you wanted in the first place. Kyle will never get to know his older sister."

My mother's expression changes once again from sad to worried. "I… I don't want you to leave. I'm sorry I didn't run to you when you showed up. You have to understand that it has been hard on us too. I'm sorry." I can't blame her. I know I have caused her pain, but that was the past. I'm here, right now, in the flesh. But I know that I'm not wanted.

"I understand," I say and stand up. I start to walk to the door but then stop, turn, and walk upstairs instead. I have to say goodbye to Kyle before I leave.

I haven't been upstairs since I left, but it doesn't look much different. The bathroom is still in the same place, one foot to the right of the stairwell, and my room is next to that. But my room is a storage room now. I walk to where Kyle's room was before I left and find him asleep in the bed. He has clothes all over the floor and toys everywhere you look. I quietly tiptoe over to his bedside and sit on the edge, quietly, so I don't wake him.

"Kyle," I say, my voice hushed. "It's me, Zandrea. I'm so sorry, but I have to leave you. I have to go and live my life. Stay here with Mother, where you're safe. I love you so much, don't ever forget that." Then I slip something under his pillow, next to the picture frame. It's a phone-like device that you can text and call with. I bought a pair for my flying partner slash best friend and I to use on the exploration to find the Stoneard, in case we got lost or separated. I asked for it back, and he was willing to give it up, since his boss was going to give him something better. I have the other one in my satchel. After it's behind the pillow, I stand up, kiss him lightly on his forehead, and walk out of the room.

I take my time getting downstairs, because I catch myself looking at the pictures on the stairway. Most of the pictures are of my mother and Kyle, like the ones downstairs, but in one of the pictures, I see Chris, with his arm around my mother, and she's laughing. There's something about his eyes that bothers me, like I've seen them before, but I can't remember where.

I feel anger boiling up inside of me. I think of a picture I saw once before I left. It was of my parents' wedding. My mother was wearing a golden, silky dress that flowed and came down to her ankles. My dad was wearing a white tuxedo and a red tie. They looked like a couple that everyone else would envy. The only problem: neither my mother nor my father was smiling. It's not like they ever hated each other, or even disliked, but just that they weren't ready, like how my mother isn't ready to let Chris into her life. She's probably doing it so she can forget about everything and try to move on. I wonder if Chris knows about my father. Has Mother told him she lost her husband because he wanted to help the family? *Father could still be alive, and maybe he's out there, and he needs help.*

I walk quietly down the rest of the stairs until I hear the soft laughter of two voices. I stop short. Who else is here? Then the laughter turns to whisper. "Why did she come back? Doesn't she understand that no one wants her here," a deep, scratchy voice whispers.

"I thought so," my mother says. "I don't know why she came back. Especially after all this time. And to make matters worse, she's old enough to get married. That's going to cost money, and that's something I don't have."

"I have an idea," the deep voice says. "My son is coming over tomorrow so he can meet you. He's very excited. I told him that you had a daughter, which he said he would also like to meet. Would that be okay?"

"Sure," my mother says. "I'm sure she would love to meet him. I know I can't wait. Maybe we can arrange something." I can't leave now; I don't want her to see me.

"Yes, he'll be nineteen in three months." I'm sure our children, whether they want to or not, will get along well with each other." The deep voice is back.

"Yes, well, my daughter has already left. I really wanted you to meet her, but she's mad at me right now, and she wants to go and live her own life, one without us. I wish she had never come back. She's making everything more difficult than it needs to be," it's my mother's voice again. Is she talking about me? I'm making things more difficult? She's the one who's turned my life around, from okay to not okay. *That's it. I'm for sure leaving now. There is no way I'm staying here. I'll take Kyle with me....*

I quietly creep back upstairs and into my brother's bedroom. I gently shake him awake. He looks around in confusion until he sees me, sitting on his bed. "We have to go, now," I tell him, my voice hushed but firm.

"Why? I'm too tired. Five more minutes," he says and flips back over.

"We don't have five minutes. We have to go now before she notices," I say.

He flips back over. "What are you talking about? She's going to notice if we leave. The door is right in front of the living room. How are we supposed to get out?"

I look around the room and find a small window on the far wall of the room. He follows my glance and looks out the window.

"No, no, no, and no! There is no way I'm going out through the window. Get that idea out of your head, right now," Kyle says.

I look back at him. "Well, do you have any better ideas?" I ask him. He looks around the room and then down at his shirt.

"No, but it's a crazy idea. I like crazy, sort of. I guess we could try it, even if it fails," he says quietly.

"Good, so do you have any rope or anything at all? I mean, even towels could work. We could, you know, tie them together or something," I say, frantically. He looks up at me like I'm the craziest person alive.

"Yes, as a matter of fact I do, because I just keep a rope in my room," he says sarcastically. "Look, I'm tired, and cold, and would like to get back to sleep. So if you have a plan, let me know, but for now, I'm going back to bed."

"Fine," I say under my breath. "I'll do this myself." I stand up and walk around the room, trying not to step on anything. I find a pile of clothes and blankets on one side of the room and sift through them. I grab enough and start tying them together, making a long chain. Then I open the small window and lower the blankets and clothes down to the snow-covered ground. I wrap the top of the handmade rope around the leg of Kyle's bed.

"Kyle, the rope is secure and ready to climb down," I say in a hushed voice. He turns over and looks at me.

"Why are you doing this? You have a nice warm house now, and it's so cold out there. We'll be safe here," he says.

I roll my eyes. "Come on, we don't have much time." He stands up like he believes me and reaches for something under his bed. A moment later, he pulls out an overstuffed suitcase. He reaches behind his pillow and grabs the picture frame and the device I gave him.

"What's this?" he asks me.

"Oh that. That's a communication device that I used with my partner, in case we got split up or lost. I wanted you to have it, in case we get separated," I tell him. He looks at it and turns it over in his hands.

"Cool," he says with enthusiasm. Then he looks back up at me. "Let's go."

As we climb down the rope made of clothes and reach the ground, I realize this might be harder than I expected. I climb down first to make sure it's safe. There are a couple of dimly lit street lamps across the road from us. That's the only source of light.

"Okay," I softly yell up to Kyle. At first I don't see anything, and I think maybe he chickened out. But a couple of seconds later, Kyle emerges from the window two stories up, clinging to the handmade rope with all his life.

"Come on, you're doing good," I call up to him. "Just don't look down. Look at the pretty snow that's falling." He looks out at the snow and then, for some reason, looks down at me. He's so far up that if he fell at this height, he would die. I push the thought aside.

Kyle secures the rope between his hands and crosses his legs around it. He jumps from the window and swings out, away from the house. If he hits the house, at this speed, he'll fall. I grab the rope to keep him from hitting the house. After he's secure, he slowly lowers himself down the rest of the rope. As soon as he's landed safely on the ground, I grab him by the shoulders and pull him into a hug. A rescue mission failed, not an option. That's what my partner always said.

"Would you let go, I didn't die," he says.

"Sorry," I say and let go.

"It's fine. Now let's get on with this night. I'm cold and kind of hungry," he tells me. I laugh.

"I know a place where we can go," I say. "It's not too far from here. It's where my ship came in before I came to the house." He nods and starts walking. We take a left down the road, the same way I came, and walk toward the landing pad I was at. I check my watch to see what time it is and find it's 3:00 am.

Great, I don't know any place that's open at 3 am. I should have brought some food. At least I have my satchel. If only I could have sold that Stoneard....

"Why are we doing this?" my brother asks.

I roll my eyes. "I'm sorry, but do you really want to stay in that prison cell?" I ask him.

"At least that prison cell had food," Kyle mumbles under his breath. I roll my eyes again and then laugh.

"What's so funny?" he asks me.

"Nothing," I say and laugh some more. He looks down at the ground and kicks some snow. It creates a flurry, and the wind carries it high up into the sky. I laugh again and he looks at me.

"What is so funny?" he practically yells. I stop laughing.

"Nothing. You're just funny. That's nothing bad. At least this trip won't be boring," I say and keep walking.

"Sorry," he says. "Sorry I yelled at you." I look back at him.

"Don't worry about it. I shouldn't laugh at you," I say back. He just smiles up at me, and we continue walking in silence.

The landing pad is only another four blocks up the road. "We have been traveling for almost an hour now," I say as I look down at my watch.

It's not an hour's walk, but we keep stopping because Kyle needs to catch his breath. The walk should only take about twenty minutes, it's only like ten blocks, but I know it can be tiring, especially in the snow and sleet.

It begins to rain, and I realize this is even worse. The rain weighs us down and makes us shiver. I look back at Kyle and realize he's in an even worse condition than me. His lips have turned a shade of blue, and he's shivering a lot. I wish I had thought to bring an extra coat, but in the split-second decision to leave, I didn't think about it.

"You can do it, we're almost there," I yell back to him.

The rain is so loud it's hard to hear anything. He doesn't say anything, probably too cold. I look back at him only to find him on the ground in a heap.

"Kyle!" I scream. He doesn't move and doesn't even make a noise. I run and crouch down beside him. He groans and rolls over. I pull him into a hug, mostly to keep him warm. I stand up, with Kyle still wrapped in my arms, and keep walking.

The rain, which has now turned to sleet, starts blinding me, so I turn my head and keep pressing forward. I still hold Kyle in my arms, mostly to keep us both warm. I feel like if I let go, one of us will be blown away. We only have a few more blocks to go, but I can't see two feet in front of me and keep tripping over snow banks.

I finally see the landing pad only fifty yards away. I know we can make it, we have to, if we want to be warm. They have fires inside the building and food. But they only offer it to people who will pay for a flight. So technically it's not free.

We make it to the landing pad about ten minutes later, and with the sleet out of our eyes, I wipe my face and cup my hands over my cheeks. Kyle and I walk over to the nearest bonfire and sit down to rest or legs. "I'm going to go and get us a flight. I'll be right back," I say to Kyle and walk toward the main office.

The landing pad is huge. It has fourteen hangers for the different ships that come and go. The front office is off to the side of the main landing strip. I open the giant glass and steel door and walk into the small room. The room barely contains a long desk with papers stacked high into the air. There is a chair that sits behind the desk that also holds stacks of papers. On the left side, next to the desk, there is a small chair, outlined in velvet, and next to that, a tall, fake plant that's about three times the size of the chair. I walk in a little further and ring the bell on the desk. "Hello?" I call out. Nobody answers. The main office has a hall on the far side of the room that leads into another bigger room where you can fill out the paperwork to get a flight. I decide to walk back there.

The hall is dark, and I can only see a dimly lit room at the end of the hall. I start to get nervous, even though I've been here before. The man who runs everything here is tall and kind of scary.

The first time I saw him, I almost started crying. But I didn't because I knew he wouldn't take me seriously if I did. I sat up straight, looked him in the eye, said what I needed to, and got out of there. Being the insecure little twelve-year old I was, I couldn't have lasted in that room more than ten minutes. I think he could tell I was a little on the edge, so he spoke in a soothing voice and then told me he would assign me a partner. He pressed a button on the phone that was on his desk.

Then he said, "Daniel, can you come down to my office please? There's someone I'd like you to meet." He grabbed a pile of papers from the drawer of his desk and sorted through them. About five minutes later, a teenaged-looking boy walked into the room. I assumed he was Daniel.

He had shaggy brownish-blonde hair and deep blue eyes. He was tall and had a stocky build, but he wasn't fat. "Ah, Daniel, right on time! Come in, come in! This is the person I'd like you to meet, Zandrea. She is twelve years old and has never flown before. I'd like you to show her the basics," the man had said.

"Sure thing, Mr. Smith. Come on Zandrea, I have lots to show you." Blushing, I stood up and walked out of the room and down the hall that I'm walking in right now.

Thinking back, I think I had a little crush on Daniel. Now, I wish I could see him again. I knock on the door that was slightly open. I push it open a little further and feel a rush of warm air. I begin to step into the room when I hear a voice behind me.

"He's not here. He's out training some teenagers," the voice says. I turn around and immediately recognize the person that stands in front of me.

"Daniel!" I shout out and rush over to him. I stop a few inches away from him. He throws his arms around me. He's three years older than me, so I consider him a big brother. He still smells like oil and clove, his signature scent. He pulls away first.

"What are you doing here? I thought you were going to stay with your family after you gave up trying to sell the Stoneard," he says. I blush slightly.

"I'm running away, with my brother," I answer. "I decided he should come with me and enjoy the galaxy, like I did." He looks up at the ceiling and back at me.

"I told you never to come back. You barely made it out of there alive, and now you want to go back? With your brother?" he asks.

"It's complicated," I say. "I can explain on the way, but I need to get a flight, somewhere away from here. Far away."

We find my brother sleeping next to the fire where I left him by. He's curled up into a ball, with his sweatshirt draped over him like a blanket and his arm as a pillow. I gently shake him awake. He slowly opens his eyes and lifts his head up. "I thought I was dreaming," he says. I know what he means. It was a nightmare the first time I left home and came here too.

"Sorry to disappoint you," I say. "I want you to meet someone. His name is Daniel, and he helped me when I was gone. He'll be helping us escape." Kyle looks from me to Daniel and back to me.

"Why are we escaping? I like it here," he complains.

"It's not what you think it is," Daniel explains. "Sacmuntas is not how most people imagine it. Coreno, and many other planets in the galaxy, has been at war with a group of people called the Intergalactic Corps for as long as I can remember, and the government here is doing nothing about it. Before you know it, everyone and everything you know won't be here. Your mother, she won't be the mother you know. We have to get out of here before it's too late."

"Then we should bring Mother with us," Kyle says. "It's only fair. She raised us, and you think we should just leave her behind?"

"No, you're right, it is wrong to leave her behind, but she has already turned into one of them," I explain. "We can't risk it. We'll come back for her, but unless we can free her from the Corps' spell, she has to stay." Kyle's expression goes from horrified to scared. I wish it didn't have to be this way. I don't want him growing up with fear the only word in his vocabulary.

"We can try to change her back," Kyle says, his voice shaking.

"The only way to do that is by going to Vulcona and stopping the war from the inside of the Corps' headquarters. That's the only way to get our mother back," I say.

Kyle brightens up a little at that and pulls his jacket around him.

"Daniel," I say. "Can you get us a flight out of here?"

"Yeah, I was going to see what kinds of ships they have left. I'll be right back."

He swiftly walks over to the main office and pulls the door open. I look over at Kyle, who yawns so big I think he might pop an eardrum. "So what do you think of Daniel?" I ask him. He shrugs.

"He's okay, I guess," he says tiredly. "I just wish he wasn't right, you know, about our mother being under some sort of spell, and we have to travel around the galaxy to help her. I just want my mother back, my real mother." He looks back at the fire as I put my arm around him.

"Don't worry, as soon as we defeat the Corps, we'll get Mother back, I promise," I say as I look him straight in the eye. I don't even know where to begin looking, but I know Daniel does, and that's why I need him on this mission. I think bringing Kyle with us is going to make things difficult, because he doesn't seem to want to cooperate. I have to remind him that it's all for our mother. I realize now why she didn't seem like her normal self.

Daniel comes back a couple of minutes later with some papers in his hand. Kyle had fallen back to sleep, his head on my leg and jacket draped over his feet. "I talked to the chief's second-in-command, and he said all we needed to do was sign a few spots and we would be good to go," Daniel says with fake enthusiasm.

"Where does he want us to sign?" I ask. He points to a few different lines. I take a pen out of my satchel and sign the lines that are required. I hand the pen over to Daniel, and he signs as well. We just need one signature from Kyle, but he's fast asleep. I gently shake him, and he stirs. He turns over and sits up.

"Yes?" he asks. I hand him the paper and show him where to sign. He signs his name quickly and sloppily and turns back over.

It's good enough, I just want to get out of here, I think. I hand the papers back to Daniel and he takes them back to the office. I sit there and think about what I'm about to do. I'm leaving again, but this time, I have Kyle with me. I don't feel as bad this time. *It's because of you that your mother has fallen into the hands of the Corps. She would be fine if you never left her and Kyle*, a voice in my head tells me. If Kyle ever found out it was because of me that our mother has fallen into the Corps' trap, he would never forgive me. He wouldn't be able to bring himself to do so. I may not have seen him in a while, but I know Kyle. And I know that if the roles were reversed, I wouldn't be able to forgive him.

Daniel comes back with the second-in-command. They stop right in front of us.

"Are these the people you're going to take?" asks the second-in-command. He has a deep voice, kind of like the chief's.

"Yes. This is Zandrea, and that over there is Kyle. I need one of your ships to take us away from here," Daniel answers. The man looks at me, as if he recognizes me.

"I've seen you before. I don't know where though," the man says to me.

"I've been here before. I just got back yesterday. I left six years ago," I say.

"Still doesn't ring a bell. Anyway, come with me. I have your ship all ready to go," the man says. Daniel looks at me and shrugs.

I wake Kyle up again, but this time he looks mad. "Stop waking me up," he yells.

"Kyle, it's time. We have to leave. You can sleep on the ship," I say. He stands up and grabs his backpack and jacket, a scowl still on his face. We follow Daniel around the corner to another part of the landing pad. This is where the ships are stored and stay until someone wants to fly one out like us. The man leads us down to the fifth hanger and goes inside. There are a few people in the hanger already. One of them looks up to see the second-in-command walk in. He dries his hands off on his pants and walks over.

The second-in-command starts explaining the situation to the other man. The other man nods his head and yells something over to the rest of his crew. The second-in-command walks back over to us. "These men are just readying the ship. They should be done in five minutes," he says.

"That's fine," Daniel says. The man walks away, back toward the main office.

"It's so big," Kyle says in astonishment. He looks all around him.

"Yeah, no kidding," I say and follow his gaze to a ship that's about to land on the runway. As soon as the ship lands, three men jump out of the door, and a team of cleaners jump inside and find a hangar for the ship. I look back over to Daniel, who is now talking to one of the workers that was cleaning the ship we are about to use. The worker walks away and Daniel walks toward us.

"He said the ship is ready for us. We can get on, and I'll show you how to work the controls," he says.

"But I already know how to," I say.

"These are slightly different," he says.

He's not kidding. The ship is slightly bigger than the ones I'm used to flying. This one is meant for four people instead of only two.

Kyle and I board the ship and he takes his seat in the back. I set my stuff down in the seat next to Kyle and go up to the cockpit for my training lesson. Daniel takes the seat next to me a few minutes later. For the next ten minutes, I learn about all of the controls and buttons and whistles. After my training lesson, Daniel gets out of the ship and goes to find the second-in-command.

"Are you excited?" I ask Kyle. He shrugs.

"Mother always said to never leave her side. That's what I'm doing right now. I didn't ask to be here. I can stay and keep her company," Kyle says.

"You can come with us or stay here with Mother, but just know that we need you on this mission. It isn't safe for you to be here with her, and without you, we can't bring down the Corps. The mission won't be a success," I say, almost cheerful. He just shrugs again.

Daniel comes back five minutes later with the second-in-command, and he gives us the all clear to go. *Finally*, I think. *Finally we can go.* Daniel puts the ship in drive and steers the ship down the runway. There's the sound of engines whirring, and before I know it, we're launched into the nothingness of space.

"Our route is from here, and then we head to Techario where we will fuel up and then head back out," Daniel says. I nod and look back at Kyle, who has fallen asleep.

"I feel bad," I say. "I didn't give him a choice. I didn't ask his opinion on anything. I basically kidnapped him." Daniel looks over at me.

"You're doing the right thing. Plus, he needs to get out in the world. He'll have so much fun!" *Yeah, that's what I'm afraid about.*

We stop on Techario about a half hour later. It's cold there as well, even though it's the middle of summer. Daniel jumps out of the ship and goes into a little convenience store to ask about fuel prices. I hear Kyle stir and then moan. "No, no. Don't take her. Take me instead. No," Kyle says in his sleep. I climb to the back and shake him awake. He sits up fast and almost hits his head on a low-lying bar.

"Are you okay?" I ask.

"I was dreaming that they took Mother with them to the Corps, and there was nothing I could do to stop them," he says, frantic. I pull him into a tight hug.

"Don't worry," I whisper. "As long as you help with the mission, no one will take Mother." I hear his breathing slow down, but I can tell he's still worried.

Daniel comes back a little later with some news. "I asked the man that worked in there where the Corps' headquarters is, and he said we have to go to Vulcona. He said it might take a few days to get there, so we need to get going right away." I get in the front seat, next to Daniel. We shoot off into space again and head toward Vulcona.

Four days later, we arrive in Vulcona with barely enough fuel to go any further. Vulcona is the industrial planet in our solar system. They have a really nice landing pad station, complete with 200 hangars and a heated runway to prevent ice damage.

As soon as we pull into the station, a cleanup crew helps us get out and then jumps in to clean out the ship so it can be used for other people. Daniel leads us to the main office so we can check in. I hold Kyle's hand, making sure I don't lose him.

Daniel opens the door for Kyle and me, and we take a seat in the comfy, velvet chairs that line the wall. The room is much bigger than the main office on Coreno's landing pad. The ceiling is much higher, and the desk isn't as crowded. The office here doesn't have a little hallway that leads to another room, though.

On the right side of Daniel sits a girl I think I know. She looks to be about eighteen, like me. She's really pretty, with long brown hair and light pink cheeks. She keeps trying to put her hand on top of Daniel's, like she's flirting with him or something. Daniel looks down at her hand and smiles, and I get this knot in the pit of my stomach. Almost like I'm jealous, but I'm not. I don't have a crush on Daniel anymore, or so I think….

A few minutes later, a really tall, skinny man walks through the front door and looks us all in the eye. I see Kyle squirm in his seat next to me. "Sorry about the wait. My wife likes to talk, a lot," he says. "Anyways, let's get down to business. My name is Andrew and I will be helping you, so your stay is more enjoyable. Who would like to go first? Come on, don't be shy! I promise I don't bite." He says it with fake cheer in his voice, like he's done this a million times. The girl looks over at Daniel.

"We'll go first," Daniel says, and Kyle and I stand up and follow Andrew out of the room.

"So, have any of you traveled before?" Andrew asks.

"I have before," I say. "And so has Daniel. But never here."

"Very nice," he says, his voice distant, as if he really could care less. We stop just before we get to another room across from the main office. "So, which one of you is Daniel?" asks Andrew. Daniel raises his hand and then turns to Kyle and me.

"This is Zandrea and Kyle. They will be helping with this mission," Daniel says. I whip my head around to look at Daniel.

He just told this man about the mission! Why would he do that? He looks over at me, and as if he can read my thoughts, he winks.

"Right! I almost forgot," Andrew says. "You guys are going to the Corps' headquarters. How could I forget?" Daniel laughs, which makes me laugh, but it's my nervous laugh. Andrew opens the door that was behind him and lets us in. A man sits behind a giant desk containing only a small computer and a small stack of paper. "They're here Smith," Andrew says and walks out the door. The man, who I assume is Smith, stands up and looks at us.

"The only people who come in here bring down the Corps," Smith says gruffly.

"Yes, sir. That's why we're here," Daniel says, his voice shaking slightly. Smith walks around the desk and over to where we're standing.

"If you want to bring them down, go to their headquarters," he says, his rough voice edgy and tough. "It's located in the center of Vulcona, in the capital, Irangas. It's in a big building, labeled 'Corps.' But you need a plan, because everyone who has gone in never comes out. So good luck."

Daniel looks at me, his eyes saying: *You can back out now if you want to.* I send him a telepathic message saying: *Don't worry about us.*

"Thank you, sir. We won't disappoint you," I say. He shows us out the door and tells us to go out to the street and take the airbus downtown.

"The airbus should be there in a couple of minutes, but you can stay here and out of the cold," Smith says. We stand next to the door, waiting for the airbus to arrive. It comes three minutes later, and we board. The airbus is pretty full, so we find a seat and let Kyle sit, while Daniel and I stand next to him. The airbus is fast and can get you anywhere on the planet in a day or less, and we arrive in the capital only fifteen minutes later.

The Corps' headquarters is huge and very hard to miss. We walk over to the building and stand below it. There are security guards all around, guarding every side.

"What are you doing? This is private property, unless you have a badge to get in," one of the security guards says to us.

"Sorry, sir. We were just examining this beautiful architectural design," Daniel says. He puts his arm around my waist and his other arm around Kyle's shoulders. "My wife and son and I would like to build a house someday. We were just getting some design ideas." Daniel looks at Kyle and me and winks.

"That's fine, but you must stand behind the yellow line," the guard says. Daniel nods, bows, and gracefully walks away, motioning for us to follow him. I wave at the guard so we don't seem suspicious.

We walk to the park across the street from the Corps' headquarters and find a bench to sit on. The trees around us sway in the cool breeze. A few people walk on the outlined paths near us. They seem peaceful and happy, and I feel a kind of longing panging from my chest.

Daniel drops his arm from Kyle's shoulders but keeps his hand on my waist. Some part of me wishes this was not just an act, but that it was real. *No*, I have to remind myself. *Daniel is just your business partner, and nothing more. Just a friend, who happens to be very cute and nice and… no, stop it! He's just a friend.*

"Let's just act like a normal, happy family of three. I know we look young, but just go along with it," Daniel says.

"Okay," I say. *Trust me Daniel, I won't be pretending to love you.* I decide that even though we are traveling partners, and this is strictly business, I can't help but love him. I'm old enough to be looking for someone, and I guess I didn't have to go far. Daniel is perfect, and he likes to travel like me. Everything I've wanted is right in front of me, and yet I can't seem to reach it.

Daniel tells us the plan: we change our clothes so we look more professional, and we make fake ID badges so we can get past the security. Once we get past them, we take the elevator up to the top floor, where we infiltrate the building and find the secret codes, and release everyone captured.

I like the plan, but what clothes do I have that would look professional? And I couldn't just make fake ID badges without them looking like frauds. I don't think they would buy it. We try it anyway, I mean the worst that could happen would be that they take us inside, which is where we wanted to go in the first place, and lock us up. Kyle thinks the plan will work, which goes to show he has no experience with the Corps.

"Come on, Zandrea. Think about your mother. We can do this, I know we can," Daniel says. If Daniel thinks we can, then why not give it a try. I still don't think it will work, but what choice do we have? We've made it this far, there's no turning back.

Daniel, Kyle, and I walk up to a different security guard and ask for permission to go in. "Do you have an ID?" the guard asks. Daniel shows him the ID badge, and amazingly, he lets us in, without even doing a scan or body search.

"That was easy," Kyle says. *Yeah… too easy*, I think.

We walk in, and immediately it feels like a whole new world. The walls are covered in a lining of golds and silvers, and the ceiling rises up three stories. A golden elevator comes down, but it's not like most elevators I've seen. The elevator goes up, down, left, right, and diagonal, you name it. The desk that stands in front of us is ten times bigger, and less crowded, than the one back at the landing pad on Coreno. The desk is silver, and I can perfectly see my reflection. I look tired and not professional at all, but I don't have time to worry about that. I tuck a lock of hair behind my ear.

The tiles on the floor are checkered gold and silver. The whole building is some variation of the colors. Kyle and I both stand in awe and take it all in. Daniel acts like he's been here before, but I can tell he's amazed as well.

A woman stands behind the desk, tapping something on her gold computer. She has straight black hair, with gold and silver highlights which match the rest of the lobby. Her medium-length black, gold, and silver dress is perfectly ironed. Her makeup is minimal but striking.

"Can I help you?" she asks in a monotone voice.

"Yes, we have a meeting on the top floor in a couple of minutes, and we don't want to be late," Daniel says.

"All of you?" she asks in the same voice. Daniel gulps.

"Yes, and we are running behind, so if you wouldn't mind speeding up the process, that would be great." She checks the golden computer on her desk.

"There are no meetings scheduled for today," she says. Daniel gulps again and looks over at me for help. I do some quick thinking and come up with an idea. I smack my head.

"Of course *you* wouldn't know about it. It's a secret meeting, and only the people invited to the meeting know about it. So if you wouldn't mind, we really have to be going. Besides, I don't think you want to lose your *job* because you refused us service," I say. Daniel looks over at me and smiles. I smile back. The woman looks at me.

"My mistake. I guess you do have a meeting today. Please don't tell the boss. I had no idea," she says in a non-monotone voice, as if she finally found some feeling inside of her.

"I won't, but this is the last time you do something like this, understood? Because the boss will be informed the next time something like this happens," I say with authority. She presses a button on her computer, and a gold door opens to reveal a really long hallway with hundreds of doors on each side.

We step into the elevator next to us, but there are so many buttons with numbers and letters to press that I'm not sure which one will take us to the top. Even Daniel seems confused. I want to ask the woman behind the desk, but that would give us away. I press the button that would make the most sense: 102C. I know from studying the Corps that their building goes up 102 stories, and I was guessing that C was the highest letter. As soon as I press the button, we shoot straight up into the air and over three spots. The door opens, and we step out of the elevator on floor 102.

"Where do we go now?" I whisper.

"I don't know. Let's check around the corner," Daniel says. Kyle and I follow him around the corner. This floor seems to be completely blue: light shades to dark. The ceiling allows light to come in, but since the roof is blue stained glass, the light comes in light blue. The walls are a mixture of baby blue and turquoise, and the floor is a navy blue. There are multiple office rooms down a long hall, with each of the doors a different shade of blue. We walk down the hall and stop in front of one of the office rooms. Inside, the carpet is navy and the windows are stained light blue. Each of the chairs is a different blue, and the giant screen in the front of the room is tinted blue.

"Why does each of the floors have a different color?" Kyle asks.

"I don't know. Maybe so the workers can determine what floor they're on," I say, but Daniel stops me.

"No, I think they mean something." I look at him.

"What could they possibly mean?" I ask.

"I read somewhere that a long time ago, a planet on the far side of the galaxy had different colors, based on what tribe you came from. Maybe these colors have to do with where the people come from," Daniel says.

"That's impossible," I say. "The Corps get all of their people from here. On Vulcona. They say it's because they can't trust anyone else, and Vulcona is the center of the galaxy. It's the capital planet. *I* read that they once tried hiring people from other planets, and some of them who got the job hacked into their most secure files and stopped the war for a little while so they could reorganize themselves. They couldn't trust anyone from outside Vulcona."

Daniel rolls his eyes. "Okay, you win. But still, Kyle has a point. What do the colors mean?" I keep walking past the multi-shaded doors toward the giant window on the far end of the hall. To the right of the window, there is a door, painted really dark blue, which reads "Entrance to Roof." I reach for the door handle and then stop.

There's probably some silent alarm that goes off downstairs that will blow our cover. Kyle and Daniel walk up behind me.

"Open it," Kyle says. I shake my head.

"It could set off an alarm, and then we'll get caught. It's too dangerous." I walk away from the door like it's haunting me.

"Fine, then I will," Kyle says, and before I can stop him, he opens the door. Nothing happens. No alarms, at least that I can hear, just a cool breeze from outside. Kyle closes the door. "Oh well. It was getting hot in here anyway." All of a sudden, I hear a little yelp, and I jump. Kyle and Daniel look at me like I'm crazy.

"Did you guys hear that? It was like a yelp or something," I say. Their expressions don't change. "Fine. I'll just have to figure out what it was, by myself." I walk off, but I'm completely lost without them. They must have noticed I didn't know where I was going because they follow me around the corner and then in a circle.

"So, how is finding this 'little sound' of yours going?" Daniel asks, and Kyle giggles.

"It's not funny! Someone could be hurt," I say fiercely, but it's really hard keeping the smile off my face. Kyle has made me laugh since he was a baby, and Daniel jokes around all the time. They both see me holding back my laughter, and we all fall to the navy floor, laughing.

This has probably been the most fun we've had this whole trip, I think.

Everything else has been all serious and boring. After we've calmed down a little bit, I stand up, and I hear the noise again. I think they hear it too. "See, I told you I wasn't hearing things," I say.

"Come on, let's go see if we can find out what it is," Daniel says. We follow him down a hall and then around a corner. The whole building seems really nice and fancy, but I soon find out that I'm wrong. Kyle opens the door to one of the rooms, and inside are a bunch of steel cages, each containing a person inside of them.

"This can't be real," I say. "Why are all of these people here?" All of the people stay quiet. I walk up to one of the cages, with a tired-looking woman inside. She's huddled on the floor, her legs stretched out across the cage. "Excuse me, but do you know what's going on here?" The woman slowly turns her head to look at me.

"No, but ask some other people who have been here longer," the woman says in a creaky voice.

Been here longer? She looks like she's been here decades, with little food or water. I back away from the cage, like it's on fire, and rush over to where Daniel and Kyle stand.

"We have to go talk to the others. I have to know what's going on," I say, my voice panicked and rushed. Daniel puts his arms on my shoulders to calm me down.

"Kyle and I will both help you. Come on, let's not waste a second," Daniel says. We each pick a cage and start talking to the people inside. The first person I choose is an older man with scratches on his face and dried blood on his hands and clothes. He says he's only been here for three weeks and doesn't know why they captured him.

"All I know is, I did something the Corps didn't like, and now I'm in this prison cell," the man said. Next, I went to a cage where a woman sat with two children, a boy and a girl. The children looked fine and unharmed, but the woman was a different story.

Her face and hands were tattered and her clothes were ripped to shreds. She had dried blood covering her hands and face and an opened wound on the side of her head that trickled blood. She was a mess, but she held the children with all the strength she had left. The kids looked to be about five and three years old, not old enough to take care of themselves yet. The kids were playing with each other, but the woman shivered uncontrollably, not like she was cold, but like she was afraid of something. I put my hand on the cage, and she jumps with fright. She looks at me, startled, but then softens her gaze.

"I'm sorry I startled you," I say softly. "Can I ask why you're here? Do you know what is going on?"

She looks away from me. "A couple of years ago, my husband and I got into a fight. A really big one. He started hitting me, and then he threatened to call the Corps on me. He worked for them, the Corps. He could easily have turned any of us in sooner, but as long as I did what he said, he would refrain. One night, I couldn't take it any longer, and I snapped. The Corps came within an hour and took my children and me here. They locked us up in these cages and barely fed us. They turn the temperature way down, especially at night. Sometimes they beat us, if they feel like it," she tells me. I almost start crying.

This poor woman has gone through so much, and I can't even help her. "I'm… I'm so sorry," I choke back the tears, stand up straight, and try again. "We are going to try our best to get you out of here. My team and I are here on a rescue mission." Her eyes widen, and she looks almost giddy. "I have to go talk to them, but I'll be back for you and your children." I walk away and start looking for Kyle and Daniel. I need to let them know that plans have changed, that we'll have to put a pause on helping my mother and help these people instead. I find Daniel, only a couple of yards away, when suddenly I hear a voice.

It's faint, but I can hear it. It sounds close and familiar. I follow the voice for a long time, around many cages and crying people. I don't know how I can hear the voice, or why I'm drawn to it, but it seems to be pulling me like I can't control my own body. Finally, after a couple of minutes, the voice stops. I'm standing in front of a cage with a young man inside, probably in his forties. All of a sudden, I realize why I was drawn to this cage, why the voice lured me here. "Father," I say.

I don't even know how to react; I haven't seen my father in ten years. He doesn't look beaten or hurt, just tired. "How long have you been here? What's going on? How can I help?" The questions just seem to be pouring out; some of the questions I ask don't even matter to me, but I can't stop. My father holds up his hand, and it's as if that motion alone stopped the flow of words coming from my mouth.

"Give me a second," he says. "When you haven't seen someone in ten years, you tend to forget things. But look at you, you've grown to be so beautiful, and talented, with words anyway. I've tried to escape for eight years, hoping I would get to see you and your brother again. Where is he? Who am I kidding, you wouldn't have brought him here. Or would you? It doesn't matter. All that matters is that you're here." He just keeps on rambling, but I stop listening.

I have to figure a way to get him out of here.

"Father, I have to get you out of here. Do you know of any weak spots?" I ask. He nods his head and looks up. At the top of the cage hangs a steel cable. I do some quick thinking and figure out that if I can get up there and unhook the cable, the suspended cage will fall, and I can cut my father loose. I climb the cage to the top and unlatch the cable, sending it falling a couple of feet to the ground. With a loud clang, the bars split open, and my father steps out of the cage.

I run to him with my arms stretched outward toward him. He returns the hug, pulling me close. He doesn't let go for a long time, and neither do I. I let go first with tears in my eyes.

"Come with me. I have some people I want you to meet," I say and lead him around some empty cages toward where I last saw Daniel.

A couple of minutes later, I find Daniel and Kyle at a woman's cage. She's in tears, and I can hear Kyle trying to soothe her.

Daniel sees us first and taps on Kyle's shoulder and then motions over to us. I can see Kyle's face turn from confused to excitement and back to confused.

"Daniel," I say, breathless. "I want you to meet my father. He's also

Kyle's father, but I'm sure he doesn't remember him. Kyle was three when he left."

Daniel immediately sticks out his hand, but my father doesn't return the favor. Instead, he pulls him into a hug. Daniel's facial expression goes from serious to shocked in a matter of seconds. My father pulls away and looks down at Kyle, smiling. Kyle's confusion turns into a huge smile, and I realize he looks exactly like my father. He has hazel eyes and a small nose like my father. He also has the will to help people. I like that about him.

Kyle wraps his arms around my father and holds on for a long time. When they finally release, I can see tears in both of their eyes. I want to start crying as well, but I stay strong for them. I want my father to see how strong I've been all these years. I start to realize how quiet the people around us are, not making any sound.

"Father, why is it so quiet?" I ask. He looks around and realizes I'm right.

"I don't know," he says, but about two seconds later, he knows. "We have to get out of here. It's not safe. Climb one of those ropes over there and wait for my signal." He points to a thin rope a few yards from us that leads up to a platform.

We run over to the ropes and start to climb. Kyle tries to pull himself up but doesn't get very far up the rope. He lets go and falls to the ground, which, thankfully, isn't too far. Daniel, who is already higher than my head, climbs back down and tells Kyle to grab his shoulders. Kyle does as he's told, and Daniel slowly climbs back up the rope. I'm already at the top when they reach the platform we were told to meet at. I look for my father on the ground but don't see anyone. Kyle taps me on the shoulder and points his finger over at the wall across from us.

A large door opens, and some men walk in carrying guns, large guns. They have them pointed at the civilians in the cages, and I can hear the screams of fright from within them. I hear mothers cry and children whimper. I reach for the rope so I can go back down and save the people in the cages, but Daniel puts his hand on my shoulder.

"You can't help them. You'll get shot, and die, and then they will know there are spies in the building and come looking for us. It's too dangerous," he says.

"If I don't go down there, they will kill those innocent people, and I can't let that happen. Not when I can do something," I say fiercely.

"I made a promise to myself to keep both of you safe, and I'm not going back on that promise. I can't let you go," he says. I look back at the people, but I let go of the rope. The best thing I can do now is hope.

My father stays on the ground trying to help the people in the cages. He moves quietly through the rows, silently unlocking the people trapped inside. We watch helplessly from the platform above, in the shadows, waiting for my father's signal. Kyle sits in the corner, with his knees pulled close to his chest. I walk over to him and sit down.

"Hey, are you okay?" I ask. He looks up at me.

"Yeah, I'm fine. It's just weird seeing Father again after all of these years. He's been gone for so long I almost forgot him. How did you remember him after all of these years?" Kyle asks. I look down at my feet and back up to him.

"When I was trying to find you and Daniel, I heard a voice calling my name. I followed it, and I came upon Father's cage. I saw him inside, and I knew right away that it was him. I don't know how I knew, but I did. I guess it was instinct or something," I say. He just nods his head and looks back to his feet. I stand up and walk over to my spot on the edge of the platform, behind some empty barrels and steel beams.

Down on the ground, I see that my father has helped release at least a dozen people. Some of them make their way over to the platform where Daniel, Kyle, and I stand. Some of them wander around aimlessly but don't get caught. The Corps' guards walk around to all of the cages, checking to make sure everyone is where they're supposed to be. I see a woman wandering toward the platform, and I think she's going to make it to the rope, but a Corps' guard comes out from behind a cage and shoots the woman. I close my eyes before he pulls the trigger, but I can still hear the loud *bang*.

I fall to my knees, as if I'm the one who got shot. Daniel rushes to my side to make sure I'm okay. I'm fine physically, but mentally is a different story. I just witnessed a murder, and that is something that can never be erased. I'm crying now, quietly, so no one can hear me. Daniel puts his arms around me, trying to comfort me, but nothing can.

I could have stopped that from happening if I was down there. If I hadn't listened to Daniel, that woman would still be alive. I stop crying. I look over at Daniel. "This is all your fault! If you had let me go down there, she would still be alive right now!" I almost yell but stop before I expose us.

"That's not true, and you know it," he says. "There was nothing you could have done here *or* down there, on the ground. Don't make it my fault. I made a promise and I intend to keep it." I know what he says is the truth; I probably couldn't have saved her no matter where I was. I calm down.

"Still…" I say, but I can't think of anything to say back.

"I know it's upsetting to see someone get killed and not be able to do anything about it, but you have to get past it," he says sympathetically. "The Corps do this kind of thing, and they get away with it, so we need to stop them. Are you with me?"

I look down to where the woman was killed, blood staining the floor, and then back to Daniel. I nod my head. We both stand up and go back to our positions. The guards continue to walk around, finding empty cages. I see a guard a few feet away from my father, and he sees him too. Quickly, gracefully, he moves around the cage and continues moving, releasing people and showing them to safety. A few people make it up the rope and onto the platform, and it starts to get a little crowded. The children have the hardest time getting up, their arms too weak to pull themselves up. Daniel climbs down the rope and helps the children up to the platform. Some of the men help the women and children up the rope.

I keep lookout, to make sure no guards are around. After everyone is on the platform, Daniel climbs up. There's not much room for anyone else. I see a window a few yards above my head, and I try to find a ladder or another rope. If I can find an escape, I'm going for it. I ask Daniel once he gets to the platform, and he thinks it's a good idea. I see my father on the ground, looking around to be sure he got everyone. He gives me a nod when no one is left, and I start helping people up the thin rope I found. Daniel is at the top, grabbing arms and pulling them up. I don't know what's on the other side of the window, or how far down it goes, but I'm guessing Daniel is taking care of it. I see the rope moving, and I know my father is climbing up, but when I look down, my father is nowhere in sight. All I see is a Corps' guard climbing up the rope that leads to the platform where all of us stand.

He's coming quick, and I know I won't be able to find a knife or anything sharp by the time he reaches the top. So instead, I grab one of the steel poles and hide in the shadows. He reaches the top in fifteen seconds and pulls himself on the platform. I slowly step out of the shadows but remain hidden. He looks down, his hands on his knees, and tries to catch his breath. I'm guessing he was running from one end of the building to the other. He stands there, with his breathing slowing down. That's when I hear him utter the first words: "I can see you."

I pull him by the arm, back into the shadows where I thought I could go unseen. "You better start talking *right now*. Who are you and what do you want?" I ask, my voice a fierce whisper. He looks up and into my eyes.

"Why do you care? I'm just trying to do my job," he says.

"*Your job* is to kill or capture people. Why shouldn't I push you off this platform right now? Give me *one* good reason," I say fiercely.

"Because I'm on your side," he says.

A long time ago, before my father left, he would tell me stories of heroes who did great things in their lifetime. The one I always remember, and love the most, is the one about a girl who saves a whole army of people by going undercover. She was a little older than me at the time.

The story is that she dressed as a man, because women weren't allowed in the armed forces. She trained day and night and finally was recruited. They shot down the enemy base, with her on the inside. She set off a bomb that killed the enemy and almost killed her. She made it out just in time, and it wasn't until later that she told the world her secret.

I liked that story because she was a lot like me, never giving up, even when everyone else told her she couldn't do it. I always wished to be like her one day but never had my chance, until now.

Daniel is helping the last few people up the rope as I make my way over to him. My father still hasn't reached the platform, and I have to wait for him. "Let's go, Zandrea! Everyone has made it out," he says. I lean over the edge of the platform, but I still don't see my father. I begin to wonder if the Corps took my father somewhere else. "Zandrea, we have to go before they come back!"

"Hold on! My father's not here yet," I call back.

"We don't have much time. They'll be here any minute. We have to go, *now*," Daniel says.

"Then go without me. I'm not leaving here without my father," I say. "If we leave now, then my mission will be a failure, and I can't let that happen." I know Daniel won't leave me; he told me once that the number one rule of airspace is to never leave a man behind. He can't wait forever, and I know that. *Where are you Father? Why haven't you shown yourself?*

I haven't told Daniel about the Corps' guard I found, but I can see him out of the corner of my eye. I told him to stay in the shadows until I gave him the all clear. I stand up and walk over to him.

"Listen, I know how you can prove yourself. If you go down there, and find my father, and bring him back, you can be part of the team and escape forever. Understand?" I say.

He looks at me. "Yeah, sure. Let's just get this over with. I just want to get out of here." He walks around me and climbs back down the rope, disappearing into the darkness. Daniel walks up behind me.

"Who was that?" he asks casually.

"Nobody, just a guard that climbed up here and wanted to escape with us. He says he's tired of being pushed around. I don't blame him, so I let him join us if he could find my father. So far nothing," I say. Daniel looks down to the ground and sees the guard walking around the cages, his gun pointed in front of him.

"You're very gullible, you know that right?"

"Yeah, I guess."

"Do you think he can do it? I mean, what do we really know about this guy. He could find your father and then kill him. Do you really trust a guy you just met?" he asks. I look over to him, but he's still looking at the ground.

"I trusted you when I first met you," I say. He finally looks at me.

"You didn't exactly have a choice, and neither did I. I didn't choose to be your partner, but I'm glad I am. I would probably regret it if I didn't. You've shown me what it's like to trust someone, and that's hard for me to do," he says. I start to ask why, but then I remember.

His mother and father never got along well. They always fought and never kept their promises. He trusted his mother until she went to work for the Corps, and his father left shortly after that, leaving him all alone. His "friends" made fun of him, and they got him in trouble, a lot. He had a tough childhood, so no wonder he hasn't been able to trust anyone.

I put my hand on his shoulder, but I don't think he notices. Even in the dim light of the building, I can see that his eyes are red. A tear spills over the edge of his eyelid, and he quickly moves his hand to brush it away. He doesn't want me to see him cry, but he trusts me with other things.

"You know you can cry in front of me. You don't always have to be so strong," I say, my voice soothing and calm. He looks up at the ceiling and swallows hard.

"Thank you, but it's not that simple," he says. "Before my father left, he always told me to be strong, for him. Never to show emotion, because that's how we get into danger. That's why people are weak. So, I promised I would stay strong and not let my emotions get in the way of things." He looks back at me and gives me a small, half-hearted smile. I can tell he's tired and just wants a place to rest for a while. We look at each other for a long time, silence filling the void that words never could. I'm about to say something when I hear a voice.

"I hope I'm not interrupting anything, but I found your father," the guard says. "He's over on the far side of the room. I couldn't bring him, he was too heavy." I immediately rush to the rope, Daniel close behind me.

"We'll be right back. It shouldn't take too long," I say and slide down the rope. I hear Daniel land a couple of seconds after me. We start weaving our way around the cages toward the far side of the building. Just before we round the next corner, Daniel puts his arm out to stop me.

"It could easily be a trap. This guy is a Corps' guard. You can't trust him or anything he says," Daniel whispers. I nod my head and continue to move toward where the guard said my father was. I see the far wall, just a few yards away, but I don't see my father. I move slower, but my father is nowhere on this side of the building. By the time I realize this, though, it's too late.

I wake up later in a cold cell, the walls and floors tinted a light green. I figure this is the green floor. I hear Daniel moaning across the hall from me, and I see he's tied to a post. I try to reach out for him, but I realize I'm tied to a post as well. I twist and turn hoping to get free, but the shackles pull me down. *It's pointless to put us in shackles if we can't go anywhere.* I sit still, hoping someone will come, but no one does.

If you hadn't listened to that guard, you would still be out there. You should have looked for yourself, but instead you trusted a Corps' guard. Who knows what happened to the people we rescued.

"It's not your fault," Daniel says. "He was very convincing." I roll my eyes.

"It *is* my fault," I say. "You can't trust a Corps' guard, no matter how convincing he is. Our rescue mission was a fail. The worst part is, we could have saved them, everyone in those cages, but we let them down. *I* let them down."

"Maybe Kyle can help them," Daniel says.

Kyle! I totally forgot about him! Where is he? Did he make it out? Does he know we're gone? I start moving around again, trying to break free from the shackles.

"Forget it, Zandrea. You can't get out, I've tried. Either wait for someone to come, or think of something else, but no one can hear us."

No, the Corps can't hear us, but Kyle can.... I fall to my side and flop around like a fish. "What are you doing?" Daniel asks. Finally, my walkie-talkie falls out of my satchel, and I wonder why they didn't take it. I press the 'talk' button with my foot and start talking.

"Kyle," I whisper. "Kyle, can you read me?" Static. Silence. I'm about to press the 'talk' button again when I hear a quiet voice break the silence.

"Hello? Zandrea? Where are you?" Kyle asks. I have no idea where I am.

"Um… we're in some kind of cell," I say. "I'm not sure where, though. They hit us and caused us to blackout." Daniel looks at the ceiling, and I realize that there are numbers on the cell. "I'm in cell number 22, and I think Daniel is in 23. Can you come and get us?" I ask.

"I'll try my best, but these areas are guarded well. I might have to take a different route. Hold on, I'm coming," Kyle says and then I hear more static. I'm happy I got through when I did, because any later and I would have been out cold.

I wake up to screams, faint but clear. They stop and then get louder. I look over to Daniel, kicking and screaming in his sleep. *He's having another nightmare, his fifth one this trip.* "Daniel! It's just a dream, it's not real," I yell across the hall. He still thrashes, but he's calmed down. He slowly starts to wake up, trembling. I hope Kyle gets here soon. If they keep knocking us out, Daniel is going to keep having the same nightmare.

Back when we started our first mission, when I was twelve, Daniel woke up frequently in the night screaming. From my corner in the far back of the ship, I could understand that this was no ordinary nightmare. The next morning I asked him what caused him to scream like that, but he just said, "Sometimes, dreams are your reality." I left it at that, not wanting to pry. Later, he told me what the real reason was.

"My mother was killed right in front of me," he once told me. "She went against the Corps, and they threatened to kill her. They found us. There was nothing I could do but stand there and hope someone heard my screams. The murderer left right away before the city military got there, but he didn't wear a mask. I saw every detail of his face, and I will never forget it."

"My father came home an hour later, and he was upset. He asked me what happened and I told him mother let a man in the house. At first they were laughing and talking, but then something happened, and the next thing I knew, he dragged my mother out to the living room and shot her in the head. I didn't even move, I just stood there and wished her to be alive again. I screamed when she didn't move. My father gave her body to the city military, and we never heard from them again. He married some lady right away, because in my neighborhood, if you weren't married, you could get relocated, by yourself. They fought all the time, and after they got divorced, she went to work for the Corps. My father couldn't live in the house anymore, because he wasn't married, and he had to leave me all alone. I was eight at the time. The memories keep coming back to haunt me." I never mention his past. The thought of it is too traumatic, and I don't want to be the cause of his pain.

They bring us a small portion of food that I only eat about two bites of. Daniel on the other hand doesn't eat any of it. He pushes it away. "We can't give into them. We have to stay strong or die in the process," he says.

I'm not going to die of starvation; it's too slow and painful. I'm not strong like Daniel or even Kyle. He was there all of these years, waiting for me to come back. I came, but it was too late. Mother had moved on, but so did I.... Static. My walkie-talkie is making noise. I scramble to try and find the 'talk' button. I hear Kyle's voice trying to break through the static.

"I... think... found... guys..." Kyle says. It's hard to understand, but I can gather the fact that he found us. But where is he? Why isn't he here yet?

I press the 'talk' button. "Kyle, can you hear me? Where are you?" I say and let up. More static. The silence is unbearable, and it takes all of my strength not to scream out his name. A guard comes around the corner, and I quickly kick my walkie-talkie behind me so he can't see it. I look up to make it seem like I'm looking at something interesting, but the guard walks past without even acknowledging either of us. Looking up wasn't a complete waste of time, though, because that's when I see it, a camera in the corner of the cell, moving up and down.

Kyle and I used to play this game, where one person would be look-out and the other would write things down. Kyle was always the lookout because he didn't know how to write yet. Every time something would happen that I needed to write down, he would nod his head. That told me to get ready to write something down. The camera moving up and down is a signal to me that he's looking at something important. I almost scream with excitement, but remember to stay undercover.

"Daniel," I say and he looks over at me. "Kyle is in the camera. He sees us, and he's coming." My tone of voice is almost gleeful. He nods his head and tries to move. I don't know if Kyle can hear us, but I talk to him anyway. I still look at Daniel, so not to get caught, but my words are for my brother only. "Come save us." But Kyle is not the only one who can hear me.

My walkie-talkie comes to life again, but this time there's no static and no Kyle. "I did what I had to do. Kyle's coming to save you, though," the voice says. "Your father is with us, back on the platform. Don't worry, he's fine." The guard who deceived us. Now he wants to help us again. Why does he have the other walkie-talkie? Did Kyle give it to him? Or did he steal it? My questions get answered quickly, because Kyle comes casually walking down the corridor. He unlocks the cell door and breaks off my handcuffs.

"What took you so long," I say with a laugh. He unlocks Daniel's door as well, and we walk down the long corridor the same direction he came from. Cell after cell line the wall, and I begin to think we will never make it to the end. A few minutes later, Kyle opens a door that leads down a spiral staircase and back into the room full of cages. We carefully run across to the platform and climb the rope, once again.

The first thing I notice is the ship full of the now uncaged people is gone. They must have finished loading while we were gone. I scan the area to see if anyone is left and find my father sitting on one of the steel poles. He looks worn out, and sweat drips from his forehead. I run over to him immediately and wrap my arms around his neck. "I was looking all over for you, but then I fell into a trap and…" My father cuts me off.

"I'm just glad you're here now," he says dismissively. "I've missed you, and Kyle has been a big help. He gave that guard the walkie-talkie so he could get in touch with you. I think there's better reception out here anyway." My arms stay wrapped around him for awhile, but I pull away because I feel a tap on my shoulder. I turn around and see the Corps' guard standing there, with the walkie-talkie in his hand. My fists clench immediately, ready to swing a punch, but he stands there, seeming defenseless and tired.

"Can I talk to you?" he asks me, his voice quiet. I nod, glancing at my father, who nods his head approvingly. He leads me over to a corner of the platform.

"What?" I ask, annoyed. I'm still mad about the walkie-talkie and the abandoning.

"I'm… sorry for lying about your father. I didn't have a choice," the guard begins. "They said they would kill all of you, and I couldn't let that happen. That's why I told your brother, and he knew how to get past the guards. I had to get security entrance so he could get to the camera booth. Your brother gave me his walkie-talkie so I could communicate with you. They cut off signals in booth, so there was no way for him to contact you. He thought I could if necessary." He's talking a mile a minute. I look over to my father, but he's talking to Daniel.

"What happened to all of the people trying to escape? Did you deceive them too?" I ask, my tone fiery. I'm not about to forgive him. He allowed for me to trust him and then turned against me. Why should I trust what he says now?

"No, of course not," he says. "I called for some airships and they took them to their hometowns. I told you, I did what I had to do." I look down at my mud-stained shoes and wonder how I ever got in here.

I should've pushed him off the platform when I had the chance, I think. *He works for the Corps. He's a bad guy. We're supposed to be against anyone who works for the Corps, and yet, he saved Daniel and me. He came back for us. The Corps never do that, unless they don't work for the Corps....* I look back at him.

People from Vulcona usually have dark brown hair and dark eyes. The guard has light brown hair and blue-green eyes. All the Corps' guards and workers were born on, and lived in, Vulcona their whole lives. "Who are you?" I ask without really thinking. I don't think he was expecting that question, and to be honest neither was I. Confusion takes over his blank expression.

"I... um... well... I'm a Corps' guard," he says and gestures toward his uniform.

"No, I mean what's your name, where do you come from, why do you want to escape, those kinds of things," I say.

"I'm Kelton, Kelton Brown," he says surprisingly fast. "I'm not from here, but I came here one day and stole a uniform. I was going undercover, like you, but they caught me and turned me into one of their soldiers. I've tried to escape many times, but they found me and tortured me until I agreed never to try and escape again. You would've thought that after a couple of escape fails I would have learned my lesson, but I will never stop trying to get away from this place. It's evil, they're evil, and they will stop at nothing to get what they want: total domination of the entire galaxy," he says.

Now I have *to trust him. He wants to stop them just as much as we do, maybe more. He didn't even start out as a Corps' guard, just going undercover and happened to get caught.* "You do understand that if you *dare* lie to me, I will kill you on the spot. You have to earn my trust back, and that's not easy. I trusted you, and you stabbed me in the back. Thankfully not literally," I say and almost start laughing, but I stop myself. He giggles nervously, which makes it even harder to hold back *my* giggles. Finally, I give in. He sort of snorts when he laughs, which just makes me laugh even harder. I look over to where Daniel and my father were talking, and they both look at us like we've gone insane.

Maybe it's not that hard for me to trust him, but I can't let my guard down that easy. Stay strong, Daniel once told me. I've been trying to, but it's hard. My mother gave up on me, I just saw my father for the first time in ten years, and trusting is something I have always been able to do easily. Now that I can't even trust my own mother, all of my assurance has been shattered. Except for Daniel and Kyle, and I haven't been around my father enough to completely trust him either.

Kelton looks at me and then looks at his feet. He pushes his shaggy brown hair out of his eyes. "Oh, I almost forgot," he says and hands me the walkie-talkie.

"Thank you," I say. "But it belongs to Kyle, my brother. He's probably wondering what happened to it." Kelton walks over to where Kyle sits by the window, and I go over to Daniel and my father. I could tell they were just laughing at something really funny. They both look at me like they're expecting a big announcement or something.

"What did *he* have to say?" Daniel asks. He sounds annoyed, and I can almost hear a hint of jealousy in his voice, but I don't know why he would sound like that.

"He just wanted to apologize for earlier and tell me his backstory. He says he's been trying to escape, but every time he tried, they caught him and tortured him. What were you guys talking about?" I ask.

"Zandrea, I think Daniel has something he needs to tell you," my father says. I turn toward Daniel, and a slow smile creeps across his face.

"Yes?" I ask. He looks at my father, and he nods. Daniel grabs my hand and leads me over to another corner of the platform. I'm pretty sure corners and big announcements are associated with each other somehow. "Yes?" I ask again.

"Um, there's something I've been meaning to tell you," he says, his voice rushed. "I've been too scared and nervous to ask before, but your father approves."

"What is it?" I ask. He takes a deep breath.

"Well, I've been thinking about this for a while, actually. I mean not too long, just awhile, and I figured now is a better time than any and-"

"Daniel, just say it."

"Will you marry me?" he asks.

The law in our part of the galaxy is no romantic social interaction before marriage. In other sides of the galaxy, you can, and are required to, but here in the North Galaxy, you are not allowed to interact romantically.

If a boy asks you to marry him, and you are of age and your parents agree, you must marry him. Another condition is you must be married by age thirty, or something bad, like maybe execution, could happen. I haven't heard of that happening to anyone, so I wouldn't know, and they don't tell you the punishment either. I guess I'll never know....

I look at him, my eyes gleaming, as a huge smile spreads across my face. I have been waiting for this moment since I first met him. I never thought it would happen, though. I'm lucky he's only three years older than me, otherwise I wouldn't be able to marry him. There are lots of restrictions here, because of past experiences. If the person is four years older or more, it's considered against the law and you can be penalized. Execution is one of the most popular ways to punish someone. Daniel is perfect, and I've known that since the beginning.

"So, what's your answer?" he asks.

"Of course! Like that's even a question," I say. "*I've* been waiting forever. I'm glad we finally found my father." He smiles.

I've heard of people giving jewels and Stoneards as gifts for engagement, but I've never really been into that kind of thing. Daniel knows that. Once we get back, we'll go to the House and make everything official.

The House is a giant building in Sacmuntas where people go to get married, sentenced to prison, sign up for jobs, and even buy food. Every month, one person from each home must go to the House and receive a portion of food for each person in the household. Once, someone took more than they should have, and they were shot on site, in front of everyone. People were terrified, and no one wanted to come back, but you couldn't have bought the food anywhere else. They do that on purpose, so either you starve or come and take your exact portions.

Daniel takes my hand, kisses it, and walks away. Kyle sits by my father, so I know he will find out soon enough. I practically skip over to Kelton and almost give him a heart attack.

"You scared me, I didn't see you coming," he says and then giggles.

"Guess what?" I ask him. *This is the first time someone has made me feel giddy and happy in a long time. I don't want this feeling to ever end....*

"What?" he asks. I forgot I asked him a question.

"Daniel, you know the guy over there, asked me to marry him, and I said yes!" I say and start jumping up and down. I feel like a little girl again, jumping because I'm happy, which I haven't done in a long time. It's like the time when I found out I was going to have a baby brother.

I don't know why I tell him this information, or why he would even care, but I see the look on his face that erases all of my happiness. His expression is somewhere between mad and sad. I stop jumping and my smile fades like an old memory.

"You don't seem happy about it," I say. He looks away, and for some reason, I feel like crying. I don't know why I want his approval, even for him to be happy for me, but it feels like something is missing.

"I didn't know…" he trails off.

"What? What don't you know?" I ask.

"Never mind, it's stupid. Love is stupid and worthless and disappointing. Why do people love other people? What's the point? You end up getting your heart broken in the end, and then you know it was all for nothing. Just forget I even said anything." He walks away, leaving me alone with my swarming questions.

Love is stupid? Worthless? Disappointing? What's that supposed to mean? Why does he think that? He has no reason to be mad at me! I'm so confused right now. I can't even feel happy about my own engagement. I march over to where he stands, looking down at the ground far below, rope in his hand.

"We need to talk, *right now*," I say, and I think I startled him, because he jumps back a little.

"I told you to forget about it, okay," Kelton says defensively.

"How can I when you stole every bit of happiness I've felt in a long time? I haven't been able to smile, without someone taking it away. Besides Daniel, I'm the one who's felt the most pain around here. So you better explain yourself, because I'm *not* fooling around." I'm practically shouting at him. I want him to know I'm serious.

He takes a deep breath and looks me in the eye. His bluish-green eyes turn sad. "You don't want to know. If you want to remain happy for the rest of your life, it's better I don't tell you."

My glare hardens, which I didn't think was possible. "I don't care, I want you to tell me," I say. "I'm already miserable from your little outburst." He takes another deep breath.

"I'm too late," he says. "Too late to win your heart."

I almost fall off the platform. It couldn't have been a worse time for him to tell me that. To tell me that he's in love with me. I think I start to fall, because he grabs my hand and pulls me away from the platform.

"I told you, you wouldn't want to know," he says, sighing in a way that makes me think I should've just listened to him.

"No," I say, steadying myself with the help of his hand. "I'm glad you told me. But why didn't you tell me sooner?" He just looks down at the ground.

"I knew Daniel loved you, I mean it was obvious, and I knew that since you guys had known each other for so long, you would obviously choose him over me. It would have made things awkward between us, not that we even know each other, and I didn't want that to happen. I'm sorry, I just didn't know I had no time left to tell you."

I look over to where Daniel is talking with Kyle, wondering what he would think of all this. "It's just, I barely even know you," I say quietly. I finally make eye contact with him, the blue in his eyes like water, pulling me in. "And you barely know us. Besides the fact that you lied to us and captured us, and the only thing I know about your past is you came here to steal something and got caught." I almost start yelling at him. I take a deep breath and try again. "My point is, if things were to ever work out, I would need to know a lot more about you. I would have to be able to trust you. I trust Daniel and know lots about him. That's why I said yes to him." I can't believe I'm even entertaining the idea of being with him.

Kelton still doesn't look me in the eye. He knows I'm right, which gives me a hint to his personality. *He doesn't like to admit that he's wrong. Why?* I almost ask the question out loud but refrain. *He's probably stubborn, like my father or Daniel....* I realize my list could be a mile long with how many stubborn people I know.

"My mother hated my father, and vise versa," Kelton begins. "They only got married because they would've both turned thirty within the next couple of months. They fought, and sometimes it got violent. My mother always cared for me, but my father hated me. It was because he knew he had to share me with her. He never acknowledged me or even cared that I existed. I was fine with that, considering how mean he was to my mother."

"One day, I left home. I overheard some kids at my school say they were going to join the Rebel Base. The Rebel Base stopped anything that was Corps-related. I wanted to join, because then we wouldn't have all of those stupid laws."

He takes a breath, as if telling his story was harder work than running five miles. "So I joined, hoping that my parents would separate and I would never have to see my father again. I went to their base and signed up. The age requirement was fourteen years old, and, thank goodness, I had just turned fourteen the month before. A week later, we all got assigned our first mission, and mine was to go to the Corps' headquarters and steal one of the uniforms so they could make a copy of it. The idea was they would act like a Corps' guard and infiltrate the building. It was a brilliant plan, but I wasn't the one for the job."

He stops and waits for a reaction, but when I don't do anything, he continues. "They caught me within minutes after I got there. The mission was a failure. Everyone who was on the ship with me was either tortured or killed. Sometimes both. I knew it was all my fault, and I could never forgive myself. That's why I have to escape and get back to the base so I can explain what went wrong all of those years ago. And I need your help to get out of here. I know you don't trust me, and you have reason not to, but I don't exactly have a reason to trust you either." There's something about that question that makes me mad.

He lied to us and got us knocked out and thrown in cells, and he doesn't trust me? *I haven't done anything to him that would cause him not to trust me.* "You told me you loved me. How can you love someone you don't trust?" I ask.

"I trust you. I just want to know why I should."

"I haven't done anything that should cause your trust to falter," I say angrily.

"Look, I know you love Daniel, and there's nothing I can do about that, but if you let me prove to you that I can be trustworthy, I will," he says and once again walks away, as if somehow that's going to end the conversation. I have a million questions I want to ask him, but....

"What was *that* all about?" I hear Daniel say from behind me. I turn around and immediately feel tension between us that wasn't there before. *He shouldn't be mad at you. First, because he doesn't know what was said, and second, because even if he did hear, it's not like I love Kelton back, right?*

"Oh, I was just telling him that we were getting married, and he seemed okay with it," I say, my voice rushing. I have to be careful not to trip over my words.

"Okay with it? What, is he like, our judge, telling us what we can and can't do?" he asks, sounding exasperated. "I've never really liked him, or trusted him, and you shouldn't either." Right now, trust feels like a looming weight I can't get away from.

"Of course not, I just told him so he was aware. Definitely *not* because I care about his opinion," I say and add a little giggle for effect. Daniel slowly starts to smile, and I know he buys my act, but I'll never get past the fact that I've lied to my future husband. Guilt starts creeping into me, covering me like a shadow. I've never lied to him before, because there was never a need to. I don't want him to know about what Kelton *really* said and how he took our engagement announcement, because if he finds out, things will never be the same.

"It's time for everyone to get some sleep. We have a big day tomorrow, and we'll need all the energy we can get!" my father practically sings.

He has a good voice, or least from what I remember, but I'm too tired to care about voices. Besides, the voice in my head that keeps urging me to tell Daniel the truth is a nuisance.

My eyes may be too heavy to keep lifting and my muscles too weak to move, but I can't sleep. I know that I'll have nightmare after nightmare of things that may not seem scary to most people, but they are, and always will be, to me. I figure Daniel will be up most of the night as well, so at least I'll have him to keep me company.

This is your chance to confess your lie, the voice in my head keeps telling me. *No one else will hear, and it's not like Daniel can do anything until morning.* I almost start to believe it but stop myself. *One of the main reasons Daniel loves you is because he can trust you. If you confess, the wedding is off.* Is this what I want? To always have one lie kept from him, a really important lie? *Technically speaking, you didn't lie to him, you just didn't tell him the full truth. Don't feel guilty.*

Before I know it, I'm dreaming. *I guess my eyes couldn't handle it any longer.* I know I'm dreaming because my mother and father stand in front of me, holding hands and smiling. "My daughter, I know Daniel means the world to you, but is he the right choice?" my mother in my dream asks me. I want to ask her what she means or who would be a better choice, but Kyle wakes me up before I get the chance.

"Wake up, sleepyhead! It's time to go!" he says, way too cheery for the morning. I groan and turn over to my side, away from Kyle and the blinding light.

Sun, sun, go away; come back when I'm more awake, I think. I almost start laughing.

Kyle walks around to the other side of my body and yells in my ear "Wake up, or we're leaving you behind!" At this, my eyes dart open and I sit up. Kyle starts laughing his high-pitched laugh and then turns to Kelton. "I knew that would wake her up." They both start laughing.

"You guys are so mean," I say, rubbing my eyes. I walk over to them and take the small, flat pillow that my father found and start playfully hitting them with it. They put up their arms in defense. Kelton snatches the pillow from my grasp and starts hitting *me* with it. I run away from them, trying not to get hit, but Kelton is a lot faster than me, and he catches up to me within seconds. He picks me up and tosses me over his shoulder, swinging me around. I kick and scream and laugh until I'm dizzy and my head hurts. Kelton puts me down, and we all start laughing until our sides ache.

I catch a quick glimpse of Daniel out of the corner of my eye. He looks sad, like he wishes he could join in on the fun but considers it too childish for him. Our eyes meet for a second, but he turns away quickly. The same guilty feeling I had last night returns. I want to run over to him and give him a hug, tell him that I lied to his face and feel really bad about it, but instead I turn away and look at Kelton and Kyle, who are now wrestling with each other. It looks like Kelton is winning, but I figured that. I can tell Kelton doesn't like losing, and something tells me he doesn't lose often.

Kyle gives up after a few seconds and rolls to the side, panting. He blinks his long eyelashes, and Kelton raises his fist to give him a fist bump. A smile creeps on my face, and I realize now how much Kelton and Kyle are alike. They're both strong and willing to help others and can make me laugh without really trying. Kelton looks over at me and flashes his perfect, white, straight teeth. I look down at my mud-covered shoes and blush.

How could he love someone like me? I think to myself. *I'm not extremely pretty or smart. I'm just your average girl, who seeks adventure and thrill. There's nothing special about that.* But even as I tell myself this, I begin to realize how untrue it is. *Guys like Kelton don't look for pretty faces and the smarts of Einstein, just someone who can laugh at themselves and is not uptight about everything. I guess he thinks that person is me.*

I look back over to Kelton and Kyle, who continue wrestling each other, and think about what things would be like if we had never met Kelton. Daniel doesn't do things like wrestling and fist bumps; instead he would look at all of the reasons why it's pointless and stupid. I stand up and walk over to Daniel, who seems to be working on some kind of contraption.

"What are you doing?" I ask. He looks at me like it should be obvious, but I give him a blank expression that tells him I'm clueless.

"It's for the ship taking us back. It holds more oil than the other one did, so I figured it would get us farther. What are *you* doing?" he asks me. I know he's actually asking what Kelton and Kyle are doing, but I don't answer. If he really wanted to know, he would ask them himself.

"Seems pretty reckless to me. They could break something or get hurt. Maybe you should go and tell them to stop," Daniel says without glancing my way. I don't know why, but something about him commanding me to do things irritates me.

"You know, if you want them to stop, you should go tell them yourself," I snap. He looks up at me and rolls his eyes.

"Can't you see I'm busy? I'm trying to build this so we can leave this place," he says and lowers his head back to his work. I can tell he's jealous of Kelton, because while he's working really hard to get us out of here, Kelton can fool around and play with my younger brother. Daniel doesn't say anything more, so I turn around and walk over to Kelton and Kyle, who are now thumb wrestling. I sit down right in front of them, and Kelton turns to look at me.

"You might want to look at your competition. He looks like he could take the lead," I say with a laugh. Kelton looks back at Kyle with determination in his eyes. For a brief moment, it looks like Kyle might actually win, but Kelton moves his thumb out of the way, allowing Kyle's thumb to fall. Kelton smashes his thumb on top of Kyle's and easily takes the win. They unlock hands, and Kyle rubs his thumb with his opposite hand.

"Thanks a lot," he says to me, but I can see the smile threatening to take over his scowl. I start to laugh, and I can feel Daniel's eyes on the back of my neck, but I keep laughing anyway. If Daniel wants to play the *jealous game*, then I will definitely help him.

My father comes back in the room from who knows where. He shows Daniel a piece of metal, which he fidgets with for a while before finally placing it to the side of his contraption. My father claps him on the back and walks over to me.

"So, what do you think?" he asks. I look at him with a blank expression.

"About what?" I ask back.

"About Daniel. About his marriage proposal. I mean, I saw the way you looked at him. Anyone with a pair of working eyes could see that you loved him. I'm happy for both of you," he says cheerfully. I swallow hard, but the lump in my throat makes it hurt.

"Yeah," I barely squeak out. My throat is dry, which makes it hard for any words to come out. My father puts his hand on my shoulder and pulls me close to him. *Would he be angry if I told him that things weren't exactly working like they used to? It was his idea to let us get married, but he's not always right.* My father kisses my forehead and walks off but stops and turns around.

"By the way, I've been meaning to ask you how your mother is doing? Ever talk about me?" he asks, his voice full of hope. He doesn't know that I left the family, trying to find what he didn't.

"Um… not really," I say. His smile drops. "But, I think it's because it's a rough subject. She doesn't want the pain to come back from losing you. I'm sure she'll be excited to see you, thrilled even!" He nods, as if he understands, and walks away. The smile doesn't return. I sigh and look down to the ground below.

Life was much easier before Kelton climbed up that rope, I think. *I don't know if I love him, but I definitely don't hate him. He did what he had to do, and he came back to save me. Kyle thinks he's great, even if he always loses at the games they play. The only thing now is to convince my father that I've fallen in love with a Corps' guard.*

I need to catch my breath. *In love with him? No, that's not right. I love Daniel, not Kelton.* I keep telling myself this, because if I keep hearing it, I might actually start to believe it. *Right now, my top priority is to get these people as far from here as possible or to wherever their homes are. I can't think about stupid love right now.*

I think back to when Kelton first told me he loved me or just before that. He said love was stupid, and pointless, and disappointing. Was he referring to me, that loving me is pointless because I will never love him back? Disappointing because loving me is like loving a dangerous storm, you only get hurt the more you stick around? If that's the case, then why has he not left yet? *Because he knows you love him. He hasn't left because he's waiting for you to realize it.* It's this thought that scares me the most. But I've made up my mind, and there's no going back.

Kelton stands off to the side, picking up pieces of used metal and bringing them over to Daniel. He walks back over to the edge of the platform. This is my chance, to see how much he actually loves me. I grab a thin rope that lies on the ground next to me and tie it to my waist and then to a notch in the platform. The rope is thin enough that it won't be seen by anyone but me. I position my feet at the edge of the platform, and when I know he's looking, I cross my arms over my chest and fall backward off the platform.

It's a long way down, so he has enough time to think about what to do. I'm only about halfway down when something hits me hard, from the side, knocking the wind out of me. I close my eyes tight and don't open them until I know what hit me. I feel a strong hand wrap around my waist, and I open my eyes. Kelton holds on to me, one hand on a different rope and one hand around me. He looks straight ahead, not wanting to meet my eyes. Even in his strong grasp, I start to slip, so I throw my arms around his neck and hold on.

He saved me. I don't know why this surprises me, because I knew he would. Because he loves me….

"Hold on tight," he whispers to me, and I pull myself a little closer. The top of the platform gets closer, and I begin to wonder how we're going to stick the landing. I close my eyes, and seconds later I feel my hair go upward, over my head, and back to its normal position. I open my eyes one at a time, and when I do, we're safely on the platform. I release a breath I didn't even know I was holding, and Kelton sets me down.

My legs shake so much that I sit down, cross-legged, and start to cry. Kelton sits next to me and allows for me to cry in peace. He doesn't know *why* I'm crying. He probably thinks I was scared or something, but that's the least of my issues. He puts his arm around me, and I cry into his shirt. I eventually stop and fall asleep, his arm around me, my head on his shoulder. This time my father is in my dream.

"He's always been the right one. I was wrong. Follow your heart." I wake up only to find out it's the middle of the night and Kelton sleeps next to me. His back is propped up against a steel beam, his arm still around me. He looks peaceful but tense at the same time. His chest rises and falls in a lulling rhythm.

I now know what my mother in my dream meant. Maybe Daniel isn't the right choice. I know it was just a dream, but both of my parents agree Daniel isn't right for me. Somehow, I'll have to ask my father what he thinks, in real life. *Tomorrow, tomorrow I'll tell him…* I think before I slip back to sleep.

It comes way too soon. I have not been asleep for more than a couple of hours. The bright light from the window comes into the room, but I want to keep sleeping. Kelton is nowhere in sight, but I'm guessing he's helping my father. Kyle is standing next to Daniel, asking him about what he's doing. Daniel talks without glancing at Kyle, and I can tell he's annoyed, but not necessarily from the questions. I stand up and brush the dirt off my pants.

My father walks out from behind a pillar on the far side of the platform, but he's alone. I start to panic. Kelton is nowhere, not helping my father, not talking to Daniel or playing with Kyle. *Did he leave? Why? Where is he?* My head starts to spin, and I have to sit down to steady myself. I look down at the ground, the only thing that makes my head stop spinning. *If I fall, will he magically save me again?* I don't want to though. It was scary the first time, and it might not work again. But I almost fall without even trying. I see a shadow down on the ground move, the shadow in the shape of a person. It startles me, and I feel dizzy again. But the shadow stops moving, and the source of the shadow stops in between two cages. *Kelton…* I think, before I fall toward the ground many yards below.

I must have blacked out. My mind is awake, but my body isn't. I want to move, but I can't. "How is she doing?" I hear someone, probably my father, say.

"I ran as fast as I could. I barely caught her before she hit the ground.

I think she'll be okay, though," I hear Daniel say. I'm confused, but disappointment soon takes over. *Why didn't Kelton save me? He was closer, wasn't he?*

"Good, let her rest. She needs a break, although she hasn't been doing much. Don't bother her, okay Kyle?" I hear my father say.

"Okay," Kyle says. I hear two sets of footsteps, but it sounds more like an army. "Hello?" Kyle's voice is inches from my face.

Stop it! I want to yell, but my throat is too dry to talk. I want to open my eyes, but they feel as if they are glued shut. Kyle places one of his thin fingers on my forehead. The will for my arm to move is gone. I have no feeling, no nerves. I'm lucky I can still think. Kyle tries a few more times before he finally gives up and leaves me alone. I want to move, and I want to ask what happened to me, ask why I can't move. But as much as I try, I can't move or even open my eyes. My thoughts swirl back and forth until eventually I fall asleep.

I wake up again, but this time my eyes open. I move my arm and gulp in a huge breath of air. "She's awake!" I hear Kyle yell. Footsteps thunder on the ground, and then my father appears in front of my eyes.

"Hey there, sunshine! How are you doing?" he asks me. I turn my head to the left and see Daniel standing a few feet away, crossing his arms and smiling.

"I'm fine, I guess. How long have I been out?" Daniel uncrosses his arms and allows for his smile to fade.

"You've been out for a little over a day," my father says. "I was starting to worry." At first I smile, but then my smile fades to a frown. I remember what he said whenever I was last conscious but not really. Able to hear, but not respond. Able to formulate thoughts, but not act on them.

"Worried that I wasn't going to wake? Or that we wouldn't get to leave on time?" I say, anger clear in my tone. He gives me a puzzled look, as if he can't remember what he said, but then it seems to come back.

"Oh, you heard… I didn't mean…" I put up my hand and he stops talking.

"Save it, I don't care. What I do care about, though, is where Kelton is," I say. Out of the corner of my eye, I see Daniel squirm.

"I don't know," my father says. "I assumed he left." I shake my head in disbelief.

Kelton couldn't have left us, couldn't have left me. There are two sides to every story, and I'm going to find the other side.... I attempt to stand up. My legs wobble underneath my weight, and I start to feel dizzy again. My father grabs my arm and pulls me into a standing position. I hold on to his arm until my knuckles turn white. I steady myself and walk over to the edge of the platform and sit down. This may not be the best idea, but it's where I last saw Kelton. And maybe if I wait long enough, he'll come back.

Daniel sits next to me, dangling his legs over the edge like I do. He puts his arm around me, probably so I don't fall again. "You know, maybe it would be best if you didn't sit here. I mean the last two times you did, you fell off," he says with a laugh. I don't look at him.

"I'm fine," I say quietly. He stops laughing, removes his arm from around me, and clasps his hands in his lap.

"I'm sorry," he says. "I'm sorry he left. He really liked you, you know. He really liked hanging out with Kyle too. You probably knew that, it was kind of hard to miss." He smiles a sad smile, but I don't react. He must assume I already knew all of that. "Zandrea, you know how we made a silent promise never to lie to each other, because that would only complicate things? Well, I have a confession, and I think you do too." I can't look him in the eye, but I have to, or he'll know something's definitely wrong.

"What's your confession?" I ask. He looks down at the ground and back to me. His dark eyes hollow and sad.

"Kelton is gone because of me," he says with a sigh.

Maybe I should have listened to him when he said not to sit on the edge of the platform. That might have been smart. He holds on to me so I don't fall for the third time in the last forty-eight hours.

"I told you, you probably shouldn't have sat there, but did you listen? No! And I guess I shouldn't be surprised," he says with a small eye roll.

"Why is he gone because of *you*? What did you do?" I'm furious with him. My face grows hot, and I clench my fists.

"Because..." He pauses, and then his eyes narrow. The deep blue eyes piercing me, pinning me to what he believes is the truth. "I knew you would be angry with me. I did it for our own good. He was a distraction, and we need you to help us get out of here."

"He was *not* a distraction!" I yell at him. "He's wanted to get out of here for years now, and you just took that away. I mean, how would you like it if something you've wanted for so long is just taken from you, because of someone else?" He looks down at his feet.

"Believe me, I do. I know exactly how it feels," he says, his cold tone chilling me. He stands up, lingers for a little bit, and then walks away. He was probably expecting me to say something, but I'm speechless.

What is he talking about? When has he ever felt something like that? I stand up to chase him, but he hasn't moved much.

"What are you talking about?" I ask. He looks down at his feet again and then back to me, his eyes holding my gaze. He glides over to where I stand until he's inches from my face.

"I'm talking about you," he says.

My heart skips a beat as he walks away from me. *He's talking about me? What's that supposed to mean?* And then I get it.

My head hurts, and it's painful to think about anything besides what's in front of me. "You've loved me ever since we met?" I ask in disbelief.

"No, but after I got to know you, I started to realize how alike we were," he says. "You were twelve when we met, and I was fifteen. You were still getting used to the world, unlike me who had seen it firsthand. I didn't want to overwhelm you."

He loved me before I loved him. I liked him right away, but that's different. And he's right, I was only twelve. I was a little girl who hadn't seen the world for what it really had to offer. Everything was cupcakes and butterflies to me, until I met him and learned the other part of life—the part no one warns you about, the part everyone seems to throw under the rug until moving day.

"I hate to admit this, but I was, and still am, jealous of you and Kelton," he says, his eyes wavering from mine, not being able to look at me directly back. "I can tell you love him, and *I* was just a distraction. I wish things were different. If we hadn't met him, *we* could still be together. But I let my emotions get the best of me, and I got angry. I told him to leave, or I would hurt you. Of course, he didn't believe me considering I loved you and wouldn't hurt you if my life depended on it. So, and I regret every bit of this, I pushed him off the platform." He looks miserable and angry but mostly just sad and disappointed. I step forward and wrap my arms around him, pulling him into a hug, but he pushes me away.

"I don't deserve you," he says. "I never have, and I never will. Tell Kelton I'm sorry for what I did. I don't expect him to forgive me. Go be with him, and do me a favor, forget about me. It will be better for both of us." He pushes my arm away and walks toward the open window. I run after him, even though he's only a few paces in front of me. I grab his arm again, but he doesn't stop walking.

"Daniel, I know what you're going to do. Stop, it's not worth it and you know it. If you won't do it for yourself, do it for me," I say, my voice shaking.

"Why? We both know we're going to be miserable unless I do this. Go find Kelton. Do it for me, okay?" he says.

I take a deep breath. "Daniel," I say, and he stops walking. "Look at me. I loved you first. I liked you ever since I met you. As I got to know you and your story more, I grew to love you. I kept telling myself not to, because it could only hurt me and I couldn't handle that. I eventually couldn't help myself, and I went ahead and loved you anyway."

"When you asked me to marry you, I almost fainted I was so happy. But right after you told me you loved me, Kelton told me the same thing. I didn't want to believe it at first. I tried to convince myself that I didn't love him and that I only loved you, but it didn't work, just like it didn't with you. And now my soon-to-be husband wants to jump out of a window, just so he doesn't have to face the fact that his soon-to-be wife is in love with two people."

I take a breath. It feels weird admitting that out loud, considering I haven't completely accepted the fact myself. Yet somehow saying it to him makes the truth in it ring a little louder, calling my attention. It scares me. How could I want something so bad and still feel like giving it up is the best option?

"Zandrea, I want you to be happy, that's why I have to do this," he says and continues walking.

"I'm not going to be happy if you jump out that window," I retort.

He doesn't stop walking, and I don't stop following him. I try to pull him back, but he doesn't even glance my way. He steps onto the mini-platform and hoists one leg out the window. I can't see the ground with all of the fog the day brings, but I know how far it was to the top—a dance with death if someone were to fall or jump at this height. I grab his arm as my hair blows all over. With my free hand, I tuck the loose strands of hair behind my ear.

"Don't jump," I yell. The wind is loud enough to cause ringing in my ears.

"It's too late," he says. "I'm sorry, but I know it'll make you happier, just trust me." He knows I can't, and again trust is the issue at hand.

"Promise me something," he says over the sound of the wind. "You will forget about me and love Kelton. I don't want you thinking about what might or could have been between us, understand? Please, just do that for me." He hoists his other leg out the window. By now, I'm bawling my eyes out, begging him not to leave. He turns around for a moment, kisses my forehead, and lets go of the window frame. I reach out for him, grabbing only air as he descends far below the thick fog. Everything runs in slow motion. I sit exactly where he sat and cry until I fall asleep.

Morning doesn't come soon enough. I am awoken by many nightmares, one of the scariest was when Daniel fell to his death and I stood there holding Kelton's hand, smiling. He screamed out, yelling for me to help him, but I told him that I was happy and he was merely a memory. I woke up screaming at that and looked out the window. I wanted him to be hanging there, or sitting or something, but I only found fog. The rest of the nightmares were a variation of that.

My father must have moved me away from the window so I didn't fall out, because I wake up next to a pile of burlap bags filled with different materials, not next to the window where I remember falling asleep.

Kyle and my father are already awake, Kyle grabbing a steel rod and handing it to my father. He nods at him like he's thanking him. I remember what my father said about me not working very much when I was half blacked out. I stand up and walk over to my father. He sees me first and smiles a tired smile.

"Hey sweetheart, do you need something?" he asks.

"I was just going to ask you the same thing. I know I haven't been very productive lately," I say, smiling back.

He looks at me, his eyes gleaming, and he nods his head. He points over to a pile of steel rods and tells me what to do.

"Bring me as many of those as you can, okay. I'm going to use them to build another ship to get us out of here," he says and gets back to work.

I walk over to the pile where Kyle leans over a couple of rods, straining his back.

"Need some help?" I ask. He looks at me and smiles.

"Sure! Grab the ends of them and we can take them together," he says excitedly. I walk around to the back of the rods and grab the ends. They're a lot heavier than I expected, and I can see why Kyle was straining his back.

It makes the load lighter when you suffer together, I think, but this only makes me think of Kelton, and how he left, and Daniel, and how he jumped. My eyes start to tear up, and I sniffle. Kyle doesn't say anything, even though I know he can hear me. Maybe he just wants to let me cry in peace.

We set the rods down next to my father, and he tells us we can go and play or something.

"Go be kids! You've helped me plenty, and I'll call you back if I need you," he says. He understands I need time to process what happened last night.

I walk over to the edge of the platform, my new safe place, but I don't sit down. No one is here this time to keep me from falling. I stare at the space where I saw Kelton right before I fell for the third time. I don't know why I'm looking; maybe I'm just hoping he shows up again. It feels selfish to be wanting him considering what happened last night, but Daniel did tell me he wanted me to be happy.

Kyle walks over to where I stand, but he sits down. "Are you going to sit?" he asks me. I smile.

"Are you going to keep me from falling?" I ask while sitting down. He laughs lightly, because he knows that I've probably broken the record for How Many Times Someone Has Fallen From a Platform. I start laughing too, until I remember last night's events. My laughter stops, and so does his.

"Why did Daniel jump? Didn't he know I wasn't going to be happy without him? I mean, I love Kelton, but something's missing," I say.

"You do?" Kyle asks.

"Yes. I mean he loves me, and you guys seemed to be best friends, and I just couldn't help it. He's Kelton, and he's gone. Do you know where he went?" I ask him, not really expecting an answer.

"No, I don't. I'm sorry," he says. "Kelton told me he loved you, and I was worried at first. I could tell by the way you looked at Daniel that you liked him, and I didn't want things to get complicated or anything. He was scared to tell you, so he asked me if I could. I told him that if you were ever going to love him back, he had to tell you himself. But now I wish I hadn't told him that, because then things would be different and Daniel might still be here. I'm really sorry. This is all my fault." I can tell he's holding back tears for my sake, but I wish he wouldn't. I want someone to cry so I don't feel as alone.

Kyle and I sit there, on the edge of the platform for a very long time, not saying anything. I realize how grown up Kyle looks now compared to when I first saw him two weeks ago. He looks his age, instead of ten years old like he did when I saw him for the first time a week ago. He's taller, and stronger built, but with a smaller frame. Muscles have replaced his baby arms, and his soft brown hair falls in layers over the top of his head. His voice has dropped slightly from his high-pitched whine.

I let Kyle cry in peace and find he has soft, quiet cries, and I'm not sure if he's crying or breathing heavily. I put my arm around him, and he puts his head on my shoulder.

"Kyle, this isn't your fault," I say. "It's mine, if anyone. I loved Daniel and I shouldn't have let my feelings change. You did what you had to do, and I don't expect anything more. I love you, Kyle. I always have, and I always will. I thought of you a lot while I was searching for the Stoneards, and I didn't want to come back until I had something. You've grown up a lot this trip, and I'm very proud of you. Stay the sweet little brother I've always known you to be." I playfully nudge him in the arm. He smiles at the ground. *It's good to see you smile again*, I think.

An hour later, my father tells us it's time to eat. I open one of the sacks of food that contains oats. I grab a handful and give the sack to my father, who takes two handfuls and passes it to Kyle. He looks at it hesitantly and grabs a small handful. The oats are dry and rough on my tongue, making it hard to swallow them. One of the sacks to my right has dried carrot shavings. The sack to my left has chopped potatoes in it. I take one of the slices and pop it in my mouth. It's slightly dry and untasteful.

I don't feel like eating. My mind is elsewhere and my stomach hurts. The slice of potato I ate only adds to the uneasy feeling in my stomach. I stand up and walk over to the window. I need fresh air or I might throw up. I sit on the ledge where Daniel sat before he jumped and look down. The sky is clear tonight, and I can see moving dots on the ground far below. *Must be people enjoying their night. Must be nice to be happy all of the time.*

I can't stay next to the window for long. It brings back too many painful memories. I push all thoughts of last night away and go back to where Kyle and my father sit. They both look tired from working so hard, and I feel guilty. *If I had worked as hard as them, I would probably be as tired as they looked. Maybe I should, just to get my mind off things.*

"We should all get some rest," my father says. "We have a big day tomorrow. We'll head back to Coreno first thing in the morning. Hopefully the extra-powered turbine engine I installed will get us all the way there." He says that last part mostly for his benefit.

"I'm sorry I didn't help more. You guys did a really good job, though," I say with fake enthusiasm. I wish it was real, but ever since Kelton went missing and Daniel jumped to his death, the only emotion I feel is sadness and regret.

"Thank you!" my father says a little too cheerfully. He puts his hand on my shoulder. "It was hard work, but I couldn't have done it without you. I know things have been harder recently, but it'll get easier, I promise."

He takes his hand off my shoulder and walks over to his contraption, where he continues to work on it. Maybe that's his coping mechanism.

We're leaving tomorrow, and still no sign of Kelton. I can't just leave him here. He's wanted to get out of here ever since he first stole that uniform. Why did Daniel have to push him away?

I walk to the part of the platform where I last saw Kelton, hoping that somehow he might have returned. He's not; the area is completely empty. Something about this doesn't seem right. One would think that after the guards left, someone would have said that there were rebels in this area, but no one has come to investigate. *Where is he? Why has he not come back? Or, an even more important question is: why do I care? He's gone, and I should be happy. But I'm not, and I don't know why.*

But I do know why. I let myself love him, even when I thought I loved Daniel. Is it possible I love Kelton more than Daniel? Or just differently?

Kyle comes bouncing over to me; he looks ten times happier than I wish I felt.

"You want to do something? I'm tired of being sad all the time. I wanted to cheer you up!" he says, and I want to cry tears of joy. It's been too long of a time where someone has made me feel like crying tears of joy, and I don't want this feeling to ever leave me again.

"Sure. What do you want to do?" I don't want to make this all about me.

"I don't care. I was hoping you would tell me," he says. I think for a moment. What I truly want to do is find Kelton and leave this place for good, but I don't think that's what he had in mind. "What if we went looking for Kelton?" It's as if he can read my mind.

I shrug as if that wasn't exactly what I was thinking. He reaches down and hooks the rope that hangs loosely from the platform around his waist. He looks like the bungee jumper from a video I watched once. His arms poised out to the side, his knees bent. I put my hand on his shoulder before he jumps, and he turns around to look at me.

"Are you sure this is how you want to get down there? I've fallen plenty of times, and it seems to do the trick," I say with a laugh. He just looks at me, confidence overpowering his light blue eyes. "Alright, but don't say I didn't warn you."

He bends his knees one more time as he releases his feet from the platform's edge. He sails down the side of the platform, his head closest to the ground. Once he gets about halfway down, he spreads his arms out to the side, like he's a bird in mid-flight.

Just before his head hits the ground, he pushes his legs in front of him and lands perfectly 100 feet below. He quickly unties the knot around his waist so *I* can tie the rope around my waist. *This is the most* stupid *idea ever. I can't believe I'm doing this*, I think. Before I can talk myself out of it, I bend my legs and jump off.

My hair flies around my face, cutting my vision into parts. Every muscle in my body tenses as the air blows all around me. I'm sure I'll throw up as soon as my feet hit solid ground. The rope feels even tighter than it did before I jumped, which isn't helping my stomach. Down below on the pavement, my brother spreads his arms out to the side and nods his head yes. He's trying to tell me to open my arms, but the force of the air pushes them to my sides, and I shake my head no. He holds his arms out and continues to nod. I'm guessing he's done this before, so I have to trust him. I slowly move my arms away from my sides, like a baby bird opening its wings for the first time. I shut my eyes as tightly as possible, and when I open them, I feel as if I'm flying. I start to smile as the adrenaline rushes through me.

The wind bunches up all around me, wrinkling my shirt. Kyle is only a few feet below me, and I remember to straighten my legs, or it's basically just falling and hitting the ground. I push my legs in front of me, ten times less graceful than Kyle, and hit the ground with a thud, sending a jolt throughout my body. He starts laughing but immediately stops when he sees my facial expression.

"Well that was fun," he says. "But next time, straighten your legs sooner and spread your arms more. That might help you land more gracefully."

"Yeah, if there even is a next time," I mumble. He just shrugs and continues walking.

I haven't been down here since Kelton betrayed Daniel and me, and it feels eerie. The sudden openness feels unfamiliar. Kyle finds a flashlight in his belt and clicks it on. The sudden light hurts my eyes, and I have to blink a few times to see again. The air gets colder with each step, and the flashlight is the only thing keeping me from tripping. I hold on to Kyle's shoulder so I don't fall.

"Are you scared?" he taunts me. He looks over his shoulder and grins. I roll my eyes and let go of his shoulder. "I didn't mind. It's nice to know someone relies on me to feel safe."

I put my hand back on his shoulder. "Who said I was relying on you?" Sarcasm fills my voice. He rolls his eyes but doesn't say anything.

He points his flashlight at the different crates lining the walls. Each one is labeled with something different: food, weapons, bombs that I'm guessing could explode any minute if they wanted, and some tools used for who knows what. I'm just starting to read some of the labels when I hear the voices.

"I'm pretty sure they went that way."

"Are you sure? I saw some figures go in the opposite direction."

"I'm positive. The escapees are up on the platform. I saw one of them leave yesterday. Or maybe it was two days ago."

"I heard one of them jumped. Sad."

"Probably a good thing if there's less of them."

"Yeah, I guess so. We should go find out."

"Not until Boss gives us the orders. Remember what happened to Kelton Brown?" *Kelton?*

"You mean the skinny initiate? That kid was a joke! The only thing he cared about was getting out of here. If I were him, I would've stopped after the first time. Stupid, and then Boss tells *us* to look after him. I mean, we could have had any job, and we got stuck with babysitting."

"We lost him, remember? He ran away when our backs were turned. I heard he saw some girl and thought *she* could get him out. How stupid! And then Boss yells at us because we left trying to search for him. When I find him, I'm going to give him a piece of my mind!"

"When you find him? We're doing this together. *We* find him. And what piece are you going to give him? There's nothing left! Not that you had a brain to begin with."

"Watch it! Boss wouldn't like it if one of Kelton's babysitters ended up dead."

"If it was you, he probably wouldn't mind! And just remember who got the higher score on the accuracy test."

I see Kyle tense up next to me. He's thinking the same thing I am: these two idiots know about Kelton; they worked with him. Well, to be more accurate, they babysat him. I'm the girl they were talking about. *Who's their boss? Where is he? Why would he be mad?* I consider asking Kyle what he thinks about those guys, but I don't want them to hear me. They might tell their "boss." Kyle grabs my arm and squeezes it. In the faint light, I can see my arm turn white from the pressure of his fingers.

The two men eventually leave, and Kyle loosens his grip. I take the flashlight from him, because I can tell he's a little shaken from almost getting caught. I point it at the ground and start walking with slow, careful steps. Kyle follows close behind; I can feel his breaths on my neck. He's not too much shorter than I am, and his strong build makes him look sixteen instead of thirteen.

We find the edge of the room and skirt the outside until we find a door. I figure the door might lead to a closet or some storage area, but when I open the door, it leads to a long hallway. It's brightly lit; huge lights hang above, spaced out every few feet. The floor is made of stainless steel, so when I look down, I can see my reflection. I look worn out and my hair stands up on end on some parts of my head. *Now I know for a* fact *that Kelton doesn't love me because of my looks. I'm scared of my own reflection!* I step into the hallway, tentatively, and find the walls are made of mirrors. The mirrors reflect back the light from above, making the room even brighter. I have to squint to see the end of the hall.

The hallway is long and only a couple yards wide. The lights overhead provide a warm golden glow. Unlike the platform I'd just spent days on, the hallway looks like it gets cleaned every day, maybe even multiple times.

"Hey!" Kyle exclaims, laughing at his reflection. His voice echoes off the walls. "The mirrors make my body look really weird."

"You don't need a mirror to tell you *that*," I say with a laugh. He glares at me and then rolls his eyes.

I'm glad he's here. I would be a lot more terrified if there wasn't someone to joke around with. But then again, he is the one who brought me down here. I look back and find him examining himself in the mirror. I laugh again, but my laugh is interrupted by a loud screech. I see the door slowly closing behind me and run to stop it. But I'm too late, and the door closes with a thud. I lean my head against the cold, metal door. It feels good to stand like this, taking in the smell of freshly painted wood and metal. My eyes begin to blur, and I feel my face get hot with tears.

"It's going to be okay," Kyle says gently. "Maybe they'll come and clean this hallway out soon." I look at him sideways and smile through my tears. *Leave it to Kyle to keep me on track.* I turn toward the mirror closest to the door and smile.

Why is this room so bright and reflective? I wonder. Kyle stands at the end of the hall, flexing his baby muscles and examining his so-called perfect face. I try the door handle again and again, hoping that maybe someone would've unlocked it by now. No such luck.

My stomach growls loudly. I'm not tired anymore, just extremely hungry. I try to trick it by biting my fingernails, but it only grows louder. It only makes me think of food and how I might starve myself in here.

Kyle looks over at me and waves. I wave back, which I find to be a miracle considering how weak I feel. It's a wonder to me how he has this much energy. I try not to think about my stomach as I slide down the mirror into a sitting position. After staring at Kyle for a few minutes, I let my eyes drift into sleep.

I've always found dreaming an interesting topic. How can your brain still imagine things even after you've told it to shut down? Why are dreams so obscured all of the time? You can dream of anything from kittens and sunshine to being attacked by an animal on a rainy day. And then you wake up and forget everything you just saw. So what's the point in dreaming if you can't remember the good stuff and forget the bad?

I allow for my dreams to wander. I see Kelton running toward me, his arms outstretched. He throws his arms around my shoulders and pulls me closer. I feel his heartbeat racing and tears come from his eyes.

"I thought I would never see you again!" he says, his voice filled with tears and joy. He pulls away, and then his lips lightly touch mine.

I wake with a start, and my heart races inside my chest. I breathe heavily into the palms of my hands. I slowly stand up, putting all my weight against the wall. *Too soon*, I think. *I don't know him well enough to kiss him. But he kissed me, so technically I didn't kiss him, right? Besides, he wouldn't do that in real life. It was just a dream, right?*

I can't convince myself it's just a dream, but it's not reality either. Yet.

Kyle stands at the end of the hall, talking to someone behind the golden door. *Someone has come to rescue us*, I think. My mind is foggy, and I feel like I should be happier, but leaving this hallway only means I get to live longer and possibly see Kelton again. It's not a bad thing, but the dream made me see him differently, and not necessarily for the better.

Kyle runs toward me, grinning. The hallway is long enough that I have time to collect my thoughts before he reaches me and tells me why he's smiling from ear to ear.

"You saw the guy I was just talking to, right?" He doesn't wait for me to answer. "He's some maintenance guy who comes around every other day and cleans this floor. He came today to clean this hallway. Looks like I was right."

I give him a weary smile and let him take my hand. He grabs it and pulls me down the hall toward the giant door on the other side. My feet trip over each other, and running seems impossible, but Kyle continues to speed-walk through the golden hallway.

The man behind the door sits, eating an apple when we arrive. His hair has turned white, and the wrinkles around his forehead seem to cut deeper when he catches sight of me. His small frame reminds me of Kyle. I look away from him and to the cart that sits directly behind him. It's filled with gadgets and trinkets I can only assume are for cleaning the hallway.

The man nods at Kyle and moves gracefully around him and into the hall. I watch him go until he is behind the door. and Kyle motions for me to follow him.

I haven't explored this part of the building yet. It's fancier than the platform we've been on for the past couple of days, but not as fancy as the first floor or the hallway we were just in. The room that leads out from the mirror hallway has light red stained glass windows and blood red carpet. The three walls that don't contain any windows are painted a basic red with dark red streaks. *We must be on the Red Floor*, I think. I hadn't noticed before, but the mirror hallway descended at a steep angle. We must be on the floor below the Blue Floor.

The sun has already set for the night, and maybe has been set for a while now, so the stained glass isn't as pretty as it would be in the daylight. Kyle turns on his flashlight and points it at the end of the hall to a painting of some man. I walk around the long office table and rest my hand on the side of the painting. Underneath the painting is a caption stating who the painting is of and why he's important to the Corps' company.

"Ha! Would you look at that?" Kyle says, laughter filling his voice. "Mother's *boyfriend* is the leader of the Corps. Who would have thought that she is dating the galaxy's worst enemy? And we didn't even know it."

I look at the painting closer and see the same man who was in my home not too long ago. Chris is the leader of the Corps, our worst enemy, sitting in my house, drinking tea, and probably kissing my mother. She doesn't know that it was his order that made my father disappear. She's been depressed all of these years and didn't know she would date the reason for her depression. I suddenly get a sinking feeling in my stomach. Mother is being manipulated into thinking she's doing something good, but she might be killing hundreds of people.

"We have to get back to the platform and leave. Kelton will have to wait. I'm sorry," I say and turn to the door. Or, to be more accurate, what should have been the door.

"You're coming with us," one of the men says. He's tall and has a strong build. It's hard to see his eyes, but there is a familiar glint in them. The man standing next to him looks a lot like the first one but shorter.

I try to run, but the first one grabs my arm and pulls me back. The second guy ties a blindfold around Kyle and then me. They push us out a door I didn't know was there and make us walk for what seems like a mile. When the blindfolds are removed, and I can see again, I begin to panic. The room I'm in looks all too familiar, and not in a good way. It looks like the cell I was in when Kelton trapped Daniel and me. The only thing good about it this time is that I'm not locked to the thick post in the middle of the room. I try to stand, but my ankles are chained to the floor, which makes me just as useless as being chained to the post.

The camera in the corner of the room blinks, which lets me know it's on. I turn away and find Kyle sitting in the cell across from me, like Daniel did, crying silently. I'm pretty sure that unless you have special permission from one of the head officers, you won't be able to hear anything from outside of your cell.

I bring my knees closer to my chest and slowly rock back and forth. I realize that there is no way to get out of this cell. My father doesn't know where we are, Kelton is missing, and as far as I know, Daniel is dead. Things could not be worse right now, and the only thing I can think of is how much I want to get out of here—to save myself and then Kyle.

People used to tell me, when I was younger, that I was the most selfless person they had ever met. I would smile gratefully, but I always knew it was a lie. I would imagine myself and someone else falling off a cliff, and I would always think that saving myself would be more important. I would be safe, and then I'd go and save the other person. I never wanted others to know that I played out that scenario in my head, or they might think different of me.

Asking Daniel to take me here and finding my father *and* someone I love, it's changed my view on life, on myself. *If someone comes and asks me who, between Kyle and I, should they let out, I know my answer. It's simple, and I've always, deep down, known the answer.*

Sure enough, a tall man comes down the hall and stops in between our cells. He looks at Kyle and then turns his head and stares at me a little too long. He clears his throat so that we can hear him. *He must have permission to talk to us, otherwise I doubt we would be able to hear him*, I think.

"Kyle," he says looking at Kyle, "Zandrea. I've been meaning to talk to you before but never had the chance. My name is Rowan, and I believe I have something of yours. Unfortunately, you also have something of *mine*. Just so you know what you're trading for, let me show you what *I* have."

He walks back down the hall and slips out the door at the end. My breathing speeds up. *What do we have that he wants? We're just a couple of kids*, I think, but then another thought hits me: *What does he have that* we *would want?*

Kyle glances over at me long enough for me to see the pain in his eyes. I want to reach for him, to comfort him, but my hands stay chained together. Brute force won't break them, but maybe something else will. The man could be getting us a key, to unlock us and let us go, in exchange for whatever we have. I look back at Kyle, and he mouths a word to me.

We used to have to do that kind of thing, because we never knew who would be listening. We both got really good at it. I guess some things never change. The word becomes a phrase, and I decode it before the man gets back.

"I have what the man wants," he mouths to me. I nod my head like I understand, like he didn't need to tell me because I already knew, but I honestly had no idea what he was talking about. I need to trust that he knows what he's doing.

The man comes back a few minutes later. "I have what you want, now where is my end of the bargain?"

"Unlock me first, so I can give it to you," Kyle says defiantly. He looks at me and pouts. I translate the pout into: I'm sorry we didn't get to talk about this first, I didn't have much of a choice. I nod back.

The man unlocks Kyle's cell door and steps in. Kyle hands him a small card that reads on the outside: Corps' secret files. I gasp. If that's a card full of secret files, maybe ones that can bring down the entire galaxy, why does he hand it over like he wants to? But I know why, because I see it too. If he doesn't hand over the card, Kelton could die.

Rowan tugs on a thin chain and that's when I see our end of the deal. Kelton's face has scratch marks running from east to west. Blood drips from his mouth and hands, and chains weigh him down. He looks smaller and weaker, and I can't help but think that it's all my fault. I try to stand up to reach him, but the chains around my ankles pull me back down. He doesn't look up, not even when I pound on the glass wall. *Why can't he hear me? Why isn't he looking? Does he even remember me?* These questions spin out of control, and I sit sobbing, tears flowing from my eyes to the dirt-littered ground. I don't know if either of them can hear me, but I speak anyway.

"Sir, can I please talk to Kelton? The boy sitting over there. You promised if we gave you what you wanted, then you would give us what we wanted. Right?" I ask, my eyes pleading.

"No. You can't be trusted." He swipes the card from Kyle's hand. "Besides, he's not even there." He quickly steps out of the cell and closes the door. Kyle screams, but it's silent to me because of the soundproof walls. He pounds his fists on the glass, but the man doesn't stop hurrying down the hall. Kelton disappears like the hologram he is.

My screams don't come. Only my sobs echo in the small cell. Kyle continues to pound his fist on the glass, but his screams have stopped as well. Tears streak his face, and his eyes are puffy and red. *I should be trying to find a way out of here, trying to find a way back to Kelton. Why can't I think of a way out? Think, Zandrea, think! There must be some way out of here.*

Kyle looks at me, his eyes still red from the endless tears and the anger that comes with dishonesty. I know the pain I see in his eyes is from seeing Kelton hurt and not being able to do anything about it. He mouths words that I can't make out, maybe they aren't words. I mouth back words that he can understand, and hopefully he can help me.

"Kelton is alive. We'll find him. Can you think of any way to get out of here?" I mouth to him. He understands what I'm asking, because he starts glancing around the cell for anything that might be of use. The man forgot to lock Kyle back up, so he roams freely in his cell. He pushes his hands against the walls, trying to find an opening. I start glancing around the small cell. My eyes land on the small security camera across from me, watching my every move.

Someone can probably see me. They must have someone watch over us at all times, I think. Then another thought hits me. *If all of the guards are out fighting for complete control over the galaxy, then who did they tell to watch us? They need every soldier they have to help fight the other planets. I wonder, is Kelton watching?*

Kyle looks over at me and shrugs. He's found nothing to help us escape. They'll have to feed us, unless they plan to have us starve. I wouldn't be surprised if that was the case, but they have to have some use for us, right?

Kyle crouches down and breathes on the glass. He writes something fast before his breath fades. It reads: ask guards for food, will they bring it? I nod my head, and he starts talking to the wall. After a minute, he smiles and sits back down next to the post. I had no idea that it was a two-way communication system. They can hear us and respond if they want. I wave my hands to get Kyle's attention.

"What did they say to you?" I mouth. He starts to mouth something back when we both hear the door at the end of the hallway open. Kyle stands up and braces himself against the wall, like he's been waiting for this moment his whole life. I realize I have been too when I see who it is that brings us our food.

"Father!" I cry out as he pulls a ring of cards from his belt loop. I shift closer to the glass, hoping my father will see me first but then remember that I'm supposed to be saving Kyle, which means he goes first.

My father finds the right card and inserts it into the slot. Kyle's cell door opens, and he leaps out, hugging our father. He points over at me, and Kyle releases him. He finds a different card and opens my door. I start to jump up, but my chains pull me back down. My father looks at me and laughs.

After we've all shared our hugs and cries of joy, my father leads us down the hall and toward a different room with millions of buttons. He tells us that each one does something different, from opening doors to sending out messages. It takes a lot of restraint not to press any of them, but somehow I refrain.

"So, how did you find us?" I say with a laugh. "I didn't think anyone would be able to find us or even come."

"I saw that you both went missing. I heard you jump off the platform. Your scream is much louder than I thought," he says, holding his ears playfully. "I saw which way you went, so eventually I followed you. I lost you both when you went into that hallway, so I went to the control room and looked at the cameras. I knew neither of you could see me, so I had to find some other way to communicate with you. Eventually, Kyle asked for food, and I knew I found a way to get to you."

I stare at him in awe for a few moments longer than necessary. He gives me a confused grin and I look away. I glance at a door off to the side of the room that has no windows, only a sturdy, metal handle. He follows my gaze to the door and clears his throat.

"I've been trying to open that door since I found it," he says. "I've tried all of the cards, but none of them seem to work. I do want to see what's behind it, though." He walks over to the door and tries pulling on the handle, straining his back, but the door doesn't budge. It's too thick to hear anything from the other side, so for all we know, there could be a whole room full of guards just waiting for someone to come by.

"Maybe one of these buttons does something," Kyle suggests. "I mean, it's worth a shot. There has to be some way to open the door." He walks over to one of the control panels and presses a button. Nothing happens.

"We have to be careful," my father says. "We don't know what will happen if we press the wrong one." He carefully examines the buttons on the panel before pressing one that's colored blue. Nothing happens in the room, but I'm guessing that somewhere in the galaxy, something happened. Whether it was good or bad, I do not know.

He presses another one after careful examination, but we only hear a small click. Kyle tries the door, but it doesn't open. I try to pull open the door we came in, but it stays closed, which means we're locked in here. I start to scream but remember my father is in here with us; we are not alone anymore.

After a few more tries, with no success, they both give up, but my curiosity gets the better of me, so I keep going. I find a lever, but before I push it down, I think: *the Corps would never leave their control room that contains life-or-death buttons and levers unattended. Maybe this isn't the head control room. Maybe this room has only the unimportant buttons, the real one is somewhere else in this enormous building, and we have locked ourselves in the most unimportant room in the entire building. Who are we saving by sitting here and pushing different buttons? Who are we harming?*

I pull the lever and a quiet alarm sounds out in the hall. Eight guards run past the room, guns hoisted in their hands and belts. There are a million things they could be running for, or a million things they think they're running for, but will never find. They pass by our room without glancing our way, which makes me think that *they* think it's something really important, and I want to find out what it is exactly.

Neither of the doors open, and I start to panic. No one else knows that we're in here, so dying of starvation or dehydration seems likely a chance of death. The walls of the room seem to be getting smaller, but I think it's just my imagination. Kyle doesn't move as fast as he used to. My father looks tired and pale. I begin to think none of us will make it out of here alive, that one day someone will come in here and find three piles of bones. The thought makes me shiver, and I push the thought away.

I stand up from my sitting position with renewed energy and start across the room toward one of the control panels. *One of these buttons* has *to do something. Whether it opens a door or sends us food, I don't care. Hopefully I'm not hurting other people's lives by pressing random buttons.* I stare at my father, who lies still on the floor, sleeping.

I look over to Kyle who sits bug-eyed and stares into space. "You saw Kelton, right? I wasn't hallucinating when I saw him, was I?" I ask Kyle.

"No," he says. "Unless I was hallucinating too. I think it was a hologram, some kind of projection, but I didn't see any light beams. As soon as Rowan ran off with the card, Kelton disappeared. He had something to do with it."

"Do you think that the hologram was really Kelton, like a projection of him from somewhere else in the building?" I ask nervously.

"I don't know. We studied some forms of holograms in school, and I remember hearing something about how the projection can be anywhere from seconds to weeks old. That could have been recorded weeks ago, but it also could have been present-day images. Hopefully it's present day, otherwise he might be..." His voice trails off. He doesn't have to finish, because I know exactly what he means. If we don't get out of here and find Kelton, chances are I may never get to see him again.

One of these buttons has *to do something important. I'm going to find which one it is, and I'm going to get to Kelton.* I repeat these words over and over in my head, trying to believe them. Eventually, we've each tried over two thirds of the buttons in total, but still nothing significant.

With every minute that I waste trying to figure out which button will take me to Kelton, the closer he is to death, if he isn't already dead. But I can't afford to think like that.

Two guards stop outside of our room. They start talking, quietly, and I have to strain to hear them.

"What was that alarm for? It scared me half to death."

"Why do you think I know? I'm guessing Commander pulled it, maybe as a drill. He does a lot of things for no reason."

"Commander's on the third floor, you idiot. The control room where all of the alarm buttons are is on *this* floor! Man, you are so dumb. Sometimes I wonder how I got stuck with you as my partner. If Commander didn't threaten to kill me every time I complained, we would *not* be partners right now!"

"Well, I'd rather be partners with that kid who left any day! At least he was nice."

"I'd be a lot nicer if you weren't so stupid. And anyways, we've been over this. Kelton left because he saw a way to escape and took what might have been his only chance."

"Oh, that's his name! I always forget! Oh, and by the way, I'm smarter than you think. I know that Kelton is still here. Commander found him and brought him to some room. He also found some other kid who was with him. They never escaped, and I don't think they ever will. I wonder what happened to that girl he saw. She was really pretty. I can see why Kelton followed her up to that platform."

"Be quiet, you've never even met her. She was probably really mean or snotty, like most females. And people wonder why Commander doesn't hire girls."

This makes me mad. I know they're talking about me. And most people *don't* wonder why he never hires girls. He probably thinks they can't fight as well as boys can, but whatever. They gave me some really useful information: Kelton is still here, most likely alive because "Commander" took him as prisoner, and something tells me he won't kill him just yet. But something keeps nagging at me. One of the guards mentioned that Commander found someone else with Kelton. Who would that be?

I start pressing all of the buttons with renewed energy. The guards talked about Kelton being kept in a room, and I need to get to him. My father wakes with a start when he sees me pushing all of the buttons. He's about to reach for my hand to stop, but before he can, the door behind me opens slightly, revealing a small room. I run to it, wanting to see what's inside.

My heart stops when I realize what—who—is in there. "Kelton!" I scream, adrenaline rushing through me, making me propel toward him. He's chained to the wall, the shackles tight, making his hands purple. I pull my hardest against them, but they don't move. I stop trying when I see him wince.

I wrap my arms around his neck, but he doesn't move. I pull back and examine his face. He's scratched and bleeding, and one eye is swollen, the purple enveloping his blue-green eyes. He looks almost the same as the hologram did, so I assume the recording was taken recently.

"What happened?" I ask quietly.

"Commander found me," he says hoarsely. "He knew I was trying to escape, so he brought me to the Torturing Room, on the fifth floor, and tortured me until I was nearly dead. He took me here, hoping I would eventually die. Thanks for finding me." He gives me a weak smile, trying to show how strong he is, but I know better.

I fight back tears. "Kyle and I saw a projection of you. We knew you were still alive, but we didn't know for how much longer. I can't believe they did this to you and then left you to die. How long have you been here?" I ask gently.

"A couple of days. There wasn't anything you could have done. I kept hoping someone would find me, but I began to lose hope. You don't know how long it's been, just sitting here, waiting for death or someone to find me," he says.

"Kyle and I were trying to find you, but these guys captured us and brought us to the cells," I explain to him. "This guy named Rowan wanted to trade with us; he said we had something he needed. He was going to give you back to us, but instead he ran off with some card that contained a bunch of codes. He tricked us by showing a projection of you, making us think he was going to trade fairly. I'm so sorry we didn't get here sooner."

"Those codes are important," he says, his tone serious. "They were going to use them to hack into the government's data systems and take control over the galaxy. That card was the only thing stopping them from full control of the galaxy."

Kyle clears his throat. "I'm sorry Kelton. I didn't know what the card contained. This older man gave it to me. He told me he was an undercover agent, disguised as a sanitation worker. He thought I could be trusted with it for some reason." I realize Kyle is talking about the man who let us out of the golden mirror hallway. That's what they were talking about that took so long.

"I didn't expect you to know," Kelton says. "Let's just hope something goes wrong with the card." He looks at me, but I turn away. I can't look at him, not after what happened to him.

My father moves around both of us and around to the wall opposite us. He uses one of his cards to unlock the shackles from his wrists. His arms fall forward, and he winces when he pulls them close to his chest. My father and Kyle help him stand up and move out of the room. I go first to help keep the door to the control room open but remember that it's still locked shut. Kelton looks from me to my father and back to me.

"Do you see that pink button over there?" he asks weakly. I nod. "Press it, it'll unlock the door." I run over to the button flashing pink, the only one on this control panel, and press it like my life depends on it, which in some ways is true.

The door gives a resounding click, and I pull it open so fast that I think I might break the door handle. I sneak my head into the hall and look to the left and then to the right, to make sure no one will see our escape. Fortunately, the hall is relatively quiet.

Two guards quietly talk at the end of the gray-brown hallway. They don't notice us, but I recognize them as the two guards who had been talking about Kelton by the mirrored hallway. One of the guards, the smarter of the two, stands with his gun at his side. He's medium height and rounder than the other guard. His brown, bowl-shaped haircut makes him look like he's in his forties. The other guard leans against the wall, his gun resting next to his leg. He's taller, thinner, and younger-looking than the first guard. His dark blonde hair flops over one side of his head, making him look like an older teenager instead of in his twenties or thirties.

The hall is dimly lit, which makes it hard to determine which way they are looking. I can't risk being out in the open, especially not with Kelton not being able to fully walk. I can tell they're getting impatient with me, so I turn around and tell them the news.

"There are two guards at the end of the hall. I don't know if they can see us, so I think we should wait," I whisper. Kelton slowly hobbles to the doorframe and sticks his head out far enough to see the guards. And just when I think we couldn't be in a worse position, Kelton yells out to them.

"Hey!" he yells. I pull him back into the room before they can see him, but I'm not fast enough. They come running down the hall, guns positioned to shoot. I almost shout "Run!" to the others, but then I remember that Kelton can barely *walk*. My first instinct is to hide behind the door and punch them in the face when they get close enough, but something stops me. If these guards catch us, they will most likely bring us to Commander, who will torture us, like he did to Kelton. Kelton should know this, and I'm pretty sure he does. So why did he yell to them?

The words get stuck in my throat. I want to ask him why he wanted to get their attention, but before I can do that, the guards reach the door. I brace for impact, squeezing my eyes shut, only to hear the sounds of laughter.

"Kelton? Is that really you? Man, we've missed you!" the tall, skinny guard exclaims.

"It's good to see you too David. Where have you guys been?" Kelton asks.

"Sipping tea and relaxing," the shorter guard says sarcastically. "What do you think we've been doing?"

I step in the middle of the three of them and hold my hands up, as if to signal that it's my turn to comment.

"You guys *know* each other? How?" I ask, bewildered.

"We worked in the same squadron for a few years. They were already here when I joined, so they showed me the basics and the best ways to escape. They're like older brothers," Kelton says with a laugh. "Remember? I told you I had been working here for a while."

"Of course," I laugh, as if *I* was the stupid one. "How could I forget? So is that why you got their attention?"

"Yeah," the shorter guard says. "We said that once Kelton was found and we could break him free, we would stick together. Sorry man, I wish we had come sooner. We couldn't find you, though. Luckily, these guys did."

"It's alright Max. This place is so big, I'm surprised anyone found me at all," Kelton says. Then he turns toward me. "Thank you." I blush and turn my head to the ground.

"By the way," David says, breaking the silence, "did you hear any of our conversation?" He's looking at me, his light eyes anxious.

"Yeah, pretty much all of it," I say with a giggle. I look at David. "Thank you." I wink at him. Now it's *his* turn to blush.

Kelton glances at me sideways. "What did he say?"

"Oh, he just mentioned that I was really pretty and he understood why you followed me. Max, on the other hand, didn't agree," I say with a mini eye roll. "Still think I'm snobby?" I'm taunting him now.

"Yes," he fires back. "In fact, you just proved what I already thought. So there." I start laughing. Everyone else follows in my laughter, except Max, who rolls his eyes. "We're going to get caught if you don't keep it down," he says annoyed. I laugh even harder.

Fortunately, no one hears us, or if they do, they don't care. David and Max take over carrying Kelton, and I walk in the back with Kyle and my father. Kelton's talking to Max about something, their tones serious, not at all like what I heard earlier. I freeze when I hear what Max and Kelton are talking about.

"Where are they keeping the other guy they found?" Kelton asks.

"Somewhere on the third floor, I think. Right near Commander's office. I think he's doing that on purpose, though. To lure us. Commander is using that kid as bait. So the question is: are we going to take it? Is this kid really worth it?" Max asks.

Kelton looks back at me, our eyes meeting for only a second before he turns around. "Yes, he is definitely worth it. You've known me long enough to know that I would risk anything for the people I care about." He looks back at me again.

"Of course," Max says, like he should have known the answer all along. "It was stupid of me to ask. Come on, I'll show you where he's keeping him." He turns his head down, like he's ashamed for asking such a ridiculous question. I start to pity him, but then remember he and Kelton are friends, or at least close acquaintances. Friends don't take things personally. At least, I hope that's true.

Before I met Daniel, and before I went on my journey, I had a best friend at school. Her name was Layla, and she had the prettiest blonde hair. It flowed down her back in waves and had a certain shimmer that you could recognize anywhere. She had her own group of popular friends, but I was desperate for someone to talk to. I walked up to her one day and asked if she wanted to be my friend. She laughed and walked away to talk with her group of friends.

I was really confused at first, but then I realized she was laughing because she thought I was joking. At the time, people called me a freak, because I talked to myself a lot, but I stopped after a while. They still told me I was a freak. A couple days later, she came up to me after school and told me how she felt sorry for me.

"I didn't mean to laugh at you the other day," she said then. "My friends say I shouldn't talk to you because you're a freak. What they don't know is that I used to talk to myself also." She winked at me and walked off for the second time that week, but this time I felt better about myself. We were friends ever since, until her family moved to a different planet and never came back.

I never knew why she left, other than the fact that she had to move, but most people don't leave unless they have to. You can't guarantee any homes in most areas in the galaxy, so some people end up living homeless for a while until the government has to do something about it.

There were plenty of things I didn't tell Layla. I considered her my best friend, but things didn't click like they did with her other friends. We talked about how we spent our days away from school, what kinds of makeup we found to have the best results, and what we thought of the work they gave us to do at home, but never anything deep. I didn't know how to have a deep conversation until I met Daniel, who changed the way I viewed people. He spoke his mind and what he thought of other people and didn't mind that I had no idea who he was talking about. I liked to think that he was like me, talking to whoever wanted to listen, but since no one ever did, people thought he was talking to himself.

I think that was when I started to have feelings for him. I saw myself in him more than I had in anyone else, and I could tell him whatever I wanted without him judging. Layla judged me on everything I said, so I let her do most of the talking and only spoke when necessary. Daniel allowed for me to be my true self, and that's what I miss most about him.

Max leads us to an elevator that will take us down to the third floor, where we can find this mystery person Kelton and Max were talking about. We step into the elevator, and a gate shuts in front of us, and then steel doors slide in front of the gate. David pushes a button that has a small number 3 written on it. The elevator jolts as it begins to bring us back down to the ground, and I feel my ears pop. I look over at Kyle, who's holding his ears. Elevators are a luxury, and many people have never been in them before. I have a few times before today. The launch pad back on Coreno had a few of them.

"You three might want to step back," Max says when we reach the third floor. "At least until we can make sure it's secure."

My father steps back, grabbing Kyle's shoulders. I follow him but wonder why Kelton doesn't follow. He can't do anything in the state he's in. He grabs one of the railings on the side of the elevator and lets go of David's shoulder. He looks at me, embarrassment registering on his face.

"What?" I ask gently, hoping that he can explain his current facial expression.

"It's just, I don't want you to see me like this," he says sheepishly. "I've always felt the need to be strong around you. And I do feel stronger, at least more than I used to. Whatever happens, I don't ever want to go back to the way I used to be." I nod.

With Kyle and my father standing right there, it makes it hard to say anything back to him. I haven't had the chance to tell him how I feel about him, Daniel jumping, and even the fact that my father is still alive. I'm not the type of person who opens up easily to other people. Daniel was the only person I was comfortable with telling things to. But the more I think about Daniel, the more my chest tightens with longing, wanting him to be right here next to me. And what hurts the most is that I'm the reason he isn't here.

Max and David position their guns on the door so that when it opens, they're prepared to shoot whoever fires at us. They explain the plan to us: they will go out first to make sure the coast is clear, and then they will signal us to leave the elevator. Once that happens, Kelton leads Kyle, my father, and me down the hall. He knows where the room is that holds this mysterious person. We will find the person and bring him or her back to the platform along with Max and David and return home.

"As long as no one deviates from the plan, we should be in and out in less than a couple of minutes. Any questions?" Max asks making me think of a drill sergeant. We all shake our heads no. "Good, then move out!"

I stand back as Max and David storm out of the elevator. Kelton's arms are around my father and Kyle's shoulders. I stand at the edge of the elevator, ready to give the signal. As soon as I do, the plan is to run down the hall and into one of the rooms, whichever one Kelton chooses. According to Max, Kelton is the only one of us who knows which room this person is in.

This floor, unlike the rest of the floors in this building, doesn't have a specific color. The walls on all sides of us glow blue and white, as if there are light generators behind them. Plastic borders line each of the office rooms, which also glow blue and white. All of the bordered rooms look the same, as in small, cramped cubicles.

"Kelton," I say gently, "do you really know which room it is?"

"Yes, there is no way I would forget," he says back, his voice full of sorrow. I try to respond, but the words stick to my throat. Kelton hasn't shown emotion like this since I've known him. It makes me want to cry, and hug him, and laugh all at once. I keep my face straight, making sure no emotion gets to it. I don't want to make him feel worse.

A few minutes later, after weaving around a few office cubicles, he finds the room that we are supposed to go to and knocks on the door. I get that feeling of regret again, but last time he did something spontaneous, we found Max and David. I trust him; he knows this place better than me.

"Can I see the ring of cards?" Kelton asks my father. He hands them over without hesitating but never takes his eyes off of Kelton. "Thank you."

Fingering through the ring of cards, he chooses one of them labeled: Office Rooms (203). I look at the room number next to the door and find that they match. I shouldn't have second-guessed him, but sometimes I can't help it. He slides the card into a slot underneath the door number, and the pressurized door unlocks with a *hiss*. I begin to wonder if all of the doors make that sound, but I know they do. Why would this door be different from the others?

Kyle pulls on the door, just enough to see inside. The door looks light, like only a thin tarp, but from the way Kyle strains, it seems to be much heavier than I thought. My father slips inside, followed by Kelton and then Kyle. I hesitate, which seems stupid considering Kyle and my father went into the room without a second thought. I move toward the door but don't make it more than a few steps before I hear two gunshots, and everything goes black.

"Zandrea, come back. Zandrea," a voice says, distantly. I try to respond, but my mouth doesn't move like I want it to. I try to move my arm, but I'm met by an extreme sense of pain. If I could move, my whole body would tense. My eyes seem to be glued shut, but I can see a faint red glow from behind my eyelids. "Zandrea," the voice says again. The voice sounds angelic, and I wonder if I'm dead. Someone else starts to talk, but the voice isn't as angelic and smooth.

"Zandrea! Wake up! You have to. We found someone who wants to see you!" The voice belongs to Kyle, I realize, and I'm not dead. But I also can't move. Why? Every muscle in my body feels locked, tense, but I can't release them. I have to, I have to see this mystery person. Why does my whole world stop right when I feel like I'm finally getting what I want?

There is one voice that will always bring me back, no matter what. But that voice died a few days ago. A voice so sweet and musical, like there was always a song in it but never had the chance to release it. The only voice strong enough to bring me back, I discern, is Daniel's.

Daniel is dead, I tell myself. *Nothing will bring him back. I am the reason he jumped. He wanted me to be happy and thought jumping was the best way to solve that problem. It only made it worse, because now, I feel like nothing is worth living for. I might as well not even try and let death slowly eat away at me, until I am nothing anymore. At least that way, I'll be with Daniel again.*

My plan to let death eat away at me must work, because eventually, I hear Daniel's voice, telling me I have to wake up. For him. To come back to him. *That's strange,* I think. *If Daniel wants me to come back to life, why would he be contradicting himself? Does he want me to live or go to him?* And then I understand what he means. The thought sounds ridiculous, even before I have time to think it through, but I know what he's trying to tell me. *He's alive somehow and wants me to come back to him.*

If I wasn't trying before, I am now. Fighting every instinct to push the darkness aside and see him. A sad but wonderful thought hits me. *I have four people I love who are waiting for my return to consciousness. Others don't even have one.* It's this thought, combined with Daniel living, that makes me fight the hardest to get back.

The darkness of being unconscious gradually begins to fade. *This is it,* I think. *I'm almost back. I can almost see him right in front of me, guiding me back to life.* I'm going crazy. Now that I have a little more time to think, I realize how impossible it would be for Daniel to be here right now. But the darkness fades, and my vision becomes blurry. I can make out three figures, but I can't tell which one is which. I command my eyes to blink, and somehow they do. I try to wiggle my fingers and move my arm. It's slow, but they do move.

"Wha-" I try to say, but I can't finish my question before Kyle throws his arms around me, nearly tackling me, and pulls me closer to him.

"Zandrea!" Kyle squeals with delight. "I'm so glad you're back! We thought you were dead." He squeezes me so hard I begin to feel a little lightheaded. I gasp. He pulls back, grinning from ear to ear. Kelton sits behind him, smiling, but it's a sad smile. I look around, trying to find my father, but my eyes land on someone else.

I try to say his name, but the words get caught in my throat. It comes out sounding more like a groan. He is sitting three feet in front of me, and yet my brain can't believe what my eyes are seeing. He can't be there, but he is. My head starts to hurt from trying to process all of this information, and I have to blink a few times to clear my vision. Everything blurs, and I don't know why until I feel a tear stream down my cheek. My brain has finally processed the fact that he really is here, in front of me, saying my name.

"Daniel. You're alive," are the only words I manage before more tears choke me, making my throat swell. Kyle moves over a little, allowing for Daniel to come and sit next to me. He wraps his warm arms around my shoulders and pulls me close to his body. I tremble, but my vision only blurs more. His hand rests at the back of my head as he smooths my hair, a comforting gesture that makes me feel like a child. "How… are you… alive?" I sob so hard my voice comes out in sputters.

"I can tell you that later," he says gently. "Right now, you need to rest and get better. You got shot in your stomach. Thankfully, the bullet didn't hit any vital organs. Your father went to go get some aid for you."

"Where would he get aid for me in this building?" I ask him tiredly through breaths. The bullet wound in my stomach explains me not being able to breathe completely.

"I don't know. Hopefully he comes back soon. He's been gone for almost a half hour. How are you feeling?" He says it so casually that I begin to panic. If my father has been gone for almost a half hour, then he could be in serious danger.

I place my hands on the ground next to me and try to push up. The feeling of lightheadedness is back, but I fight it off. My father might need me, and I can't leave him stranded when he has been there to help *me* so many times.

"What do you think you're doing?" Daniel's voice sounds almost like a command. "Sit back down. There is no way you're going to get anywhere in this condition." Despite our reunion, his tone is serious, almost scolding.

"My father could be in trouble. I have to do something. I owe that to him," I tell him.

"You don't owe him anything. He wanted to do this for you. If someone is going, it should be Kelton or I. We know this place the best."

I'm about to ask him what he means by that last comment when my father emerges from around one of the office cubicles. "Father!" I say as I try to stand up but then remember I was shot. The pain surges through me, and I wince.

He rushes over to me with a medical kit in his hand. "Don't stand up unless you have someone to help you. You could injure yourself even more if you do that." He sighs. "Finding this kit was difficult, but you know I would do anything for you. Where does it hurt the most?"

I pull my shirt up slightly and point to the wound. This is the first time I've looked at it, and I almost throw up. I've never been good with blood, and it seems to have soaked part of my shirt. I touch the wound gingerly before turning to Daniel, searching for the comfort I've longed for. My father opens the kit and digs around for something to help my wound. He finds some disinfectant, but as he touches my bullet wound, I wince. He retracts but tries again when I've stopped moving. I fight every urge in my body to tell him to stop; I know he's helping me, but it feels like he's only making it worse.

To distract myself from the pain, I decide to ask about the wound itself. "What happened? Who shot me?"

"We were trying to get Daniel out of his containment cell," Kelton begins, "but Max and David couldn't keep everything contained. Two of the guards ran past them and aimed their guns at you. I think they both shot, but one of them missed. The other caught you in your stomach." He looks at me, his eyes filled with grief. "I should've let you go in first. I guess I wasn't thinking. I should've checked to make sure we were all clear, I-" He stops talking because tears threaten to spill over his bottom eyelid. He turns away from me.

"Kelton," I say softly. "You didn't know what was going to happen. It might have happened to any of us, but they were just lucky and got me. It's not your fault. No one is blaming you but yourself. Trust me, I would have rather taken the bullet than let it hit you." He looks at me but doesn't seem convinced.

Something hits me hard emotionally. I had to choose between Daniel and Kelton before, and then Daniel supposedly jumped off a building. I thought that, even though it made me upset, I was going to choose Kelton in the end, because that's what Daniel told me to do. Now that I know Daniel is alive, it's a lot more complicated. I stare at him a little longer than necessary, and he gives me a weird look back. My eyes glance over at Kelton, who playfully slugs Kyle in the arm, his eyes still red. I smile. They get along really well, almost like the brother Kyle never had. Instead, he got a sister who dragged him right into the middle of danger, almost got him killed, and was forced to grow up seeing the galaxy for what it really is: a power-hungry war zone controlled by the Corps.

A sudden flashback hits me, and I am forced to remember the week before my father left. We were sitting in the living room, and I heard a forceful knock on our front door and tapped my mother on her leg. She was holding Kyle in her arms, sleeping peacefully, not knowing what was about to happen to any of us.

My mother walked over to the door, opened it slightly, and peered out into the night. Two Corps guards stood on the porch, neither one smiling.

"Sorry for coming by so late in the night, but we have some important information to discuss with you," the first guard said. My father walked around the corner. He looked upset by the late night visit.

"What is going on? Why are you here at this hour?" My father almost shouted at them. If he had, they could have arrested him on the spot. I held onto my father's pant leg, hoping the guards couldn't see me and hoping that if they did decide to arrest him, maybe I could hold him back.

"Again, we are sorry for coming by so late. We have a message for Jordan Knowles. We need to speak to you in private. Please show us to a room," the second guard says.

My father allowed them in and showed them to a room around the corner. Our house was smaller, but it had many rooms. We could each have our own room, if we wanted, plus a room for toys and books, one for clothes, a guest room, and two bathrooms. To me, it was heaven. And being so little and young, it made the world seem even bigger, which allowed for my creative genes to be put to the test.

My mother had held me back, telling me not to go with my father. "That's a conversation for adults, not children. Besides, it's time for you to get to bed." She walked me up the stairs, Kyle in her arms, into my pink and blue room and helped me get my pajamas on: a long pink dress with flowers printed on the front and sides. "You look very pretty," my mother had told me. I spun around so my nightgown ballooned outward like a tornado.

I jumped into bed, and my mother pulled the covers up to my chin. "Sleep tight," she told me. "I'll see you in the morning. And I'll tell your father to come and say goodnight once he finishes with those two men, okay?" She kissed my forehead and stood up to leave.

"Okay, but tell him to hurry," I said, and she nodded. I waved goodbye as she turned out the lights, and then she disappeared. I fell asleep right away, and never knew if my father came to say goodnight. I slept for awhile until I heard the door shut, and my parents start talking, their voices hushed and panicked. I walked over to the top of the stairs so I could hear them.

"What did they want?" My mother's usually soothing voice sounded rough, like it didn't belong to her.

"They told me I could no longer trade my Stoneards," my father said with a sigh. "They said it made their business go down because they couldn't keep up with me. I told them that it was my job, issued by the government, but they said they didn't care. I would have to find a different job, one that had nothing to do with trading or Stoneards. I argued that the jobs here were all taken, so they suggested I move to another planet and search there. We eventually came to an agreement."

"And what, exactly, did you agree on? I heard they rarely make agreements with anyone unless they work for the Corps," my mother asked.

"That's just it. We agreed that if I could find a Stoneard, on the other side of the galaxy, they would let me keep my job. If I didn't, I had to work for them, as a slave." My father delivered the news slowly so my mother could have time to process the information.

"We could move you know," my mother reasoned.

"Not with Zandrea and Kyle being so little," my father said. "Besides, who knows if we would be able to find a new home, let alone a new job? I think it would be best if we just stayed here." My mother nodded slowly.

"So, are you going to do it?" Her rough tone was back, and it scared me.

"Yes. I will be leaving in a week," he said sadly. "I'm sorry, but it's for the best."

"I understand," she said quietly. "Just promise you will return to us as soon as possible."

"I promise," my father said. He kissed my mother on the cheek and walked upstairs. I ran to my bed as fast as I could so he wouldn't catch me. But he only walked down the hall past my room and toward his room. He looked tired, sad, almost, but my father is one of the strongest people I know. I knew this was hard for him.

A week later, his bags were packed, and he said his last goodbyes. My mother cried silently off to the side of the hallway. My father gave me a hug, holding on for too long. He knew something else but didn't tell my mother. Kyle held onto my father's leg, but he had no idea why we were all hugging and crying. He didn't understand yet, being only three years old. I didn't really understand yet either, but I also knew I didn't want my father to leave.

A week went by, and he still never came home. I would stay awake late at night, hoping and praying that he would find his way back to us. He told us the day before he left that if he couldn't find a Stoneard, and he was forced to work for them, he would still come back to tell us the news and say goodbye again. That was one of their agreements. But since months had passed, my mother believed he was dead, which made me believe he was dead as well. I never thought ten years later I would find him, alive and in fairly good condition. And now it's my fault that he isn't safely home yet.

"Zandrea," Kyle says now, waving his hand in front of my face. "Man are you out of it."

Daniel rests his hand on Kyle's shoulder. "She was just shot with a bullet. What do you expect from her? To stand up and lead us all into battle?" I roll my eyes at both of them. Daniel's use of sarcasm is definitely not appreciated at the moment.

"Of course I do," Kyle says. "This is Zandrea we're talking about. She's the strongest person I know." I look at him with confusion. I was just thinking the same thing about our father. I know he's not kidding, but it doesn't seem like something he would say. I turn my confused expression into a smile so no one will ask.

Kelton and Daniel help me stand up so we can find a place to sleep for the night. My father walks ahead of us, and Kyle to the left of Kelton. I feel relaxed, knowing that they would not let anything happen to me. I'm comforted until I remember that Daniel is here, and I still don't know how. I make a mental note to ask him once the pain in my stomach lessens.

My father finds a sleeping area in a hallway that lies around the corner and assigns us each a room. They are all empty, which makes me wonder when they were last occupied. The guards who slept here must be out in the war, otherwise most of these rooms would be full and we would already be caught.

I walk to the room my father assigns me and slide open the thin metal door. The air in the small room feels cold against my skin, and I don't see any heaters. There is a thin mattress on top of a short bed frame and a neatly folded blanket on top of the mattress. I sit in a chair across from the bed that's positioned adjacent to the door and lean against the two-drawer dresser. I open the bottom drawer and find two shirts that look about two sizes too big, but I could use a change of clothes.

The walls of the room are poorly decorated, painted gray with only one picture frame on the wall across from the bed. There's no picture in it, just a newspaper article that tells about the war. It must be a newer article, considering the war has only been going on for a few months. Whoever was here last took care of their room. Everything was folded neatly, and the furniture seemed recently polished. I idly stroke my hand along the dresser, checking for dust. Nothing floats off, so the person must have left recently, or maybe someone came by and dusted. Either way, I'm impressed.

There is a small knock on my door. I move to try to open it, but my stomach reminds me that I am incapable of walking on my own. "Come in," I say. The door opens and Daniel walks in.

"Hey, mind if I sit down?" He gestures to the bed.

"Go ahead. I'm not busy," I say with a smile. His facial expression is serious, and I figure he wants to talk to me about something.

"I figure now is a better time than any. You wanted to know what happened when I jumped, right?" There is no smile on his face. I can tell he wants to get this over with. I nod. "I had to wait for the right moment. There had to be clouds so you couldn't see anything. Kelton and I had planned that I jump out the window. After I told him to leave, which was a setup, he found some boards and made a platform for me to jump on. We had gone exploring on the floor below the platform while you were unconscious and found a window with a huge hole in it that would be perfect to set up a small platform." He pauses to make sure I'm catching all of this. "I had to convince you that Kelton was the better choice for you. I knew you would choose me unless you had a motivation to choose otherwise. My death might make you forget about us and you could move on. After I jumped, I told Kelton that he should go back to you and pretend he didn't know what had just happened. I would have escaped and flown around the galaxy, lived a new life."

"You did all of that for me? Just to make my decision easier?" I can't help but let the cheerfulness enter my voice.

"Yes, I would do anything to make sure you were happy," he says. "That was the one thing that I told you that day that was not a lie. Things would've continued perfectly, but two Corps guards found us." My hands fly up to my mouth to hold back a gasp. It's like he's telling me a ghost story, and the ghost just ate someone. He continues. "We fought with them for a while, but they eventually took over and hauled us both away. On the way, Kelton whispered to me that he knew where they were taking us and that he had been there before. His face was pale, and he was shaking. I could tell that this place wasn't going to be fun. I found out the place was called the Torturing Room. The name is pretty self-explanatory."

"What happened in there?" My voice shakes, and I stop talking. He shakes his head.

"I don't want to remember the pain from that room, but just imagine someone prolonging your death until you become useless. Every ounce of strength and energy drained from your body. Kelton told me the Corps do this kind of thing to all of their prisoners. It burned me to hear that, which I guess made me stronger in that room," he spits. I don't press him anymore. He's like a nut, and my questions are the nutcracker. He stands up to leave. "Did I answer your questions?"

I look up at him, wondering if he was being serious. It's not like him to leave so abruptly. I clear my throat. "Yes," I say. "You definitely answered my question."

Kyle comes in my room later that night. I'm already half asleep, uncomfortably, on my thin mattress. He pulls the chair over to the side of the mattress and sits down.

"Can I get you anything? Water? A blanket?" His eyes gleam in the soft glow of the nightlight, and he looks older, stronger. A sudden pang of grief hits me as I realize he's not my little brother, but more accurately, my younger brother. He is old enough to take care of himself. He doesn't need me anymore to tie his shoes or comfort him when he has a nightmare.

I missed out on him growing up. That is one thing I will never get back. At least my mother has pictures of him, or I would never know what he was like as a child. If I stare at him any longer, he's going to leave.

"Maybe some water. My throat is a little dry. Thank you," I say. He pushes back the chair and walks out of the room, slightly closing the door behind him. Through the silence of the room, I can hear Kelton breathing lightly. It almost lulls me back to sleep until Kyle comes back with a glass of water.

"Here you go," he whispers. He sits down in the chair again.

"Where did you get this?" I take a sip and feel the icy water slip down my parched throat.

"There was a bathroom at the end of the hall. It had a few glasses in it and a bucket of ice," he says and then squints his eyes at me. "It was weird that the ice wasn't melted. It must have been put there recently."

I shrug and take another sip of the water, my mind too groggy to form any somewhat reasonable thoughts. "Maybe someone keeps the bathroom stocked. I mean they must have some kind of maintenance staff to keep the building clean," I say.

"I know, I'm just saying it's kind of weird," he says, like he's trying to prove a point. I decide to change the subject so he doesn't wake anyone up.

"Did you mean what you said earlier? About me being the strongest person you know?" I ask him quietly.

He looks at me. "Of course. I meant every word, but I was also saying it to get Daniel to be quiet. I was actually surprised that he said that about you. He thought that you couldn't lead us into battle. I mean, sure, you got shot in the stomach with a bullet. Who wouldn't be out of it? But I know you. You're a fighter, you always have been, and I want to be just like you someday." His eyes look hopeful in this light.

"Kyle, you already are a fighter," I say. "You're braver than I am, and I mean that. You came all this way to save our mother, and you're still young. You have a long life ahead of you to do great things. I think *you* should be the one to lead us into battle, if we ever encounter one." I almost start shouting, but then I remember it's the middle of the night.

"I don't feel brave," he says quietly. "I feel like I can't do anything."

I open my mouth to protest but shut it when I remember something my mother once told me. "Mother said something to me before I left all those years ago, something I will never forget. She told me that even the strongest people have things they can't do. As long as I remember who I am, and what I was made to do, nothing can stand in my way."

He eyes me, like he's trying to figure out what I'm saying. "I guess that makes sense," he finally says. Then he yawns. "I should probably get some sleep. Do you need anything else?"

"No," I say. "Thank you for everything." He smiles, returns the chair to its corner, and shuts the door behind him. I slip off to sleep, a smile on my face, and dream calm, happy dreams.

To my relief, my dreams are not nightmares. I hear Daniel across the hall wake in the night, breathing deeply, and I ache. I wish his nightmares would go away, but they aren't just nightmares. They are his reality, something he can never unsee—his mother leaving and then getting murdered for coming back, and his father arguing with his second wife and then leaving him because he had to. I thought my own childhood was bad enough with my father leaving, but at least I found him again, and my mother never physically left, but she wasn't always present emotionally.

After that, I have trouble sleeping. The light from the small window in the corner of the room keeps me awake. I want to sleep; my stomach aches from the bullet wound. I toss and turn but can't get comfortable. The night wears on for far too long.

It feels like I have only been sleeping for a minute when Kyle bursts into my room. "Zandrea! Wake up! It's time for breakfast," he says excitedly. I turn over and moan. The bullet wound sends jolts through my body as I try to stand up. I slowly make my way over to the dresser and pull out a shirt. I keep my same pants on because they don't seem too dirty yet. I slip the shirt over my head, which requires a lot of effort, tuck the shirt into the waistband of my pants, and limp down the hall. My leg didn't get injured, but limping makes the wound hurt less.

Kelton hands me a thin slice of bread when I reach the end of the hall. A small table has been set up, and food fills it. They couldn't have found all of this food; someone would have had to put it here on their own terms. It makes me recoil and refuse the bread, my trust issues kicking into high gear.

"Okay," Kelton says wearily. "It tastes good. No complaining later if you're hungry." He winks at me, and I smile. Daniel rolls his eyes and finishes his piece.

"Good morning sweetheart," my father says. "How did you sleep?"

"Fine," I reply. "The wound made it harder though."

"I'm sorry that happened," he says. "It should heal soon."

I stare down at my feet and realize everyone seems a little extra cheery this morning, at least everyone, except Daniel, who seems extra grumpy. I decide to sit next to him to see what's bothering him.

"Hey, are you okay?" His eyes meet mine for a second, but then he turns away.

"Why do you care?" His tone surprises me, but I don't flinch.

"I don't know, maybe because I care about you," I say, nudging him in the shoulder.

"Oh really? Because it seems to me that you care more about *Kelton* than me," he spits. I've played this "game" with him before. He acts like he's mad at me, but then I make him smile, and he gives up, although this time, he seems to be serious.

"Why would you say that?" I use the same fiery tone he used with me.

"Of course you go and find what cell he's locked in before me. I mean why not? He lied to you and then trapped you. Who wouldn't go help someone like that first?" He fake-laughs, so I know he's being sarcastic.

"You jumped out of a window," I almost yell. "I knew he was alive, but you convinced me that you died. You're right, who wouldn't help some-one that they knew was alive? Maybe because they know and that would make the most sense! Helping someone alive versus helping someone who is dead. Think about it Daniel! Would you rather help someone alive or dead?"

"He lied to you and then got us both trapped! How can you trust someone like that? Tell me," he demands.

"How can you? You're the one who trusted him enough to jump out of a building and hope that there was something below to catch you. I'd like to understand that, because right now, I'm having trust issues with everyone at this table, and in the entire galaxy," I retort. His face softens, but his tone is still hard.

"You're right," he says calmly. "I can't trust anyone either. You want to know why? Because my parents lied to me and left me to fend for myself at a very young age! If anyone at this table should have trust issues, it's me." His fiery tone is back.

I scowl at him. "I know you had a rough childhood, but that has nothing to do with now. You trusted me, and we didn't even know each other. I didn't trust Kelton right away, but I learned to let my guard down because sometimes that's the only way to get to know somebody."

Daniel stands up, kicking his chair back. "Do whatever you want; I'm not going to stop you. But don't think for one second that we're back to being friends or anything." He storms off down the hall and goes into his bedroom. I look at my father, but he doesn't say a word. Neither do Kelton or Kyle.

"Did you guys hear most of that?" I look at each of them in turn. It's a stupid question, really. Of course they heard us yelling at each other.

"The sun is shining bright sweetheart," my father says without looking at me. "Come and enjoy the bread that has been put out for us." Kelton nods, and Kyle hands me a slice. I shove it away, scowling. My father would never say something like that. He would never force me to eat something I didn't want to.

I walk over to Kyle and playfully shove him. Kyle would usually retaliate and shove me back, but he doesn't. He stands there, buttering another piece of bread. "Today is a lovely day, wouldn't you agree?" He finally looks at me, but the irises in his eyes are a deep black. I step back, as if he is on fire. I hobble down the hall toward Daniel's room, my wound burning my insides. I knock, but he doesn't answer. Kyle, Kelton, and my father slowly move toward me like zombies but with their hands at their sides.

"Daniel, open up," I shout, banging on the door. "They're coming!" The door finally opens.

"Who's coming?" He looks down the hall and pulls me into his room before I can answer.

"What's going on?" His eyes are as unforgiving as they were only a moment before. I don't know what changed between us, except that I have feelings for Kelton instead of him. He hasn't been mad at me like this before, so I feel like it's something different.

I hear three knocks that actually sound more like scratches, and I limp to the other side of the room. "What are we going to do?" My voice sounds panicked.

"First, tell me what's going on," he demands.

"After you left, I started talking to them, but they weren't themselves," I begin. "They had deep black pits for eyes, and they remind me of zombies. All I know is they aren't Kyle, Kelton, and my father anymore." He stares at me for a while, not saying anything. Then he finally speaks.

"They were eating the bread. Maybe that has something to do with it," he says.

"How is that supposed to work? You were eating the bread too, and you aren't a zombie right now," I say.

"Maybe the poison was in the crust. I don't eat the crust, remember? Or maybe you forgot while you went googly eyes for Kelton." His fiery tone is back.

"Daniel, this is not the time," I say with a sigh. "We can discuss my feelings for Kelton later. Right now, we need to figure out how to turn them back."

"*We*," he asks, not missing my use of the pronoun. "Why should I help you?"

"Do you not remember what we were before we came here? Let me remind you," I say, annoyance flooding my voice. "We were best friends, who told each other everything and didn't keep secrets. Before that night on the platform, when you asked me to marry you, you never made any indication that you loved me or saw a future with me besides as flying partners. Your proposal came out of nowhere. You can't go from loving me like a best friend to loving me more than that. Not without some kind of warning, or heads-up. I am allowed to love *who*ever I choose, and nothing is going to stop me!" Arguing is not something I want to do right now, but I feel like I have no choice. He walks across the room but stops just before he runs into me.

He presses his forehead against mine, and I can feel his breath on my nose. "I'm sorry," he whispers. "You're right. I should have given some indication to you before I asked you to marry me. It was sudden, and I'm sorry." His hands find my cheeks, and for a moment I think he might kiss me. My heart starts racing. Before I can think of what to do, he pulls away, his eyes closed. He looks relaxed, in a tense sort of way. "How do you plan to turn them back?" I realize he's talking about the three maniacs outside his door.

"I thought you'd never ask," I say.

I find the pillowcase on his bed and fill it with two shirts and three pairs of pants, enough to make the pillowcase a nonlethal weapon. On the count of three, I open the door, and Daniel runs out with the pillowcase in his hand. He swings it over his head, hard, and knocks Kyle back, causing him to fall to the ground and hit his head. I wince. Kelton and my father still claw at Daniel and the pillowcase.

As Daniel distracts them, I run to Kelton's room and find his gun, which is positioned next to his bed. I limp back into the hallway and fire the gun once in the air. Kelton and my father look at me and then slowly walk toward me. Once they get in reach, I swing the gun at their jaws, knocking them off balance enough to make them fall to the ground, both out cold.

Hopefully it doesn't hurt, I think before turning my attention to Daniel. He smiles, and I return the favor. It's nice to have my best friend back.

Kyle is the first one to come back. His irises have turned back to their light blue shade, and he blinks at me a couple of times. Kelton and my father come back a few minutes later.

"How long have I been out?" My father rubs his jaw and stares at the ground.

"About an hour," I say, pretending to glance at my invisible watch.

He doesn't say anything and just continues to rub his jaw.

I walk down the hall and back toward where the table with the bread was at. The bread is gone, and five glasses of water replace it. I'm tired of being tricked. My hands find the edge of the table, curl underneath, and with as much strength as possible, I flip the table and the glasses over. The glasses crash to the ground but don't break. I hear footsteps behind me and turn around to find Daniel standing, arms at his sides, scowling.

"What?" My voice sounds distant and accusing. He just stares at me.

"What makes you think you can flip over tables? Someone could hear you and send guards or something," he says finally.

"I'm tired of living in fear all the time. Let them come, we have guns," I say nonchalantly.

"You can get killed on your own terms," he says to me. "But don't bring the rest of us down with you. We have lives worth living, so don't take that away."

"*Excuse me*," I demand. "You have a life worth living and *I* don't?" I'm furious now. He gives me an exasperated sigh and an eye roll before finally speaking.

"That's not what I meant," he begins. "I'm saying that *some* of us would like to live long lives, and you're putting us in danger. Don't you want to keep them safe?" He gestures to my father, Kyle, and Kelton.

"You aren't the boss of me," I retort. "I will protect them when the time comes, but that isn't right now. If *you* want to keep them safe, I suggest you let me get my anger out over here and not by them." I kick the table one last time and rush past Daniel, bumping into his arm on the way. *Oh well*, I think. *He deserved it.*

I sit down next to Kelton. He's fiddling with one of his shoe laces.

My hand finds his, and he winces slightly. I look from him to our hands intertwined and take a deep breath.

"Can I talk to you?" My voice is barely above a whisper.

"Sure. What's up?" His eyes move from our hands to my eyes, and I feel my face turn red.

"Not now. Tonight. After everyone is asleep," I say, turning my head to look at the gray wall behind me. He nods.

"By the way, thanks for saving me. From whatever I was. I don't know what happened. One minute I was eating a slice of bread, and the next everything was black. If something moved, blue or pink dots moved in sync with the object. It was like something or someone was controlling me, and I couldn't stop myself. Somehow I knew it was you, but I couldn't talk, couldn't do anything but pursue whatever moved. Anyway, I just wanted to say thanks." He smiles at me, and my face goes red again, but I smile back.

"Well," I barely squeak out, "You saved my life too. On the platform. I never thanked you for that."

"You mean when you jumped?" He almost starts laughing. "I saw the rope tied around your waist. I knew you would be fine. I went after you because I knew that's what you wanted. Besides, I thought it would be kind of fun. You know you aren't that good with hiding your feelings, right?"

I feel like a tomato, my face is so red. "What*ever*," I say, trying to laugh it off. "You're such a dork." He grins, flashing his perfect white teeth. I stand up and walk to my room. I sit on the bed and ease myself until my head hits the pillow. My eyelids feel too heavy, and I fall asleep before I can talk myself out of a nap.

Kelton wakes me a minute later, or so I think. He tells me that I've been asleep for six hours, but I still feel groggy. He sits on the chair across from me, and I sit up, which I find to not hurt as much anymore.

"What did you want to talk to me about?" The dim glow of the room makes it hard to see him, so I have to squint to adjust.

"I wanted to hear your side of the story before and after Daniel jumped," I say directly.

"Didn't he already explain what happened?" he asks with a slight tone of accusation.

"Yes, but I wanted to know your side. There are two sides to every story, you know."

"Well," he begins, sounding slightly irritated. "At first, we were fighting. We were arguing over you. He claimed that he had known you longer and you had already said yes to his proposal. I decided that we should just let you choose, but he didn't like that idea. He said he knew you were going to choose me, but I wasn't sure. Eventually, he pushed me off the platform and told me not to come back. I barely got a hold of the rope, and I have burn marks on my hands, but I'll be alright."

I take his hands in mine again but turn them over to look at the marks. Nothing. No marks, not even a hint of redness or irritation.

"They must have healed," he says quickly. He pulls his hands away from me, casually, but suspicion seeps into me.

"So what happened next?" My voice sounds strained and distant. I choke through my words.

"I wandered around the cages, waiting for you," he says. "I was hoping you would see me and, I don't know, come looking for me. Instead, Daniel came and apologized. I didn't care, but I listened to him anyway. I'm glad I did, because he said he was going to pretend to jump out the window, and if I built a platform below, he would leave all of us alone. He wanted to go and live his life somewhere else, with some*one* else. He didn't tell me who."

My eyes widen at the last sentence. *Has Daniel been in love with someone else this whole time? Who could she be?* My mind is still racing when I remember her. The girl from the Vulcona landing pad office. She had long brown, wavy hair and was about our age. I remember her hand on top of his when we were waiting in the office on the landing pad. She looked familiar, and Daniel seemed to know who she was. He didn't seem to mind her hand on top of his. *Why did I never think of this? That there are other girls in the galaxy and he might not love me the way he does someone else. But how do you explain his proposal to me? Fighting with Kelton for me? Was it all just an act?*

"Did Daniel tell you that? That he wanted to go live his life with someone, somewhere else?"

"Yes," he says. "He told me that he wanted to leave, but he needed my help. So I helped him. Things were going just fine. I was about to come up to the platform again, but these two guards found us. They were both taller and stronger than us, and they had guns. We fistfought for a bit before they pulled out their revolvers and threatened to shoot us. Daniel gave in, but I couldn't because I knew where they were going to take us if we did."

I'm shaking my head now. I can't believe this happened, and all I did was sit there and grieve over Daniel jumping. Kelton still has a scar from the Torturing Room across his left cheek. My bullet wound hardly seems worth the complaining.

He clears his throat. "That's my side of the story. I don't know what Daniel said, but I wouldn't lie to you." He stares at me, but all I can do is let the tears stream down my cheeks. I don't know why I'm crying, but it feels nice to let some of the pain in my chest dissolve.

"Thank you," I whisper through tears. He stands up but doesn't leave. Instead, he sits down next to me and puts his arm around my shoulders. It makes me think of a brother or a friend trying to comfort when the pain seems unbearable. I relax and breathe deeper, trying to calm and steady my tears.

I fall asleep a few minutes later, my head against his shoulder. But when I wake up, he's gone, and the chair is back in the corner of the room. I slip on my shoes and walk down the hall toward the bathroom. I need a shower, and something tells me we're going to head back to the platform soon. Two neatly folded towels rest on the counter by the sink. I bring the top towel and a bar of soap over to the shower area. A small nozzle hangs a foot above my head, and I turn the faucet over to the middle left. The water runs out in a steady stream, but it makes my wound ache.

I stay in the warm water long after I'm done washing myself. It feels nice and relaxing, seeing all the dirt and grime leave my skin. Eventually I hear Kyle come into the bathroom, and I turn off the water and slip a shirt over my head. The shirt falls just above my knees, and the pants are a size too big. I scrub my dirt-covered shoes in the sink until the water is a light shade of brown. I forgot my shoes were a dark shade of blue.

Daniel walks into the bathroom, towel wrapped around his arm. He glances my way, his eyes pleading with me. I look back to my shoes, scoop them up, and walk out of the room. *If he wants to talk, he better learn to try harder.* My room is warmer than it was last night, and the heat overwhelms me. I decide that wandering around aimlessly is the best option I have at the moment.

The table at the end of the hall that contained the poisonous bread has been removed. That's probably a good thing, because I might have kicked it again if it was still there. I need to get my anger out on something. Ever since last night's conversation with Kelton, my mind has been in a blur. I have to talk to Daniel, but I can't bring myself to do so. *He's right*, I think. *Our lives would be much easier if Kelton wasn't here, but they might also be full of lies and dread. Who is Daniel going to choose, me or that other girl at the landing pad?* I realize then that I'm not the one who has the impossible decision, he is. Daniel. The person I fell in love with all those years ago. Maybe it's okay that Kelton is here. If he wasn't, would Daniel feel obligated to marry me? Or would he break my heart and marry that girl at the landing pad instead?

Someone taps my shoulder. I turn around, half expecting Kyle or Kelton to be standing there, teasing me. Instead, Daniel stands in front of me, his hair wet from the shower. I fold my arms, trying to look as annoyed as possible, so maybe he will take me seriously and tell me the truth.

"How was your *shower*?" My voice comes out sharper than I intended, but I don't care anymore.

"The water was cold, and Kyle stole my towel, but thanks for asking." He uses the same tone I use, which irritates me more than I like.

"Remind me to thank Kyle later," I say coldly.

"Whatever," he says back.

I roll my eyes. "Did you need something?"

"I was going to ask what you and Kelton talked about last night," he says.

"Oh, so now you're interested," I say, annoyed. Daniel only crosses his arms. I sigh. "I wanted to hear his side of the story before and after you jumped. He told me everything, including the real reason why you thought you were doing me a favor by pretending to take your own life."

"And what is that reason?" He's taunting me.

"There was someone else you wanted to be with besides me. You didn't know how to tell me so I wouldn't be hurt, so you decided that jumping out of a window was the best way to do it." I'm guessing at that last part, but I figure it's true.

His eyes open wider, like I wasn't supposed to know that. Then he squints at something over my shoulder briefly before turning back to me. "How do you know Kelton isn't lying?"

"Is he?" I retort.

"Well… no… not exactly. But you don't know all of the details."

"Enlighten me." I sound bored, even though my body is screaming on the inside.

He sighs, realizing there is no way to get out of telling me the truth. "You're right, Kelton's right. There is someone else I would not rather *be* with, but I know her better. Her name is Callie Raymond. We used to go to school together, and then we were sent on a mission together. We were really good friends until she was moved to a different division. That's when I met you. I told Callie about you, and she said she hoped she could meet you sometime. We almost had the chance on the landing pad here, but I told her that it wasn't a good time."

"Why did you tell her that?"

"Well, I asked her what she thought of me, and she said she loved me. I didn't want to make things awkward between you and me, so I thought that if I could escape, fake my death, then it would save you the heartbreak." He says it like it should be obvious.

"That doesn't explain why you proposed to me, fought with Kelton over me, and then pushed him off the platform!" I'm so enraged I want to hit something.

"I love you! That's why I did those things," he cries. "Callie told me she loved me, not the other way around. I liked her enough that if things didn't work out between us, I would still have her."

"Well, you got what you wanted. Things didn't work out between us, and I should've known they were never going to work. You don't want to make me happy, you don't care about me. You only care about yourself and how *you* feel. I don't *want* that, I don't *need* that!" I'm on the brink of tears, but I don't want him to see that this is breaking me. Kyle told me how strong I was that he wanted to be like me. I don't think he was referring to my broken, crying self that's here currently.

"You're right. I-"

"Of course I'm right," I interrupt. "I'm the one getting hurt, which I know doesn't mean I'm right, but it certainly doesn't mean you are either. Now leave me alone! I don't ever want to see you again." At that, his jaw tenses, and he stands up a little straighter.

"Fine," he says. "If you want it that way. I tried, so don't come running back. This is what you want, not me."

"This is exactly what *you* wanted," I scream. "I'm sure you're *glad* that things didn't work out, otherwise you would have *had* to marry me, and love me, but something would always be missing. Don't you understand, you've *crushed* me, my life. I was exhilarated when you asked me to marry you. You don't understand the agony I've been through."

"What about Kelton? Is he not enough for you?" His voice is thick with irritation.

"This is not about him! This is about us. Why can't you understand that?" I'm crying now, my voice dripping with dejection. Why doesn't he understand what's going on?

"You didn't answer my question," he says calmly.

"You didn't answer mine," I say idly.

"I understand that this is about us only," he begins. "There has never been anyone else."

"Then how do you explain Callie?" I demand.

"I don't love her! I never have," he screams.

"Yeah, sure, whatever," I say with casual sarcasm. "How do you explain the looks you gave each other at the landing pad or her hand constantly on yours? I'm sure there have been plenty of other things too that I haven't been around for. Please, just tell me the truth." I'm tired of arguing with him, and my tone gives that away. I wish he would understand my side of the story.

"Look, I said I didn't *love* her. Not that I didn't *like* her. There's a difference. I'll try to understand if you will too, okay?" His eyes lock with mine, but I can't hold his gaze, his pleading eyes. He uses the same voice he used when we first met and he was trying to show me how the ship worked. It's the same voice my parents used when trying to explain something to me. I never liked the tone; it always made me feel smaller and unimportant and childish.

"I understand that you wanted to fake your death so you could go live with some girl I've never met," I say. "Just let me know if there are any details I'm missing." He sighs, understanding my sarcasm.

"You forgot the part about me loving you," he says.

"No, I think I covered everything," I retort. He sighs again, giving a tiny eye roll but not saying anything. I clench my fist; I really want to hit something right now, but that wouldn't do anything to our current situation. I'm not known to be a violent person, but sometimes I slip.

I remember one time, Kyle was annoying me so much I punched him in the gut. He screamed and ran to my mother, who told me to go to my room and that she would talk to me later. I stormed up the stairs, but instead of going to my room, I went to Kyle's. I found one of his favorite toys and smashed it against the ground. He came upstairs later and found his toy in bits and pieces on the ground. He started crying, and my mother came running again. I was in my room at this time, trying to act as innocent as I could considering the circumstances. My mother immediately came to my room and scolded me. Then she asked me where my jar of Stoneians was. I showed it to her proudly, because I had just saved up enough to buy a game I really wanted. She took the jar and poured all of the Stoneians out into her hand. My mother walked out of my room and down to Kyle's room. I followed her, curious of what she was planning to do with them.

"Zandrea, why did you break your brother's toy?" Her voice was as smooth as silk.

I blinked and said as innocently as possible, "Why do you think I broke it?"

"Who else in this house would have broken his toy?"

"I don't know, the wind," I said sarcastically. She rolled her eyes.

"I want this to be a lesson to you; don't break people's things," she said and handed my brother the Stoneians. I screamed and tried to swipe them away, but my mother grabbed my wrist, stopping me from reaching my destination. I proceeded to scream until my throat hurt. My mother tried to calm me down, but nothing could stop my screaming. First, I got punished for punching my brother, and then I had my Stoneians stolen by my mother, and now my throat hurt from screaming. What next?

My mother came to talk to me that night to tell me why she took my Stoneians. "I wanted you to learn a lesson," she said. "Hitting people and things is not right. It's not good, do you understand? It never solves any problems. It only gets you into trouble."

I pretended that I understood, but I just wanted my Stoneians back. Now, I realize what she was saying. It's like fighting fire with fire inside of a house made of paper—it hurts everyone within reaching distance and further.

Daniel stands in front of me, arms crossed, a crease between his eyebrows. He looks worn out but still trying to stay strong. He knows better than to give in, because every time he does, I end up winning the argument. We usually don't argue, but when we do, I tend to win. My parents agree I'm the most stubborn person they know, although they don't know very many people. Our neighborhood back on Coreno is small, mostly because everyone around us has moved away to find a job. One of my mother's friends left just before I did, and she was heartbroken. They were really close, but her husband had to leave to find work on another planet.

Before Layla, I had a friend who lived three doors down from me. We played games together and had sleepovers. Her parents and mine were talking one night about the Corps and how they were planning to take control of Coreno. Her parents said they were leaving as soon as they could to find a place on the other side of the galaxy where the Corps hadn't gained control. They asked if we wanted to join them, but my father said no and that we would be fine here. They left the next day, and we never saw them again.

The Corps have taken over our lives more than any of us would like, but no one is willing to stand up to them, until now. They have ruined my life: taking away my father, making some of my friends too scared to stick around, and turning my own mother against everything that my family stood for. They have to be brought down, otherwise they're just going to keep going up.

"Daniel," I say. "I'm sorry." He looks at me as if I've just admitted to killing someone.

"You're what?" he asks, astonished.

"You heard me," I say. "I don't want to keep fighting, especially not with you. I just want to go home, see my mother again, and reunite my family. I want the Corps to be brought down so we don't have to live in fear anymore. Is that too much to ask?"

He looks at me, and his gaze softens. "No, it's not too much. You're right; the Corps needs to be obliterated. Where are the others?"

I glance over my shoulder and find Kyle and Kelton at the end of the hall by the bathroom. Kyle is flinging soap at Kelton, who brings his arms up to protect himself. While Kelton is distracted, Kyle lunges at him, knocking him off balance. I glance back at Daniel, and he wears a worried expression on his face. I understand what he means, although he's not saying anything. If it's up to us five to save the galaxy, we could be in trouble.

Nobody here knows what's going on outside the Corps' headquarters. We've tried to guess, but we have no way of knowing what's true or what's false. The only way to find out is to leave and to go back to help the people who were once trapped here. After my father showers, we pack up our belongings and start our trek back to the platform. Kelton says he knows his way around here, so we trust him. I start thinking about all of the things that have happened since we got here: finding my father, meeting Kelton, and Daniel faking his death so he could go live with Callie, which I'm still mad at him for.

It dawns on me how free we have been these last few days. Besides the day we first came here, we haven't seen many signs of life. We haven't seen Max or David since I got shot, so who knows where they went. It's eerie how alone we've been, with no one around trying to stop us. I wonder if they even know we're here. But they must, because two guards found Kelton and Daniel, and they found Kyle and me. I wonder if Rowan taking that card from Kyle gave them access to anything and everything in the galaxy. I shudder at the thought that we gave them exactly what they needed. I rub my arms that are crossed over my chest, trying to relax my stiff body. It doesn't work until Kyle wraps his arm around my shoulder and pulls me closer to him. I smile gratefully, hoping he understands why I'm shaking. He returns the smile, but I don't think he gets the message.

The building seemed smaller from the platform. The trek back takes far too long, and my feet begin to hurt after a while. I almost start complaining, but I remember there are lots of other people who deal with much worse—people in the war, people who are bystanders during the war, and my parents and friends, the list is endless. I keep telling myself this, to the beat of my footsteps, and try to focus on other things.

Kelton holds the only gun we have in front of him and checks around every corner before motioning to us that it's all clear. We swiftly move to the other side of the hall and continue walking. We round the next corner and then walk down a long stretch of hallway, painted a dark gray, the ceiling a bright red. Some of the paint has chipped off the walls, and underneath lies an ugly shade of green. Kelton looks around the next corner, but before he has a chance to motion us backward, the shouting begins.

My legs can't move fast enough, and two large hands rest on my shoulders, pulling me backward. I slam onto the ground with a *thud* and the hands grab my wrists. I try to yank free, but I'm not strong enough. I hear Kyle scream, but it gets cut off abruptly. The hands drag me along the ground toward the end of the hall. Everyone else is being pulled the same way as me, including Kelton, who fired his gun at one of them. They drag us past the body, and I almost throw up. They soon knock us out with a poison gas, and everything goes black.

I wake a few hours later, or so I think, with my arms and legs chained to the wall behind me. The room is a dank, gray cell. This one isn't like the ones I've been in before. The doors are not transparent, and to the best of my knowledge, there are no cameras. The walls look like they are made of concrete, and the floor is white tile, with a drain in the middle. I start to get a really bad feeling, and I can't shake it. I begin to scream until my throat hurts, and a white smoke fills the room, knocking me out again.

I look up and see Kelton walking into my cell. I try to smile, but it's impossible with how much physical pain I'm in. He looks at me, examining my every move.

"Hello," he says finally.

"Hi," I croak out.

"On a scale of one to ten, how much pain are you in?"

"Eleven," I say without thinking.

"That's good, that's good." He looks at a clipboard that just appeared in his hands. He marks something down.

"How exactly is that a good thing," I manage to squeak out.

"Well, would you consider it a bad thing?" He looks back at me.

"Um… yes, I would actually." I sigh, and he gives me a confused frown. "Kelton, what's going on? How did you manage to escape your cell?"

"Well, I-" He doesn't finish his sentence. Instead, he crumples to the floor, blood pooling underneath him. A man stands behind him, knife in hand, black hood over his head so I can't see his face. I nudge Kelton a little, but his body remains cold, lifeless. I start to scream, shaking the chains that hold me to the floor. It's a rage scream that makes my body shudder with grief. The love of my life, killed, stabbed, right before my eyes, and there was nothing I could do to save him.

It's that thought that brings me back to reality. My biggest fear: not being able to save someone I love. They set up that scenario on purpose. And I know what room, what cell, I'm in—the Torturing Room, the one that Kelton has been in multiple times, seeing the same, or maybe different, fear over and over again. This is what the Torturing Room does to you: shows you your biggest fear, over and over, until you can't take it anymore, and grief and fear have taken over your entire body. If this keeps happening, I will be worth nothing, too far gone to come back. I just have to be able to overcome it, and now that I know what's going to happen, I can be ready.

The door creaks open, and Daniel walks in. Somehow, I remember that I'm still mad at him, and the scenario generators don't know that. *This should be easy*, I think, but immediately after I say it, I know it's not true. Daniel is my best friend, and there is no way that losing him would ever be easy.

"Zandrea," he begins. "There's someone I'd like you to meet." A girl steps into the room behind him, and I recognize her as the girl from the launch pad. *Callie*, I think. Suddenly there's a bitter taste in my mouth, and I want to throw up. Callie gives Daniel a quick kiss on the cheek and turns to look at me. Her overly makeup-done eyes look at me intensely. I glare back at her.

"What a pleasure it is to meet you," I spit.

"Wish I could say the same about you," she retorts. "Oh wait, it is. I forgot that Daniel chose me over you. I'm glad I could meet my competition, if you could even call it that."

I try to thrash out at her, but the chains on my hands and ankles pull me back. She takes a step away from me as if I'm going to bite her. The thought did cross my mind.

"Vicious little thing, isn't she," she snarls. "I don't know how you ever could have loved her."

"I didn't," Daniel says. "But I had to go along with it."

"You told me you loved me," I scream. "You proposed to me and everything. You crushed my dreams! And you know what? Kelton is twice the man you'll ever be! Good luck, *Callie*. You're going to need it!" The tears stream hotly down my face, and I make no attempt to stop the flow.

Callie crouches down in front of me and smacks my cheek hard. "Don't worry, you were never a threat to me anyway." She stands up, and a moment later I hear the door slam shut.

The tears keep coming, but I can only think about what they said. Daniel said he never loved me and that it was only an act. Callie isn't the kind person I thought she was, and she told me that I was never a threat to her relationship with Daniel. A new thought crosses my mind: Daniel is being held captive too. I wonder what kinds of things he's seeing.

I think I fall asleep, but I'm awoken by the sleep-inducing gas, and I'm launched into a different scenario. This time, Kyle appears, but not like Kelton and Daniel did. My mother is here too, and so are some medical workers. They don't acknowledge me. The edge of my vision is blurry, almost like a dream, but it's not, because I know exactly what is happening.

Kyle sits on an operating table while the doctors talk to my mother. Kyle sits as still as a statue, and his eyes don't move, don't even blink. His blue eyes staring but not seeing. I touch his face with the tip of my finger, but he doesn't even flinch.

"So explain to me what's going to happen?" It's my mother's voice.

"Of course," says one of the medical workers. "We've already put him in a deep sleep, and now we are going to operate on his brain. I'm going to inject this purple liquid into his head, which will allow us to access all of his memories. You tell us which ones you want removed."

"How do you remove the memories?" It's my mother's voice again.

"Good question," says a different medical worker. "We don't actually remove them, just gloss them over. This is why you can't say anything to him about the memories we've taken away. If you do, the memory resurfaces and he'll be able to remember that specific memory. The purple liquid was designed to modify a part of your brain called the hippocampus, which helps transfer short-term memories to long-term memories. The hippocampus grows neurons to help retain memory. But the purple liquid also stops the hippocampus from growing certain neurons to retain the memories we took away. And that, in short, is how the purple liquid works."

"Fascinating," says my mother flatly. "I think we can begin."

"I just need you to sign some paperwork that states we are not responsible if this doesn't work because you told him something."

My mother grabs a pen and signs her name. "I'm ready," she says.

"Excellent, now tell me what memories you want us to get rid of," the medical worker says. My mother reads off a short list of things she doesn't want him to remember, and the medical workers begin operating. A tear slips down my face when she says my name, and I begin sobbing after she reads my father's name. Thankfully, no one can hear me sobbing in the corner of the small room. Everything goes black after that, and I'm sobbing in reality. Only do I stop when I hear a knock on the door.

The door opens slowly, creaking as if it's 100 years old. A dark figure walks in, tall with a big frame. "Hello," the voice says. "Remember me?" Rowan steps into the light where I can see him more clearly. He's still intimidating, and I shrink back against the wall. Last time I saw him, he stole a card from Kyle and pretended he was going to give us Kelton. I'm still furious with him for that.

"Oh, sure," I say smugly. "You're the coward who couldn't keep up his end of the bargain." At the mention of him being a coward, he scowls at me, making his wrinkled face even more wrinkled. He soon releases his scowl and gives an airy chuckle.

"I think you misunderstood what my intentions were. Besides, you were roaming free up until about six hours ago. I couldn't let you go, but it was fun while it lasted, right?" He looks happy, in a very menacing sort of way, and it makes my stomach hurt. "Anyway, I was planning on having you as personal bodyguards, but I figured with everything that I've done to you, you wouldn't agree. So then I got to thinking, what if I *made* you help me? But I also thought making you wouldn't be enough. You would have to be so depressed, barely even living, for you to agree, and so, here you are now!" He says it as if it's his biggest success ever, and I'm guessing it probably is.

"How exactly would you make us so depressed that we would help you automatically?"

"That's a good question, but I think you already know the answer. You see, I need an army, because eventually, they're coming for me. And as much as I would love to fight, I'm too old." I roll my eyes at this remark because he doesn't look a day over thirty-five, but I keep quiet. "It would be so easy to destroy each of you, but where would the fun in that be? No, I decided you would much rather be in here than out fighting alongside the Corps. Correct me if I'm wrong, but I think all of these people, even Daniel, mean a lot more to you than you let on. Tell me again why you allowed Kelton to be a part of your group. And don't leave out any details, especially the one about you falling for him instead of your best friend. I find that part to be really intriguing and not really like you at all."

My voice shakes a little as the next words come out. "How do you know all that?"

He motions toward the cell I'm in and the surrounding walls. "Do you not see that you are in the Corps' headquarters? I know everything about everyone."

"I hadn't noticed," I say sarcastically. "But thank you for pointing that out. By the way, I was just wondering, if you know everything about everyone, why do you want me to tell you about my personal life? You should already know all of the details, right?"

"Ha ha, very funny," he says like I have time for laughing when I'm in my death cell. "You know, I think you're the most fiery out of them all. You would be perfect for my force. You have the right skill set. I could slowly kill all of the other ones, and you would be the only one left. Brilliant, right?"

I feel all of the color drain from my face. I want to thrash out at him for even mentioning that idea, but the more uncivilized I become, the less chance I have of getting out of here alive, with my family and friends.

The walkie-talkie around his belt crackles to life, and he steps out of the cell to answer the call. He comes back a few minutes later, checking his watch. "Sorry, that was my boss. He needs me downstairs now. Besides, I'm guessing you need some time to process this information. Tell you what, I'm going to go talk to some of my supervisors about enlisting you for my army. I think you would be perfect!" He opens the door, winks, and briskly walks out, leaving the door ajar.

It occurs to me that Rowan must take his orders from Chris, and if Chris knows who I am, he might want me on their "force" even more than I thought they would. If only my mother were on our side and not brainwashed by him.

Rowan and Chris are complete opposites. Rowan is friendly and not extremely bright. I think that he would be a really nice and fun person if he didn't work for the Corps. But then again, Kelton worked for them too, and he turned out fine, at least, as far as I know.

Chris, on the other hand, is strict and firm and has no emotion. His laugh might sound like nails on a chalkboard, if he knew how to laugh. I guess I can see why he chose to work as the Corps' first-in-command. His personality is just as appealing as the company he works for. I wonder if Chris brainwashed Rowan to get him to work here, and his personality would make them seem like an organization that wanted to help people, not kill for fun and brainwash innocent people.

I'm about to drift off to sleep, hoping it would make things go slower, and maybe imagine my family one last time, but I'm awoken by something. Or, to be more accurate, someone. Someone I know well. I have to blink a few times to make sure I'm not dreaming again, but I'm not. He stands right in front of me, the overhead light illuminating his face. I whisper his name, but he's already unlocking the chains around my hands and feet. I bring my hands in front of my face and examine them really closely. His hands wrap around mine and he pulls me to my feet.

"How did you escape?" I manage.

"Max and David found me," Kelton says. "They said they knew my screams all too well, but I think they saw me in one of the cameras. Anyway, we have to go. They knew my cell was unlocked, so they could be here any minute." I look at his gleaming eyes and find actual fear behind them. I can't tell if he's worried we might be caught or he's still reliving the nightmares from the cell, or both. I've never truly seen him afraid before, but it scares me more than it should. I try to calm myself by wrapping my arms around his neck. He wraps his arms around my waist. It reminds me of when I used to hug my father when he came home from work.

He pulls away a few seconds later. "What was that for?"

"I'll tell you later," I say. "We have to go right now. Rowan said that he'll be back soon, and I can only imagine what would happen if he found out you escaped." He grabs my hand and pulls me down a row of cells, each one with a heavy metal door in front of it.

"Do you know which cell my father and Kyle are in?" I purposefully leave out Daniel's name, because even though it was just a scenario, it doesn't mean it couldn't happen some day. Kelton looks at me funnily as if he just smelled something awful.

"Yes," he says wearily. "And Daniel?"

"Did I forget about someone," I ask. "Oh well, I guess we can get him too."

Kelton stops running, which makes me jerk forward a little. "What did you see in that cell that had to do with Daniel?" He asks the question accusingly, and I cross my arms and scowl.

"Nothing, just him introducing *Callie* to me," I spit.

"Who's Callie?"

"The girl that Daniel faked his death for. She was really rude and uptight about everything. It made me sick the way she clung on to him. But she can have him, I found someone better anyway." I wink at him, and a smile creeps onto his face. "Anyways, we should probably get going." He nods and we take off running again.

Kelton stops in front of a cell and pulls out a ring of cards around his belt loop. He selects one of the cards and slides it through a slot next to the door. The door opens with a *hiss*, and I push it open further to see who's inside. The cell looks just like mine did, except it holds my brother instead of me. I run over to him and wrap my arms around him, pulling him close to me. He doesn't move, and I can barely feel his breaths against my neck. I pull away and find his eyes open and his body limp. A tear rolls down my cheek as I recall what he looked like in my dream. I look away, at the blurry ground, before I stand up and sob into Kelton's shoulder.

He doesn't ask for a while, but eventually he can't wait any longer. "Kyle's going to be okay, you know that?" he assures me. "He's in one of the simulations that you and I were in, except there's no emotion, so maybe he's seeing the beginning of his dream. I've heard you don't show much emotion on the outside until the middle to end."

"He was in one of my hallucinations," I blurt out. "Except that it wasn't futuristic. It was the past. It was from when my mother took him to get the Procedure. His face was blank and slack and his eyes open but not seeing anything. He looked like he did after he ate the bread, except younger and less frightening."

Kelton nods at me thoughtfully, contemplating what he should say next. "Was I in one of your hallucinations?" he asks me. I nod. "What was it about?"

"You walked in my cell," I begin. "You asked me to rate my pain, and I told you I was an eleven. You told me that was good. I asked you how you escaped, but before you could answer, someone, I didn't see who, came up behind you and stabbed you in the heart. You crumpled to the ground and blood started pooling around you. I screamed until I woke up and realized I was just hallucinating. It felt so real, though."

"Yeah, they're designed to target your worst fears and make you imagine them," he says. "It's actually a pretty genius way to torture your enemies. I would give them more credit, but they've been using it against the people I care about most. I'm so sorry. This is all my fault. I should've been protecting you more. If you want, I can go find your father and Daniel and you can stay here with Kyle until he wakes up."

I nod in agreement, and he shows me how to unlock the chains around his ankles and hands.

"I'll be back soon," he says. "If he wakes up before I get back, come and look for me." He runs out of the cell and to the right. I watch him run for a while until I hear Kyle scream. I whip around, finding him trying to clutch at his neck. I start to pull his hands off his neck, but I realize that he's doing it for a reason. He screams again, but this time, his face turns blue. He closes his eyes and starts throwing up blood and saliva, but his screaming still continues. Finally, after what seems like too long, his eyes open. He blinks a few times, adjusting to the sudden source of light. His gaze lands on me, and he screams.

"Kyle," I shout at him, trying to raise my voice over his. "Kyle! It's me, Zandrea, your sister. I'm not going to hurt you." He stops screaming and begins panting to slow his heart rate. "I'm going to get you out of here, okay." I unlock the chains, just like Kelton showed me how to do. He rubs his hands where the cuffs were and starts crying.

"You were dead," he says to me. "Everyone was. It was all my fault, too. I was brainwashed to think that you were the enemy. You told me to stay strong, and I did, but it was too late. I also had to kill Mother because Chris said I had to." He starts sobbing, so I wrap my arms around him. He buries his face into my shirt and cries until the tears stop flowing. Kyle wipes his eyes and stands. "How did you get in here?"

"Kelton unlocked my cell and we found yours," I say calmly, like it was no big deal. "His friends Max and David heard him and helped him get out. We have to go find him." Kyle and I start down the corridor until we find an open room. No one is inside, but it looks like it was used recently.

Kyle runs ahead as I examine the room. It looks the same as all of the others, but the chains start a little higher up. This room is meant for taller people, like my father. The thought scares me, so I keep running to catch up to Kyle, who is stopped in front of a doorway. He's hugging someone, my father, their cheeks stained with tears. I join the group hug, and my father pulls me close to his side.

"I thought I would never see you two again," he says. "I'm glad I was wrong." A smile crawls onto my father's face, one I haven't seen since I was little, the smile that reads: everything is going to be alright, nothing can hurt us. I saw the smile when he would embrace my mother after a long day at work. It made me realize that nothing can separate our family, not the Corps, and definitely not Chris.

"Father," I begin. He looks at me expectantly. "Let's go home." His smile grows bigger, and he pulls me even closer to him.

I walk into the cell that contains Daniel. Kelton crouches on the floor next to him, waiting for him to wake up from his nightmare. He looks very calm, considering his worst fears are playing across his mind like a movie screen. His eyes flutter open a few minutes later, and he looks around the cell, blinking in the new source of light.

"What's going on?" He demands. I sit down next to Daniel. "How did you get out?"

"Kelton helped me," I say. "At least he would care enough."

"I would've too if I wasn't chained up like a dog," he retorts. "It's not like there was much I could do."

"Kelton helped me," I say again. "Why couldn't you?"

"In case you haven't noticed," he begins. "I'm sort of tied up. So maybe if you could stop treating me like your enemy, maybe I can stop feeling like one. At least I didn't betray you." His eyes flicker over to Kelton, hatred brewing underneath his blue irises.

Kelton winces next to me. "You did, actually," I say.

"Not like he did," Daniel fires back.

"No, you're right," I say. "My best friend faked his death so he could go and spend the rest of his life with his *girlfriend* after he already proposed to his best friend. So yeah, you didn't betray me like he did. What you did was much worse." I pause, my voice dropping to a whisper. "And I will never be able to forgive you for it." I stand up and walk out of the cell, tears threatening to slip down my face.

Later, my father comes out of the cell and stands next to me, leaning against the wall. “I’m so sorry, sweetheart. I didn’t know how bad things have been with you and Daniel. I thought you were working things out.” He takes a deep breath and closes his eyes.

We stand in silence for a while before I muster up the courage to ask him a question that’s been nagging at me since we first found him here. “Do you still love Mother?”

The question must come as a surprise, because his eyelids fly open and he whips his head to look at me. “Of course,” he says, like the answer should have been obvious. “Why do you ask?”

“I don’t know,” I say quietly. “Even though they weren’t together at the time, her boyfriend is the one who got you into this mess. It was his idea to bring you here.”

“Well, I guess we should get back before anything else happens.” He smiles at me, and the warmth of his smile is enough to make me smile back. He pats my shoulder in a reassuring gesture and looks from me to where Kyle is in the cell.

“He’s grown up a lot,” my father says. “And you’ve done a good job taking care of him.”

“I haven’t done much,” I admit. “I think just being here has helped him to grow. You should have seen how scared he was to leave home.”

“It is a lot to process,” he says. “But I think it was good for him, and you for that matter, to see the galaxy, get out of your comfort zone a little bit. It gives you a new perspective on things.”

I nod, not really sure what else to say.

Kelton, Kyle, and Daniel come out of the cell a few minutes later. Daniel looks tired until his eyes meet up with mine. He straightens up, trying to make himself look bigger and stronger than Kelton. I would start laughing, but I remember I’m still angry with him.

I walk faster to join Kelton, who playfully slugs Kyle in the arm. “Kelton,” I say, and he turns around. “I need to talk to you.” He falls in step with me, leaving Kyle to walk with my father and Daniel. I begin discussing the conversation I had with Rowan. “He came into my cell and told me he wanted me to be a part of his army. He said I had enough skill for it."

"He actually thought you were going to help him? He must really be desperate," Kelton replies.

"Here's the weird part: he left my cell open enough for me to escape. I was still locked up, but I probably could've got out of those chains if I wanted to. And the way he left, it just seemed too… setup. Like he was planning for his walkie-talkie to interrupt our conversation. And he winked at me, as if he was trying to tell me something."

"Yeah, probably that you're beautiful and he would probably like to go out with you."

I shake my head. "That's disgusting. He's like twenty years older than me. And besides, he works for the Corps. Like I would date anyone from the Corps." Kelton looks offended by this, and I remember that he used to work for them. "I didn't mean it like that. And anyways, you were working undercover. That doesn't count." He smiles and does something I never saw coming. He kisses me. It's like the dream I had, back when Kyle and I were trapped in the mirror hallway, except real. I feel Daniel's eyes on the back of my head. This is my way of showing him I've moved on and don't need him.

I smile as he pulls back and reaches for my hand. I can't keep the smile off my face, not even when Kyle turns around and starts mimicking us. Kelton laughs, and so do I, making me feel more free than I have in weeks.

The corridor that we're in is very long and lit dimly. We don't reach the end for a few minutes. Kelton pulls out his card loop and opens the door. Max and David wait outside for us, guns poised and ready to fire at will.

"What took you guys so long?" David asks it like it was supposed to be a joke, but I don't find it very funny.

"Thanks for getting us out of there," Kelton says. "Now, we all need to get to the main hangar, where we'll find some kind of ship to get us back to Coreno. From there, we can head in our own directions. I know

Zandrea, Kyle, their father, and Daniel live there. I have some friends who live there as well. Where are you guys heading?"

"I'm heading to Xeltron with David," Max says. "His sister lives there. And, from what we've heard, it seems to have the least amount of war there. Good luck on Coreno, it has the most fighting in the entire galaxy."

"Thanks," Kelton says. "We'll keep that in mind."

"So," Daniel begins. "What's the best way to get out of here?"

"The hangar is on the first floor and about half a mile north of here," David informs us. "The best way to get there would be to go the half mile up here, then take an elevator down to the first floor, and go from there. They might not have many ships, considering how many they have had to use for warfare, but the Corps have been planning this attack for several years. Hopefully they have enough ships left. Once we get there, stay put until Max and I find a ship we can use."

"Let's go then," I say. "I have to get back to my mother before she does something she'll regret for the rest of her life."

We take off running in the direction David said we should go. We get there a little later, panting and sweating. The roar of the ships taking off shakes the ground. The vibration is enough to make my stomach hurt where the bullet pierced me. I lean against the wall until the vibrating stops.

"You okay?" Daniel approaches me, looking defeated and tired.

"Now you care?" I'm not letting my guard down with him for even a second. I've seen him do this kind of thing before, pretending to care so the person will open up to him. It's a great gift to have, especially when your job is to interrogate people. He has a specific tone of voice he reserves for times like this. He uses it when we get in fights, but this time is different. This time, I don't have to come running back to him.

"Look, I didn't come over here to fight with you," he says. "I seriously want to know if you're okay. Even if you don't think so, you're still my best friend. That hasn't changed, and will never change, for me anyway. And I'm sorry I didn't tell you about Callie. I knew it would break you, and I couldn't do that. I realized when Kelton kissed you that things were different between us, you had moved on. I hope someday you can at least forgive me."

He sounds so sincere that it almost kills me to keep pushing the subject, but there's something I have to know. "Why did you propose to me if you were in love with Callie?"

"I don't know," he answers. "I never really was in love with her like I was with you. Callie has liked me since we were young, we went to the same school and everything, but I never felt the same way. I knew you were falling for Kelton, so I decided to take drastic measures, like faking my death. I didn't realize how much our relationship would be affected."

"Listen Daniel," I begin. "If you had told me that there was someone else, before you proposed, I would have told you to be with her instead of me. Sure, it would have hurt for a while, but I could have got over it. Now, when I look at you, all I see is a liar, and I can't trust you like I used to. Things change, nothing is ever going to be definite, and that's why there's such thing as risk. If there's no risk, there's no thrill. And now, there's no us."

It kills me to talk to him the way I just did, especially after he apologized, but I have to hold my ground. If I don't, he will reel me in like he does every time we get in a fight. He looks at the ground, probably contemplating what I said. He finally looks up at me, his eyes red with tears. I look away. One thing that hasn't changed since I left home almost three weeks ago is my compassion for other people. My mother told me I get it from my father. He's the kind of person that would help no matter what the circumstance. I can't bring my eyes to his, no matter how hard I try. Part of me aches for him, because I understand what he's going through. I know what it's like, coming so close to something, only for it to be taken away. My eyes fill with tears, but I blink them away, not wanting to show weakness and defeat.

"I should probably go and find us a way out of here," he says quietly. "I thought you should know that Callie is only a name to me. But Zandrea is a name that means so much more to me. Hope and inspiration. Love. I'm not asking for you to take me back. I'm just asking for a second chance, at least at being friends."

He walks away, back to the big picture window. The ships outside rumble down the runway, jetting off somewhere into the galaxy. As far as I know, the war is still waging on the North side of the galaxy. The South has been safe for a while, but no one knows when war will strike next.

I walk along the length of a glass wall, overlooking the runways. Different size crates line the wall, each one labeled with different weapons and tools. I figure it's the supplies for the soldiers in the war, brought to the areas where the fighting is the strongest. The Corps had already taken control over half of the galaxy when I returned home. The numbers must have grown immensely since then. I hope my mother is out of the war zones and in neutral territory. I push the thought away immediately; she's dating the leader of the Corps, of course she's safe.

I find an empty space between two crates and wedge myself into the snug area. Snow litters the ground outside, and the cold seeps in through the windows, making me shiver. Of the ships that are stationary, only a few remain on the runways, the snow covering them like a blanket. I bring my knees closer to my chest to keep warm, but the frosty glass prevents any warmth from reaching my body. I stare out at the runway until I drift off to sleep.

My mother always told me I had a creative imagination. I used to believe I was a superhero who could save our galaxy from any harm the Corps threw at us. I would make up stories about other heroes that lived far away. Kyle loved story night. I would dress up in a sheet that I used as a cape and tell the story of some guy that fought against the Corps. He would join me and act like my sidekick. He was too little to understand that the Corps was real and they needed heroes, real ones, to save the galaxy. To him, it was fake. An act. But to the rest of the galaxy, it was a real-life nightmare.

I let my dreams take me wherever they want. It starts out great, wonderful even. The Corps have long been deceased, and the peace that once was present had been restored. In my dream, I'm married to someone with light brown hair and big blue-green eyes. I couldn't have asked for a happier dream right now, in the mix of all this mess. I can almost feel myself smiling in reality.

My dreams start to take a wrong turn a little later. I find out my husband is the leader of the Corps, and he's planning to take revenge on the galaxy yet once again. I try to stop him and tell him it's not worth the loss of so many lives. It reminds me of the woman I met in the cage. She told me she and her husband got into a fight, and he was the reason she was beaten and put into a cage with her children. I worry that I may turn out like her, beat and tired with no hope and nowhere to go.

I wake with a start later, hoping no one asks why. I stand up, my legs cramped from sitting in the same position for who knows how long. I find that most of our group has left the area I last saw them in. Only Kyle and Kelton sit on the ground, playing some kind of hand slapping game. I walk over to where they sit and watch them play. They pretend like they don't notice me, though, which I guess is better. I have other things I need to worry about, things that are more important than a silly game.

"Do you want to play?" Kyle's voice catches me off guard.

I stare at him blankly before finally finding my voice. "I guess," I say, even though I'm not sure I want to. "How do you play?"

He explains the rules to me, but my mind is elsewhere. I nod along, pretending I'm listening, but all I can think about is how we're going to get out of here.

"Do you get it?" Kyle's voice interrupts my thoughts and snaps me back into focus.

"Oh sure, it's simple," I say absentmindedly.

"You weren't listening at all, were you?" Kyle asks the question so nonchalantly I smile and laugh.

"It's nothing personal," I say after a few minutes. "I've just been really distracted lately."

"No kidding," Kelton chimes in. "I've been trying to get your attention for like the last two minutes as Kyle was explaining the game. I think you need more sleep or something."

"I just need to get out of here," I say tiredly. I rest my head in Kelton's lap, and he smooths my hair like a mother would to her child. The touch soothes me, and I close my eyes, dreaming of home.

Chris sits in my father's favorite chair. His hands are clasped and rest on the armrests of the chair. He looks almost comfortable, except his back is straight, alert, and his eyebrows furrow into each other. His eyes are fixed on something behind me, but I don't turn to see what it is. I don't need to. I already know what's there.

"That's my chair," my father says calmly from behind me. "I need you to move."

"That's not going to happen," Chris says back, calmly. The tones of their voices scare me. No one should be that calm while arguing with someone.

I step out of the way as my father moves gracefully toward Chris. Chris doesn't move, not even flinch, as my father eyes him up and down, sizing him up. My father could probably take on Chris any day, but something is stopping him. That something is my mother.

Her entrance into the room draws the attention of both men, causing them to momentarily forget their differences. By the way they look at her, you would think she is the highest form of honor there is. My mother, being who she is, ignores their stares and steps farther into the room.

"I thought I heard bickering," she says in a monotone voice. "I don't allow bickering in my house." Her eyes move back and forth between Chris and my father, not staying on either one for longer than necessary.

"We weren't bickering," Chris begins. "I was explaining that this is my chair and my house. He's the one who got testy with me."

"That is not true, and you know it," my father chimes in. "None of that was true. That is not your chair, and this is most definitely not your house. I'm the one who bought it, and I intend to keep it."

"You need to-" Chris starts, but my mother interrupts him.

"Chris is right, Jordan," my mother says. "You left *us*, remember? Chris has taken your place, in my house, and especially in my heart. You can leave whenever you feel like it." She turns on her heel and walks out of the room with just as much flair as she had when she walked in.

My father turns to run after her, but Chris puts his hand on my father's shoulders. "From what I've learned, once she exits a conversation, she likes to leave it that way," Chris says.

My father slaps Chris's hand away and, in one smooth motion, punches Chris in the jaw. "Don't ever touch me again," my father growls. Chris holds his jaw with one hand and swings his other hand up to connect with my father's nose. They begin fighting, each one taking a turn and holding their injuries with their free hand.

I try to shout above the noise, but my voice gets drowned out. I run outside before I'm forced to choose sides. I could care less about Chris, but I know now that my mother would side with him no matter what.

The chilly air outside freezes me to the bone, but I can't go back to my house. I look over my shoulder at what once was my safe haven before I continue walking down the street and try to ignore my body's cry for heat. I hear the shuffling of feet behind me and turn to see who's following me.

"Kelton?" My voice comes out barely above a whisper. "What are you doing here?"

"I came to see how you're doing," he says casually. "Am I not allowed to do that?"

"Of course you are," I reply. "I just wasn't expecting to see you around here."

"Yeah, I work up the road a little ways," he says as he stuffs his hands in his pockets.

I nod and continue walking. I'm not sure where I'm going, but I have to get away from my house. Kelton trots up next to me and slips his hand into mine. For once, I feel like we're a normal couple, going for a walk in the cold, laughing about random things.

"I didn't realize I was that funny," a man in front of us says. I look from Kelton to the man, who I realize is Daniel.

"Hey Daniel," I say in a relaxed tone. I haven't seen him since we got back.

"Looks like you two are getting along just fine," he says harshly.

"Obviously," Kelton retorts, pulling me closer to his side. "People don't hold hands because they hate each other." His sarcasm makes me laugh until I see the look on Daniel's face. "Also, people don't do this if they hate each other." His free hand moves to my chin, and his lips press against mine. Just like the first time we kissed, I can feel Daniel's eyes on me, but this time I don't feel great about the kiss. I just feel sad, because I know this is killing Daniel, and I know that all of the problems I have with Callie don't compare to what he must be feeling.

About two seconds later, a force pulls Kelton away from me, fast. I open my eyes to find Daniel tackling Kelton to the ground. I step back, and my hands fly to my face, astonished by what is happening.

"Daniel!" I try to yell, but my voice gets lost in the air. "Daniel, stop!"

He glances up at me, hatred seeping in his eyes, and goes back to fighting Kelton, landing a punch square in his nose. I feel bad for even thinking this, but Kelton kind of deserves what Daniel is giving him. He doesn't take jealousy lightly.

One time, a few years ago, as Daniel and I were at a ship repair shop on Techario, one of the workers came over to me and started flirting with me. I tried to smile, but I could see Daniel out of the corner of my eye. The scowl on his face was all I needed to see to know he was jealous. I quickly ended the conversation with the worker and walked over to where Daniel stood. He didn't look at me for about a day after that until I finally broke him by threatening to leave.

It has always puzzled me how Daniel can pretend he has no interest in me until someone else tries to take me away from him. I'm like a dog on a leash, always having to do what my owner wants, instead of what I want. What Daniel has taught me though is how much I dislike being a dog on a leash.

I can't stand to see Kelton get beat up, especially by Daniel, but I know that nothing I say or do will change anything; Daniel hates Kelton, and there is nothing I can do about it. I decide running is the best option for me.

I run toward the landing pad, which is only a few minutes from my house. The cold air burns my lungs as I take in breaths. The wind whips at my face, stinging it. Even though I am breathless and my legs feel like jelly, I keep pushing myself to go faster, further. I have to leave the life of fighting behind.

I see the landing pad about a block away, and relief overwhelms me. As I near the landing pad, I see someone who looks familiar.

"Kyle!" I shout, and my voice carries through the air. He turns to look at me and then lifts his hand to wave. With an extra burst of strength, I run even faster to catch up to him.

"Hey," he says casually. "What are you doing here?"

"Trying to escape my past," I say, realizing how deep that sounds.

"Um, okay," he tries. "That's nice. Anyway, how have you been?"

"Father found Chris in his chair and started fighting him," I start. "I ran out of the house and found Kelton, who I walked with for a little, and then Daniel showed up. Kelton kissed me, Daniel tackled him, and, as far as I know, they're still at it."

"Well who can blame him," Kyle snaps. "You and Kelton are always together, and it's kind of making us both sick. And while you were planning your wedding, Mother was ill and could barely lift a finger. She asked about you all the time, like when you were coming back and if you were helping me at all. I simply answered with, 'I don't know' and left it at that."

"I'm sorry," I say. "I don't mean to be like that, but things have been different ever since we got back here. I saw Mother earlier today, before Chris and our father started fighting. She told Father that she had moved on without him; I thought that meant me too, since I had been gone for so long."

"Well, if you weren't so stuck up all the time and started to care about the other people in your life, besides Kelton, maybe things would be different," he shouts. "You only care about yourself!"

"That is not true," I say indignantly. "I do care about the other people in my life, but I've been busy lately. I'm back now and you still seem upset. Why?"

"You know exactly why," he says quietly, but he's still furious. "Don't pretend that because you've been gone for so long, you have no idea what's happening."

"I'm not pretending," I say, my voice a half step louder than necessary. "But I will pretend that everything is fine if you don't tell me something soon."

"I'm surprised he hasn't told you anything," Kyle says. "I thought you would have been the first person he would tell anything to. He really hasn't told you anything?"

"Who? Tell me what?"

"Kelton!" he yells. "Kelton hasn't told you anything, has he? About taking over the galaxy again?"

"What are you talking about?" I ask incredulously.

"From what I've heard," Kyle says, his voice a whisper. "He wants to do what his father never could. He wants to enslave every planet in our universe and to make them each work for him. He's already taken control of Demephebis and plans to enslave more."

I gasp at this news, because Demephebis is one of the most heavily fortified planets in our universe. Chris could never enslave Demephebis because of its security measures and the fact that most of our soldiers come from there. Kyle said something about how Kelton's father could never do something that he can. I haven't met Kelton's father, or have I? I gasp again.

I wake with a start, my heart beating too fast. Kelton sits in the same place he did before I fell asleep, my head still in his lap. He looks down at me, concern filling his eyes. I sit up and look around for Kyle.

"Are you okay?" he asks.

The truth is I don't think I am. Being away from home for this length of time with long days and short nights has finally taken its toll. I don't like seeing people I care about worried or concerned, though. "Yeah, I'm fine. I just thought I overslept or something."

He looks at me for a little longer before standing up. He offers me his hand, but I waive his offer away. I just feel like sitting and thinking.

Somehow, I think he understands this and walks away without saying anything. I cross my legs and put my elbows on my knees, my hands holding my head upright.

My mind races with thoughts of my mother, back at home; of Kyle, who appeared in my dream and has now disappeared; and of my father, who has tried so hard to get back to us all of these years. I think about how my mother wrote him off years ago, because she assumed he was dead. She never tried to go looking for him or me for that matter. I'm beginning to wonder if she ever wanted us to come back or if she would have been happy if we stayed away forever. I refuse to believe this. My mother loved both my father and me; she cried the days we decided to leave. It was Chris who changed her point of view. It's Chris who has been killing innocent people for a living with the war that he started. And it's Chris who will pay for everything he has done.

As I snap out of my thoughts, I overhear Daniel talking to my father. "I cannot believe that's how you two met," Daniel exclaims.

"Oh yeah, it was a very funny story," my father says. "She felt so bad, and I felt so bad for her that I had to see her again. We laughed about it every time I came in."

"So she really spilled a steaming cup of coffee on you, and you still came back," Daniel replies. "I would've found some new place to drink my coffee after that."

"That's just it," my father says. "If I had, I never would have married the woman I love to this day, and Zandrea and Kyle wouldn't exist. And who knows, maybe she did it on purpose." He stares off into space for a while before noticing me.

"Zandrea," my father declares. "We were just talking about how your mother and I met. I've told you the story before, right?"

"I'm not sure, maybe," I say absentmindedly.

He laughs before launching into the romantic story of my parents falling in love because my mother spilled coffee on him and felt terrible, which led him to come in every day just to see her.

"Ah, yes," my father sighs. "Samantha was the light of my life. I should never have let her go." He looks down, as if ashamed by what he did. Kyle puts his arm around my father.

"She doesn't blame you, and neither do we," Kyle says sympathetically. "I think she understood what had to be done. You were trying to protect us. It wasn't your fault that they tricked you."

"Yeah, I guess you're right," he replies. "I just wished I had tried harder to break free. I was gone for so long. I didn't get to see you or your sister grow up, and that has been my biggest regret. That is something that can't be reversed."

"From what I've heard," Kyle says. "I was pretty annoying as a toddler, so I don't think you missed much there."

My father laughs his tired laugh and hugs Kyle. "I'm so lucky to have you," he says quietly.

Max returns later, with news about the ship he and David managed to steal. "So I have good news and bad news. Good news, we've found a ship that should get us to our destinations. Bad news is we don't have a pilot to fly the ship."

"Yeah you do," Kelton says. "I thought you guys knew me better than this." He rolls his eyes and playfully slugs Max in the arm.

"Ow, come on man," Max complains. "You know I'm just joking around. Anyway, David is with the ship, so we should start moving."

Max and Kelton lead us to a back stairwell that leads belowground to where the Corps keep most of their ships. The basement is vast, bigger than the base of the aboveground Corps' building. The room is bright and the walls are an off-white color, the ground a deep black. I look down and see my reflection in the shiny tiles below my feet. I look worn down and grimy. I'm suddenly very self-aware of the stench rising up around me. Once I get back, I'm definitely taking a shower.

The basement contains a few ships that look to be in good condition, but the rest are broken down and have parts strewn across the floor. I look to my left, which has two giant sliding doors, which I assume must be used to get the ships out of here. The doors appear to be locked by some kind of chain, which will be hard to maneuver.

David waves us over to where he stands by one of the only fully put-together ships in the area. The ship is small but big enough for everyone to fit in. I glance at Kelton who seems very confident about his flying abilities. He steps onto the ship first and moves to the front, where most of the controls are.

"You might need a copilot," I say softly to him as he adjusts some switches overhead.

"No thanks," he says without looking. "I've got Max for that." He finally peers at me over his shoulder. I look at the ground like a kid might after being scolded.

"I didn't mean that you couldn't, just that I don't need anyone," he says apologetically. "Max is one of the best pilots I know, and he has been trained extensively. But maybe you could be my co-copilot." He laughs lightly at his own joke, but I just frown at him.

"In case you didn't know," I retort. "Daniel and I used to fly everywhere together, and I was his copilot. So if you think I can't do it or something, talk to Daniel, because he's one of the best pilots *I* know."

Daniel looks at me and smiles, but I'm too enraged at the moment to return the favor. He goes back to reading a thin manual book he found in one of the seats.

"I didn't mean to offend you," Kelton says. "I'm just saying that-"

"That because I'm a girl I can't fly a ship?" I can feel my face flush red with anger.

"No, that Max and I have already agreed on everything," he retorts. "Besides, one of the pilots I trained with was a girl, and she flew better than anyone else in the class, including me."

"What happened?"

"I'm not sure. I think she flew to one of the war sites to help the Corps."

"Too bad," I say. "She could have really helped our side."

"Yeah," Kelton says absentmindedly. He turns back to the control panel next to the flight controls and fidgets with the levers some more.

"Excuse me," Max says, coming up from behind me.

"Sorry," I say. "But can I sit next to him? You can still be copilot, just back there." I point to behind the pilot's chair.

"Hey Max," Kelton says, eyeing him carefully. "Just this once, I'll let her sit next to me. You can next time, I promise."

"Sure," Max says.

I grow very suspicious, considering Max never agrees to anything without arguing about it first, but I take my seat anyway, next to Kelton. Not once, though, until after takeoff do I take my eyes off Max, and he does the same to me.

The takeoff is loud, the engines roaring from the back of the ship. Kelton keeps his eyes focused ahead, not aware of anything else around him. Max sits behind Kelton, and David behind me. They whisper about something, but every time I look back, they sit upright and pretend nothing had happened.

"It's time," Max says.

"I know," Kelton replies.

"So are you going to do something?"

"Hold on a minute," Kelton says.

"By then it will be too late," Max says back.

"I said, hold on," Kelton says through gritted teeth. Then he turns to me. "Put this on, and don't ask any questions." I take the pack he hands me and strap it to my back.

Max goes back to whispering to David, who is paler than usual. He taps his foot rapidly on the ground and never takes his eyes off the seat in front of him. Max, however, looks calm, confident, nothing out of the ordinary, except his eyes bounce from object to object and don't land until he catches me looking at him.

"Kelton," David says, panic flooding his voice. "I think we're high enough."

"Not yet," he replies.

"Are you afraid of heights?" I ask.

"No," he says. "But there is something I'm afraid of."

He ends the conversation with that, but I want to know what it is that he would be afraid of right now. Kelton lets go of the controllers. Max straightens his back, and David shifts uncomfortably in his seat. It all happens so fast that I almost don't notice anything until it's too late.

"I'm not who you think I am," Kelton says before smoke fills the ship and everything goes black.

I've never been fond of heights. I remember one time when I went to the neighborhood water hole, kids would swim for hours, but the main attraction was the board resting fourteen feet above the ground. Children would climb a ladder to get to the top and then jump off into the clear water below. The board didn't seem too high up, so one day my friends and I went to the base of the ladder and waited for our turn to climb to the top. I was the last to go, and with each rung of the ladder I climbed, the more afraid I became of jumping off. Once I finally reached the top of the ladder, and stepped on the board, my legs quivered beneath my body. I walked to the edge and looked down at the water below. My friends waved up at me and urged me to jump, but I couldn't bring myself to do it. I could tell the kids at the base of the ladder were growing restless as they were waiting for me, and yet I couldn't seem to do it.

Finally, one of the older kids came to the top and asked if I was alright. I told him no and that I couldn't do it.

"Have you ever wanted to fly?" The question was unexpected, and I blinked my confusion.

I processed his question before finally answering, "Yeah, I guess."

"When you jump, it feels like you're flying," he assured me. "Try it. It's the only real way to fly." With that he climbed down a few rungs to give me space.

I walked to the edge again, but instead of looking down, I looked out, closed my eyes, and believed I could fly. Moments later, I was wet. The water was cold, considering I had pretty much dried off waiting at the top of the board. The lack of oxygen burned my lungs, and I realized I had been under the water for too long. I kicked my legs and raced back to the surface. The first thing I heard when I emerged was the sound of cheering.

Since then, I still haven't loved heights, and I never jumped off the board again, but I can tolerate it now. I guess I should be glad that kid helped me with my fear of heights, because free falling from a ship that was flying just barely above the clouds is not something I would have been able to handle.

At first, I don't know what happened on the ship. Darkness surrounds me, and air rushes up around me. I'm reminded of the time Kyle made me jump off the platform when we went to find Kelton. I was terrified then, and I'm terrified now. The difference is there's no rope tied around my waist to ensure my safe landing and I'm much higher up now. I force myself to look down and realize I'm much closer to the ground than I thought. If I hit the ground at this rate, I will die, but I don't see many other options.

Snap! Something hits me in the face. The cord from my backpack hits me, and I know exactly what Kelton gave me. I pull the cord and a parachute erupts over my head. The air catches in the tarp as I feel a slight tug upward.

"Ahhhhh," I hear someone scream. I look to my right and see Kyle falling much faster than me toward the ground. I pull the cord again and the tarp folds back into the pack. I start falling faster and the ground becomes clearer. I reach out and grab Kyle's shirt, which is ballooning up around him.

I pull the cord once more, but nothing happens. I look up and see that the latch on the pack is jammed. I whip my free hand back, find the latch, and unclasp it. By now, I can see some of the details on the pavement below. We're getting close enough that the landing won't be soft, but we also won't die. The tarp has ballooned upward again and I feel a slight tug.

"Don't worry," I say. He looks at me and smiles.

We reach the ground safely a minute later, and I realize there's a lake five feet in front of us. The water is dark and murky and I can only imagine what must live beneath the surface.

"Are you okay?" Kyle's voice cuts the silence that filled the air.

"Yeah, I'm fine," I say, breathless. "What happened?"

"All I remember is an explosion and Daniel pushing me. Everything went black after that."

"Daniel," I say before looking to the water. I take the pack off my back and dive into the lake, even though I know I won't be able to see anything. I hear Kyle's muffled voice shout to me, but I can't make out what he says. I kick down farther into the water, my outstretched arms pulling water behind me and pushing me forward. I try to feel around in the dark, see if there's anything familiar.

Too long. I've been under for too long, and my lungs burn because of the lack of oxygen. I paddle up to the surface, take a quick breath, and dive under once more. Nothing. I push back to the surface and nearly run into Kyle.

"What are you doing here?" My voice comes out breathless and rushed.

"I've been trying to tell you that I found him," he says. "He's closer to the shore. Come on, I'll show you."

He swims back to the shore and motions for me to follow him. He stops before he gets on land and points toward a body, lying facedown in the water. I swim faster than before and reach him in no time. Kyle and I pull him onshore and lay him on his back.

"What should we do?" Kyle asks. "Do you think he's dead?"

"I don't know," I say, tears flooding my eyes and mixing with the water from the lake. *He can't be dead*, I think. *Not Daniel. Not again.* I step away from his limp body and turn toward the lake. I can see smoke off in the distance, which I assume to be from the ship. Before I can stop myself, I scream at the top of my lungs and sink to my knees.

Kyle touches my shoulder, trying to comfort me, but my vision remains blurry with tears. My sobs make my whole body shudder. *The last thing we did was fight, and I never truly forgave him. And now I never will be able to.*

"What just happened?" My voice trails off and I realize that I already know the answer. I should have realized it sooner, but I was busy. With what, I'm not sure. "I should have just left right away and married Daniel like I've always wanted."

"You didn't know this was going to happen," Kyle says, his voice comforting. "Even if you did, how could we have prevented it from happening? They were one step ahead the whole time."

"They," I whisper, absentmindedly. Then I snap back to focus. "Their plan all along was to kill us. They were never on our side. I should have listened to you guys when you told me not to trust him."

"You didn't know what was going to happen," he says again. "None of us knew."

"I knew," a voice from behind me says, a voice that I know too well. *Daniel.*

I turn around and blink at him in disbelief for a moment, not trusting what my eyes are seeing. I must be imagining things. I must be delusional. But no, he's lying on his back, his eyes open, and his chest moving up and down to the rhythm of his breathing. I blink again, trying to clear the image of him, alive, right before me. He turns his head slightly, so he's facing Kyle and me, and offers a weak smile.

"You're... alive?" The words barely escape my mouth, and when they do, they're barely above a whisper. I spin around fast and tackle him with an embrace. "You're alive," I say with more assurance.

"Yeah," he says as he sits up slowly, resting his hand on my back to steady me in his lap. "I think I just went unconscious. What happened?"

"Kelton blew up the ship," I say releasing him.

"Yeah, he told me," Daniel says. "He told me everything."

"Why would he tell you everything? *When* did he tell you everything?"

"He told me the night when I jumped out of the window," he says.

"Why didn't you say anything?" My tone comes out louder and fiercer than I wanted, but I'm infuriated. "All of this could have been prevented-"

"I didn't say anything because he threatened to kill you," he says softly.

I stare at him in shock, not wanting to believe what he's saying.

"Why would he kill Zandrea?" Kyle's voice comes out small and weak, unusual for him.

"Because he's Chris's son," Daniel says bluntly. "Why wouldn't he?"

My jaw drops at this news as I realize everything that I had done. "I'm no better than my mother," I say. They turn their heads to look at me. "I was always so concerned about what was going to happen to her with Chris, but I really should have been worrying about myself with Kelton. How could I have been so stupid? Here I am criticizing my mother about her boyfriend when I'm probably worse off anyway."

"You didn't know," Daniel says. "I should have at least hinted to you about it. I guess I didn't do everything I could have. I'm so sorry."

Kyle says, "So everything was fake?"

"Yeah, I guess so," Daniel replies.

"I wonder if our mother knew," I comment.

"It depends on how much Chris told her, but my guess is she knew something about the whole operation," Daniel says. "He can't keep a secret forever."

"I don't think he was planning on saying anything about Kelton, though, either," I say.

"Probably not," Daniel replies. "I think that was part of his plan."

"So," Kyle starts. "When did he tell you? That he was Chris's son, I mean."

"Well, the story begins with me jumping out of a window and landing on a platform below," he states. "As soon as he saw me, he punched me clear in the jaw. Max and David came soon to help him out. Before I completely go unconscious, he whispers to me who he really is. At that point, I was too out of it to fight back. He locked me in a cage and told me I would never see the light of day again. Obviously, that didn't happen."

"It was his idea to get you back," Kyle points out. "He could've left you to die, and we never would have suspected a thing. Why would he do that?"

"I don't know," Daniel replies. "Maybe he decided to prolong my death. Make sure you guys were there to see it."

"He's dramatic, I'll give him that," I say.

"Speaking of dramatic," Kyle says. "The leader of the Corps' son decides to take us up in a ship and crash it. Does he realize he just as easily could've locked us up and killed us that way?"

"Yeah, because his idea went totally wrong, and we're all still alive," I say. "I mean, if he wanted us dead, why did he give me that parachute?"

"Who knows why evil geniuses do anything that they do?" Daniel slowly brings himself to his feet. "Anyways, we should probably get back to the hangar and find a ship to really take us home."

"Hold on," I say, sudden panic taking over because I'm thinking of my father and how we didn't see him after the crash. After everything that has happened these last few weeks, I'm surprised he wasn't my first concern. "I have to go check something."

"We'll come with you," Kyle says.

"No," I reply. "It's too dangerous."

"That's why we're coming with you," Daniel says. "It's too dangerous to go alone."

"Shouldn't you go find us a ship?" They both shake their heads. I sigh. "Alright. Follow me."

We walk for a little while, toward the site of the crash. The shadows from the buildings help us blend into the night. The wind brushes my hair back and forth in front of my face, causing my vision to break. Kyle stays close behind me and Daniel leads the way through mazes of streets and pathways. The whole time we walk, I'm distracted by the thought of Kelton being related to Chris. I think back to the conversation I overheard before I left. My mom was with Chris, talking about his son and how she was excited to meet him. I recall all of the lies he told me while we were together. My face flushes with anger.

"Are you okay?" Kyle's voice breaks my angry trance and forces me back to reality. He points at my hand, which I find is curled in a fist.

I release my grip and reply with a calm, "Yes."

"You don't always have to be okay, you know that right?" He says it quietly, as if he's not sure this advice would suffice.

"I know," I say. "Really, though, I'm fine. Just lost in thought I guess."

"Understandable," he says. "A lot has happened these last few weeks."

More than you know, I want to tell him, but I can't, and I'm not sure if he would understand.

Daniel stops a few minutes after walking in silence for a while. The alleys created by the lofty buildings around us provide a path back to the Corps' headquarters. The shadows of the buildings make the night seem even darker and our path seem even more dangerous than it once was. Kyle hangs close behind me, and me behind Daniel. Something, a bottle, drops and crashes on the pavement next to us. Me, being as on edge as I am, jump and grab Daniel's hand. The warmth of it calms me because I feel as though it connects me to him, and I'm jolted by the feeling of longing panging inside my chest. He glances back at me and I release my grip, but his hand doesn't return to his side. Instead he reaches back and I tentatively grasp his hand in mine, the heat a reassurance that he isn't going anywhere.

He looks around the corner of the building we've reached, but nothing greets us. I wonder if maybe the bottle crashing was just some animal or homeless person. Coreno was full of homeless people until a few months before I left six years ago. The government made a new policy, the first one in decades, that if you did not have a government-issued house and were living on the streets, you must enroll in the military forces. To some people, that seemed better than starving and freezing every day and night, but others didn't like the idea of being forced to do things, like putting your life on the line for some strangers.

The government told us that it was because they cared about their citizens and wanted to take care of them, but everyone knew the real reason was because they didn't have enough soldiers in the military forces. At the time, the Corps were more powerful than anyone could have imagined, but with enough opposition from the outer planets, the Corps began to dwindle. Sure, their forces are technically still winning, but I've heard rumors that their ammo supply is diminishing.

I recall the dream I had a few nights ago. My dad was fighting Chris, Kelton was fighting Daniel, and Kyle was fighting me. Kyle told me that Kelton was going to do the one thing his dad never could. So far, the dream has been right. Kelton and Chris are related, and I'm sure my father would fight either of them if provoked. My father. I stop suddenly and Kyle runs into me.

"What?" Concern registers on his face.

"How come we haven't seen Father yet?" My voice escapes in an alarming tone, and Kyle's face goes white.

"What do you -"

"Don't worry about that," a voice says from behind us. "He's in good hands."

Before I can turn around and discover the informer, two hands fold around my neck, and my vision goes black around the edges. Daniel's hand is ripped from mine. Kyle's shriek comes out raspy and choked. I swing my leg back, but nothing happens.

"Wait," I call out with my last breath. "Let my father go."

"Why should I? What have you done for me?"

"I don't know who you ar-" My voice cuts out and my vision goes almost completely black.

"Let her go," the voice says. The hands around my neck fall and I drop to the ground. The voice steps out of the shadows and into the light of the street lamp overhead.

I gasp.

"Thought I was dead?" Kelton asks. "So did I. But you see, the mission wasn't complete. And my father's orders hadn't been carried out thoroughly, so I mean, can't die yet."

His face is scarred and burned, probably from the crash, and he reeks of smoke. I still see the same face that I once fell in love with, but the memories behind it were destroyed along with any feelings I have left for him. He tried killing my friends and family, something that I will never be able to look past.

I try to make eye contact with him, to show him the pain that sits behind my eyes, but he doesn't look directly my way. He seems to look everywhere but at me, which I figure is because he had the closest tie to me and it's me who he's hurt the most. Me who stood by him even when everyone else thought it was a trap. Me who saw him as I wanted to see him, not as he was. Me who is going to feel the pain most of all.

"If you want your father back," he begins, "I can take you to him. But once you go inside, you will never come back out. And only one of you may go. Make your choice."

One of us continues. Two of us go home, the place we've longed for since we got here. The only place I want to be right now....

"I'll go," I say. Kyle and Daniel look at me.

"Zandrea, you can't do this," Daniel pleads. "I've seen what the Corps do to people firsthand. You can't go." The worried, pained expression on Daniel's face tells me everything I need to know: I have to go.

It has to be me. I got us into this mess, and I'm going to get us out. If it hadn't been for me, we could have all left ages ago. I never would have been shot, Daniel wouldn't have been captured, and Kyle and my father could be home with my mother, fixing everything that went wrong while he was gone.

"I'll go," I say again, turning to face Kelton. "But under one condition."

"What's that?" he snarls.

"You let everyone else go. My father, Daniel, and Kyle. Let them all go, and I will come back with you. I have to see them get on a ship and leave. That is my condition."

"Interesting," he says. "Your father said the same thing before I..." He trails off.

"Before you what?" My tone of voice is the same that I used when I first met him.

"Are you coming with me or not?"

"Let them go first."

"*You*," he says, pointing at me, "don't get to tell me what to do. I make the rules around here."

"Let them go, and I will do whatever you want me to do."

"Zandrea," Kyle says. I turn my head to face him. "You can't do this. Let someone else go. I'll go."

"No Kyle," I say. "Go home and find Mother and fix whatever mess is waiting at home."

"I don't know if he'll be able to do that, but go ahead and try," Kelton says.

"Give them a ship to get home in and I will come with you," I say, my tone unwavering.

"What makes you think I'm going to listen to you?" he says. "What leverage do you have over me? Why would I grant your wishes when I have everything you want?"

"I know that somewhere deep down inside you, you still care," I say soothingly. "That you care about me. Prove me wrong."

He leans in close to my face and for the first time makes direct eye contact. "I don't know who you think you are, but I don't listen or *care* about civilians. Is that clear?"

"Yes," I gulp. "But I know you better than this. This isn't you. You do care. Quit trying to be your father. You're better than he is."

"I'm nothing like my father," he says as he rolls his eyes but motions for us to follow him. I know I've broken through to him, but I don't know how long this will last. He's stronger than me, both physically and mentally. He knows how to play people to their weaknesses and highlight them just enough that it becomes very clear that he will always come out on top. No matter what. And that's how I broke him.

Kelton leads us through a labyrinth of streets that lead back to the Corps' headquarters. The roads have an ominous feel which makes me uneasy. The three guards follow closely behind us in case one of us tries to run. I won't; I can't afford to. I've abandoned my father before, a mistake I won't make again. If I run now, my father will never be let out of the nightmare he's been living in for the last ten years. I hope I can see him before I'm locked up for good.

Kelton walks ahead of us, leading the way back to the headquarters. My stomach twists in knots. I can only imagine what they have in store for me in exchange for my father's life. I quicken my pace and fall in step with Kelton.

"We need to talk," I say.

He looks at me but doesn't say anything.

"Fine," I say. "I'll just talk to you."

He smirks. "You have always made me smile."

I shake my head, trying to focus on the subject that's been bothering me. "What did you do to my father?"

His expression turns serious, more like it was earlier when I first saw him. "I didn't do anything. My father on the other hand, well, that's a different story."

"Please," I beg. "Tell me what happened to him."

"You'll just have to wait and see."

We walk in silence for a while before I finally ask the question that's been eating away at me. "Why?"

The question catches him off guard. "Why what?"

"Why any of this?"

"Because," he says. "This world is not perfect. We can achieve perfection. There are so many flawed systems in this universe, and we're trying to make it better."

"By hurting innocent lives?"

"They aren't innocent," he retorts. "Most of the people in this galaxy are the farthest thing from innocent. They want what is best for themselves. The Corps are trying to eliminate that. Make all systems and all people the same."

"But it's the diversity in the systems, in the people, that makes this universe so amazing," I say. "If everyone was like you, this world would be more corrupt than it already is."

"Are you saying I'm corrupt?"

"I'm saying that you and your father are a lot alike, and he's corrupt."

"I am nothing like my father."

"Yes, you are. You do whatever he says, go wherever he goes. You're like a clone of him."

His face gets really close to mine as he spits, "I am not a clone of him. I am nothing like him."

"Would you kill any or all of us if given the chance?"

"In a heartbeat."

"Then I rest my case."

He glares at me but doesn't say anything. He knows I'm right, whether he wants to accept it or not. I plaster a look of triumph on my face and hope he notices.

The buildings become more sporadic the closer we get to the Corps' headquarters. My stomach turns in knots again and my head starts to pound. The building illuminates the night, and I have to shield my eyes from the sudden source of light. I stop walking so Daniel can catch up to me.

"How are you doing? I mean, this is a lot to take in," he says.

"I'll be alright," I say. "How about you and Kyle?"

"Don't worry about us, we'll be fine."

"I know," I whisper.

We walk in silence for a little bit longer before he speaks again. "None of this would have happened if I had just told you everything from the beginning."

"You can't blame yourself for what happened," I say. "There are plenty of things I could have done to prevent any of this."

"Yeah," he agrees. "But if I had told you something, anything, given you some kind of hint to who he really was, maybe we could have left sooner. You wouldn't have been shot, Kyle and your father wouldn't have been brainwashed, and none of us would have gone in the Torturing Room, the list is endless. And all of it is my fault."

"Or who knows? Maybe I would've resented you even more for thinking Kelton had a larger plan up his sleeve. Don't blame yourself." I don't know what comes over me, maybe it's the thought that I will never be able to see him again or I feel bad for everything, but I grab his head and pull his face, his lips toward mine. It's the kiss I should have given him a long time ago, but I never felt like it mattered. Until now, when my life is on the line in exchange for my father's.

I pull away first. "This is not your fault, understand?"

"Yes," he answers.

He leans in to kiss me again, but before he can, Kyle yells, "Gross!"

I start laughing, but it's my nervous laugh.

"Keep it down back there," Kelton yells. Then he mumbles something to himself.

We reach the front doors of the building a minute later. The doors open up to the same gold and silver lobby we first encountered a week ago. The same lady still stands there. She looks exactly the same as she did at our first meeting, except she wears a black pencil skirt with a gold and silver checkered top. Her long, flowing, straight black hair with gold and silver highlights is tucked back in a low bun. She seems older now than she did a week ago, creases lining her face.

"Do you have an ID?" she asks, her monotone voice ever present and still as annoying as ever.

Kelton shows her his ID and she lets him through. "Have a wonderful day," he says to her. She nods and goes back to typing on her computer.

"She didn't ask us for an ID when we went through," I say.

"Yeah," Daniel replies. "Maybe it's only for authorized personnel."

We take two elevators up to the fourth floor. Daniel, Kyle, and I ride in one with two guards. Kelton takes the other one with his personal guard. Kelton gets there before us, with my father at his feet. He has a gun trained next to his brain, ready to shoot in a moment's notice. I run to my father, but Kelton stops me.

"You may not touch him," he says. "I will give him to Daniel and Kyle in exchange for you. Say your last goodbyes. I will give you exactly one minute starting now."

I hug Kyle first and whisper in his ear, "I love you. I hope you know that. Take care of our father and mother."

Tears stream down his cheeks as he says, "You know, these last few weeks knowing I have a sister who's alive has been the best few weeks of my life. Promise me you will try to escape."

"Of course," I say. "Nothing's going to happen to me. I'll see you soon." He knows the lie as soon as it has escaped my lips, but I hope he finds some comfort in what I said.

I turn to Daniel. Before I can say anything, though, his warm hands find my face and he kisses me. I know Kelton is looking at me, and I hope somewhere, deep inside him, he is hurting that same way I was hurt. I know he is.

My father lies limp next to us on the floor. Cuts and bruises have formed from where I'm sure he was stricken. I pull his cold body close to mine and hold him for the rest of the time I have remaining. I whisper in his ear that I love him and hope he can hear me.

Kelton pulls my father into a standing position, hands him to one of the guards, and tells him to escort Daniel, Kyle, and my father to the landing pad where a ship will be waiting for them. A tear slips over my bottom eyelid, and I make no attempt to fight it off. I turn around and punch Kelton square in his jaw. He stumbles back a little, but before I can take my next swing, one of his guards pushes me to the ground.

"Follow me," he says as he gingerly rubs his jaw. "My father will be notified of this little outburst of yours."

"Tell him whatever you want," I say. "There is nothing you can do that will break me any more than you already have."

"We'll see about that," he replies quietly.

Chris's office is not far from the elevators, but multiple guards surround it, each one carrying a gun positioned to shoot. I gulp.

"Do you have an ID?" one of the guards asks.

"Of course," Kelton replies. "Like I would walk around without one."

The guard curls his upper lip into a half smile and lets us pass. He never takes his eyes off me, and I don't take my eyes off him. There is something about this particular guard that makes me feel uneasy. Maybe it's the look in his eye or that his smile grows when I pass him, but he's not like the rest of them. He's friendlier, which scares me.

What scares me even more, though, is Chris's office room. It looks like a laboratory, with machines lining every wall. Some of them have lasers, others a sharp wheel that rotates quickly, enough to see sparks. The walls are painted white and the floor is a shiny black, making the room seem even larger than it is. In the middle of the room, though, lies an operating table lined in a white bed cloth. The knots return to my stomach once again.

"Hello there," a man, who I recognize as Chris, says. "Welcome to my office."

I begin to huddle back, but a guard pushes me forward, closer to Chris than I was before. "What," I sputter, "do you plan to do with me?"

"Wouldn't you like to know," he taunts.

"Yes, I would."

"I'll tell you sometime, but for now, just sit on the table over there. I'll be right back."

I slowly walk over to the table, making every step twice as long as it needs to be. I boost myself up onto the white bed cloth and lay back. Immediately, two women in white robes hover over me, adjusting some lights overhead. One of them injects a needle into my neck, and I slowly drift off to a dreamless sleep.

I wake up later. How much later, I don't know. The room is empty, except for two guards who stand near the door. I try to stand up, but the restraints on my wrists and ankles keep me in place.

"Comfortable?" The voice startles me.

"Not really," I answer.

"Good," the voice says. "Now, did you dream anything?"

"What?"

Chris comes into view. "I said, did you dream anything?"

"No," I answer.

"Good, so it's working."

"What's working?"

"Our experiment," he says. "We needed a test subject, and I think you are the perfect candidate."

"What's the experiment?"

"I really shouldn't tell you," he says, "but I will anyway. Since you're going to die, I'm guessing you want to know how, right?"

I don't answer.

"So basically, we inject you with a serum that stimulates your brain, causing rapid eye movement. Rapid eye movement is when your brain is highly active, and it resembles being awake. In other words, rapid eye movement is what causes dreams." He looks at me to make sure I'm following along with what he's saying. "Then we watch and monitor your dreams."

"So you can see everything that I dream?"

"Exactly," he responds. "The key is we get to manipulate the dreams into nightmares, and eventually you won't be able to take any more of it. You go completely insane, become useless, and then we kill you. Now, you are our first test subject, so I don't know how this will go. Who knows? Maybe you will die quickly." He walks off into some other part of the lab on a different floor.

The women in white robes come back, masks over their mouths, and adjust the lighting once again. A third woman comes from behind the table, cleans a spot on the left side of my neck, and plunges a thick needle into the disinfected area. I fight to stay awake, but the serum pulls me away from consciousness.

My mother stands in front of me. Her hair is pulled back, defining the shape of her face. She looks younger, and the creases in her forehead have subsided. Her hand wraps around my arm, in a gentle, motherly touch. She kisses my forehead and I'm brought back to my childhood. And for what seems like an eternity, we just stand there gazing at each other, neither one of us talking for fear we might ruin the moment. Somehow in my conscious brain, I realize this will probably be the last time I see her, the last time I get to feel her motherly touch, protecting me from the outside world.

Bang! Her eyes get bloodshot and she grips my arm even harder than she once did. My mother, who I love so dearly, crumbles at my feet in a pool of blood. I scream, but no sound comes out. I cry, but no tears fall down my face. Then I look up and see the face of her murderer. I'm not shocked to see Chris standing behind her, gun slowly lowered back down to his side.

"You should have listened to her," he tells me. "You shouldn't have left."

I charge at him, but before I can make contact with his jaw, everything goes black once more. I try to reason with myself that she's not dead, as far as I know, in real life. This was just a dream, more of a nightmare, but still just a dream, one that my brain, along with Chris's serum, made up.

I slowly come back to consciousness, the women in white robes still working overhead. Chris's voice comes over the loudspeaker, but I can't make out what he's saying. Then moments later, his face appears in front of mine, blocking out the blinding lights behind him. He says something, but I don't hear anything. I try to respond, but I don't know if any words are coming out. Then I realize he was talking to the women in the white robes.

"How are you feeling?" His voice is sickly sweet. If I didn't have restraints over my wrists right now, he surely would have had a black eye by now.

"You killed my mother," I say through gritted teeth.

"Yeah," he says cheerfully. "Pretty cool right?"

"If I didn't have these restraints on," I start, "you would be dead."

"And that's why you have the restraints on," he says, smiling the whole time.

"Let me go," I say.

"Then bring your father back here," he says tauntingly. He knows I won't.

"Why are you doing this?"

"Because I can," he replies. "Because the fate of the galaxy depends on this. You are helping a lot of people by doing this. Don't you think one life traded for millions is worth it?"

"I don't understand why you have to kill me for this to work," I say.

"I have to see how much pain and fear someone can take," he tells me. "And besides, I don't want you running around telling people my secret so they can use it for themselves. I can't have that happen, so I need you to stay here."

"Who would I tell?"

"You probably have friends in high places, people that could ruin me if given the chance."

"What are you trying to accomplish here, because I see no progress."

"Domination of the entire galaxy," he says like it's no big deal. "I've been trying to do this for years. If all the leaders went insane, like you're going to be, then who would run the galaxy? Everyone would live in fear. Until one day, I come out on top, seeming like the cure for this disease which we call home. They would make me their leader because they have no one else to turn to. Then I would impose my new laws on them and make the galaxy in my image."

"I think you've gone mad," I say. "Besides, you said they wouldn't want an insane leader, so obviously you wouldn't be their first choice."

"Careful with what you say," he taunts. "I can end your life right now if I wanted. I've tried to prolong it in case someone came back for you. Then I would have another prisoner."

"Do whatever you want," I say. "No one is coming back for me. If you kill me now, no one will know, but you also won't have a test subject. Remember how much work it was bringing me here? I don't think you want to go through that again."

He mimics me in a childish way, something that Kyle used to do, but he doesn't say anything more. He knows I'm right; he knows he can't kill me yet. He returns to his viewing room as the nurses plunge yet another syringe in my neck. This time, I don't fight the darkness.

"Zandrea," a voice calls. I look around and find Kelton standing behind me with a gun pointed at my head.

"Shoot me," I say. "I don't care."

"I'm not going to shoot you," he says soothingly. "I'm going to shoot them." He points his gun over at a small group of people consisting of my mother, my father, Kyle, and Daniel, their faces pale with anticipation.

"No! Don't shoot them," I say.

"If I don't, you have to," he tells me. "And don't worry. Only one of them has to die. You get to choose which one."

Now my face goes pale. I have to choose between the four people I love most which one I have to kill. I take the gun from Kelton's outstretched hand, but I'm smarter than the simulation. I point it at Kelton's head and fire.

I don't wake up in a cold sweat this time. I didn't kill anyone that I loved. Chris comes into the room, shock registering on his face. He starts yelling at some of the women in the robes, and they begin moving faster, scrambling to fix whatever mistake they made.

He runs up next to me and gets close to my face as he says, "You won't be so lucky next time."

"We'll see about that," I say before getting hit with another syringe and fall asleep.

It's the same dream as before. Everyone I love stands in a group and Kelton holds a gun out to me.

"Which one?" he asks.

I take the gun and fire it at his head like before. This time, however, it ricochets off his head and lands on the ground. I gulp, realizing that the only way to get out is to shoot one of them. Somehow, I tell myself that this is just a dream, not reality, and that they are still alive in real life. So I point the gun, turn around, and fire, not knowing which one I killed.

I wake up again. Chris is still yelling. I can't imagine how hoarse of a voice he has at this point. I know that this is driving him crazy. He can't get through to me. Somehow, I'm still conscious in my unconsciousness.

Before I drift off again, the woman who plunges the syringe in my neck shakes her head at me. Her eyes look sad, thoughtful. She looks almost like she feels bad for me, but she gives me the shot anyway.

I'm on the front step of someone's house. The house is bigger than mine, nicer than mine. The door opens and a rush of heat blasts me. A woman, who looks about my age, steps in the doorframe, blocking the golden light from inside. She's laughing and doesn't notice me right away. When she finally sees me, she goes pale.

"You need to leave," she tells me.

"I don't know what I'm doing here," I respond.

"Don't play dumb," she says. "You know he doesn't want you around."

"Who?" I ask.

"My husband, who else?"

"Can I talk to him please?"

"You guys haven't spoken in years," she tells me. "Why start now? He doesn't want you in his life."

"Just tell him it's an emergency," I explain.

"Fine, I'll tell him you're here, but I don't make any promises."

She walks away, leaving the door ajar. I open it slightly, allowing more light outside. Two children sit on the ground in the living room next to the entrance hallway. They play with metal cubes and spheres, stacking them and knocking them down. One of them squeals loudly as the cubes fall to the ground. I imagine Kyle and me where they are, playing peacefully, with no cares in the world. I wish life was that easy.

Footsteps pound on the ground and I step back from the door so I don't intrude. A man steps around the ajar door and glances at me.

"Daniel?" I say incredulously.

He glares down at me and then begins to shut the door.

"Wait," I say. "Can I talk to you?"

"Why would you want to?"

"Because I love you," I say.

"I think you have the wrong person," he retorts.

"No, I don't," I say. "You're the only person I've ever truly loved."

"That's not what you said last time I saw you."

"Remind me what I said."

"Right before you shot me in the leg so you could go live with your fiancé?"

"What are you talking about?"

"Did you lose all of your memories or something? You and Kelton got engaged. *You* pushed *me* away, remember? I kept trying to get you back, but all you thought about was you and Kelton. To keep me away, you shot my leg, hoping I would back off. I realized that any feelings we used to have for each other were gone. Do you not remember any of this?"

"No," I say. "And I don't believe any of it either. You were the first person I loved, and you will be the last. Whatever I said, whatever I did, let it go. I didn't mean any of it."

"I have a metal leg now because of you," he shouts. "How can I just forget a metal leg?"

I look down at his leg and tears begin to form on my bottom eyelid. "I'm so sorry," I say.

"You should be," he spits. "It's changed my life, and not for the better. Now, leave, please. I don't think you want a metal leg as well."

I walk down the steps but turn around before I get to the bottom. "Kelton and I aren't together anymore. I hate him, in fact. I'm not asking for you to love me again, just a shot at being friends." I realize he asked me something similar back at the Corps' headquarters before we got in the ship that exploded. I know this isn't real, but my chest aches at the thought of what happened between us in this scenario. I shot him to be with Kelton? What kind of person would do that? I continue walking down the stairs, down the street, not sure where I'm heading.

Tears pour down my cheeks, the cool air freezing them. I pull my jacket tighter around me trying to keep the warmth inside. All of a sudden, a wind comes and blows my jacket off me, leaving me to shiver my way back to the landing pad. Rain and then sleet begin to fall from the sky, weighing me down.

I wake up shivering. The lights blind me. Chris stands over me, nodding to someone behind him. He leans in close to my face, pulling my eyelids apart with his fingers. He examines each eye before reporting his findings to whoever is behind him.

"You aren't as shaken up as I thought you would be," he says almost disappointed. "But I'm hoping we can change that."

Darkness. I'm so used to being injected with this serum that I barely notice any difference now. The blackness lessens and reveals a room decorated with pictures of a family of three: a mother, a father, and a little boy. I pick up one of the frames and stare at the happy family. The little boy is smiling the biggest, his arms wrapped around his parents' necks. Something about the boy, maybe his eyes, makes me think of Kyle with my mother after I left. The boy does look familiar though, but it's not Kyle.

A gunshot. Loud. Right behind me. I spin around to find the source of the noise. A woman, being held by her neck, crumples to the ground, a bullet wound in her head. I look to the left of the woman and see a little boy, the one from the picture, standing in front of her. Shock registers on his face but is immediately replaced with horror. He screams a blood-curdling scream loud enough to wake the entire neighborhood.

The man who killed the woman looks at the little boy. "She's told me a lot about you," he snarls. "Daniel."

I drop to my knees as I realize this is the moment that haunted his sleep. This is the moment he woke up screaming to every night. This is the moment that changed everything. Daniel's younger self doesn't know it, but the man who murdered his mother is slowly killing me too.

Chris disappears as I run over to Daniel to try to comfort him. It doesn't work. He doesn't know I'm here. This is all a dream, but at one point it was a reality. *Sometimes, dreams can be your reality,* Daniel once told me. It hurts me to know how accurate that statement was for him. Chris knows this memory scarred Daniel, and when he told me, it scarred me too. I couldn't imagine what it would be like to have one of your parents murdered in front of you.

It hits me like a bullet. Daniel said that his mother and Chris were laughing and talking before it all went downhill and he killed her. My mother was laughing and talking with Chris right before I left. I scream.

The darkness fades physically, but not emotionally. I have to get back home. I scream until my throat goes dry. The room is dark, and everyone has left, including Chris. Only two guards stand by the entrance to the room. I know there are more on the other side of the door, guarding the room from the outside.

Suddenly, I hear a gunshot, and think I must be dreaming. But no, I'm not. I'm in the same room I was before when I got my numerous injections. I turn my head in the direction of the sound. One of the guards lies on the ground, while the other hoists the dead guard's gun over his shoulder. Then he runs in my direction.

He stops next to the table I lay on and points the gun at me. I scream again. "Don't worry," he tells me. "Just take the gun."

"I can't," I say wiggling my hands.

"Oh, right," he says and pushes a button on a panel across from the table. "There you go."

The restraints release with a *hiss* and I sit up. "Why did you do that?"

He pulls off his mask.

"Rowan?" I say incredulous.

"Fancy seeing you here," he responds.

"What are you doing? Are you helping me? Why are you helping me? We're going to get caught."

"I know," he says. "That's why we have to go. Hurry, I'll explain on the way."

"How do you plan to get us out of here?" I ask.

"Lie on the table, and act dead or something," he explains. "Then I'll tell them Chris gave me strict orders to take you to another room."

"Where is Chris, by the way," I ask.

"He's in his other office, on the seventh floor," he says. "Now hurry. We don't have much time."

I jump on the table again and loosely put the bands around my wrists. Then I close my eyes and breathe in small breaths as Rowan pushes the table toward the door. I glance at the guard he killed, who now lies limply on the ground by the door.

Rowan pushes a button on a panel to the right of the door and it slides open. The guards on the outside stand at attention, except for one who looks like he's in charge.

"What is your reason for bringing her out of the lab?"

"Chris asked me to," Rowan responds. "He said he was going to do some experiments with her in his seventh floor office."

"I would have received a transmission first," he says. "She's not going anywhere until I get a transmission."

If we wait any longer, he won't let us go for sure. Something has to happen. He's not going to be getting a transmission, and Rowan will probably be put in my shoes after they're through with me.

Something in me, survival instinct maybe, fires up. At first, I don't even realize what I'm doing, and then I understand. My eyes fly open, my arms rip from their restraints. I sit up, almost in a wired, mechanical sort of way. Rowan's eyes grow huge, but I give him a slight nod as if to reassure him. Everything happens in slow motion. No one moves. The guards stand in awe, as if me waking up from a deep sleep is something they've never seen before. If I wait any longer, they will come out of their shocked trances and fire, surely killing Rowan and me.

I punch the head guard square in the jaw and knock him off balance. What happens next is a blur. Rowan throws me the gun he grabbed from the guard he killed. I catch it and fire at the unsuspecting guards. Rowan does the same. The guards fire back, so I duck behind the operating table and fire from the ground. They come so fast.

I hit one guard in the arm and another in the stomach. Then a bullet catches me in the shoulder and I fall back. Black spots dance around my vision, but the mission is not over yet, so I'm not over yet. Rowan hits many of them in the heart or the head, something I'm guessing he learned in training. I hear one of the guards laying on the ground whisper something into his communications device. I shoot him dead before he can finish his sentence.

Rowan gets hit and stumbles back, clutching at the table. I shoot the guard in return and rapid-fire others until most are either dead or wounded. I run over to Rowan, who clutches his side, blood spilling out.

"You'll be fine," I say, trying my best not to sound panicked. "Can you walk?"

"The mission isn't over," he says. "I'm coming with you."

I help him to his feet and shoot the half-dead guards once again to make sure they don't follow us or send backup transmissions. Rowan limps down the hall, one arm across my shoulders. I wince with every step, the bullet wound sending a piercing pain through my body. I check around each corner, my gun positioned to shoot at a moment's notice. I finally see the elevators where I said my goodbyes to Kyle, Daniel, and my father. I thought it was going to be my last. Not anymore. I'm more determined than ever to get out of here.

I press the 'up' arrow and the doors to the elevator slide open. Once inside, I press the seventh floor button, but nothing happens.

"Here," Rowan says, handing me a card. "It only works if you have an ID."

"That's not what happened when we first showed up," I recall. "It moved automatically for us."

"That's because it was a trap," he explains. "Everything seemed so easy to get through, the security on the outside of the building, the front desk, and the elevators. You thought you were wandering free, but we were watching you the whole time."

"I don't understand," I say. "Why?"

"We wanted to see what you were going to do," he says. "We had to single one of you out so we could do the experiments. So we chose Daniel. He seemed the strongest, the best person to test things on. But he wasn't. He broke down almost immediately."

"I don't believe you," I say flatly.

"It's true," he says. "I can show you the videos if you want."

"No, it's fine," I say. "Continue."

"We discovered we needed someone better to test, so then we tried singling you out," he continues. "We realized you were the person we needed to experiment on. That's why Kelton stayed around a little longer. We thought he was able to keep you here so eventually we could operate on you. It worked for a while until things went south. You wanted to go home, but we couldn't let our test subject get away, so we had Kelton blow up the ship to get you by yourself. Remember the parachute? We were planning on either letting Daniel and Kyle go or kill them."

"I can't believe this," I say. "All of this was planned. I had no knowledge of any of this. You just messed with my life for the past few weeks and I didn't even know it. Why? Why would you do this and then decide to help me escape?"

"I'm Chris's right-hand man," he claims. "Do you honestly think I'm going to do everything he says?"

"Um, yeah, that's exactly what I think," I say.

"I needed a job," he says. "I ended up here. Chris needed someone to help him with the things he was otherwise too busy to do. They paid well. Chris revealed his big plan to me, the complete domination of the entire galaxy. I didn't agree with this, but he threatened to kill everyone who didn't follow his plan. I, of course, never shared with him my own plans."

"Which is?"

"To take down the Corps even if it costs me my life," he explains.

I drop my voice down to a whisper. "Aren't you worried he will hear you?"

"No," he says casually. "I turned off all radio and camera communications before coming to help you escape."

"Why are you doing this?" I ask.

"Because," he says. "He killed my family, just like he did to Daniel's. My mother was murdered in front of me. I was slightly older and took a few swings at him. His guards quickly beat me down, and he fled so fast it was almost a blur. He killed both my brothers and my father shortly after."

"Did your family go up against the Corps?"

"Yes, they all did," he says sadly. "Chris said he would kill them all, but they didn't believe him. They kept fighting. I tried to convince them to do what he said, but they told me they didn't want to live in fear."

The doors open revealing the seventh floor. "Are you sure you can fight?" I ask.

"I will always fight for what I believe, no matter the cost."

He says it so dramatically I almost start laughing. "Did you just come up with that?" I ask.

"Yeah, you like it? I've been working on it for a while."

I roll my eyes but smile. Only Rowan would be making jokes at a time like this.

The seventh floor doesn't look much different than the other floors of this building. Unlike most of the floors, this one doesn't have a specific color. To the left of the elevator lies a long stretch of hallway with doors on either side. To the right lies one giant room with stained glass doors. Lights from the other side of the doors indicate someone is in there. Two shadows move around; one looks like a person pacing, and the other looks like someone swiveling on a desk chair.

Rowan pulls a pair of linked chains out of his pocket and hands them to me. "Put these on," he says. "I'll pretend you escaped from the room."

"That doesn't sound very believable," I comment. "You saw how many guards were outside of that room."

"Just go with it," he says. "He'll be dead soon anyways."

His overconfidence is enough to make me worry. "If I die tonight," I say, "I'm blaming you."

He smiles and knocks on the door. I slip the linked chains loosely over my wrists.

The doors open and who should appear but Kelton, in a suit, dressed to impress. "What is she doing here?"

"She tried escaping," Rowan explains. "Luckily I was there or she would have made a run for it."

Kelton turns around to consult his father. He motions us in. Rowan shoves me hard in the square of my back, forcing me forward. He positions his gun on my right temple, threatening to shoot me.

"What do you want me to do with her?" he asks.

"Bring her back and tie her up again," Chris responds. "Why didn't you do that in the first place?"

"I thought you would want to know," Rowan says, his tone unwavering but his eyes filled with worry.

"Why would I care? Bring her back, tie her up, and I'll be there shortly to finish experimenting. I've been working on something new."

"Sir-"

"Rowan," Chris begins, "I thought you were better than this. Why the delay? Hurry, I fear she's seen too much. You know what happened to your parents."

He smiles his evil smile, a sickening grin only he could master.

"You can leave now," Kelton chimes in, defending his father as usual. How could I have ever loved someone like him?

"Why are you stalling? What do you have to hide?" Chris demands.

Again, everything seems to happen in slow motion. Rowan turns his gun from my head to Chris's chest. He fires and a loud *bang* bounces off the walls. Chris falls back into his chair, but no bullet wound stains his chest. In a second, Kelton turns, pulling out his own gun. He fires at Rowan, who falls to the ground. Blood pools at my feet, dark red liquid staining my shoes.

Kelton points his gun at me and I raise my arms over my head. "Did you know about this?"

"He... He brought me here," I stammer. "Why would I know anything?"

Rowan moans on the ground. He's still alive, but he won't be much longer. I grab the gun out of his hand and point it at Kelton.

"Don't make me," I say. "I don't want to do this."

"You couldn't anyway," he sneers. "You're weak. Pathetic."

"I cared for you once, a mistake I won't make again."

"You would have shot me by now if you didn't care," he fires back.

"You would have too!"

He stops and squints at me. He knows I'm right; I've trapped him. Again.

"Do it," I say calmly. "Shoot me. Bring me back to the laboratory. Do whatever you want, I don't care enough to fight you for it."

I lower my gun to my side. Either I will see black or the face of a man who imprisoned himself with his own foolishness. Whatever the outcome, I'm satisfied with my choice. I take a step forward and rest my head against the muzzle of the gun.

"Shoot me," I say. His eyes narrow.

"I will," he threatens.

"Then do it," I say. "I don't care." My heart beats in my chest. I hope he can't hear it. I close my eyes and picture Kyle's face, his happy, baby cheeks. He smiles that warm, brotherly smile. I grin and open my eyes.

"Shoot her," Chris says wearily. "I can find someone else to experiment on. If you don't, she will ruin everything."

"Why don't you shoot her then?" Kelton asks.

"It would be my pleasure," he says. "Hand me the gun."

"No," Rowan shouts hoarsely. "Don't let him."

"Are you still alive?" Chris asks. "Really, Kelton, I expected more out of you. You can't even kill Rowan, let alone your girlfriend."

"She's not my girlfriend," he retorts.

"Must be my mistake," Chris says. "I thought I remember someone falling for her willingly."

"You're wrong," Kelton growls. "I never loved her."

"Then you should have no problem killing her," Chris taunts.

"I-"

"Just do it," I say.

"That's what I thought," Chris says. "Give me the gun."

"No," Kelton says. "It's mine. I'll do whatever I want with it. I don't want to get blood on it."

"Excuses," Chris sighs. "What kind of son have I raised?"

"*You* didn't raise me," Kelton retorts, seeming to have found a loophole out of the current situation. "Mother did. Before you killed her. You took everything from me."

"This is not the time for sob stories from your childhood," Chris says. "I have a galaxy to rule, you have a girl to dispose of. No one cares about your childhood backstories."

"You're right," he says. "No one worth mentioning cares about me."

He aims his gun at Chris's head and squeezes the trigger for good measure.

"You wouldn't do it," Chris says. "If you can't kill her, you wouldn't have the guts to kill your own father."

"Watch me," Kelton says.

Chris pulls his own gun out from a drawer underneath his desk. He fixes his gun on me and looks Kelton square in the eye. "I, on the other hand, have no problem shooting," he says. "Put your gun down or she dies."

He holds his ground a little longer before lowering the gun to his side.

"Right choice," Chris says. "Now excuse me. I have a new formula for the serum to test out and a galaxy to rule. I'll come back for her soon when I'm ready for testing." He walks out of the room, locking the door behind him. Great, now I'm trapped with a psychotic maniac and a half-dead man.

"He was going to kill you," Kelton says quietly.

"Do you want me to thank you?" I retort.

"You don't have to be rude about it," he fires back. "I saved your life."

"You want a pat on the back?" I ask.

"A simple thank you would suffice," he says.

"Thank you," I shout. "Happy now?"

"No," he says. "I'm still stuck in here with you."

"Well, I'm sorry your father is a psycho but it's not my fault we're trapped in here!"

"Did you really think you could just walk in here, put a gun to his chest, and expect him to surrender?"

"I wasn't the one who came up with the plan!"

"Would you guys please stop fighting?" Rowan shouts. It sounds like that might have been his last breath.

I sit next to him and examine the wound. It's not as bad as it looks, but he won't last much longer if the bullet doesn't come out and the bleeding doesn't stop. I stand up and search the room for a piece of cloth large enough to wrap around the wound. Thankfully, Chris likes curtains, so I tear a part off of one covering the window.

"Here," I say, propping his body up so I can loop the cloth underneath him. "Apply some pressure to the wound." He does as I say.

I walk over to Kelton, who sits in his father's chair, rocking it slightly back and forth. "Can you believe I used to want to be like him?" he asks. "I mean, I would come up here every day and just sit in this chair. I loved him."

I don't know how to respond, so I don't. A tear slips down his cheek, but he swipes at it fast. He glances at me quickly, looking to see if I saw his weakness.

"I don't expect you to understand," he says. "You still have both of your parents. Alive and not evil."

"Yes, but I didn't always," I say. "My father left when I was little. When he didn't come back, I assumed he was dead. I didn't understand at the time, but I do now. It changed my outlook on life. I've changed a lot since then."

"But he came back," he says. "My mother is never coming back no matter how much I miss her. She's dead, gone."

"Because Chris killed her," I finish for him. "This is why I need your help getting out of here."

"What, so you can go be with your family and boyfriend and live happily ever after while I sit here living out my days alone? No thank you."

"I came here with one mission and that was to bring this organization to its knees," I explain. "And I intend to finish my mission. I'm getting out of here whether you help me or not."

I walk over to the giant picture window and stare down to the ground. It's far. Seven stories is an insane height to jump from. I will most likely die. I try the door handles, but they don't move. However, I do see a card slot next to the door. Rowan has a card that opens doors.

"What kind of psycho puts a card reader on the inside?" I wonder aloud.

"My father," Kelton responds. "In case he somehow got locked inside the room."

"Bingo," I say. "Our way out."

I insert the card I pulled from Rowan's jacket pocket into the card reader. Nothing happens. I try again. Still nothing.

"Did you think that was going to work?" Kelton asks. "Only he has the key to open it."

"It was worth a shot," I say and shrug. "I don't see you coming up with any better ideas."

"Why should I?" he asks. "He'll be back soon enough to collect you for further experimenting."

"Are you just going to let him take me?"

"It's easier than trying to fight him about it," he says casually.

"You are the biggest coward I know," I say. "He killed your mother and you still act like his slave."

"Yes, I am his slave," he says. "He promised me the company after he died. Zandrea, we're trying to help people here, not hurt them. You've been blind to the fact that the galaxy is controlling us more than we realize. We can't do anything without them butting in and giving their opinions. I want to change that, so yes, I do what he says. He's right."

"No," I say. "He isn't. He's trying to conform us to one way of thinking. I don't want to be a mindless drone. He isn't giving people freedom, he's taking it away, and I'm sorry but I'm not sticking around to witness the end of mankind."

"You are so blind-"

"Don't say that," I practically shout. "I have seen this world for what it really is. It may not be perfect, but it's the only home I have, and I intend to keep it the way it is."

"We're trying to help-"

"You think you're helping us? You aren't. You're hurting us more than you already have!"

"Stop interrupting me! You don't know enough about the galaxy to even start a debate with me. My father is helping people, not hurting. If you think otherwise-"

"Did he help you when he killed your mother?" I riposte.

His mouth opens but nothing comes out. He silently stutters before standing up and marching toward me. He gets close to my face before spitting, "Don't ever mention her again. Understand?" He steps away from me.

"It's not my problem you have family issues," I snap.

He stops in his tracks, whirls around, and says, "I don't know how Daniel could ever have fallen for someone like you."

"Don't talk about him like that," I scold.

"Then don't talk about my mother," he says calmly.

All of a sudden, there's a knock at the door.

"It's locked," I yell.

"The room is soundproof," Kelton says. "They can't hear you."

The door opens a moment later, revealing an older man, a cleaning cart behind him. His white hair, the wrinkles cutting deep in his forehead. I've seen him before.

"You're the man who gave Kyle that card in the mirrored hallway," I say excitedly. I almost start dancing.

"Who's Kyle?" he asks. His voice sounds like it could break down any moment.

"Oh sorry, he's my brother," I say. "You saved our lives. I thought I was going to die in that hallway."

He shrugs and moves into the room, pulling his cart behind him. "I remember the boy," he says. "I have faint memories of you. Anyways, where is Chris? I was scheduled to clean his room right now. Should I come back?"

"No-"

"Yes-"

Kelton and I speak at the same time. I look at him.

"Do as I say, Gregory," Kelton says. "Leave us to our meeting and come back tomorrow."

"Sure thing, Kelton, see you tomorrow."

"Wait," I say and hold the door with my foot. Kelton wraps his hand around the handle and tries to pull the door closed. "I'm not-" I say struggling against him, "letting you take away my freedom again."

"Try stopping me," he says.

"I already am," I say through gritted teeth. He lets go of the handle and sends me flying backward into the hallway. I see Rowan through a crack in the door. His eyes are wide, fearful. He tries to move but winces from the pain.

"You can't save the galaxy," Kelton shouts. "You can't save anyone."

"Is that what Chris told you before he murdered your mother?"

"I said to never mention her again!"

"And I said my mission wasn't over until the Corps were destroyed."

"Then you have to kill me," he says. "Because this company will be mine for the taking."

"The company isn't yours until Chris dies," I say.

"I know," he says. He grins his evil grin and everything clicks.

"You're going to murder him, aren't you?" I ask.

He grins again and lets the door slowly shut. "Aren't you a little detective?" The door closes, and I get one final look at Rowan's shoe. Kelton locks the door with the swipe of a card and takes a few steps toward me.

"Rowan will die," I say. "You have to let him go."

"Why?" he asks. "So he can betray the company once again? Anyone who gets in the way of me and my company will be shot on site. Now move."

"No," I say. "I can't let you go. You told me you weren't like your father, but here you are, willing to kill anyone who interferes with your plans. You are just like him."

"I am nothing like him," he retorts. "He was weak. If his company could be destroyed by a little girl like you, then he wasn't doing his job. He promised that once he won the war, he would take over the entire galaxy. He would be a leader. But what leader cowers behind a desk and allows for a girl to run his company into the ground?"

"Don't-"

"I'm going to be the leader he never could," he says. "This galaxy will finally know what true power is. No one, and I repeat no one, will be able to stop me."

He steps over me and continues walking to the elevator. I wait until he's inside before standing up and rushing to Chris's office door. "Rowan,"

I say. "I won't be able to hear your response, but I wanted to thank you for saving my life. I wish I could do the same for you. I feel so helpless sometimes. Kelton is on his way to find Chris and take over the company. I'm so sorry. I have to go." I tear away from the door and head to the elevator.

I don't know where Chris is hiding this time, but I check his laboratory first. The guards still lie on the floor, their blood seeped into the ground. I step over a couple of limp bodies, staying clear of arms and legs. I quiver. These guards must have had families to take care of, wives and children waiting for their return. I do my best to look straight ahead at the laboratory door instead of at the faces of my fallen enemies.

The laboratory door is card-locked but ajar. It seems like a trap to me, so I don't open it any further. Instead, I press my ear to the closed half of the door and listen. Silence. I try peeking in through the crack of the door but don't see much besides the machines that line the wall. I glance down at one of the limp guards, still holding his gun in his left hand. I pry it out, kick open the ajar door, and stand behind the closed one. Nothing happens. I look around the corner but find no one. The quietness is eerie. I almost step inside of the room until I hear the sound of a gun being cocked. Before I can turn around, the gun fires and I fall to my knees.

"I told you not to get in my way," says the voice of the man who shot me. Kelton. "I thought you were smarter than that."

"He's not in there," I say in a weak voice. "I don't know where he is."

"Did you check the entire room?" he asks. He doesn't wait for an answer. "Didn't think so."

I moan.

"So tell me," he says. "Why are you trying to stop *me* from completing *your* mission? You should be thanking me. You told me that you wanted him dead, that was your mission."

"I told you I was going to destroy this organization. That doesn't necessarily mean killing him," I respond.

"But you know you want to," he taunts. "You could help me. We would make a great team."

"You shot me!" I cry.

"You got in my way," he fires back.

"Teammates don't shoot teammates," I say through gritted teeth.

"I offered it to you," he says. "We weren't teammates yet."

"You could have just asked me to move," I complain. "I'm not a threat to you."

"You could be."

"Then you're just like your father," I say. "You said so yourself: you wouldn't be taken down by some little girl."

He kicks me in the side where I previously took a bullet. "You have some nerve, don't you?" he retorts.

I curl up into a ball and groan. My side still hurts. I don't respond.

He leans in close to my face. "Don't follow me," he whispers harshly. "Don't ever get in my way again."

He marches away from the laboratory, kicking one of the guards to his right, and continues left down the hall. I prop myself up against the wall to examine the wound. It brushed my other side, so now I have almost matching bullet wounds. I touch the infected area but wince as my hand grazes the bullet, tucked just beneath the skin. Blood runs down my side, and I realize I will bleed out if I don't treat it.

I attempt to stand up, gingerly holding my side so blood won't trail everywhere. I remember there were cloth pads inside the laboratory used for disinfecting the area where they injected me. They weren't very big, but I figure it's the closest thing to medical help I can get.

The lab is dark, ominous. The only source of light comes from a small bulb across the room. I sneak over to the area where the operating table used to be. A small cart with multiple shelves sits next to the empty space. A syringe, the sleep serum, and a few of the cloth pads rest on the top shelf, everything in perfect order. I grab a few of the cloth pads and apply pressure to my grazed hip. The pads are soaked through immediately.

I walk over to another table in search of something that would last longer. One of the white robes that the women wore lies idly across the back of a chair. I rip a piece of cloth from it and tie it around my waist to stop the flow of blood. Part of it gets soaked through, but it should at least help with the flow.

I walk back out to the hall and pry the first gun I see out of a guard's hand. I position it in front of me and follow the path Kelton took. The corridor is long and dark. Rooms line each side, each door glowing a yellow-blue tone. I don't believe Chris would be hiding in one of these rooms, but Kelton knows his father more than I do. I check each door handle, and if it's unlocked, I peek in. Every room I check is empty, except for a few which contain long tables and chairs with wheels. I bypass each room before finding a stairwell that only leads up.

The stairwell leads up two floors and opens into a small business room. The room contains a small table with four chairs circling it. A screen lays flat on the table presenting the Corps' intricate insignia. I touch the screen and a voice screams from the speakers.

"Welcome, employee," the monotone recording says. "Please enter your ID number."

I begin to panic because I don't have an ID number. My eyes dart around the room as I try to come up with a solution. Then I remember I still have Rowan's card, so I flip it out and scan the card. I find his number on the top and enter it into the database.

"Welcome, Rowan," the voice says. "You have no new messages. Would you like to browse the site?"

I click the 'yes' button and a series of apps appear. I scroll through the list and click 'cameras.' Maybe I'll be able to find Chris or Kelton this way.

"You have selected 'cameras.' Would you like to continue?" the voice asks.

I click 'yes' and the app opens, revealing a selection of over five thousand cameras. I spin through the options, pausing every time I see a person. I see a camera labeled 'Chris's Office.' Maybe one of them went back there.

"You have selected 'Chris's Office' camera. This camera requires an ID number to continue. Continue anyway?"

I select 'yes' and type in Rowan's ID number again. I don't understand, though, why you would need another ID number if you already entered one to get into the system. Another one of the mysteries of the Corps.

The camera enlarges and I can hear everything that is happening in his office, which isn't much, but I do find Rowan lying on the ground. Blood still pools around him, but I no longer see the rise and fall of his chest. I assume he lost any strength he had left in his arm and was no longer able to hold the ripped curtain over the wound. I hold his card against my heart for a moment and stifle a cry. I didn't know him that well; he was just the man that saved my life.

I exit out of the camera and continue my search. I find multiple cameras focused on the laboratory. The bodies of the dead guards have been cleared away; I hope the janitor—Gregory—didn't have to clean the area. I have to add him to the list of people who have saved my life.

Some of the cameras later in the list are turned off. Their room numbers correlate with the upper floors. However, I happen to see one camera that is turned on. Two men stand opposite each other. One man holds a gun, pointing it at the other man's head. My hopes are lifted when I see an insignia stitched onto the left sleeve of the man with the gun. A raid. The adversaries of the Corps have stormed the building. I click on the camera and zoom in, taking everything in. But I realize the insignia is that of the Corps. The man being held at gunpoint is Chris. And the man holding Chris at gunpoint is Kelton.

I frantically scramble to find the right button to push so I can listen in. The computerized voice asks again if I would like to continue, so I press 'yes,' turn on the audio, and wait.

"I can't believe you're doing this," Chris says. "To your own father."

"You were never much of a father, now were you," Kelton retorts.

"Is this because of your mother?" Chris asks. "I killed her because she was a threat to my-our-company. This organization wouldn't be what it is today if she were still here."

"You could've locked her up with the rest of your prisoners," Kelton offers.

"That's just so inhumane," Chris responds. "She was my wife, not my slave."

"She was my mother!" Kelton cries. A tear slips down his face. "I watched her die in front of me."

Welcome to the club, I think, but I realize I'm not part of that club. My mother is still alive as far as I know. I hope the meeting that I walked in on back at my house went well.

A tear falls down my own cheek as I think of Daniel and his mother. Chris murdered her, in front of him, as a child. Every decision he made was because of her. He told me once on one of our longer flights how everything he did was to avenge her death. He told me that one thing she always said was to never live in fear, otherwise it would consume you. Daniel mentioned later that he almost went after Chris himself until Mr. Smith assigned him to be my partner.

"I couldn't have taken a scared little twelve-year old with me," he said once. "I'd like to believe you saved my life." He didn't like to admit to weakness, so this speech of his caught me off guard. I blushed slightly and he slugged me playfully in the arm.

I almost begin bawling at the memory. Daniel and I were best friends, even though I always secretly hoped it would be something more. At first, he would tell me about this girl that he knew; he talked about her all the time. One day I exploded.

"Do you have anything better to talk about?" I asked furiously.

"What?"

"This girl, Callie or whatever, you talk about her all the time," I said, a little more calmly this time.

"Oh, sorry," he said. "I didn't realize you were the jealous type."

I exploded again. "I am *not* the jealous type! I just think it's annoying when the only thing you talk about is some girl I've never met!"

"If you met her, would you change your mind?"

"Probably not," I said, still very angry with him. "Besides, I know enough about her from you blabbing all the time to probably pick her out in a lineup."

"Ha!" he said. "I knew you were the jealous type. You could *not* pick her out in a lineup."

"I could-"

"She's made up!" he shouts above me. "I made her up to get under your skin. She's not real. I don't know anyone named Callie."

I was speechless. All of this—these stories about their adventures—was made up to make me mad. I don't remember if it made me more mad or just more annoyed. He playfully punched me in the arm and smiled.

"Don't be so uptight," he joked. "I'm just trying to have some fun."

"You had me believe she was real," I said, on the verge of tears.

"Look, I'm sorry for wanting to have fun, but liven up a little," he said. "You only live once."

Thinking back, I should've realized the story of Daniel jumping off a building to go be with some other girl named Callie was all a hoax. I guess I was just too caught up in things to realize he *had* given me a clue to Kelton's deception. I can't believe I let Kelton get in my head enough to make me forget about Daniel's made-up girlfriend named Callie, created to make me mad. I smile at the memory.

Daniel's tone did get more serious after revealing Callie was fake, though. I'd always wondered why. He woke up the next night screaming. It startled me so bad I got mad at him the next morning. I accused him of messing around too much. I thought he was trying to scare me. Turns out he was having another nightmare, the one I would later learn would be from Chris killing his mother.

Bang! A loud noise snaps me back to reality. I look at the screen again and see Chris slowly falling backward to the ground. A bullet pierces him through his head. His eyes remain open but lifeless, like the rest of him. He hits the ground with a thud and his body quivers with the impact.

I gasp as I realize what happened. Chris—the leader of the Corps—is dead. Mission accomplished, right? I think back to my dream where Kyle told me Kelton was going to do what his father never could. That dream foreshadowed more than I thought. Creepy. If my dream comes completely true, Kelton will run the Corps and possibly bring even more fear to the galaxy. I know what I have to do. It will be difficult, it will be dangerous, but it will be worth it.

I look at the room number that correlates to the camera and exit out of the app. The room is on the tenth floor, so I head there next. I carry my gun in front of me, extending it around each corner. I climb four floors to the level where the room is and walk down the hall a few paces before finding a spacious area with open cubicles lining the walls. On the far end, opposite the door I entered, Chris's body lays flat, motionless against the ground. Kelton stands above him. He snatches his ID card and leaves the room.

I run across the expanse of the room, my heart beating and my lungs burning. I run as fast as I can. The center of the room slopes down slightly and I lose my footing. My left leg trips over my right and I go flying. My knee scrapes the concrete floor, and my fresh bullet wound hits the pavement. I scream out from the excruciating pain. No one comes. The only person in the room is dead.

I slowly stand up and limp the rest of the way to where Chris lies, still, peaceful. I sit next to him and examine the bullet wound in his forehead. There's no blood surrounding him on the ground. His eyes remain open but unwavering. I use my fingers to shut them. Then I place my hand on his chest to see if he's still breathing. But I don't feel flesh. My hand touches something hard and smooth. I lift his shirt up slightly and find a chest plate made of a strong metal. That, I realize, is why the bullet Rowan shot didn't kill him. It ricocheted off the metal plate. Kelton must have known he was wearing body armor because he aimed for his head, not his chest. Maybe he knew because he too was wearing body armor. It's effective, I'll give them that.

I get up to leave the room, nearly running into Gregory. He doesn't look the slightest bit shocked or surprised to see me standing there. He pulls his cart behind him and moves around me, whistling. He glances at Chris, but his expression doesn't falter. The dead body doesn't even faze him.

"I found him like this," I say. "It looks like he was shot."

He nods but stays silent. I don't understand how he could be so calm at a time like this. The man who employed him, his leader, is now dead. Then it hits me like a dozen flying bricks. He's like Rowan, who pretends to help Chris, be his friend, his staff member, but really helps destroy the Corps from the inside.

"Are you-" I start, "a spy?"

He glances at me, the wrinkles in his forehead crease, deepen. "I don't understand the question," he replies.

I try to think of a different way to word the question. "Do you work for someone else, besides Chris?"

"First of all," he starts. "I wouldn't share that information with you. And second, even if I did, what would it matter. I clean the largest building on this side of the galaxy. I don't work for Chris, I clean for him. There's a difference."

"Then who do you work for?"

"That, my dear, is confidential," he says. "Sorry." He pulls a bag from his cart large enough to fit a body.

"You just happen to carry body bags with you?" I say surprised.

"This is the Corps, darling, not the Mardina government." He gives a weak smile.

His joke is funny, but I don't laugh. Mardina is a planet in the very center of the galaxy. It has to keep a pretty tight ship over there because it could be attacked from all sides at once. The military system is great. The guards don't carry guns or anything, they just wear extremely protective body suits and fight everyone bare-handed. They don't even allow guns on their premises.

I focus back to Gregory, who neatly slips Chris's body into the bag. But instead of bringing it somewhere to dispose of it, he leaves it where it is. Then he proceeds to push his cart to the opposite end of the room, the side where I came in.

"Wait," I shout. He turns around. "Aren't you going to take his body? If you can't lift it, I can help you."

"You're a naive little girl, aren't you?" he responds. "If I disposed every body of Chris's that I found, I'd wear myself to death."

"What do you-"

"Bye-bye now!" he sings over his shoulder. Then he carries on with his whistling.

I could follow him, see where he goes next. I figure he won't talk to me anymore though. He's stubborn that way. The room is so vast and empty that he would see me if I followed him. I could go out the way Kelton did, but I don't know if it connects with the other door, and by the time I get to the other exit, he'll probably already be gone. I'm running out of options and time, so I decide to chase after him. I cross my fingers and hope he's in a talkative mood.

For an older man, he's pretty fast. He's halfway across the room before I make up my mind. I run to catch up, being careful of the slope in the middle. When I reach him, I slow my pace down to a walk and try to catch my breath.

"Why are you following me?"

"I need answers," I respond through breaths.

"And you think I have the answers?"

"I think you know more than you're letting on."

"What makes you think that?"

"I don't know," I say still panting. "You just seem like you have a lot of insight on the Corps and what they plan to do."

"I clean for them, don't I? I would have to know something."

"Look, I'm on your side. I just want to know some information."

"How do you know I'm on *your* side?" he taunts. "You have been deceived many times in this building; what makes you think now would be any different?"

"I've learned to trust people," I say. "I don't know if that's a good thing, but it's who I am. It's what I do."

He looks at me sideways.

"Look, I've been through a lot these last few weeks. My mother is at home, either dead or barely living. I may never get to see the man I love again. I may not get to see my younger brother or my father, both of whom I hadn't seen for many years before this excursion. If you want to help me complete my mission, follow me. We have to find Kelton and stop him from taking over this operation. He cannot follow in his father's footsteps."

"Why are you so adamant about destroying the organization?"

I stop to think about this. The question throws me off guard because I haven't really found a specific answer except for the fact that they split my family apart and ruined countless others. But I tell him, "Because they're bad people. Bad people set out to do bad things."

"Are they bad because they *do* evil things, or are they bad because their views don't align with yours?"

"I-" I stop. I don't respond. Maybe he's right. Maybe I believe they're evil because they do the opposite of what I do. Maybe I'm the bad one, corrupted, evil. I can't come to terms with this though.

"Everyone was raised to believe they are doing the right thing," he says. "Everyone believes they are good and they are doing things for the good of others. No one ever stops and thinks they are doing evil until someone else points it out. I'm not saying you're an evil person. I'm saying that you need to open your eyes. Don't be so narrow-minded that you can't see something right next to you."

He pushes past me and continues pulling his cart to the entrance of the room. Before he reaches the door, he looks back and smiles tiredly.

"You're brother was right," he says. "You only see what you want to see." Then he disappears around the corner leaving me speechless.

My brain is tired from information overload. *Sleep*, I think. *I need sleep.* I find an office cubicle pressed against the wall and curl up under the chair. Hopefully no one finds me. I slip off to a sweet, well-needed rest.

The darkness of my eyelids fades and I'm in the mirrored hallway again. I stand up from my lying position on the ground and brush myself off. Then I look ahead and find a face staring back at me. But it's not my face. The girl in the mirror looks like me in a way but at the same time completely different. When I turn my head, she turns hers the same way.

Her pale blue eyes reflect mine, but hers seem to sparkle in a way my eyes never did. She's older but still looks my age. I look down and notice she wears a clean dark green shirt and tight black pants. Compared to my ratty pullover and muddy pants, she looks beautiful.

I put my left hand up against the glass as her right hand goes up to meet mine. Her hands are fresh, and her nails are filed to a perfect roundness. My nails are dirty and rough. I look to my left and then to my right; she copies me. Then I put my right hand up. She puts up her left, but I notice something else different about her. She wears a beautiful, sparkly ring around her second to the left finger. I glance at it closer and she does the same. Then she breaks our synchronizing rhythm by looking from my finger to my face and back.

"He did not propose?" the girl in the mirror asks.

The question takes me by surprise because I didn't say anything. "Who didn't?"

"You know exactly who I'm talking about," she replies.

I do know. I know it, and I almost say his name, but I don't want to burst into tears.

"It's okay," she says. "I know how you're feeling."

"You know nothing about me!" I scream, tears threatening to spill over my eyelids.

"My dear, there is still so much you need to learn," she says, her voice angelic and sweet.

"You can't and won't teach me anything," I say sternly.

"Of course not," she says. "Everything you know, I know."

"Then how am I supposed to learn anything from you?"

"You aren't," she says. "Look around you, Zandrea. Your mind is like a tunnel, you can't see anything except what's in front of you."

"What's your point?" I ask flatly.

"These people, this organization, they've been playing you like a fiddle," she says. "You don't know left from right, right from wrong, light from dark. Be a bridge, not a tunnel."

Then she disappears and I'm left staring at my real reflection. I look to my left and then my right. I place my right hand on the glass and her left hand follows. This time, there is no ring. Only dirty, hollow fingers that I know belong to me.

The door that leads out from the mirrored hallway opens and reveals a light so bright I have to shield my eyes. Some force, a feeling in my gut, pulls me toward the light. A voice repeats my name until I am out of the hallway and into a clouded kingdom. The voice gets louder and more persistent. I keep walking to where I believe the source of the noise lies.

An alarm. It sounds overhead. How long has it been going off? How long was I asleep? I try to stand up but realize there's a desk over me. I scoot out briefly from under the desk; that is until I see about 100 Corps' guards running through the room. I scoot back under the desk until they leave the room through the same door Gregory did. Then I wait until the coast is clear before making a run in the same direction as the guards.

Most of them are too far ahead to catch up to, but there are a few stragglers who seem very out of shape. One of them slows down to a jog and then to a fast walk. I could easily catch up to him without any strain, but I don't know what side he remains on. Could he be a spy? Probably not, but it's always nice to hope.

I come up with a plan to join the group and find out what they're running for. I run up next to the closest straggler and tap him on the shoulder. He jerks and aims his gun at me, but I point mine at his head and pull the trigger slightly. He throws his hands up in a surrendering sort of way, and I point to a room behind him. I poke him in the head with my gun, and he moves into the room. I follow behind him, checking to make sure no one saw us.

As we enter the room, I find the door and shut it closed. "What's going-"

I pull my trigger and he falls back toward the ground. I slip off his helmet and uniform and pull it on over myself. I hide his gun in a storage closet opposite the door and then leave and catch up with the rest of the group. They jog to somewhere on the opposite end of the building. The alarm overhead is piercing, but the beat of my heart and the thump of my footsteps pounding on the cement floor help me tune it out.

We reach the area a little later; almost everyone stops running as soon as we get to the site and pants like they've never ran before. I'm in better shape than some of the people here, but I'm still worn out. Whatever it is we ran for, it better be worth it.

A guard, who I assume to be the leader, stands on a small podium in front of the crowd. He yells some things about this group being the laziest bunch of nobodies he's ever met and how they should try harder if they want to stay alive. I tune out for the most part; none of this applies to me. Instead I walk over to the big picture windows that line the side of the building.

The view is pretty in the daytime. It's the same view of the runway that I got to see before we left the building and our ship exploded, except now, it's a few stories higher in the air and it's daylight hours. The lake shimmers with the source of light reflecting off of it. The lake goes for what seems like miles in every direction. I can faintly see the shore where Daniel landed. It looks peaceful, beautiful, and not at all menacing like it was the first time I saw it.

The leader of the group yells a few more commands and the group disbands. Some go back the same way we came, and I can tell by their body posture that they aren't happy. The leader looks down at his list and then turns his head to each direction in turn to watch the groups depart. Then he turns toward me. He eyes me carefully. I gulp. He'll know I'm not supposed to be there. I wait as his look decides my fate. He opens his mouth to speak, but all he yells is for me to get moving and there's no time for sightseeing.

I run in the direction of one of the groups toward an area I haven't been yet. I catch up to them pretty easily; they jog so slowly I could run to the front of the group and be ahead of them in an instant. I decide not to though and slow down to a fast walk.

The hallway is long, narrow, and dark. The windows are tinted a dark color and allow in very little natural light. The hallway gets darker quickly, and some of the soldiers turn on lights on top of their guns. I find the switch and activate my light. I point it at the walls and find light writings scribbled all over. Some of the scribblings are legible, while others are just drawings or carvings. One reads: *Kelton is crazy*. Then below it: *Don't trust him*. Then another below that: *David was here*. I tap one of the soldiers on the shoulder and lower my voice.

"Do you know who this David is?" I ask, even though I'm pretty sure I already know the answer.

"I think he was one of the recruits that got to work alongside Chris's son. I heard he died recently in a ship crash."

"How did that happen?" I ask. "I thought the Corps' ships weren't supposed to crash."

"From what I heard, it got hijacked by some spy who also died in the crash."

"Hijacked?"

"Yeah, the pilot hijacked the ship, crashed it, and took off unharmed. I think he had a parachute with him because you don't just fall from the air and come out unscathed."

"Was there anyone else in the ship?" I ask.

"I'm not sure," he replies. "Maybe. The guy who told me said he heard from some other guy that he saw two people with parachutes, but it could be incorrect information."

"Right," I say. "Of course."

We walk a little longer in silence. My mind wanders to Daniel and Kyle. I have more hope now than I did before about seeing them again. Maybe when I get back, Daniel and I can finally have that wedding I've dreamt so much about. I can picture the dress my mother wore for her wedding. She looked gorgeous in it, and I even remember as a little girl asking her if I could wear it when I got married one day. She told me yes, that when that day came, she wanted to be the first to see me in it. One day she let me try it on. It was big, but it made me feel special, high class. I didn't want to take it off, but my mother had told me it would get ruined if it stayed out of the box any longer. I would sometimes take peeks at it when she wasn't around.

Once, she caught me. At first she scolded me, but then she explained the story of when she first wore it. It was the day before she has planned to marry my father. Her mother was helping her try it on, making sure it fit.

"You look so beautiful," her mother said. "Jordan is a very lucky man."

"Thanks Mother," she replied. "I hope these are the best years of my life."

"They will be," she assured her. "They will be."

She got married the next day at the House and kept her dress tucked away safely. When I was old enough, she told me it was going to be mine someday. I've waited forever to wear the dress for real. Hopefully that day comes soon.

The hallway is long, very long. My feet start to ache, and I slow my pace down until I'm almost at the back of the group. I notice more writings on the walls, some of them tallies reaching into the hundreds. One of the soldiers catches my gaze and points to one of the tally charts scratched into the wall.

"These used to be prison cells before they relocated them to one of the higher floor levels," he explains as if reading my thoughts. "The tallies were left by prisoners."

"Interesting," I respond. Then I point to a single scratch on the wall. "Why is there only one?"

"Chris took the prisoners to his lab and did experiments on them," he says. "Something to do with dreams becoming nightmares. Whoever was here was probably brought to his use pretty fast."

I look closer at the walls. Underneath one of the scratchings is another scratching, this one reading a name. *Jcrdan Kncules*, it reads. I can tell, even though some of it was not scratched very deeply, that this is my father's name. He was in a cell in this spot probably not too long ago. I count the marks next to his name. Two-thousand marks, roughly. I shiver.

"Did all of the prisoners in this area get relocated?"

"For the most part, yes," he says. "Unless Chris needed them for his experiments."

"Do you know where the prisoners were moved to?"

"Some cages on the higher levels of the building," he responds. "I heard most of them escaped though. Not sure how, but the Corps let them loose."

I know, I think but I keep my mouth shut. I study more of the wall, trying to find clues of anyone else's escape. Nothing. I keep walking down further until the wall changes color from an off-white to a light brown. The scratches become infrequent and then stop altogether. I shiver.

"Are you cold?" the soldier asks.

"No, I'm fine," I say. "Just thinking about what it would have been like to be stuck in one of those cages." I know though. I'm too familiar with the feeling.

"It probably wasn't that bad," he says. "They bring you food and you can sleep whenever."

"That doesn't mean it's all fine and dandy in there," I snap.

"Sorry, didn't mean to offend you," he says. "Did you know someone in there?"

"Why do you care?" I ask.

"Well," he starts. "I care because I knew someone in there. Someone I was close to."

"What happened?" I ask flatly.

He turns away from me and swipes at his cheek.

"What happened to them?" I ask quieter.

"Nothing," he says. "It doesn't matter."

"Over the years," I say. "I've learned that when someone cries about something, it's because it's significant. Nobody cries for the fun of it. You don't have to tell me, but don't lie to me either. I've been lied to enough in my life."

We walk a little longer in silence, except for a few sniffles coming from my left. Finally, he turns to me.

"She was my best friend," he begins. "We told each other everything, never lied to each other. She was like family. One day, and I don't know how this happened, but one day I started liking her as more than just a best friend. I eventually told her this, and she told me she had felt the same way for a long time. We got married that summer and had two children, two years apart."

He glances at me to see if I'm paying attention. I am. This story sounds like my own.

"Anyway," he says. "We didn't have much money, so I left and joined the Corps because I knew they were hiring and paid good. But what I didn't know was what they expected of us. They said that anyone who didn't believe in what the Corps stood for was to be tortured and killed. If they found out, and they always would, they would kill us and our families. I couldn't do that. Well, as fate would have it, my wife didn't agree with the Corps to any degree. I was forced to beat her so she wouldn't die. I hated it. We fought so often. Of course, I couldn't tell her anything or she would be killed. One day she snapped. Knowing that the Corps could see everything that happened, I had to report her to protect her."

My eyes grow wide. His story reminds me of one I've heard before. I can't think of who or what it was.

"The Corps came and took her away along with my two beloved children. I cried for weeks straight. When I finally returned to work, one of the group leaders took us through this hallway and showed us all of the prisoners they captured. As I was walking, I saw my wife and children huddled in one of the cages. I put my hand on one of the bars and told her someday I was going to break her free. She shrieked and told me she wanted nothing to do with me, that the children were hers, and if she ever got out she would never allow me to see them again. I cried even more after that."

He teared up again and swiped at his eyes.

"I was relieved when I heard that some enemy ship came by and helped the prisoners escape. By that point, most of the prisoners had been relocated to one of the higher levels of the building. I tried going back to see them but she had moved far away from the Corps and its evil clutches.

If I knew where they were, I would fly there immediately and apologize for everything that I did."

"I'm sure you'll be able to find her," I say. "The Corps have so many fancy gadgets; I'm sure it wouldn't be too hard to locate them."

"I'm just, afraid," he says softly. "Afraid I'll find her but she won't listen to my apology. She'll shut the door in my face and tell my children that I'm nobody to be concerned about. They were so little when I left; I doubt they would remember me."

"You'd be surprised by what kids can remember," I say quietly. I remember every last detail about the day my father left. He was calm and controlled but sad. He picked up his bag, kissed each of us in turn, and told us that he loved us with all of his heart.

I wonder what my mother would have done if my father came back before me. Would she have slammed the door in his face or be delighted to see him? What if Chris had been there? Would she break up with him? Or would she be too afraid? He could kill her. Maybe he would. And then my father would be next. Or maybe he would force her to watch him die. Would he have killed Kyle too?

"My children mean the world to me," he says, interrupting my thoughts. "I just hope that my wife took care of them all these years."

That's when it hits me. I know who he's talking about. The woman and her children in one of the first cages I saw when we first arrived here. She told me that she and her husband had a fight and he worked for the Corps and turned them in. I gasp.

"She's fine," I say.

"How do you know?" he says.

"I saw them leave. Your kids were in good condition. Your wife, well..."

"How do you know it was them?"

"I just have this hunch," I say. "They got on the ship. I don't know where they went though."

"Just as long as they're alive," he says. "That's all that matters to me."

We walk awhile more in silence as I stare at the wall for any other signs of scratchings. He catches my gaze again.

"You never told me who you knew in there," he says.

"Nobody," I respond. "Just forget it."

"I won't force you to tell me, but I've found that sometimes it helps."

I continue staring at the wall. This guy, this soldier, I don't trust him. It's not that he's suspicious, but I've learned my lesson about letting my guard down with people who work for the Corps. I can tell he's waiting for me to say something, but I can't. It hurts too much to bring it up.

"I can't," I say. "It's something I've been trying to forget."

"It's these kinds of memories that you don't ever want to forget," he says sympathetically. "I never wanted to forget my wife or kids because it was the thought of them that controlled every decision that I made."

I get a feeling he's telling me this so I'll explain what happened. I can't though. He's right, but I choose to ignore this fact.

"The longer you bottle something up, the bigger the explosion," he says.

"Will you stop?" I say a little too fiercely. "I didn't make you tell *me* anything, did I?"

"No, but-"

"Right, so stop pestering me," I say. "It's something I don't want to talk about. I don't even know you. Why would I tell you my whole life's story?"

"I'm not asking you to," he says holding up his hands as if he's surrendering. "I just figure it might be better if you talked to someone about it. It helped me when I told you."

"Well, I operate differently than you," I say. "For me, the farther I push things away, the lesser it hurts."

"Fine," he says tiredly. "Don't tell me anything. I'm just going to say that hiding things, pushing them away, that's what hurts the most. I hid things from my wife and pushed her away, and now she never wants to see me again. Things may be different for you, but I've gone through somewhat similar circumstances. I know the pain it brings."

"It's not even that big of a deal," I protest.

"Then you should have no problem confronting it."

"Why do you care so much?"

"Because I want to help you," he says. "I've made a huge mistake, and I don't want you to do the same thing."

A tear slips down my cheek. I know he's right, and yet I can't bring myself to say anything. My throat swells with tears I try to choke back. Pretty soon, I'm bawling, but only loud enough for him to hear.

"I had everything I'd ever wanted, right in my arms," I say. "The person I fell in love with proposed to me. I couldn't have been happier. There was this other guy though. He told me he loved me. I had just met him, and he had tricked me into thinking he was helping my fiancé and me. Turns out I was stupid enough to listen to his lies. I thought that he was the one I truly loved. Everything was a lie. He didn't care that I existed. He only wanted me so his father could use me as a test subject. Everything else he told me was so far from the truth it kills me to think I ever believed it."

I look up at the guard, but he stares straight ahead. I continue with my story anyway.

"My fiancé faked his death so I wouldn't be burdened by him," I say. "He loved me so much that he was willing to die for me to be happy. I didn't realize that until it was already too late. I'm furious with myself for everything. I deserve to be punished by never seeing him again or something of the sort."

"Sure," he says. "But also realize that he loves you so much that he realized your mistake as well and already forgave you for it. He forgave you before you did the same for yourself. Sometimes you need to let go of the past and start over completely."

"You should take your own advice," I say.

He smiles. "Maybe I should."

We continue our trek in silence for a while. I think about everything he told me. Maybe he's right. I should forgive myself since Daniel already did. He loved me enough to sacrifice everything. I wish I had seen all of this sooner.

This guard and I have both been through a lot in our lives. I compare my story to his. We both let the people we love slip through our grasp like sand through a sifter. Except that my story seems to have a better outcome. Daniel is like a rock. Rocks don't go through sifters so easily. They hang on for as long as possible even when it seems like all strength had been lost. I smile the biggest, most real grin I've smiled in a long time.

The hallway is a maze of other hallways joining up together and leading off to separate rooms. It's dark enough that without the lights from our guns I wouldn't be able to see the person in front of me. I don't know what could be this far off the beaten path that would require our assistance, but I can't lose the group now. Besides, I would have no idea how to get back to the main building.

We go down a few flights of stairs and end up walking in another tunnel under the surface. Small, rectangular windows line the top of the walls near the ceiling. They let in just enough light that the guards in front of me turn off their lights. I look ahead to see how long this hallway is. A door sits on the left a few yards in front of us. As I get closer, I see a label next to the door that reads: *To Outside Facility*. I can only assume what the outside facility would be used for.

All of a sudden, a noise roars so loud my body begins to shake. The thunder shakes the ground and I grip the wall. Then it's done. A loud *whooshing* sound follows the thunderous noise, and I notice that the runway is on our right. A ship must have taken off.

Once I straighten up, the guard looks at me and laughs. "What? You've never heard a ship take off before?"

"Not this close," I say.

"You'll get used to it," he responds.

The group continues to move down the hallway. The footsteps beating against the ground lull me into a trance, and I feel tired again. Something tells me, though, that we aren't stopping for a while. The hallway leads to another set of stairs and we descend even further into the ground. A few more ships take off, but by now I'm used to the rumble of the ground. One of the ships passes us overhead. I cover my ears.

Eventually we reach a room not much wider than the hallway. Ten hooks line the right wall, three of them holding shot rifles. The leader of the group grabs two of them, handing one to a guard behind him. The group continues to move, filing into another hallway just beyond the room. I replace my gun with the one left on the hook and then follow the rest of the group into the next hallway. This hallway is even narrower than the last one; everyone moves in a single file. The lights overhead are dim, making it hard to see the people in front of me.

We walk a little further until we reach a medium-sized room. It's cold and dark and has a strong odor that makes me think no one has been here in a while. Something green grows at the edges of the room and ceiling. The black faded tiles on the ground look worn and grimy.

"When was the last time someone was in here?" I ask the guard.

He chuckles. "Probably awhile," he says and looks around. "It could probably use a cleanup."

The group comes to a halt so fast I almost run into the guard in front of me. Then I hear the leader of our group saying something, but not to us. He's talking to someone in front of us.

"… this is where we're supposed to meet, correct?" the leader of our group says.

"Yes, didn't they tell you to come here?" The voice sounds awfully familiar, and my stomach lurches at the thought of who it is. I push my way to the front of the crowd.

"They told me to stop when we found you," our leader says. "I wasn't sure how far we had to go. Man, this place is a maze I almost got lost a couple of times-"

"Wonderful," the familiar voice says in a bored tone. Then he gets more excited. "Well, here you are. I have tasks for each of you."

I almost make it to the front but someone grabs my shoulder and pulls me back. "Don't go up there," the new voice whispers. "If we aren't invited, we're not supposed to move." I realize it's the same guard who I've been talking with this whole trek.

"Let go of me," I whisper harshly. "I'm just trying to see who it is."

"They'll shoot you," he warns.

"Let them," I say. "It's one less guard they have to fight for them."

He lets me go but stays close behind me as I move toward the front again. I push past many people, but when I get to the front, a line of bodies block my view. I stand on my tiptoes and try to see past them. I get a glimpse of someone very familiar, someone who's going to be dead soon.

I pull my gun up and position it against my shoulder. It's much heavier than my last one. I aim it at him and cock the gun. The sound is just loud enough for him to see me. I squeeze the trigger slightly, letting him know I'm not messing around this time. I won't let him slip through my grasp again.

"What are you doing?" he asks. Then he turns toward our group leader. "Is she okay?"

I pull my helmet off and his eyes widen. "Hello, Kelton," I say.

He stares at me and blinks. "Hey," he offers, slightly raising his hand to wave. "How have you been?"

"I've been better," I say. The soldiers in front of me step to the side, allowing me to move closer to Kelton.

He nods.

"So," I say, changing subjects. "What are you planning to do with all these soldiers?"

"Wouldn't you like to know."

"I have a few minutes to spare," I respond.

He shrugs and looks at the ground.

"Well," I say, shifting my gun from my right shoulder to my left. "I'm sure we would all like to know what we're in for."

"Too bad," he snarls. Then he explodes. "You think you're so special, don't you? My father chose you for a reason? He said because you were stronger mentally than Daniel. I say it's because he wanted to hurt you the most!"

"Why does he care about me?" I fire back. "It's not like his son cared for me or anything!"

"I don't!"

"You lied to me," I say. "And I told you, if you lied to me, I would kill you." I position my gun again and aim at him. All eyes are on me. Everyone holds their breath. I'm surprised no one tries to stop me. Do they all want him dead too?

"You can't do it," Kelton says. "My father thought you were strong mentally. He told me he's never seen someone survive as long as you did under simulation. But I think my father was the weak one in the family. He said he was going to push you to your limits, and then he let you get away. I'm not going to let that happen."

He pulls his own gun from out of his pocket. It's a small one, barely bigger than his hand. He raises it slowly, taunting me. He aims it so I'm looking into the barrel of my certain doom.

"Not so special now, are you?"

"I was never special, not now, not ever," I say. "At least, I wasn't special to myself. You, well, you're a different story. See, there were so many times you could have killed me, destroyed me, but you didn't. You think your father was the weak one in the family? You're wrong. It's you. And it's because of your love for me that made you weak."

"I-"

"Don't try to deny it either," I continue. "You tried pretending for everyone else but never for me. There were countless times you could've killed me, and you didn't. Take your father's office, for example, or just after that by the laboratory. So many chances, Kelton. And I may have been lied to by you more times than I can count, but your love for me was the one truth you spoke. And if I'm wrong, shoot me."

He hoists his gun up even higher, repositioning it so it would pierce my head and kill me in a second. He scowls, embarrassment and hostility registering all over his face. I notice something else too.

"Your hand is trembling," I say matter-of-factly. "Just do it. Get it over with. Make your father proud!"

"Stop!" he screams.

"It kills you to have come so far only to be whittled down to pieces in front of an army of your soldiers."

"I will kill you!"

"Then do it! What's taking so long?"

A hand rests on my shoulder followed by a voice. "Don't," the voice, who I assume is the guard's voice, says. "He cares about no one. Don't test him."

"He won't shoot me," I whisper. "He can't."

"Oh, is this your friend?" Kelton snarls. "Isn't that sweet. Daniel just wasn't enough for you?"

"Don't ever say his name again," I say fiercely. "He's a thousand times the man you'll ever be."

"Really? Because I remember you falling for me even after he proposed to you."

"How do you know it wasn't a setup?"

"From the look in your eye when you finally decided he wasn't the right one for you," he says back.

"I don't know what look you're talking about," I say.

"Don't be so naive," he replies. "You trusted a Corps' guard! It doesn't get more naive than that."

I look back at the guard behind me, who looks almost sad and regretful.

"How do you know he isn't lying to you?" Kelton asks.

"I have a hunch," I retort.

"Yeah, and where did that get you last time?"

I look at my feet.

"Right, trapped and alone," he answers for me. "Now let me ask you this, why do you trust him?"

"Because his story lines up with the story his wife told me," I say.

The guard looks at me. "You knew my wife?" He sounds hopeful.

"Not personally, but I knew someone who shared the same story as you," I say. "I told you, it was just a hunch."

"Well, isn't that sweet," Kelton says.

"You need to keep your mouth shut," I say to Kelton.

"And you need to stop being so altruistic," he fires back. He positions his gun again, but this time he points it at the guard. In a split second, my ears ring from the backlash of the shot. The guard falls back, his head nearly hitting the ground. Before I can think, I tackle Kelton to the ground and punch him square in the jaw. He aims his gun at me, but I fling it away and punch him in the nose.

After that, the room becomes a madhouse. The spies begin firing at the genuine Corps' guards, who, in return, fire back. The next few moments go by in a blur. Kelton grabs my arms and stops me long enough to whisper, "You were right, I did love you." Another shot. I could hear this one whiz by my ear before it landed in Kelton's heart. The rapid rise and fall of his chest slows down until it becomes nonexistent.

I don't even wonder where the bullet came from. Probably just a misfire by one of the guards behind me. Except… except it was too accurate. Too spot-on to be a failed attempt. I look into his eyes before they go lifeless, recalling everything that happened between us. At first, sad tears flow down my cheeks, and then relief tears, followed by hot, angry tears at everything he did to mess up my life. He told me he loved me and then tried to kill me, only for me to be right in the first place.

I glance behind me. The guard Kelton shot sits propped up behind me, a small pistol in his right hand, the same pistol Kelton held only moments earlier. The guard looks from Kelton's stark eyes to mine, relief and euphoria displayed on his face.

"He drove my wife and me apart," he says. "He's lucky I didn't strangle him."

A small smile appears on my face. "Yeah, and he almost killed everyone I love." We both start laughing, our states of delusion clearly written across our faces. "Don't worry, I'm going to help you first, and then you can go find your wife and explain everything."

"I don't know if I can do it alone," he says.

"Who said anything about doing it alone?" I ask. I grab his hand and pull him to his feet. He stands up, limping slightly.

"At least the bullet didn't hit you anywhere vital," I say, trying to reassure him. I wrap my arm around his waist for support and lead him through the entrance of the room, careful to dodge any wandering bullets that might cross our path.

"You know, I never did catch your name," I say.

"Eli," he replies. "What's yours?"

"Zandrea."

"My wife's name is Andrea," Eli says chuckling slightly. Then his smile turns into a frown, followed by a slight whimpering.

"Hey," I say softly. "Are you okay?"

"It's just," he begins. "I don't think you understand what it's like for someone you love to be ripped away from you, turned against you. It's the saddest way to lose someone."

I frown at his comment. "And to think I was the only one in the galaxy who knew that kind of pain firsthand," I say sarcastically.

"I'm sorry," he says. "These last few weeks have been really hard for me."

"Look," I say a little too harsh. "You can mope all you want about losing your wife and kids, but at the end of the day, sulking gets you nowhere. Trust me, I've done my fair share of sulking in the past, and I can distinctly remember that nothing good came out of it."

He looks at me, his eyes red. "Alright," he says quietly.

We take the long trek back the same way we came the first time. It feels even longer this time because Eli can't walk. He's a lot heavier than he looks. We stop a couple of times, me to catch my breath and him because his pain level is too extreme to continue. The trek takes all night and most of the next day. I almost start sleepwalking until I hear the vibrations of the ships taking off overhead.

"We should be there soon," I reassure Eli. He nods but winces at the sudden exposure to pain.

Once we get back to the main building, I check around to see where the camera room was where I saw Kelton attempt to kill his father. I wonder what Chris would think if he knew his son died at the hands of one of his own.

We move to the elevator and I punch the ninth floor button. The doors close, and we're whisked to the ninth floor. The doors slowly open. I wrap my arm around Eli's waist, and he drapes his arm across my shoulders. He hobbles out the doors and peeks around the side of the hallway.

"All clear," he says weakly.

We walk down to the end of the hall and stop at a door that reads: *Documentary and Surveillance*. "This is the room," I say and grab Rowan's card from my pocket. I swipe the card through the slot and hear a click. I twist the doorknob and reveal the camera room.

"What are we doing here?" Eli asks.

"Finding your wife," I reply.

I prop him up on a chair and attempt to use Rowan's ID card to access the cameras.

"This ID is out of use," the computerized voice says. "The user of this ID card is deceased. Please try a different ID card."

"You've got to be kidding me," I scream at the computer.

"Try mine," Eli mutters. "It's in my chest pocket."

I open the pouch and grab his ID card. Then I hold it against the scanner and wait for it to read the card.

"Welcome Eli," the computerized voice says again. "Please enter your code."

"220331," Eli replies.

"Access granted," says the computer. "What would you like to see?"

"Andrea Parker, code name 220332," Eli commands.

After a few seconds, the computer registers a location. Then a map pops up and gives the exact coordinates of where she is. Then the camera zooms in on her and picks up an audio sensor.

"… be back by three," she says. "Your father will be home by then."

"Bye Mother," one of the children says.

A door slams shut. The woman, who I assume to be Andrea, lifts a small child into her arms and cradles him. She starts singing softly into the child's ear, rocking him gently back and forth in her arms. I notice a few scars on her arms and face, most likely from the beatings she endured.

Out of the corner of my eye, I see Eli start to rise in his seat. "Can you rewind the video?" he asks.

I search the control panel and find a rewind button. The video bounces back a few seconds, stopping on an image of Andrea handing the older child a small bag.

"Make sure you eat all of it," she says to the child. "No wasting like yesterday."

"Yes Mother," the girl says.

"And promise me you'll be back by three," she says. "Your father will be home by then."

"Pause the video," Eli says, his voice rough and strained.

"What's wrong?" I ask.

"Didn't you hear what she said?" he asks.

"Yeah," I say slowly. "She wants her to eat her food and be back by three."

"Why does she want her back by three?" he asks, trying to make a point.

"How would I-" I turn my head back to the video fast. "Oh. She's not talking about you, is she?"

"Bingo," he says quietly.

I stare at him in complete silence. His jawline goes slack, his eyes vacant. He begins to slip away from the chair. I stand up fast and help prop him up again. The look in his hollow, dark eyes is enough to make me believe the bullet wound in his lower torso is nothing compared to what he just heard.

"Hey," I say gently. "It's going to be alright. Maybe she tells her children that so they think you're coming back."

"Do you even hear yourself," he asks harshly. "Can you look me in the eyes and honestly tell me that she's talking about me?"

"Well…"

"Right," he says. "Didn't think so." Then he winces.

"Let me help with your wound," I say. "At least that way I can be useful."

"What's the point?" he asks.

"What do you mean?"

"The only reason I've been fighting this hard to stay alive was so I could go back and see her, see them," he says. "But you heard what she said. She's moved on. There is no reason to go back."

"Obviously you don't love her then," I say.

"What do you mean? Of course I do."

"No, you don't. Because if you did, you would be doing everything in your power to get back to her, no matter what you heard on that recording. For the longest time, I thought Daniel would never love me the way I loved him."

"Who's Daniel?"

"But I was always there," I say ignoring him. "I stood by his side even when he told me there was someone else he loved. Turns out he was messing with me, but that's besides the point. Ever since I made the sacrifice to stay here and let them be free, I've been fighting my way back to him. And I will keep on fighting until the last breath in my body escapes from me. Because I love him. I always have, and I always will."

Saying it out loud scares me because it makes it true. It makes me feel vulnerable, in a way that both terrifies and excites me. The feeling that's pounding in my chest is so different from any other feeling. Different than when I was with Kelton and different than when I was with my mother, my father, and even Kyle. It's something brand-new. And only now, after saying it out loud, do I feel its truth rising in my chest.

I turn to Eli. "Let's go," I say. "And don't argue with me."

He stares at me blankly but doesn't say anything. I help him to his feet, wrapping my arm once again around his waist as he drapes his arm across my shoulders. I log out of the computer and leave the room, pulling the door closed behind me. We make our way to the end of the hall and almost to the elevators until I feel a heavy tug on my left side, one that almost drags me down. Eli collapses to the floor next to me, his arm gripping my shoulder hard. I slowly lower him to the floor, carefully removing my left arm from around his waist.

"I can't," he says quietly. He takes in a sharp breath.

"You have to," I say and try picking him up.

"No," he says gripping my forearm. "I can't make it any further."

A tear slips down my cheek, though I don't exactly know why. Even though his story is similar to mine, I did just meet him. "Eli..."

"Tell her I... I love her," he says before sinking to the floor and the last breath in his body escapes.

I rest my head on his chest, sobbing. The source of my grief is dead. I should be grateful. But all I can think about is how he is taking lives from beyond the grave. Eli should be alive; I should have killed Kelton when I had the chance. Eli took a bullet for my ignorance. That is something I will never be rid of. Unless I fulfill his dying wish.

I run back to the *Documentary and Surveillance* room and enter Eli's code. Thankfully the codes always work, unlike the ID cards. I click on *Personal Information* and scroll down to find his address. According to the database card, it says his wife and children have moved to a planet on the South side of the galaxy called Juema, which is known for their agriculture and gardens. I check the address and print out a copy. I double-check to make sure the information is correct and fold the paper to fit inside my pocket. Hopefully she doesn't move by the time I get out there.

I shut the door to the *Documentary and Surveillance* room once again and make my way back down the hallway to where I left Eli. His body is no longer there, but a note lies where the body should have been. I pick it up, hesitant, and begin reading.

"I'm sorry to hear about Eli. He was an excellent soldier with a good head on his shoulders. I'd always hoped he would go far in life. I hope you accomplish his final desire as I know he would do the same for you. Since you can't exactly walk to the home of his wife and children, there will be a ship ready for you in hangar 22. The keys are in a small black box in the back of the ship. I know you know what to do. Also, in the black box you will find a paper with a list of numbers. Each one represents a person in your family, including Daniel. If you ever wanted to check up on them, you can find many Codereaders throughout the galaxy. You'll know what to do when you find one. Best wishes."

I know exactly who the letter is from, and it's hard for me to think I may never see him again. But he left me a ship, and that is something I won't pass up. I fold the note, stick it in the same pocket as the address sheet, and take off running.

Hangar 22 is on the main floor of the building, behind the primary runway. It's a smaller hangar that only about two ships would fit in it. However, only one sits in it now. The ship is small, easily maneuverable. It reminds me of the ship I used to train in with Daniel before I officially became his copilot.

I remember one day when he was trying to teach me how to land on the runway without scraping the wheels. I was getting frustrated since he could do it so perfectly and I kept failing. He would show me and then let me try it for myself. I focused so much on trying to land better than him that I almost crashed during one of my landings. Daniel gripped the armrests on his seat so hard his knuckles turned white.

"You need to focus," he told me.

"I'm trying," I said, my frustration edging into my voice.

"I meant focus on actually landing the ship," he said. "I can tell you're focused on something else."

"Well, yeah," I said flustered. "I'm focusing on landing as perfectly as you did."

He chuckled. "I've had years of experience," he explained. "You've had a week. The landings will become smoother the more you practice, but don't expect to get things right on the first try. Focus on one thing at a time."

I took off from the runway again, turned the ship around, and tried to land it again. The landing was smoother but not anywhere close to perfect. However, instead of getting frustrated, I just tried it again and again, until the landing was so smooth you wouldn't be able to tell the difference from flying and hitting the ground. Daniel congratulated me and told me I was ready to fly by myself. My smile dropped.

"Oh," I said disappointed. "So that's it."

He put his hand on top of mine, which was resting on the armrest. "You don't have to," he said quietly. "I forgot to mention that part."

He smiled, which was enough to light up an entire planet. A slow smile crept across my face. Thinking back, I think that was the first time I realized he was more than just a crush to me. I liked him as more than just my flying partner, my friend. He wasn't even my best friend at this point, more of an acquaintance. Somehow I knew, though, that from that moment on, things between us would never be the same.

Gregory left me a really nice ship. I open the side door that leads into a somewhat spacious cockpit. The ship looks to be an older model but still nicer than any of the ones I'd ever flown or copiloted. I maneuver my way to the back of the ship and find the black box Gregory told me about in the note. Inside are the keys he promised along with a folded piece of paper. I take them out and return to the front of the ship, inserting the keys in the ignition. The ship starts with a grumble and coughs to life.

I fish the piece of paper with Eli's wife's address out of my pocket and replace it with the list of numbers Gregory left. I enter the coordinates of her address into the ship's database and autodrive takes over. The ship soars down the runway and takes off almost as smooth as I can. I sit back in my seat and begin to feel free for the first time in weeks.

I must have fallen asleep. I wake up to a bumpy landing that jostles the ship around. I grab the controls and straighten it out, something I learned from Daniel. I look outside the front window and notice I've landed at the small, run-down landing strip on Juema. I was here one other time on a mission. When Daniel told me we would go on missions sometimes, I expected them to be thrill-seeking adventures. Taking down the Corps, rescuing someone. I was wrong. Their term "mission" literally meant "errand."

Juema has never had enough resources to fix up anything on their planet. Everyone was too focused on making sure there was enough food to go around. The houses were all average in size and had yards stretching for acres. Almost everyone farmed or gardened. The planet as a whole was quaint; people would retire here when they weren't able to do anything else. It was warm year round, great for growing season. A majority of the population was elderly or people with larger families. And since Juema wasn't taking sides in the war, it was peaceful all throughout the planet.

The hangar the control guard directs me to is small and falling apart. One of the stilts holding up the roof is tilted, and grass grows in between the cracks in the sidewalk. I park the ship under the wooden roof, remove the keys from the ignition, and hop out the door in the middle of the ship.

The air smells clean and refreshing. The breeze brushes my hair away from my face. It's chilly but not cold. The trees rustle with the wind, the leaves falling and moving every which way. It's so calm, so unlike Vulcona, so unlike the past few weeks that I don't move. I don't want this moment to end.

"The next airbus will be leaving in five minutes. Please make your way to the station," a recorded voice says through the overhead speakers.

I walk over to the control booth which regulates traffic flow. A guard is working there, his head bent over a booklet containing numbers and locations.

"Excuse me," I say. He looks up at me. "Does this airbus go to the Northeastern Ward?"

"Let me check," he says turning from his booklet to the computer on his left. I wait a few seconds, taking in the breeze. "Looks like it doesn't, but there is one leaving for the North Ward in ten minutes. You can take that one and catch another one that goes to the East."

"Sure, that's fine," I say. "I'll just wait."

He nods and goes back to hovering over his booklet. I take a seat on a bench near the airbus lane and pull out the list of names and numbers Gregory left me. There's no other context next to the numbers, which will force me to find a Codereader. They most likely will have one at either the capital building or the Agricultural and Science Center.

The airbus pulls up a few minutes later and I hop on. Three other people sit in the car, each one holding a small tablet. I take a seat in the far back and wait for my stop to come.

I'm nervous about meeting with Eli's wife. She might not even be home, but I have to try. She needs to know what Eli's last words were. Maybe she'll be relieved to hear he's passed. Maybe she'll be upset. I wonder if she'll remember me. I get more nervous as each stop comes and goes. Two more left before I get off. One stop.

The doors open minutes later, cold breeze filling the car. I step out onto the platform and feel a rush of wind behind me as the airbus leaves the station. I make my way over to the other lane where an airbus should show up and take me East to the Northeastern Ward where she lives. The airbus shows up about a minute after I get to the lane. This time, the car is fuller, and I end up sitting next to an older woman carrying a woven basket with fresh food. She looks at me and smiles.

"Where are you headed to," she asks.

"I'm visiting a… a friend of mine's wife," I respond.

"A friend?" she clarifies.

"Yes," I say. I'm not exactly sure what Eli was to me. More than an acquaintance, but I'm not sure friend is the right word.

The woman hands me something from her basket. "Here," she says. "Take this. Never show up empty handed at someone's house if they invited you."

"Thank you," I say. "I just got here this morning, so I haven't had much time to shop."

"Oh how nice," she beams. "Where did you travel from?"

"I live on Coreno, but I went to Vulcona for… work," I respond.

"For work?" she asks, tensing up a bit. "Like with the Corps?"

"Actually," I say with a laugh to help ease her. "I'm working against them."

"Oh, wonderful," she says, her bright tone back. "We don't like to engage in war here. Peace is what we enjoy most. I think I enjoy it more than most people. You see, I used to live on Dquartis, and as you probably know it's not a peaceful planet. So I left. I met my husband here. Great life, great kids. Couldn't imagine anything better."

Dquartis was taken over by the Corps a few years ago and has remained under their control ever since. Most of the children who are born there grow up and learn to fight from a young age. A lot of the Corps' soldiers are born and bred there. Almost like robots, they're trained to kill anything and everything that opposes the Corps.

"That is a much different scene," I say.

She nods. "I didn't hate it there, but it wasn't exactly the life for me. I've never been a fan of violence."

"Did you participate in any of the training notions they offer over there?" I ask.

"A couple," she responds. "Although it isn't like what you've heard I'm sure. Dquartis is viewed as a dark, grim, war-hungry planet. Not all of the training sessions are about killing. I took a survival class; it was pretty interesting."

The airbus stops and the woman begins to stand up. "I'm afraid this is my stop," she says. "It was nice talking to you. Oh, I never did quite catch your name."

"Zandrea," I say. "What's yours?"

"Mauve." She scoots around me and slips off the airbus. For being an older woman, she sure moved swiftly.

The airbus takes off again; this time the car is empty except for a man sitting three rows in front of me. A computer sits on his lap, although he doesn't look at it. Instead, he taps furiously on the small tablet he holds in his hands. Then he picks the tablet up and puts it to his ear.

"How could you let this happen?" the man yells into his tablet. "How could you let her go?" He waits a few seconds before transferring the tablet between his shoulder and ear and types something into his computer. Suddenly, my name and face appear on his screen.

He begins talking again. "Well, how did she know there were keys in there? Is she a spy?" Then I see the case protecting his tablet. The Corps' symbol. He works for the Corps. And he's searching for me.

The next stop is still far away. Eli's wife lives very far into the country. I'm debating whether I should get off at the next stop even though it's still too far from Eli's wife's house or if I should just play things cool and hope he doesn't notice me when he stands up all of a sudden. He closes his computer, puts it in his case, and moves over near the door. He's still talking on his tablet.

"I would fire you, but you're too valuable to the company," he says to whoever is on the other end of the line. "You know I was supposed to go home to see my wife this week. Somehow we got lucky with where she landed."

My stop is next. So is his. I'll wait until the next stop and backtrack.

"Well, Juema is a nice planet to kick back and relax," he says. "She probably thought this was a safe place. Maybe she has family here?" He pauses. "Coreno? That's on the other side of the galaxy. You're sure she doesn't have family here? Any friends or close ties?"

The doors open and he grabs his computer case and steps off. The doors slide close and we're moving again. I grip the armrests on the seat. He knows I'm here, on this planet. Juema is fair in size, but with the technology the Corps have, I'm surprised he didn't know I was right behind him.

The next stop isn't too far away, short enough that it wouldn't be too much of a problem to walk to Eli's wife's house. The airbus pulls up to the station, and I hop off. Two women get on, both chatting to someone on the other end of their tablet lines. Their lives seem so simple, so safe. Safe, I feel, will never be a reality for me.

I feel a rush of air behind me as the airbus leaves the station. The cool breeze has me pulling my light jacket around me, keeping the warmth from escaping.

The Northeastern Ward is much different than the Central Ward. The houses are bigger and way more spread out. On average, the closest neighbors live about a half a mile away from each other. I check the sheet with her address on it one more time and make my way over to a shuttle service.

"Where do you want to go?" the driver asks. I show him the slip of paper. "May I keep this until we get there, for direction purposes?"

"Sure," I say. "No rush."

He punches the coordinates of her address into a medium-sized tablet and pulls away from the station. The ride is smooth and short. We pull up on the opposite side of the street from her house. He hands me back the paper and I slip out the side door. I hand him three Stoneians and he drives away. I glance at the paper one more time to make sure the address is right and shove it back into my pocket. I smooth my hair and tuck in my shirt. I probably should have showered before coming here and put on new clothes. I can't turn back now so I cross the street.

Her house is big. More than enough for four people. I walk up the large staircase that leads to the front door of the house. The patio is nice; it extends around the entire house. I knock on one side of the double wooden doors and wait for someone to answer. My nerves remind me of a few weeks ago when I was standing on the doorsteps to my own home. I was nervous then too but for a different reason.

Finally, footsteps sound from the other side of the door. As if in slow motion, the knob slowly turns and is pulled away from me. "Can I help you?" a woman, who I assume to be Eli's wife, asks.

"Are you Andrea Parker?" I ask hesitantly.

"Yes," she says just as hesitantly.

"Who's at the door?" a voice calls from behind her.

"Some girl," Andrea yells back. I hear footsteps approach and a man shows up behind her, half of his face covered up by the door. Then he steps out from behind the door and I almost faint. It's the man from the airbus. The one looking for me. I duck my head and peer at the ground.

"What's your name?" Andrea asks.

My mind is foggy. I can't think straight. "Callie," I say, still looking at the ground.

"Can I help you with something Callie?" Andrea says.

"I was wondering if I could talk to you about something, something personal," I say.

"Um, sure. Do you want to come inside?"

"Oh, I have to go soon. Could we do it on the porch?"

"I suppose so," she says hesitantly. She steps over the doorway barrier and pulls the door until it's ajar. "What's up?"

"I have two things I need to inform you about," I say. "One, Eli's dead." It's blunt, I realize, but I don't really care at this point.

I wait for her reaction, but she doesn't even flinch.

"We knew each other from the Corps."

"You work with the Corps?" she says, outraged by this new news.

"No," I say. "I was a spy. So was Eli. His dying wish was for me to tell you that he loved you."

"You must have the wrong person," she says. "Because the Eli I knew didn't love me. At least not when it mattered."

"He did though," I say. "He was trying to protect you."

"By abusing me and turning me over to the Corps?"

"He did it because otherwise they would have killed you, and he thought that he could save you," I explain.

"I don't understand," she says.

"Anyone who doesn't believe in what the Corps stands for will be killed," I explain slowly. "And since you didn't, you would have been killed. As twisted as it sounds, he beat you to save your life and your children's lives."

"What's the second thing?" she asks after a few moments.

"What?"

"You said there were two things you had to tell me, what's the second one?"

"Oh," I say, somewhat stunned that she doesn't care to know more about Eli. "Well, I have reason to believe that the man in your house right now works for the Corps. Just making sure you're aware."

"My husband?" she says, bewildered. "James wouldn't hurt a fly. What makes you think he works for the Corps? I mean, he hates it about the same amount I do."

I lower my voice. "I escaped from the Corps' headquarters last night. I saw him on the airbus this morning. My face was on his computer screen, and he was talking to someone on his tablet about me. There was the Corps' logo in the background of his computer screen."

"Look, I don't know who you are, or what you want, but you can't just come here and claim my ex-husband is dead and my new husband works for the Corps," she says raising her voice. "You need to leave."

"Fine," I say. "But I know how much you've endured. I'm sure you want it to stop. Don't say I didn't warn you." I turn on my heel and bounce down the steps. I can tell she's still looking at me. From the wavering tone in her voice, I know she is questioning what I'm saying, whether what I told her was true or not.

I walk down the block and circle back to her house. This time, I enter the porch from the opposite side of the house. Through the windows, I can see her and her husband. She's crying. He has his arm around her, comforting her. I can make out some of the things she says.

"Why did this have to happen?" she says. "All of the memories are coming back."

"Just do what you did before and don't think about him," her husband says.

"You don't understand," she says. "He was my best friend. It's because of him that I hate the Corps. They turned him on me. They made him something he wasn't. That girl just reminded me of everything I hate about the organization."

I shouldn't be here. Every minute that I stand here watching them is a minute that I'll never get back. He could have sent an army after me. He probably knows I'm standing here right now. He probably knows exactly what I'm thinking. And yet, I don't move. Not a muscle twitches. I am frozen.

His head moves. His eyes turn up and catch mine. A pull, like a magnet. I can't take my eyes off him. He knows I'm here. Neither of us moves. Andrea still sobs, but he's no longer focused on her. He knows me. He knows that I'm a valuable asset to the Corps, yet he doesn't even acknowledge I'm here except for the fact that he won't take his eyes off me. Is he a spy, like Eli was? Or is he waiting for the right moment? Why can't I move? If I run, he'll know something is up, and if I stay still any longer, he'll know something is up.

Then, his lips part. He says something. What is he saying? I step toward the window. He says it again. Then his body jolts to the left and men fill the room. Andrea stumbles as James falls to the ground. Then she stands up and slowly turns so her gaze meets each of the men in the room in turn. They all have the same logo on their backs. The same logo that was on James's computer screen. Before my brain even connects all these things together, my feet switch directions, and I run as fast and hard as I can.

My pulse climbs into my throat. My heart races. I don't know the exact way back to the airbus station, but I run in the direction I came from earlier. My legs hurt and my chest burns. I try to gulp for air but the wind stings my throat.

I don't know if James is dead or alive, and at this point, I'm not sure I care. Even if Andrea didn't believe me, she was still the ex-wife of Eli, and I had to honor his wish. Andrea might be dead now too for all I know. And if she is… I stop. If she's dead and James is dead, who is going to watch out for her children? They're too young to take care of themselves.

But I can't go back. But I should. I told Eli his kids were safe and I intend to keep it that way. Even if I don't take them back to Coreno, I at least have to get them out of that house. Despite every muscle in my body telling me to get as far away from that house as I can, I start running back to that dreaded house. My last thought before I break into a full-on sprint is *I hope I can get there before the Corps' guards do*.

I return to the house, silent and still. It's eerie enough as it is to be walking into a house that may contain people who want me dead, but the silence is unsettling. I don't even make it onto the back porch before I hear a gunshot and a scream. I peer inside the window where the Corps' guards have formed a semicircle around Andrea and James's lifeless bodies. Then, one by one, the guards disband and make their way to the front door. I hide behind the back of the house until I hear the screeching of tires on pavement, and the military style truck is nowhere to be seen.

I enter through the backdoor, which is slightly ajar. The stillness of the air in the house is enough to let me know that it's empty. Andrea lies on her side, a few feet away from James. I check their pulses, both were nonexistent. The color from their faces drained, lifeless. I step back and survey the house. Open, spacious. Enough for two children to play.

Pictures line the walls, some taken professionally, others drawn most likely by the kids. One in particular draws my attention. It's of Andrea with the kids, sun surrounding them, the breeze blowing back Andrea and her daughters' hair. They look peaceful, calm, almost like nothing bad could touch them. It reminds me of Kyle and my mother and how happy they seemed while I was gone. I need to get back to them.

I go up the stairs on the left which leads to a small loft. The loft has a ladder that leads to another small room in the attic of the house. I look around the small loft and find that it's empty except for a few toys scattered across the floor. I check the attic and find that it too is empty. My heart starts to race. What if they took the children? What if they're dead? What if they're still alive and don't know what to do? I start pacing in the small, dark attic and try to think of where they could be.

Then, the creaking of a door. Somewhere downstairs. I freeze. If whoever is here finds me, they'll probably kill me either for trespassing or something else entirely. I climb down the ladder to the loft and grab one of the toys on the ground. I position it over my head as the bottom stair cracks underneath the weight of a person. Then there are whispers.

"Someone could be upstairs," someone, a girl's voice, whispers.

"We should go back to the barn," someone else, a boy's voice this time, whispers back.

"Mother told us to come back to the house when the truck left," the girl says.

"She also said to stay there until it's safe," the boy points out.

"It is safe," the girl says back, louder than a whisper.

I step forward and the floorboard creaks. The whispering stops.

"Someone's here," the girl whispers. Shoes slap against the stairs, and I move toward the door. I can't lose them. I owe it to Eli.

I chase after them, down the stairs and almost out of the house before I yell, "Wait!" The boy turns around, a small blanket in his arms. He can't be older than three years old.

"Come on Cody," the girl says, pulling on his arm. She looks to be about five. "Cody, we have to go, now!"

"Hold on," he says. "I saw her talking to Mother earlier." The girl looks up at me.

"Who are you?" she asks.

"I'm a… friend of your father," I say. "The one that left a while ago. Do you remember him?" I move down the staircase and the girl takes a step back.

"Not really," she says. "Mother doesn't talk about him."

"He made some mistakes," I explain. "But he loved you both very much."

"Where is he?" the boy, Cody, asks.

"He's… gone," I say.

"Gone where?" he asks. His soft blue eyes, looking right through me, make it hard to lie to him. So I tell him what I hope to be the truth.

"Heaven," I say. "Or so I hope."

"He's dead?" the girl asks. She looks at the ground and then back to me. No emotion registers on her face. I can tell she doesn't know what to feel. She doesn't know enough about him to make a judgment.

"Did you know he saved my life?" I ask her. She shakes her head. "He was brave. And helped the galaxy out a lot. You may not understand this yet, but your father probably saved trillions of lives."

"How did he do that?" Cody asks.

"Well, he…" I trail off. He killed Kelton, but I don't want these kids to think he's a murderer. "He helped me fight against the bad guys."

Gregory's voice rings in my head. I think back to what he said about people being evil. "Are they bad because they do evil things, or are they bad because their views don't align with yours?" I didn't know how to answer then and I don't know how to answer now. Of course the Corps is evil. But then I think about Kelton and how he believed he was doing the right thing by siding with the Corps. When I first got to know him, he didn't seem evil, just mixed up in bad things. When I found out who he truly was, I was shocked, but I still believed there was good in him. Maybe the real question is *what, in their heart, do they believe is the real evil?*

"Did you guys win?" Cody asks, interrupting my thoughts.

"Not yet," I say. "Which is why we have to get back to my home planet."

"Can we come with you?" he asks.

"Of course," I say. "That's why I came back." I begin walking toward the front door, footsteps padding on the ground behind me. When I turn to look back, I find that the girl hasn't moved an inch. She bites one of her nails and looks at her deceased parents lying on the ground.

"I'm not going," she says.

"Come on Lila," Cody says. "You have to come."

"No, I don't," she says. "I'm staying here until someone comes for Mother and Father."

"I don't think anyone is going to come," I say slowly. "I think the bad guys will make sure no one finds out that they're dead."

"Why?" Cody asks looking up at me.

"Because the bad guys don't care about people who don't work for them," I say although it isn't entirely true. They just care about a select group of people.

"I'm still not going," Lila says.

"But you promised Mother that you would watch out for me," Cody says. "How can you do that if we aren't together?"

"She can watch out for you," Lila says back.

"Lila," I say softly. She turns her head up to me. "I'm taking you both to a safe place, one where the bad guys won't be able to hurt you. If you stay here, they could hurt you, and that would leave Cody all alone."

"I don't want to leave Mother and Father," she says, reasoning with herself why it would be a good idea to stay here with her parents.

"You won't," I say. "They will always be a part of you. But staying here won't make them come back to life."

She looks at me, her soft eyes reminding me of Eli's. "Okay," she says. She looks at them one more time and walks over to Cody and me. "Where are we going?"

I smile. "Home."

The trek back to the airbus station doesn't take too long. The streets are mostly empty with the occasional aircar. Aircars are more common on Coreno and other surrounding planets than they are here. They were invented on Techario about a century earlier.

The station is slightly more packed than it was when I got here. Three men holding briefcases stand next to one another talking. One man motions to the sky and the other two laugh. An older woman sits on the bench to my left holding two stitching needles and a roll of fabric. The fabric is loosely woven, the colors merging together then separating. The woman stares off into space, her hands shaking slightly and her knee bouncing up and down quickly. She looks tense but at the same time calm.

A younger woman approaches us and taps my shoulder. "Are these your children?" she asks enthusiastically.

I look down at them and then back up at the woman. "No," I say. "I'm just a family friend taking care of them for the day."

"That's nice of you," she says. "They are adorable little kids."

"Thank you," I say. "I'm lucky to have them for the day."

The woman nods and walks over to where the older woman sits on the bench and begins talking to her. The older woman shows the younger lady her loosely woven fabric, and the younger woman examines it. They begin discussing other parts of the fabric, and then they turn to the stitching needles. The older woman no longer seems tense as she smiles at the younger woman.

"That woman is our neighbor," Cody says.

"Which one?" I ask.

"The older one," he says. "She brings us treats sometimes." He waves at her and she smiles back.

The airbus pulls up and we hop on, finding a place to sit near the front. Cody points out the window, naming things he sees as we go past. In a way, he reminds me of Kyle because he was like Cody when he was his age. Even though Kyle is older, I still see some resemblances.

I look over at Lila who sits with her head propped against the window. She stares out at the open farmland, her eyes vacant and tired. I scoot over next to her and she looks at me. "Hey," I say.

"Hi," she says back.

"What are you looking at?" I ask.

"Nothing much," she says. "Just trees and hills. A few houses here and there."

"Nice," I say. I look at her a little longer but the memories come flooding back. The look on Eli's face as he uttered his last words. His eyes, full of emotion but completely drained of life. He loved Andrea. He loved Cody and Lila. He wanted to be there for them every day and every night. His heart broke when he found out they didn't feel the same way back. I look away from Lila and out the other side of the airbus.

We pull up to the station a few minutes later and everyone files off. Cody grabs my hand, and Lila trails behind us. She looks around at the surroundings, trying to take everything in.

"Have you guys ever been to the city?" I ask.

"Once," Lila says. "When I went shopping with Mother."

"I haven't," Cody says. "It's so big."

I nod and lead them to where I parked my ship. The walk isn't very long, but there are a lot of people, and trying to navigate around them is next to impossible. Some people are dressed up in nice suits or dresses, and others look like they're heading to go farm somewhere. From what I've heard, the people who work in large office corporations here on Juema are the richest and hold the highest place of power. Office jobs are rare because most of the residents are farmers or gardeners. Either that or retired. Even though it's not the best vacation spot in the galaxy, people come from all over just to relax in the warm climate here.

"I'm hungry," Cody says tugging at my hand. "Mother told us that there was a grain shop not too far from the airbus station."

I look around to see if I can find anything, and sure enough, a small building with paint chipping at the sides has what I'm looking for. "Like that?" I ask Cody.

"Yeah," he says and takes off running for the store.

"Cody!" I yell and run after him. I quickly check back and find Lila right behind me. I smile with relief. I turn my head back to the way I'm running and almost slam into a mother with three children. "Sorry!"

The store isn't too far away but I'm out of breath by the time I reach the doorway. Cody stands near the glass display case, pressing his nose against the glass and eyeing a blue and green sugar treat. "This one," he exclaims.

"All of my Stoneians are back on my ship," I tell him. "Let's go back to my ship, and we can come back here."

He gives me a look of disappointment but follows me out of the store. Lila follows behind him. I maneuver us around the groups of people congregating on the streets and sidewalks. People cluster, some talking about their days and others complaining about the work they have to do when they get home. No one talks about the war or what the Corps is doing to the galaxy. How simple their lives are. How peaceful.

The ship port isn't too far away, just a few minutes walk from the grain store. The occasional aircar passes by, stopping to pick up people and then pulling away. Juema doesn't have many tall buildings but rather longer, more drawn out complexes that are only a few stories tall. It's better to build it that way due to the texture of the soil.

We get to the ship port and check in with the front desk. "Hey," I say. "I'm here to pick up my ship."

"You'll just need to sign some papers so we know that you're the one who owns the ship," the guy tells me. He pulls out a thin stack of papers, filed neatly inside a folder, and hands them to me along with a pen.

"Is it okay if I just go to my ship and grab my satchel inside?" I ask. "I'm not leaving just yet."

"I'll have someone escort you," he says. "Just tell him what number stall you parked in and he can lead you there."

"Thank you," I say to him. Then I turn to the kids. "Follow me guys."

A man approaches us, tall and fit. He has a tan, probably from working in the sun all day. He's handsome, with a familiar appeal to him. Something about his smile makes me think of Daniel, the way the corners of his lips seem to reach his eyes. I blush slightly when he walks over.

"Hey guys," he says. "You can follow me. What's your hangar number?"

"22," I say. "But I'm not leaving yet. I just need to get something in it."

"Okay," he says. "Did you sign any of the forms?"

"No," I say. "I told him I wasn't leaving yet."

"Will you be leaving tonight?" he asks.

"Yes," I say. "We won't be long."

"Good," he says quietly.

"Is something wrong?" I ask him accusingly. "Have I inconvenienced you in some way?"

"No," he says. "Just forget I said anything."

I'm angry, but I cool down enough to ask him one more question. "What's your name?"

He hesitates. "Why do you want to know?"

"Why do you care?" I ask more angrily this time.

"I don't," he says back, not making eye contact. He waits a little longer before saying, "Damien."

We make eye contact for the first time. Something about his eyes seems so familiar. "Have we met before?" I ask, all my anger gone.

"I don't think so," he says.

"You seem so familiar," I say.

"I get that a lot," he says. Then he smiles and my stomach flutters. He looks away and checks the clipboard he's holding. "Hangar 22 is at the end of the row. We should be there shortly."

I check behind me to make sure Lila and Cody are still there. Cody looks tired and drags his feet. Lila looks around in awe. I have to remember that she's not like me, growing up with, for the most part, one parent and leaving her family at the age of twelve. I went to the city anytime my mother wanted to go. She's only been to the capital once and never to the ship port.

"This is pretty cool, isn't it?" I ask her. She nods but doesn't look at me.

"So," Damien says from next to me. "Are these your kids?"

"Yes," I say. "I mean no. I'm watching them for the day while their parents are… out of town."

"Oh," he says. "That's nice of you."

"Just trying to help the family out," I say, avoiding eye contact.

He doesn't ask any more questions until we get to the hangar, where he pulls out a pen and hands it to me along with the clipboard. "Just initial at the bottom and sign on the line below that, just so I have a record," he says.

I sign and hand him back his clipboard before turning to the ship. I climb up the side ladder and open the door that leads to a small hallway connecting the cockpit and the back of the ship. I knew I left my satchel on the copilot's seat, which is where it is when I check. I grab it and climb down the ladder, stumbling on the last rung. Damien catches me, putting his hand on my back. Heat runs through my body as I realize how warm his hands are and how cold my body is.

"You alright?" he asks.

"Yes," I say. "Thank you for catching me."

"Of course," he says. "I'm not just going to let you fall."

I remember a time similar to this. It was back when I was first training with Daniel. We were cleaning his ship one day. He was showing me the "right way" to clean an exhaust valve.

"It's all in the angle of the brush," he said, holding the brush at the exact angle I was supposed to do it at. "Because if you go too much to one side or another, it will break the valve."

He handed me the brush and I tried a couple times before he was satisfied. Then we climbed up into the ship and cleaned the inside. Eventually, we were called for lunch. Daniel went down the ladder first. I moved my feet down each rung until I got to the second to last one and slipped. I didn't have far to fall but I was still terrified. When I felt like I was about to hit the ground and possibly get a concussion, Daniel put his hand on the small of my back, catching me.

I had never really touched him before, and he had never touched me, but I could tell his hands were strong, firm, and there was no way I was going to hit the ground in that scenario. Even though I didn't really know him, I trusted him.

"Are you okay?" he asked.

"Yeah," I said. "Thanks for catching me."

"You're welcome," he said. "I wasn't going to let you fall." His smile was enough to send jolts down my spine and make my stomach flutter.

The memory makes me smile. He kept his promise. I never once fell after that as long as he was by my side. I must have a weird grin on my face because Damien looks at me funny. He starts laughing.

"What are you smiling at?" he asks in a teasing sort of manner.

"Why would you care?" I ask trying to hide my own grin.

"Well, since you've been here, I haven't really seen you smile," he says. "I was just curious if there was a special occasion."

"If you must know," I say. "I was thinking about my boyfriend."

His smile fades. "Boyfriend?" he asks quietly.

"Well, yeah," I say. "Although it's kind of complicated. We didn't technically make things official or anything, which is partly, mostly, my fault. I mean, we've known each other for years, so I think he understood, but I haven't seen him for a little over a week."

"Can I ask what his name is?" he asks.

"Daniel," I say. "Daniel Thomas. Why? Do you know him?"

"Yeah," he says. "He's flown in here a couple of times. Really great pilot. Excellent navigation."

"You must have known him before I became his flying partner because I've only been here once before," I say. "And I became his navigator as well as his copilot."

"Really?" he says. "Because he came here recently, like within the last few years. He mentioned something about this really amazing girl he met.

I can only assume he meant you. But yeah, that guy was head over heels for some girl."

"Did he ever mention the girl's name?" I ask.

"No," he says. "Just kept saying how amazing she was and how I had to meet her sometime. I guess now I did."

I nod and turn away from him. Tears start to well in my eyes, and I quickly swipe at them so he won't notice. I can feel him looking at me.

"Did I say something wrong?" he asks.

"No," I say. "I was just thinking about how much I miss him. I don't even know if he's alive."

"There's a Codereader by the capitol building," he says. "If you wanted to check."

"Could you show me?" I ask.

"Of course," he says. "I'd be happy to."

We leave the ship port and head toward the capitol building in the middle of the city. It's not too long of a walk, but we stop at the grain shop to get Cody the treat he wanted. The clerk recognizes Damien right away, and they chat while he packs the treat.

"Damien!" thunders the clerk, who I find is named Victor. "Good to see you man! What brings you in?"

"Just grabbing a treat for the little guy here," he responds in the same joyful manner.

In a quieter tone, Victor asks, "So who's the pretty lady?" Then he winks.

"It's not like that," Damien replies quickly. "I'm just taking her to the Codereader in the capitol building."

"Sounds like fun," Victor says winking again as though he doesn't believe Damien. He nods to us, and we make our way to the front door of the shop. Just as I open the door, Victor yells out, "Damien, come here a second, would you?"

He turns to me and says, "It'll only be a minute. I'll meet you outside."

He walks over to the counter and leans forward as Victor says something quietly to him. He glances in my direction briefly before continuing what he was saying. Damien nods and walks back to the store entrance.

"We can go," he says.

"What was that all about?" I ask.

"Just some business stuff," he says. "A contracting deal I signed with him. No big deal."

I nod, but I don't exactly believe him. Something about the way they were being secretive. We walk a little longer in silence, the hustle and bustle of the people around us filling the air. Lila and Cody walk behind us, Lila still in amazement and Cody eating his treat from the grain shop. I still don't know what I'm going to do with them once I get home, but it's nice having their company for the time being.

The capitol building isn't too far from the ship port. It sits in the center of town, only a couple of stories high. White marble stairs lead to the giant revolving doors that people file in and out of. People in business suits and pencil skirts, each holding a briefcase or tablet bag, go about their day. They all look so elegant. I stare down at my own clothes and wonder if they will even let me in the building.

As I walk up the marble steps, I can feel people's eyes on me. They know I don't belong in this environment. I look like one of the farmers on the outskirts of town. I don't fit in, but I have no other choice. I need to know what happened to Daniel, Kyle, and my father.

A man stands by the door wearing a green suit with silver buttons. He smiles as people pass him and enter the building. As we approach the door, his smile slowly fades. "Can I help you?" he asks, looking us once over.

"We just need to use the Codereader inside," Damien says.

"Well," the man says looking at Cody and Lila. "You're breaking many rules of protocol here. First, no children are allowed inside the building, and second, this is a formal area. Formal wear must be worn at all times unless a specific meeting is being held, which, last I checked, nothing was scheduled for today."

"Sir," I say. "I know I'm not the best dressed around, but I just need to use the Codereader inside. It won't take longer than a couple minutes."

He snickers at the "not best dressed" part. "Look," he says. "I'm sorry, but I'm not breaking protocol for you, no matter how much you plead. However, I can be bribed." He looks at me and smiles.

At first, I can't possibly think what I would have that he would want, but then my hand hits my satchel and I remember something. "I happen to have a one-of-a-kind Stoneard in my purse here," I say tauntingly, remembering my lines from the first time I tried to get rid of it. "It's a beauty and worth more than my trip inside the building, but I don't know. Maybe I should just take my business elsewhere."

I turn on my heel and start walking down the steps of the building. I've made enough trades in my life to know that when someone wants something, they'll do whatever they can to get it. If he wants the Stoneard, he'll say something.

"Miss," he shouts. "Can I have a word?"

I spin back around and look him in the eye. "Can I help you?" I ask. I start to walk up the stairs again, making sure to keep eye contact with him the entire time.

Once I get back to the top, he smiles. "Like I said," he says. "I can be bribed." He holds out his hand, a huge grin plastered across his face.

"All four of us?" I ask.

"All four of you," he confirms.

I slip the Stoneard into his hand and proceed toward the door. I hear steps behind me letting me know Damien, Cody, and Lila are following close behind me. I push on the left revolving door and step into the circular entryway. I push on the clear door and spin halfway around the circular doorway until I'm let out into a giant foyer.

Windows run floor to ceiling, and silver knit with gold strand curtains fall the length of the window. The carpet is a navy-gray shade that leads into a white-tiled floor beyond it. Purple velvet chairs surround a wooden coffee table to the right of the revolving doors. Two women sit in the chairs opposite each other, each one holding a tablet on their laps. A grand staircase sits in front of me. People scurry up and down, rushing to get to their meetings in time.

"The Codereader is over here," Damien says, placing his hand lightly on my back and directing me in the general area of the Codereader.

It's down a wide-tiled hallway. People pass on my left, giving me a once-over like the people outside. I smile, but it's so fake that I drop it. "Why are the people around here so judgmental?" I ask.

"I don't think everyone is like that here," Damien says. "It's just because these people are the richer, more privileged people on this planet, and they like letting other people know it."

I glare at the next person who walks by me, which happens to be a woman wearing a pencil skirt and matching red blouse. Her hair is pulled back into a neat bun, not a hair out of place. She's young, probably not over thirty years old. She looks at me and keeps walking.

"The Codereader is just around the corner," Damien says. We turn a corner that leads to a spacious room. People move about, some talking to one another, others staring at the tablets in their hands. On the far side of the room, two machines sit next to each other.

"Is that them?" I ask, pointing to the opposite wall.

"Yeah," Damien says. "Have you ever used one before?"

"I think so," I say. "When I was in the Corps' headquarters-"

"You were in the Corps' headquarters?" he asks incredulously.

"Yeah," I say. "I was being held captive. I went to try and stop them from mind controlling everyone, and my friend ended up killing Kelton, the leader of the organization's son."

"Wow," he says. "He's dead?"

"Yeah, I watched him die," I say shrugging it off.

"Really?" he asks.

"Yeah," I say nonchalantly. He stares at me blankly.

"Oh," he says. "Well good job."

"Thanks," I say. I start walking over to the Codereaders. Two tall box-like machines stand a couple feet apart from each other, each with a screen and a keypad. I pull the note from Gregory out of my pocket and unfold it. My hand shakes. I'm nervous. What if something happened to them during the flight? Or after they got back? My heart pounds in my chest. The man in front of me finishes and grabs his receipt.

I step up to the machine and punch in Kyle's number. The screen takes a few seconds to bring up his information. When it does, next to *Existence Status* it says ACTIVE. I sigh a breath of relief. Next, I look up my father's name. His *Existence Status* also says ACTIVE. I breath another sigh of relief. They both made it home, alive.

Damien looks over my shoulder. "Good," he says. "They're alive."

"Yeah," I say almost breathless. "I just have to check one more person."

I type in Daniel's number and the machine brings up his information. I have to scroll down a ways because he has a lot of information regarding his flight experience. Once I get to his *Existence Status*, my heart drops. It reads DECEASED.

I can't move. I can't think. I can't breathe. I'm frozen. I think I fall backward at one point because Damien's strong hands grab my sides like in a trust fall. My vision goes blurry, probably from tears. I can make out Cody's face through the blurriness. He looks concerned. Voices mumble all around me, and it's impossible to make out what any one person is saying. My head is spinning.

I'm back on my feet again, unstable but standing. Someone's hand is on my shoulder. I assume it's Damien's. I cover my face with my hands and melt to the ground on my knees. Damien wraps his arm around my waist and envelops my hand in his. He helps me stand up and then leads me to a bench near the Codereaders. I'm sobbing.

Damien says something to Cody and Lila and they run off. He turns his attention to me but doesn't say anything. Instead he strokes my hair, a comforting gesture that eases me slightly. I rest my head on his shoulder, something that both comforts and alarms me. It scares me that I've known Damien for less than a day and I already feel so comfortable around him, like I've known him my whole life.

"I loved him," I say quietly.

"I know," Damien says. I look at him questioningly. He quickly adds,

"I mean, from the way you talked about him and the way you reacted when you found out he's dead. I'm sure he loved you too."

"I never told him," I say staring blankly in front of me. "I don't think he knew because I never said anything."

"Yeah, but actions speak louder than words," he says. "I knew this girl once. She was amazing. I would have done anything for her, but I was scared."

He looks at me but I don't say anything.

"We worked together," he continues. "One day, I talked her into helping me with a project across the galaxy. She was super excited, but the Corps caught us when we stopped on Vulcona to refuel. They offered to let one of us go. I was going to sacrifice myself, but she beat me to it. The Corps took her away and let me go. I knew right then and there that she loved me because she risked her life so I would be free."

"Have you seen her since?" I ask.

"I checked the Codereader everyday to make sure she was still alive," he says. "One day I saw her. She was walking downtown, buying things at different street vendors. I was so happy, but she didn't see me, and she left to go back home. I was devastated, but there was nothing I could do."

"Why don't you go try to find her?" I ask.

"I have," he says. "I know where she is, but I don't have a ride, and I'm not sure she would want to see me. Besides, it's safer here."

"Are you a coward?" I ask. "She risked her life for you, why can't you do the same?"

"It's… complicated," he says. "It's safer for her if she stays away from me."

"Why?" I ask.

"Like I said, it's complicated," he says.

"If you love her, shouldn't you be doing everything in your power to go be with her?" I ask incredulously.

"Shouldn't you?" he retorts. He sounds mad.

"What do you think I've been doing?" I ask using the same tone.

"You should go be with your father and brother, now that you know they're alive," he says.

"How did you know that?" I ask.

"Know what?"

"That my father and brother are alive; I never told you that was who I was looking up," I say.

"I just assumed," he says, avoiding eye contact. "And I'm pretty sure you've mentioned them before."

I don't argue, but I'm sure that I never mentioned Kyle or my father. I look at him but he stares straight ahead. He looks sad, defeated, but most of all, worried. I don't know why, but I slip my hand into his, the warmth comforting against my icy palms. He looks at our hands but doesn't say anything.

Lila and Cody come back a little later, each holding a treat from the snack bar we passed on our way to the Codereaders. They look happy.

"Are you all better?" Cody asks.

I smile. "I'm doing better," I say, despite it not being completely truthful. "Thanks for asking."

He returns the smile and sits on the bench next to me. He leans his head on my arm and finishes his treat. I find that his presence is soothing, like the little brother Kyle could have been if I was there to see him grow up. I wish I could have been there for him, for my mother. I shouldn't have left them. But I wouldn't have met Daniel. And I probably wouldn't have done half the things I've done, the things that make me who I am. I wish I could have told him all of this. I wish he was sitting right next to me, holding my hand and telling me everything was going to be alright. He would tell me to go be with my family. And as if he were here, I take his advice.

"I have to go home," I announce, standing up. "I've been away from my family for too long."

"Zandrea," Damien says softly.

"Yeah?" I answer.

"Would it be okay if, and you can say no, if I went with you?" he asks hesitantly.

"Sure," I say. "But why?"

"I have to go get my girl," he says with a slight smile. "Like you said, she risked her life for me, so I should do the same."

I smile and head for the hallway outside the room. Cody slips his hand into mine. I'd like to think that Kyle would have been like this when he was younger. I can't wait to see him again. Hopefully this time I can stay with him and watch him grow into a young man.

Damien leads us out into the hallway and we follow him down the hall back to the giant foyer. People still stare at me as I pass by, but I'm too focused on getting back home to really care. Two women walk by us, and the one starts whispering to the other. I don't completely hear what they say, but I know they're talking about me.

The front foyer is bustling with people. Some of the people carry briefcases, whereas others just their tablets. People pass by with warm drinks in their hands, trying not to spill it on themselves. It's a funny scene but I follow Damien outside the building before anything happens. The man who was standing by the door when we first got here is nowhere to be seen. My guess is he went to pawn off the Stoneard I gave him.

The sun hits my face and warms me. I don't know why, but the initial sting of Daniel's death has already worn off. I don't feel sad, I don't feel anything. Something seems off though. How did Kyle and my father make it out alive and Daniel didn't? What happened? Was it the Corps' fault or his own?

A thought hits me. "Damien?" I ask, looking at him.

"Yeah?" he responds.

"Has the Codereader ever been wrong?"

"No," he says. "Not that I know of. And they're hacker-proof, so only people with access codes can alter people's information."

"Who has the access codes?" I ask.

"Mostly people who work at the Corps' headquarters," he says. "But I think they give access codes to a handful of people on each planet."

"Random people?" I ask, my hopes getting higher.

"No," he says. "Probably people who work for the government."

"Oh," I say, letting my disappointment fill my voice.

"But I'm not saying it can't be wrong," he says sensing my disappointment. "I just think it would be extremely rare for there to be a disturbance with the system."

"Right," I say. "Of course." He can tell I'm still disappointed, but he doesn't say anything. The city is busy with people moving in every direction, talking all at once, and yet I can't seem to process anything that's happening.

Damien slips his hand into mine and gives it a reassuring squeeze. The warmth of his hand feels familiar, comforting. Anyone walking past us probably assumes we're a happy family of four. But I'm not happy, and I don't want to give the illusion that I am. I pull my hand away from Damien and cross my arms protectively across my torso.

"You okay?" Damien asks. His voice is like silk.

I nod, but he knows I'm lying.

"You don't have to be okay," he says. It reminds me of what Kyle said to me after the ship crash. "You just found out that your boyfriend is dead. It's okay to mourn."

I shake my head and burst into tears. Damien wraps his arms around me. Cody leans his head on my side and gives me a small hug. "I can't do this," I say in between sobs. "I can't do this without him. I miss him so much."

Damien doesn't say anything. The silence fills the air with an explanation words never could. He lets me cry into his shoulder. The realization of Daniel's death finally hits me. I will never get to see him again, tell him anything, tease him, and fight with him. I feel empty, alone.

Damien says something, but I don't hear him. "What?" I ask, suppressing a sob.

"I said we should go," he says. "The ship port will be closing soon."

"I can't fly a ship," I say. "Not in this condition."

"That's okay," he says. "I can." He motions for me to follow him. I rub my eyes, trying to get rid of any remaining tears. Cody grabs my hand again, and Lila skips ahead to walk alongside Damien.

"Why were you crying so much today?" Cody's small voice asks.

I look down at him, his big eyes staring back at me. They remind me of Eli's, big and full of hope. I wonder how the Corps for even a second considered him to work for them; the innocence in his eyes spoke volume apparently not loud enough for the Corps to hear.

"I lost my best friend," I say. Saying it out loud hurts more than I thought it would. It hits me hard because now I'm forced to believe it's true. "And I was very close to him."

"But he wasn't anywhere near us," Cody says. "How could you be close to someone who's not next to you?"

His question is so innocent, and the look on his face is enough to tell me he's being serious. I almost start laughing at how adorable the question is.

"He wasn't physically close like you are to me," I say. "He was emotionally close, like when you love someone so much you would do anything for them. It's like you and Lila. You don't have to stand right next to each other to be close, but I know you love her because you didn't leave her in the house earlier when we had to go. You are emotionally close to her."

His face scrunches up as he tries to process this. "I guess that makes sense," he says. "I'm sorry that he's gone."

I smile a sad smile and hope he understands that I don't really want to talk about it. Thankfully, he doesn't say anything more.

We return to the ship port where I sign some release documents. Damien leaves to go talk to his manager about quitting and leaving with me. He comes back a few minutes later with a box in his hands, stuff piling inside. He waves to a couple of his coworkers before motioning me outside. We walk down the long row of hangars, eventually making it back to the one that contains my ship.

I pull the ship's keys from my pocket. "Here," I say. "Trade." I take the box from him and hand him the keys in return. He steps up the rungs of the ladder on the side of the ship, taking it two at a time. He sticks the key into the lock on the door once he reaches the top. He pushes the door to the side and steps insides, motioning for us to follow him.

"I don't think I can climb that high," Cody says, looking up at the door. It's only a few feet above my head, but Cody is much shorter than me.

"Here," I say, grabbing his hand. "I'll help you." I guide his hand to the railing, and he places his foot on the bottom rung. I place my hand on his back so he won't fall. He slowly makes his way up the ladder, and Damien helps guide him from the top.

Once he's safely inside the ship, I help Lila up the ladder, handing her off to Damien once she gets up high enough. She seems less fearful than Cody, but she doesn't let go of Damien's hand until she's all the way inside.

I ascend the ladder next, moving faster than the others. I'm used to this considering I've been copiloting and piloting a ship for the last six years. Daniel was a good teacher; he was patient and broke down instructions so I could understand them. Everything I know about flying a ship came from him. My knowledge is now limited.

"Here," Damien says, handing me a headset. "I know you might not be up to it, but I could use a copilot."

"Okay," I say. Hopefully it helps take my mind off things.

Damien begins backing out of the hangar as I check the different panels needed for taking off. He drives us over to the end of the runway and waits for the takeoff signal. The engines start roaring behind us, and I look over to see Lila and Cody covering their ears. I smile to myself because it reminds me of the first time Daniel and I flew together.

I look over at Damien, who is staring at me. "What?" I ask with a slight smile.

"Oh, nothing," he says, turning back to look at the runway.

I eye him suspiciously and he gives a small laugh.

"So," he says. "Does everything seem to be in order?"

"Yeah," I say. "Ready when you are."

The traffic control assistant motions us forward and gives us the all clear. Damien pushes the fuel lever forward, and the engines whirr even louder. I'm thrust back in my seat as we race down the runway. Pretty soon, we're in the air and the buildings below us get smaller and smaller. I hear Lila and Cody gasp in the back seat, probably because they've never been this high up.

I look over at Damien, who is smiling to himself. It puts a sad knot in my stomach. I turn away from him and look out the window. Something about his smile reminds me so much of Daniel, and it hurts to think that it's not him sitting in the pilot's seat next to me.

"So I guess I never really asked what planet you live on," Damien says, glancing at me.

I turn to face him. "Coreno," I say. "I don't think my family moved or anything."

"It's nice you have people to go back to," he says. "My mother died when I was young and my father left."

"I'm so sorry," I say. "Do you have any siblings?"

"I'm an only child," he says. "But it's okay. I've learned how to deal with things on my own. I was forced to grow up a little faster than some of the people around me."

"Was that difficult?" I ask.

"At times," he says. "But it helped me see things for what they really are."

"You remind me of my brother," I say. He glances at me questioningly. "I mean you guys are similar because he also had to grow up fast. It's a long story but it's why I'm out here and not at home."

"Why are you out here?" he asks.

"I told you, it's a long story," I say.

"It's a long ride back to Coreno," he says back.

I sigh. "My father left when I was young," I say. "He wanted to find a Stoneard. He was a regular trader. One day, some Corps' guards came to our house and told him that if he wanted to continue trading, he would have to go find the biggest Stoneard he could and bring it to them. But my father didn't know it was a trap, and he was kidnapped and held hostage until I found him and freed him a few weeks ago."

"Was he on Juema?" he asks.

"No," I say. "Vulcona. At the Corps' headquarters. I was there for a while before I came here."

"Why didn't you go straight home?" he asks.

"I needed to tell Lila and Cody's mom that her ex-husband died," I say. "It was something he wanted me to do for him."

"Were you and this guy close?" he asks, a hint of jealousy playing at the edge of his tone.

"I literally met him and within the same day he died," I say. "But I did get to hear about his ex-wife and kids and how he had to leave them to save them and stuff like that."

"It sounds like you knew this guy well," he says, the jealousy in his tone impossible to hide.

"First of all," I say getting a little frustrated. "I didn't know him that well. I didn't even really consider him a friend. And second, why do you care so much? My personal life shouldn't affect you like this. You don't even know me."

"I don't care," he says. "It just seems like you're really close to him despite your boyfriend dying so recently."

"I didn't even know he was dead until I came here!" I yell. "Stop making assumptions and accusations about my life!"

"I'm sorry," he says, holding up his palms like he's surrendering.

"You don't know anything about Eli or what he went through," I say, still upset. "Don't make assumptions about him either."

"Eli?" he asks.

"That's his name," I say, like it should have been obvious.

"Right," he says. "Of course." Then he's silent.

We don't talk for a while. He continues to fly the ship and I look out the window or talk to Lila or Cody. At first, they hesitantly ask questions about their father. I answer them to the best of my ability, but I realize I don't know as much about him as I thought. Too bad he wasn't still alive, because then they could go live with him and ask him their questions personally.

The whole time they ask questions, I can feel more and more tension building between Damien and I. At one point, I see him shift away from me. He looks out the window the whole time, keeping his face turned away from me.

And just when I was beginning to like him, I think. But then I think that thought through. Do I really like him like that? No. I can't. I push the thought away. I can't do this again. It's like what he implied, it's too early for me to be with someone else.

We stop at Dmaron, one of the smallest planets in the galaxy, to refuel. They have a small treat shop at the refueling station that Lila and Cody explore while Damien and I refuel. There is tension, and he doesn't say anything to me. Eventually, I can't take it anymore.

"Look, I'm sorry," I say. He turns to me and cocks an eyebrow. "For everything."

He turns away from me and doesn't say anything for a moment. Finally, he says, "I'm sorry too. What you do with your life is none of my business."

"True," I say. "But you aren't wrong."

He shrugs and then goes back to refueling the ship. I still feel tension in the air between us, but it's less. I feel lost, like I don't know what to do with myself, so I climb back into the ship. Instead of taking a left toward the cockpit, I make a right and head to the back.

There's a cabinet in the back, five drawers high. To pass the time, and because my curiosity is getting the better of me, I check through each of the drawers. The first one contains trinkets, most likely from the last owner. The second drawer contains clothes; a few shirts and pants stacked neatly on either side of the drawer. I grab the top shirt and replace the one I'm currently wearing with it. It's big on me but I tuck it into the new pair of pants. They smell old, like they've been sitting for a while, but they're clean, unlike my old clothes.

The next two drawers are empty except for a hairbrush in the fourth one. I don't even bother touching it. However, something peculiar catches my eye in the bottom one. A small note is folded in fourths and tucked in the back corner of the drawer. I grab it and open it.

I see you've finally found my second letter. Congratulations. I hoped the codes to your loved ones helped you out. I think no matter what you find, you'll be okay. You're one of the strongest people I know, same as Kyle. He thinks highly of you. You once asked if I remembered you from the mirrored hallway. I'm sure you know the answer now. One more thing. Since I'll probably never see you again, I wanted to clarify some things. In the rooms at the Corps' headquarters, yes those ones, it seemed a little quiet, a lack of presence if you will. That was because of me. No need to thank me, but I wanted you to know that I put that table full of brainwashing bread out for you and your friends on purpose. And yes, it was supposed to be brainwashing. I always thought you and Daniel were a better couple, so I may have pulled a few strings. No hard feelings? Thanks and good luck with the rest of your journey. Best wishes.

I pull Gregory's first note out of my pocket and compare it to this one. The handwriting is definitely the same, but somehow I miss him more after reading this one. It has more of a finality to it, a wrap-up of sorts. It also explains why nobody found us while we were in that part of the building. It's strange how I can feel so close to someone I've only talked to twice.

I hear footsteps approach from behind me, but I don't look to see who it is. Just by the sound, I can tell it's Damien.

"What do you have there?" he asks.

"Nothing," I say, folding it up with the first one and slipping it into my pocket. "Just something I found in these drawers."

"You're wearing a new shirt?" he asks.

"There's some in the second drawer," I reply.

He nods.

"Were you going to tell me something?" I ask.

"I just wanted to say that Lila and Cody are back and were helping me wash the ship a bit," he says. "It was looking a little dirty. They should be done soon, if you want to check the control panels, get things ready for takeoff."

"Thanks for letting me know," I say. I move around him and toward the cockpit, expecting him to take the hint that I want to be left alone. He doesn't move.

"Who wrote the note?" he asks suddenly.

"What?" I ask, not sure I heard him correctly.

"The note you have in your pocket," he says. "Who wrote it?"

"I don't know what you're talking about," I say.

"I read the note already," he says, sounding frustrated. "Just tell me who wrote it."

"Why do you care who wrote it?" I ask, my tone matching his.

"Why can't you just tell me?"

"Because it's personal," I say.

"I already read it!" he shouts. "I just want some context."

"You should finish helping Lila and Cody," I say, turning back to my work.

"Why is it such a big deal to you?"

"Why is it to you?" I fire back.

"Do you love him?" he asks. His tone is different, quieter, sadder.

"What do you mean?" I ask.

"Oh, so you won't even answer that question?" he asks. He sounds mad, and like he's fighting off tears.

"I just don't understand what you mean by it," I say calmly.

"Whoever wrote that note cares about you, a lot," he says. "Do you feel the same way?"

I sigh. I need to give him an explanation. "His name is Gregory," I say. "That's who wrote the letter. He was a janitor at the Corps' headquarters who helped me on multiple occasions. He's the one who gave me this ship and helped me escape."

"What happened to the first letter he gave you?"

"I have it in my pocket," I say. "He gave me the list of codes to each of my family members and Daniel."

"Oh," he says. "Remind me to thank him."

"Why?" I ask.

"Because he helped you escape," he says. "And he gave you a nice ship."

I smile. There's something about him that excites and worries me. I don't want to get too close, but I can't keep pushing him away either.

I turn back to the control panels on the side of the ship and begin fidgeting with the air pressure valve to the tires. I can feel the ship slowly rising and lowering.

"Hey!" a voice calls from outside the ship. "I can't climb when it's moving!"

I walk to the side door and see Lila trying to climb the ladder back into the ship. I try to hide my smile. Damien helps her about halfway up the ladder before I take over. He helps Cody next and then climbs the ladder himself.

"Did the air pressure seem off?" he asks once he gets inside the ship.

I close the door and head to my seat. "No," I say. "I was just having some fun."

He looks at the ground, smiles, and heads to his seat. He adjusts the takeoff controls and starts the engine. Pretty soon, we're moving. We wait for the all clear signal and then take off. The feeling of weightlessness gets my heart pumping and adrenaline courses through me. Ever since the first time I took off into the air, this feeling has been the same. It's one of the reasons I love flying so much.

I fall asleep at one point because when I wake up, we're landing again. I get really excited, until I realize we aren't at the Coreno ship port.

"Sorry," Damien says, not looking at me. "I needed to stop here on Techario for a part."

"A part for what?" I ask, still groggy.

He doesn't answer. Instead, he keeps fumbling in his bag for something before finally grabbing the whole thing. He gets up, opens the door, climbs down the ladder, and disappears. It's nighttime and I decide to fall back asleep. I check to make sure Lila and Cody are doing fine before I go to sleep. They both seem comfortable, each one covered in a shirt I assume to be from the drawer where I got mine.

I don't wake up again until I hear pounding on the door. Damien has finally come back and must have locked himself out. I open the door for him and notice that something seems slightly off.

"Are you okay?" I ask.

"Yeah, never better," he says. "Why?"

"I don't know," I reply. "Something just seems… off."

His expression changes to worry. "Oh," he says. "I wonder why that is. I think everything's fine."

"I'm sure it is," I lie. "I'm probably just tired or something."

He nods and slips into the pilot's seat. "We're almost there," he says. "Help me with the takeoff and then you can go back to sleep if you want."

"I'm awake now," I say. "I don't want to miss this."

The commander in the control tower gives us the all clear and we shoot off into space again. The feeling is back and I know I'm definitely not going back to sleep.

About an hour later, I start prepping the landing gear. I make sure the air pressure in the tires is perfect and the brakes have enough fluid in them. We touch down soon after we enter the atmosphere, and I can feel the adrenaline pump through my veins again. I'm finally going to see Kyle, my father, and hopefully my mother again.

The ship doesn't land fast enough, and I'm already starting to collect my things so I can leave. I almost forget to hit the brakes once we're near the end of the runway. Once I do, we screech to a halt.

"Come on!" I say excitedly. "Hurry up you guys!"

"What's going on?" Cody asks, waking up slowly.

"I get to go see my family soon," I say. I'm the first to climb down the ladder and the immediate shock of touching the ground sends chills through me. The air is warmer than the last time I was here. The sun is out, melting the snow outside the port.

"Zandrea!" Damien shouts from above me. "Can you help Lila and Cody?"

I turn around to see Lila halfway down the ladder and Cody beginning his descent. I help Lila the rest of the way down and wait a couple of seconds for Cody to get within arms' reach. Damien comes down a minute later after double checking that we got everything out of the ship.

"So this is Coreno," Damien comments. "Nice. It seems like a pretty great place."

"It has its moments," I say with a smile. I lead them to the front office so we can file our paperwork.

"Name," the lady at the front desk says. Then she looks up at me. "Zandrea? Is that you? I thought you were gone for good!"

She moves around the desk and gives me a warm embrace. "It's good to see you too Liv," I say with a smile.

"And who are these lovely people?" she asks. "You aren't married with kids, are you? What happened while you were away?"

"No, these aren't my kids or husband," I say. "This is Lila, Cody, and Damien." I gesture to each one as I say their name. She nods along, shaking hands with each of them.

"So," she says. "Will you be needing a place to stay or are you staying with your parents?"

"With my parents," I say.

"Which one?" she asks.

"Both," I say, like it should be obvious.

"Alternating, I presume," she says.

"Why would I alternate?"

"You didn't hear?" she asks.

"About what?" I ask getting a nervous pang in my stomach.

"Let's just say she wasn't exactly happy to see him," Liv says. "I don't know the details, but you should go be with your father." She hands me some paper and I sit down. My mind rushes through 100 different thoughts, each one entering and leaving so fast that my mind is in a whirlwind.

Damien puts his hand on my shoulder. "Are you going to be okay?" he asks.

I shake my head. "I just need to see them," I say.

We sign all the paperwork as Liv entertains Lila and Cody, and then we leave. Liv tells us my father's new address, where he lives with Kyle, and we head there right away.

The streets seem even emptier than I remember. Only one person passes us as we walk, and he seems surprised there are any people left. Little patches of snow sit around the buildings and in the yards of some of the houses. The whole scene is peaceful and quiet, not like a typical day in Coreno.

I follow the directions Liv gave me and find the house she gave me the address to. It's a nice house, slightly bigger than the one I grew up in. I walk up to the door, my heart beating double time. What if they've changed? What if they aren't happy that I'm back? What if I've changed?

"Everything is going to be okay," Damien says. "Don't worry."

"I'm just nervous," I say. "I don't know how they'll react."

"They love you," he says. "I'm sure they'll be happy to see you."

"I've walked up to a house filled with people who I thought loved me before," I say. "I was disappointed with the outcome."

"Don't let one event define the rest of them," he says. "Make a new memory, one with less sadness attached to it."

I nod and step up on the patio. I knock on the door and wait for someone to answer. Eventually, I hear footsteps and the memory of the first time I did this rushes back. Again, the knob seems to turn in slow motion and Kyle appears from behind it. However this time, he doesn't wear a confused look on his face.

"Zandrea!" he screams. "You're alive!"

He pushes the door open and runs out to embrace me. I return the hug and hold on to him for a long time. He's at the perfect height for me to hug him. My father shows up at the door a little bit later, a huge grin on his face.

"I see you've returned," he says, embracing me. "We've missed you so much. *I've* missed you so much."

Damien clears his throat. "I don't mean to interrupt, but-"

"Oh, I'm sorry," I say. "Father, Kyle, this is Damien. I met him on Juema after I picked up these kids, Lila and Cody."

They all take turns saying hi to each other and then my father invites us all inside. I take in my surroundings, noticing the lack of pictures and color.

"Are you guys living in the Funeral Hall?" I ask. The Funeral Hall is a giant room in the House where people go after their loved ones have died. The room is very lifeless and depressing because there aren't any colors or a natural source of light. Just one light hangs overhead. I went there once when I was young after one of my father's friends died.

"Somedays, it seems like we are," my father replies. "Having you here will hopefully change that. We were so worried about you. I knew you would stay strong but the Corps don't exactly play fair."

"Why are you living here?" I ask. "Instead of with Mother."

His expression goes solemn.

"What happened?" I ask, more seriously this time.

He looks away from me and at the one picture he has lying on his counter. From a quick glimpse, I can see that it's my parent's wedding photo. His eyes turn red and puffy as he looks at it. I walk over to him and put my arm around him.

"Father," I say. "I know that whatever happened between the two of you was difficult. I'm sorry I wasn't here for you. Tell me what happened, and I might be able to fix it."

"You can't fix it," he says. "What's done is done."

"Father-"

"You don't know her like I do," he snaps. His tone isn't mad, just frustrated and upset. "Once her mind is set, it can't be changed."

"What does she have her mind set on?" I ask.

"Chris," he replies.

I freeze. I thought he was gone, I thought Kelton killed him. I didn't know he was still here. And he's in my house. With my mother. Anger flows through me at the thought of him still being here.

"He's completely brainwashed her," my father says. "She wants nothing to do with me, or even Kyle."

"Did she say anything about me?" I ask.

"No," he says. "And I'm sorry, but I don't know if she'd even remember you."

My heart sinks. My own mother probably doesn't even remember me. "Oh," I say. Damien puts his hand on my shoulder, and without thinking, I whip around and bury my head in his shoulder, tears flowing uncontrollably from my eyes. He holds and comforts me until I stop crying.

Lila and Cody sit on the couch, absorbing all the information, probably not understanding half of what's being said. My father sends them off to do something to keep them occupied. My father pulls me to the side, and Damien and Kyle start talking quietly in the corner of the room, almost as if they've known each other for a long time.

I stare at Damien for a while before I realize my father is talking to me. "What did you say?" I ask him.

"I asked what they did to you at the headquarters," he says. He looks worried.

"Don't worry about me," I say. "We need to figure out how to get Mother back."

"That's why I need you to tell me what they did to you," he says.

"I'm not following," I say confused.

"My theory is that Chris has been developing some stuff to use," my father explains. "If you tell me what he did to you, we might be able to reverse it and help your mother."

"He tried controlling my dreams," I say. "Turn them into nightmares and use them against me. His intent was to make me go so insane that I would die. Somehow he wanted to use it on other people-"

My father gives me a look, and it finally hits me. Chris was testing me to get to my mother. He wasn't planning on using it on everyone, just her. And I helped him get it to the right dose. Without thinking, I turn around and run out the door.

I hear my father's voice calling behind me, but I don't stop running. I need to find my mother and Chris and somehow reverse all of this. I run in the general direction of where I used to live and come across my house. It looks the same from the outside, the attic window still ajar and the porch swing still slightly lopsided. I run up the porch and knock on the door.

The last time I did this, I was nervous but excited. Now, I'm just anxious. Who's going to open the door? Will my mother recognize me? Will Chris? The knob turns, not as slow as last time, and the door is pulled away from me. My mother stands at the door wearing the most beautiful red dress I've ever seen. It reaches to her knees and has sparkly red fringe that reaches slightly lower. I want to hug her and punch her at the same time.

"What do you want?" she asks me, leaning against the doorframe.

"Do you know who I am?" I ask.

She looks me straight in the eye before answering, "No."

My own mother doesn't even know who I am. My eyes fill with tears but I force myself to stop. I can't show her any signs of weakness. I hear loud breathing behind me and realize my father is trying to catch his breath.

"Zandrea-" he says.

"I told you to never come back!" my mother shouts at him.

Sensing the situation, I try to fight fire with ice. "Mother," I say soothingly. "It's me, Zandrea. Your daughter. I've been gone for a while, and I'm really sorry, but I'm back now and-"

She steps over the threshold as my father tries climbing the stairs. She pushes him backward and he falls down the steps. I immediately rush over and shove my mother out of the way. She stumbles a little in her clunky heels but regains enough composure to push me too. I stumble a little. I ditch my fighting fire with ice method.

"Don't you dare *touch* my father," I say fiercely. "And don't you ever touch me again either. You're a monster. And despite him being gone for so long, he was more of a parent figure than you ever were!" I motion for my father to leave, but he doesn't move.

"I'm not leaving you alone with her," he says.

"Don't worry," a voice says from behind us. "She won't be alone."

I turn around to see Damien and Kyle coming toward us. I smile immediately. Kyle begins helping my father and Damien stands next to me. My mother begins retreating inside the house, and I figure I'll probably never see her again, so I run up the steps and push the door back open.

"I'm taking Father back to the house," Kyle says. "He's really hurt."

I nod over my shoulder and begin working on my mother. She's stronger than I remember, but then again, so am I. But before I can shove her out of the way, she freezes. Her eyes become glossy and lifeless. She doesn't move, not even flinch.

"Well, well," a voice says from inside the house, one that is way too familiar. "Did you forget about me?"

A shadow appears in the doorway, and at first I can't tell who it is, but then I see him and every muscle in my body tenses. Chris.

"How have you been?" he asks like we're old friends. "Must think you're pretty tough for escaping my compound, don't you?"

"You didn't exactly stop me," I say.

"Oh Zandrea," he says. "I could have stopped you if I wanted, but that would give you the impression that I was winning. I wanted you to feel like you had some control."

He uses the same sickly sweet tone he used before tinkering with my brain. It makes me want to hurl.

"And who do we have here?" he asks, gesturing to Damien. "Have you already replaced that pathetic little boyfriend of yours? You know Kelton never liked him. I could tell he had an eye for you though."

"Kelton's dead," I inform him almost a little too triumphantly.

"Yes, he died a tragic death," he says nonchalantly. "If he had listened to his father, he would still be alive now. But he thought he could take control of the entire organization. Ha! Serves him right."

I roll my eyes. As annoying and evil as he is, he's also a bit amusing. He is very dramatic, which gives him flair. I despise him for it.

"Now," he says with a little jump in his step. "I wanted to show you this." He points to my mother like she's a new showcase that I haven't seen before.

"I've seen her before," I say with slight disgust. "She raised me."

"Ah, but she is new and enhanced," he says like a dramatic salesperson trying to get someone to buy a product. "Just watch."

He pulls out a small remote and presses a few buttons. She comes to life again, her eyes full of life, but they still have a glossy coat. He presses a different button and her head turns to me, her eyes locking with mine.

"Fancy, isn't she?" Chris asks. "Now, I know what you're thinking and no, she isn't a robot or machine. I simply attached an earpiece behind her ear that alters her brain chemistry to an electromagnetic wavelength that I can thus control her by. And all this is possible because of the experiments we did to you in the lab."

"So the remote controls her," Damien says.

"Precisely," Chris replies. "He's a smart little cookie, isn't he?"

I slap him. "How could you?" I yell. "You completely brainwashed her!"

"Fierce little one, isn't she?" he says, mostly to himself. "And I didn't brainwash her, I merely altered her brain chemistry."

"That's basically the same thing," I say.

"On the contrary," he says. "If I were to have brainwashed her, there would be no going back. She would be under my control for the rest of her life. By changing her brain chemistry, I allowed for her to be controlled by this remote and an earpiece, which is completely reversible."

"How do you reverse it?" I ask.

"Wouldn't you like to know," he taunts.

"Yes, that's why I asked," I say. "And why would you make it a reversible procedure?"

He thinks the question over for a second before sighing dramatically and saying, "My dear, do you really think I'm just going to tell you everything?"

"I was hoping you would," I say.

He sighs another dramatic sigh and out of nowhere punches Damien in the stomach. He doubles over, clutching his stomach. The blow didn't seem that hard, just unexpected.

"Well, as you're tending to his needs," Chris says. "I'm going to take my masterpiece back inside. Have fun, and get off my property."

I stand up and lunge toward him, but he's already inside the house, my mother being pulled behind him like she's nothing but a machine. I pound my fists on the patio floor and let out a scream I didn't know I was holding in.

"We should go back to your father's house," Damien says, sitting on the patio floor. "We can reassemble there."

I get up and walk over to him and offer him a hand. He accepts it and I pull him to a standing position. He doesn't let go of my hand, and I don't let go of his. We hold each other's gaze for a few seconds before a cold breeze blows by and brings us back to reality. The familiarity in his eyes mixed with the breeze sends a shiver down my spine. He releases my hand and descends down the patio stairs.

My hand feels cold now, and I miss his touch. It's weird for me to think that I've known him for a short while, and yet there seems to be a connection you only get after being with someone for a while. I try to shake the thought but I can't. My mind keeps wandering back to the patio.

The walk to my father's house isn't very long. Neither of us say anything, we just enjoy the quietness and springtime beauty of Coreno. Spring in Coreno was always my favorite time of the year. After a harsh winter, Coreno seemed to spring back to life—the warmth of the air, the slight breezes, the smell of plants blossoming to life; I never found that anywhere else.

I walk up the stairs to my father's house once again and knock on the door. This time isn't as nerve-wrecking. I hear the little pitter-patter of feet, too light to be Kyle's footsteps. Cody opens the door and gives me a huge smile.

"You guys are back!" he says excitedly. "Come on in."

Damien allows me to step across the threshold first. When I do, I see my father lying on the couch, a cloth wrapped across his forehead, and Kyle sitting next to him.

"Is he okay?" I ask Kyle.

"He'll be fine," he says. "He just needs some rest. He seemed a little warm and he might have cracked a rib or two."

"Can I take a look?" Damien asks. "I know a thing or two about stuff like this. Back on Juema, I took a few medical classes as an extracurricular."

"Thanks," Kyle says. "I have no idea what I'm doing."

We leave Damien to his work and go sit on the staircase that leads upstairs. "So," I say to Kyle. "What's up?"

"I don't know," he says. "I've been really worried about Father lately. After he found out about Mother, he sort of went into a depression. I think it's good you came back when you did, otherwise I don't know what would have happened to him."

"And what about you?" I ask.

"I'm just glad you're back," he says with a smile. He leans over and embraces me. Then he whispers in my ear, "I was beginning to lose hope."

I pull away and hold him at arm's length. "I will always come back to you," I say. "I made that promise to myself a long time ago and I don't see any reason for breaking it now."

He laughs and I pull him into another embrace. We sit there for a while before I finally feel the need to ask him something that's been on my mind the last couple of days.

"Explain to me what happened after you guys left the headquarters," I say.

"Well," he says, thinking back. "We had just taken off the runway and before we even got above some of the buildings, something hit us. Father thinks it was a missile or something. The back of the ship was smoking and we were losing altitude. Thankfully, there were some parachutes in the front near the pilot's seat, so we all grabbed one and strapped it to ourselves. Daniel helped me with mine."

I wince at his name. The memories are still too painful to think about.

"We all jumped out of the ship and barely had enough time to open our parachutes," he says. "The landing hurt more than it should have. We were all fine though. We started running in the direction of the ship port, but some guards from the Corps were chasing us, so we had to take cover."

He pauses, letting the information sink in. I'm still wondering how Daniel died when he starts up with the story again.

"We hid behind a building, and we thought for sure they would find us," he says. "But I guess the Corps aren't that smart because they ran right past us. That was when Daniel revealed his master plan to us."

"A master plan?" I ask.

"Yes," Kyle says. "He thought it would be too dangerous for all of us to stay together, so he told Father and me to go back to Coreno. That way, when you escaped or they let you go, you would be able to go back and find us. He said he couldn't go back to Coreno because it would be too easy for them to find him. He was hated by the Corps and knew they would kill him if they found him. So he went to a place where he thought they would never look: Juema."

"He went to Juema?" I ask astonished.

"Yes," Kyle says. "Since most people go there to retire and lay back, he figured it would be a good spot to blend in and not be noticed."

"Did he die on his way there or something?" I ask, the question eating away at me.

"What do you mean?" Kyle asks.

"I was given his code number and when I checked one of the Codereaders, it said he was dead," I explain. "So did he die on his way there or before he even left or what?"

"Zandrea," Kyle says softly. "Daniel isn't dead. And he's closer than you think."

I can't breathe. I can't move. I stare at Kyle in disbelief. He's dead, the Codereader said so. The Codereader is never wrong.

"He's dead Kyle," is all I can think to say. "You need to accept it."

"No," he says. "He isn't dead. I know for a fact he's alive."

He stands up and leaves me alone on the staircase. A million thoughts run through my head. How is he still alive? And what does Kyle mean by he's closer than I think? I remember the conversation I had with Cody about how someone could be emotionally or mentally close to someone without being physically close. Maybe that's what Kyle means.

Every part of me wants Kyle to be right, but I've let myself hope before and it never ends well. For once, I want to be proven wrong. I want Daniel to walk around the corner and reveal himself and tell me it was all a lie. Instead, Damien walks around the corner.

"Hey," he says.

"Hi," I say back absentmindedly.

"Can I talk to you for a second?" he asks.

I nod although I don't really feel like talking right now. He grabs my hand and leads me through the house. I'm too distracted to know where he's taking me, but eventually we stop in a small room I assume to be in the back of the house.

It's a nice room. Bookcases filled with books line every wall, floor to ceiling. A potted plant sits opposite the door, near a small window that fills the room with natural light. A large desk rests to the side of the entrance. A lamp and spherical map of Coreno sit on the left side of the desk and a small pile of books and notepad sit on the right. The floorboards creak when I step into the room.

Damien closes the door behind me and takes a step inside so he's facing me. He pulls a remote out of his pocket and I jump.

"Don't worry," he says. "I'm not going to hurt you."

He brings the remote closer to his face and presses a button. His face turns pixelated and begins to disappear, revealing a different face behind it, almost like a mask but more form-fitting. He slowly transforms into someone very familiar. Daniel.

"Wha-?" I'm too confused to understand what is going on until a thought hits me. He used a Face Transformation Unit, or FTU. Created on Techario a few decades ago, FTU's help conceal one's identity if they need to go into hiding or something of the sort. They aren't hard to find and are available almost anywhere.

"Hey," he says.

"What's going on?" I ask.

"It's me," he says. "Daniel. I'm back, although technically I've been back for a while."

I don't trust what I'm seeing. But I have to. He's right in front of me. But he can't be.

"What's happening?" I ask. "How did you just transform from Damien to Daniel?"

"Damien isn't real," he says. "That's just a name I used to conceal my identity. It's me, Daniel Thomas. You've known me for six years. I taught you how to fly a ship. I-"

Ignoring every instinct that's telling me not to trust him, I run across the room to where he's standing and wrap my arms around him. He wraps his arms around me and holds me close. I still smell his signature scent of oil and clove and know it's him. All my doubt has been erased.

"How is this possible?" I ask, half breaking away, half still holding him close.

"Well," he says. "I used a Face Transforming Unit and-"

"I assumed that part," I say.

"Then what are you confused about?" he asks.

"I looked up your code number and it said you were dead," I say. "The Codereaders have never been wrong. Why are they wrong this time? How is any of this possible?"

"I have friends," he says simply.

"What's that supposed to mean?" I ask.

"I have a friend who works at the Corps' headquarters," he says. "He works in the Codes department. They track people and when their codes stop sending information, they update the person's info. I asked him if he could change my Existence Status to deceased so I could go into hiding easier and no one would think to look for me."

"I just can't believe you've been with me this whole time," I say. Then a new thought hits me. "Why didn't you say something? Like when I first saw you or after I found out you were 'dead' or on the ship or-"

"I was trying to protect you," he says. "The less you knew, the better."

"Why is that always the case with you?" I ask. "You don't tell me anything because you think it would be better if I didn't know."

"Look, I'm sorry," he says. "You don't understand how hard it was for me to not say anything-"

"You think it was hard for you?" I ask, almost upset. "I'm the one who's had to go through these last few days thinking you were dead! And in the weeks before that, I thought I might never see you again! It's been the hardest for *me*."

"And I'm the one who thought I'd never see you again," he says. "I knew you were strong but I've seen the things Chris can do firsthand, and I was so worried. When I saw you, it took every ounce of strength I had to stay in character."

"Why didn't you just say something?" I ask quietly, the thought of him keeping Kelton's identity a secret from me for my own good starts hitting me like a stack of bricks. "Anything at all."

"Because if somehow they got you again, I didn't want them to torture you trying to get information out of you," he says softly. "I could never live with myself if that happened." He kisses my forehead and I melt into his arms.

"Just don't leave me again," I say.

"I don't think you would let me," he says with a smile.

We stand in silence for a while, his arms wrapped around me. A new thought hits me, and it makes me smile.

"Remember that story you told me back on Juema," I say. "It was about a girl that you knew and would do anything for. Was that-"

"Yes," he says. "The story was about you. And every word I said was true. Although the story itself wasn't in complete detail."

"Yeah," I say. "I realize that now."

He laughs.

"So you knew I loved you?" I ask. "Without me saying anything?"

"Of course," he says. "Like I said, actions speak louder than words."

We're quiet again for a little bit before Kyle rushes into the room. "I'm glad to see you guys are acquainted again, but there's someone at our door."

We follow Kyle out of the room and down the hall to the front entryway. Someone knocks on the door hard enough that it's a wonder the door didn't break down.

"Who is it?" I hiss, hoping whoever it is won't hear me.

"I don't know," he says. "But Father can't help us. He's resting upstairs. Cody and Lila are with him. Should we open it?"

"If you don't, they will," Daniel says. "And I'd rather not find out what would happen next."

Kyle and I move around the corner for protection. Daniel moves carefully toward the door, resting his hand on the doorknob. He pulls it open, revealing two Corps' guards standing on the porch, with Chris right in between them.

"Maybe next time you should open the door faster," Chris snarls.

"Maybe next time you should leave us alone," Daniel retorts.

"Feisty," he says. "Anyway, I thought I should warn you that Coreno is going to be home to a new base of mine, and anyone left here will be working for me."

"And what makes you think you can do that?" Daniel asks.

"Everybody, everywhere," Chris says like it should be obvious. "Wait a minute, I thought you were dead."

"Aw, did you miss me?" Daniel asks sarcastically.

"It will only make it more fun to kill you," he says.

"Do you have a gun on you?" I whisper to Kyle.

"No," he whispers back. "But there's one in Father's office. I'll go get it." He tiptoes around me and back into the office. I watch Kyle disappear around the corner and suddenly I feel alone. His presence was very comforting.

Daniel places his hand on his hip and moves it slightly back. He slips his hand into a pocket on the side of his pants near his waistline. Something metal and shiny gleams from inside. His hand lingers on the handle of the shiny object for a little while as Chris rambles.

"... I plan to mind control everyone left on this planet, use them for my army, complete my Take Over stage," Chris says with an evil grin.

"And speaking of complete Take Over, you look just like your mother." His smile grows wider.

Daniel's face turns colder, stonier. He whips the shiny object—a 22t revolver gun—and aims it at Chris's chest. He fires a bullet in one smooth motion. Excitement courses through me, until I see the bullet ricochet off Chris's chest and hit Daniel in his lower shoulder. He falls back in pain, gripping his shoulder where the bullet pierced him.

"What?" I whisper to myself. Then I remember a similar situation. Back in the Corps' headquarters in Chris's office. Kelton aimed his gun at Chris's head because he knew that was the only spot that a bullet could damage.

"Here," Kyle whispers, returning to my left. He hands me the gun and I position myself, ready to shoot. Chris starts walking toward Daniel, his henchmen following close behind.

"You're pathetic, just like your mother," Chris spits. He kicks Daniel in his side, causing him to let out a painful groan. Chris's eyes are wild as he kicks him on his other side.

I stand up slowly, aiming my gun at Chris's head. I wrap my free hand around the one with the gun to steady myself. I pop the safety out of place and cock the gun. It gives enough noise to distract Chris. He turns his head toward me. "That's enough," I say fiercely.

He throws his head back and cackles like the evil maniac he is. Without really thinking, I aim my gun lower and shoot him in the foot. His laughter is immediately replaced with a scream. I readjust my aim so the barrel of the gun faces his head again. This time, he takes things more seriously.

"You think you're so special," he says in a taunting manner. He takes a step forward and winces. "Well, I hate to be the one to break it to you sweetheart, but you aren't. And you never will be."

"Hey!" Daniel says from the floor. He turns over so his body is facing me and looks up at Chris. "Don't talk to her that way. You're-"

One of Chris's henchmen kicks Daniel again and he rolls to the side, shaking from the pain.

"If you touch him one more time, I'm going to shoot you," I say.

"I bet you wouldn't," he says tauntingly. He pulls a gun out of his back pocket and points it at Daniel. "Shoot me, and he dies."

And here we are again, at a stalemate. No one moves, no one breathes. If I lower my gun, I'm too vulnerable. If I keep it pointed on him much longer, he'll shoot Daniel. It's then that I realize how much I hate dilemmas.

Just when I feel like I'm running out of time, someone walks through the front door of the house. Everyone turns their attention in the direction of the sound. My mother stands at the door, hands on her hips. She no longer wears the beautiful red dress from before. Instead, she wears a form-fitting black uniform with a silver waistband. She looks amazing, with her long hair pulled back and shiny heeled shoes.

"Darling," Chris coos. "I thought I told you to stay home."

"I was bored," she says, providing proof to her statement in her tone. "And I wanted to join the fight."

"Well, in that case," Chris says. He pulls the remote he uses to control her out of his pocket, aims it at her, and presses a button. She pulls a revolver out from behind her and shoots, not even bothering to aim. The sound bounces off the walls, piercing my eardrum.

I scream and duck to the floor, Kyle following my lead. Chris presses another button and she starts marching toward us. She fires again, this time lower, and I cover my head with my hands. I turn to look at Daniel, who is grimacing so much and losing lots of blood. I start to think he won't make it.

"Mother!" Kyle screams from behind me.

She doesn't give him a second thought as she fires again. The window behind us shatters into a thousand pieces. Chris presses another button and it finally hits me: if the remote controls my mother, and someone controls the remote, then whoever is holding the remote controls my mother. I feel as though I'm the only one who didn't catch that the first time.

"Kyle," I say frantically. "Try to get the remote from Chris."

Suddenly, a gunshot. From upstairs. I turn my head in the direction of the staircase, and there stands my father, a gun in his right hand, aimed at my mother. At first I think he has shot and possibly killed her, but she doesn't fall forward. Instead she screams and grips the back of her arm.

Maybe my father missed. But I don't believe that to be the case. He never liked to shoot guns, but he always had some of the best aim. He told me once that when I got older, he would teach me how to use a gun properly. That never happened, but Daniel did give me a brief lesson after I learned how to fly a ship.

"I'm teaching you the basics of the two most important things known to this job," he had told me once. "To be a pilot, you need to know how to fly. And every once in a while you might need to use a gun. I think I'm killing two birds with one stone here." I guess he was right.

I focus my attention back to the scene in front of me. My mother is kneeling on the ground, grasping her arm. One of the guards moves to her side stiffly and applies pressure to the wound. The other guard runs toward my father, his gun pointed straight for my father's head. Before he can fire a shot, I aim my gun at the guard's head and fire. He stops mid-step and crumbles to the ground.

Chris goes into a fit of rage. He runs toward me, his gun outstretched. He fires once, narrowly missing me to the left of my left ear. I hear a vase shatter behind me. Chris pulls the trigger again, but nothing comes out of the barrel. He realizes this and throws the gun to the ground.

"You have been a pain in my side since the moment you walked into my building!" Chris shouts at me. He lunges forward, swinging his right arm against my jaw. I fall to the ground, and the next thing I know, Chris is hitting my face and jabbing my sides.

My whole body aches and I feel weak against his constant aggressiveness. He kicks my side and back and I roll into a ball, clutching my stomach. At one point, Kyle punches Chris in the jaw, which distracts him long enough for me to regain some composure.

Chris kicks Kyle in the stomach and he falls against the wall. I hear a crack, and I'm guessing it's his rib cage. He clutches at his abdomen and shrinks against the wall, crying to himself. I retaliate by kicking the back of Chris's knee in hard and he falls to the ground kneeling. My fist then finds his head, and through the pain, Kyle's leg finds his hip. The next time I go to punch him, he grabs my wrist and bends it back.

"Ow!" I cry and I try to pull free. Kyle swings his arm down, connecting with the inside of Chris's elbow, breaking his grip on me. I stumble backward, holding my wrist. It's at this time that my father appears in the hallway, kicking Chris in the back and buying us some time.

My father, being one of the strongest people I know, puts Chris in a choke hold and pins his arms behind his back. Chris, being more mentally tough if anything, wriggles in my father's grasp, but he has an iron lock.

"You will pay for what you did to my wife," my father says, his voice stern but smooth.

"Think again," Chris says snarkily. He turns to face the door and five more guards appear. My heart sinks.

Three of the guards storm over to my father and pull him away from Chris. They lock his arms behind his back and hold him as he tries to break free. I try to run to my father, but Chris motions another guard over and he pins my arms together behind my back. This kills my wrist and I let out a whimper. But I stop myself from full out crying. This is not the time to show weakness.

I grit my teeth and try breaking free again. Chris motions for the other guard to come over and help contain me. I examine the scene in front of me. Daniel is still on the floor, bleeding immensely from his shoulder wound. His face is pale and he looks frozen. Tears start to take shape on my lower eyelid and a lump forms in my throat. Despite me believing he was dead twice, watching him slowly fade away is a thousand times worse. I turn away to keep from crying.

My father doesn't struggle against the guards anymore. He's not tired, in fact he has more determination in his eyes than I've ever seen before. I can tell he's plotting something in his head.

My mother stands a few feet behind him, a cloth wrapped around her arm where the bullet hit her. I notice that it's her shooting arm that's wounded and I smile slightly to myself. I know my father purposely aimed there so she couldn't hurt anyone but also because I know he believes she's still somewhere inside her body. She just needs to be reprogrammed.

Kyle sits on the ground, looking defeated and tired. His face is cut and bloody but I don't think he notices. Instead, his eyes are focused on something in front of him. Chris's side pocket. And I know exactly what's inside of it.

Kyle looks over at me and I give him the smallest of nods. He gives me the smallest of smiles in return and shifts slightly. With all of the guards' gazes fixed on us, it'll be hard for him to do much. But he's fast. Kyle shifts again, and this time, he's sitting in the perfect position to spring up and grab the remote. He looks at me one more time; I give him a wink this time and before I know it, he's standing up. He moves so fast Chris doesn't know what happened until it's too late.

Kyle slips the remote out of Chris's pocket faster than he can react. The guards are so distracted with trying to contain Kyle that I stomp on my guard's foot, elbow him in the gut, and escape from his grasp. He claws at me, trying to regain his hold on me, but I'm too quick. I stand next to Kyle as he frantically pushes buttons.

My father also manages to escape and ends up punching one guard in the stomach and fistfights the other two, trying to hold them off. My heart races. Chris swings his arm and connects with my jaw. This time, though, I'm too numb to really notice, and the blow didn't hurt as much as it did last time.

Kyle still frantically tries to push buttons on the remote, trying multiple different combinations. Nothing seems to work. I'm starting to grow worried that we may never get our mother back, but I can't give up hope now.

"There's no off switch, bud," Chris says, cackling.

I let the information sink in. My mother might be an evil mindless drone the rest of her life. I can't let that happen though. I love my mother. She raised me when my father wasn't here, and even when he was. She taught me so many things in life. It's this thought, these memories, that keeps me fighting. I will get her back.

By now my knuckles have turned a dark shade of purple, but I knee Chris in the stomach really hard anyway, and he stumbles back a little, giving me time to hit him in the head and knee him again. It slows him down for a bit before one of his guards tackles me to the ground. I try gasping for breath but I can't. With the wind knocked out of me, it's hard to move or fight back.

I see my father out of the corner of my eye, fighting for his life. He's running out of steam and I can tell he won't be able to fend them off for much longer. Kyle runs around the furniture, trying to dodge one of the guards' attacks. He holds the remote in his hand, still pressing buttons. Maybe he thinks Chris is lying or something.

The guard throws a punch at Kyle, who easily dodges it. However, the guard gets enough momentum to swing a punch again, this time, knocking the remote out of Kyle's hand and onto the ground.

"Kyle!" a voice says to the left of me. It's so angelic and smooth and so familiar. I turn to the sound of the voice, wondering who it is. And then I see her. The real her. My mother. No longer a mindless machine but my actual, human mother. She looks at Kyle, a softness in her eyes, like the look a mother gives her newborn child.

I can tell Kyle's caught up in the moment, and when I look around, everyone else is too. Everyone wears a different expression on their face: Chris looks horrified, my father is in awe, and the guards just stand motionless. My expression is probably somewhere along the lines of confused. How did she turn back to normal? Is this Chris's doing? My mind races with a hundred different questions, but somehow my thoughts all swirl around one thing: the remote.

I glance over at it. It's laying right-side up, a red light that I've never seen before blinking at the top. All of the sudden, my mother starts jolting fast, like she's being electrocuted, and then her face goes stark and she's back to being a machine. Chris sighs a sigh of relief and turns quickly to Kyle.

"What did you do?" he screams.

"N-nothing," Kyle stammers. "Your guard is the one who knocked it out of my hand and-"

"You what?" Chris screams at the guard.

I don't hear his response. My mind is busy working things out. The remote fell out of Kyle's hand and hit the ground. Then my mother was back. Maybe the impact from the floor on the remote jostled something loose. Only one way to find out.

I hit the guard closest to me in the stomach, just long enough for me to get away. I run over to the remote and grab it. I stand up, hold the remote above my head, and get ready to smash it against the ground. Before I get the chance, a gun cocks.

"Drop it," Chris says, "and your family dies."

"I don't trust you," I say, the remote still above my head. "I don't think you'll stay true to your word. And even if you did, Coreno would be under your control anyway, so what's the point?"

"Your family's lives are on the line. I don't think you quite understand what's going on here," Chris says.

"You're probably right," I say nonchalantly. "I probably don't. But it's like I once said, you're a bad man set out to do bad things, and I won't let that happen."

With all my force and every last ounce of strength I have left in me, I throw the remote at the ground as hard and fast as I can, hoping it might break into a million little pieces. It hits the ground, sending tons of shards and wires all over the room. The box that contained the battery splits into two and the battery cracks.

Chris looks from me to the broken pieces of his remote and back to me in utter shock. Then anger takes over and he pulls out his gun again and aims it at my mother. A loud bang bounces off the walls and I shut my eyes, not wanting to see my mother die. I don't want to join the club of kids who have watched their mothers die in front of them and they weren't able to do anything.

I engrain a picture of my mother into my mind. She's beautiful, her long hair flowing down her back, her eyes sparkling. That's how she looked the day she married my father. One of my favorite memories I have of her was when I was about ten years old. She took me into her room one night after putting Kyle to bed.

"Shhhh," she whispered then. "There's something I want to show you." She went into her closet and brought out a picture of her and my father on their wedding day. She looked gorgeous, and I always loved the dress she wore. She looked so happy with my father's arms wrapped around her and his lips brushing her cheek. She smiled the biggest smile I had ever seen.

"Wow," was all I could say. She had another picture of them on their wedding day downstairs, but she wasn't smiling in that one. In fact, neither of them were. But that was the picture she showed everyone who came by.

"This picture is special to me," she said. "I don't want it to leave my room. Do you understand?"

I nodded my head, but I didn't exactly understand why she didn't want it to leave her room. So I asked. "Why don't you want the picture of you being happy out for everyone to see?"

"Because," she said and didn't elaborate. I knew better than to push the subject so I gave her a kiss goodnight and left the room. But no matter how hard I tried, I couldn't sleep that night. I knew there had to be some reason why that picture had to stay in her room.

One day, I went into her room and took the picture out of her closet to examine it. My mother came into the room a little later and saw me staring at it. "I don't want that moment ruined," she said.

"What?" I asked, not sure I heard her correctly.

"I leave that picture in this room because I don't want that moment to be ruined," she explained. "It's very personal to me, and if I let everyone else see it, they might give their opinions and change my view of that day. That was the happiest day of my life. When you get married someday, you'll understand what I mean."

With that, she left the room. I didn't understand what she meant at the time, but now that I'm older, I'm starting to understand. You cherish the moments that make you the most happy and you don't let anyone take them away from you. Because that's when they have power over you.

I open my eyes, not exactly sure how long has gone by since the gunshot. I examine the room, starting from my left and panning to my right. My father stands still, gaping. Kyle stands still too, but he doesn't look upset. In fact, he wears an enormous grin on his face. I scan the room again and find my mother staring at the ground, at Chris.

Chris lies on the floor, blood pooling around him. His eyes are closed, his body distorted, and his face pale. There's no rise and fall of his chest. He's dead. And this time, I'm pretty sure it's for real.

I start looking around the room again, wondering where the bullet came from. No one is holding a gun, at least not one that's aimed at Chris. I have to do a double take to make sure I'm not dreaming. I'm not. Everything is real. So where did that bullet come from?

The guards answer my question by turning to face Daniel, who is sitting sideways, propped up by his good arm. He lowers his gun down to his side and collapses to the floor. The guards begin to move toward him, one drawing a heavy-loaded machine gun from what seems like thin air. He points it at Daniel and again there's a loud bang. But I don't close my eyes this time.

Instead, I see the guard with the machine gun fall backward, the guard behind him catching him and laying him down slowly. The bullet comes from my left, and when I turn my head my father is lowering his gun. My father and I take turns firing at the remaining guards, each one somehow unsuspecting.

My ears are ringing, which I didn't even realize until all the noise stopped. The house is eerily silent. We all take turns looking at each other, relief registering on everyone's face. Daniel moans, and I rush over to his side. His condition is worse than I thought; his pale face and blank, stark eyes give that away. My father calls the local medical shop and they rush over, glad for something to do. They cart Daniel away and tell us we can visit him in a few days, but he will need a lot of medical attention before then.

After he's gone, I turn to my mother, who immediately embraces me in the warmest hug. I squeeze her so tight I think I cut off her air supply for a little bit. Kyle joins in on the embrace, and we stand there for minutes. My father finishes signing some paperwork with the medical assistants and then comes back inside. He stands outside the circle for a little bit before my mother motions him closer, and he wraps his arms around all three of us. I get a feeling of protection, one I haven't felt since before my father left.

My mother breaks away first. "You have no idea how much I've missed you all," she says, tears staining her cheeks. "I thought for sure I would never be able to communicate or hug or do anything with you guys ever again."

"I love you, Mother," I burst out. "I don't know what I would've done without you."

She smiles and embraces me again. Just when I'm finally feeling peace again, someone knocks on the door. We all jump and look at it expectantly. My father walks over to the door and opens it. A man stands on the porch, wearing a navy blue uniform with the insignia of the House on his upper breast pocket. He says something to my father, who moves out of the way to let the man through.

"Hello Mrs. Knowles," he says, looking at my mother. "Hello children. I am here on behalf of the Coreno government. They heard a lot of shooting coming from this household, and it is my job to make sure everything is alright."

"Of course," my mother says.

He looks around the room, taking in the bodies on the ground and broken pieces of the remote, furniture, and other things that fell during the fight. "Now, I can see there was a lot going on," he says. "I'll have my team come over and thoroughly search the house."

He nods to each of us in turn and leaves the house. We all stand and stare at each other, talking about what happened in the last few weeks. My father explains to my mother what happened after he left us. She starts tearing up until my father walks over to her and holds her; then she really lets the waterworks flow. My initial thought was that they would talk about everything that has happened in the decade since he left, but somehow the silence answers every question and thought that they each had.

Kyle and I turn to each other, make a silent agreement, and go outside. I walk to the left side of the patio and rest my arms on the railing. Kyle does the same. For a while, we just take in the cool breeze, the warm air that lingers after the wind, and the smell of spring.

"I missed this place," I say aloud.

Kyle turns to look at me and nods. "It's been getting warmer these last few days," he says. "I was getting tired of the snow anyway."

"Yeah," I say. "But I miss all the people too. You could hear laughter when you went outside. People used to enjoy Coreno."

"It was Chris's influence that drove them away," Kyle responds. "It's weird to think that he won't be a problem for the galaxy anymore."

I nod, thinking about everything that just happened. Chris is dead, Daniel is severely injured, my parents are reunited, I'm back home, and there isn't a threat to the galaxy anymore; the list is endless.

"By the way," Kyle says. "I've been meaning to ask you what happened after we left the headquarters. If you don't want to talk about it, I understand. I was just curious."

I look at him, not exactly wanting to reimagine what happened, but I see the curiosity dancing on his face. "You know the mind-controlling device Chris used on Mother?" I say. He nods. "He tested something similar on me. It was a serum that allowed him to alter my dreams. It was probably a prototype for what he used on Mother."

"So you were his test subject?" he says, clarifying.

"Yeah, something like that," I say. "Rowan helped me escape from the testing room and then he and I confronted Chris in his office. Chris locked us in there with Kelton, but we eventually escaped. Although, I'm pretty sure Rowan died because he was shot and we couldn't get him out of the room in time."

Kyle looks away from me. "Did you at least *try* to save him?" he asks.

"Yes," I say. "But it's not as easy as it sounds. The door was locked from the outside and I didn't really have a choice."

"Oh," he says. "So what else happened?"

"I met this guard and-"

"Zandrea!" Kyle says astonished. "Haven't you already made that mistake?"

He laughs a little and I roll my eyes, but I laugh along with him. "You didn't let me finish," I say with a smile. "He was a lot like me, except he had been married. You know Cody and Lila? Those are his kids. I brought them with me from Juema."

"You just took his kids from him?" Kyle asks, incredulous.

"No," I say exasperated. I give him a sad smile. "Eli, that was the guard's name, died before I could get him to Juema to see his ex-wife and children."

"How did he die?" Kyle asks.

"Kelton shot him," I say bluntly. "Eli survived for a while, though. After he killed Kelton-"

"Kelton's dead?" Kyle asks astounded.

"Yeah, Eli shot him," I say. "After Kelton shot Eli, I tackled him to the ground and beat him up, but Eli was the one who fired the shot. He lasted long enough to see that his wife didn't care about him and his children didn't know about him. We watched them from a security camera in the headquarters."

"That's sad," Kyle says. "But I can't believe Kelton is dead."

"Yeah, it was crazy, but I'm happy he's gone. And Eli was a good person from what I could tell," I say.

"Why did you bring his kids back with you?" he asks.

"He wanted me to tell his ex-wife that he still loved her," I explain. "That was his dying wish. So I went to Juema to tell her, but after I left her house, I came back to check on her. And so did some Corps' guards. They killed her and her current husband, leaving the children all alone. So I went back to get them."

"What are we going to do with them?" he asks. "I mean, I don't know if Mother and Father will allow them to stay."

"I don't know," I say. "I guess I hadn't really thought about it." I lean my head back and close my eyes. I couldn't imagine giving them up to the Government Child Care Agency. I've grown a special bond with Cody, and Lila seemed to like Daniel when he was disguised as Damien.

The sound of an aircar pulling up to our house interrupts my thoughts. I open my eyes and see three men file out of the aircar. Two of them move around to the back side of the vehicle and open a compartment. They each pull out a black, medium-sized briefcase and begin walking toward the house. At first, I have no idea who they are or what they want and my heart starts racing, but then I see the House's insignia on their breast pockets and relief washes over me.

One of them, the youngest looking of the three, gives me a small nod before ascending the stairs. "Hello," he says in a pleasant tone. "Is Jordan Knowles at this establishment?"

I almost start laughing at the formality of his vocabulary, but I refrain when I see he's serious about the question. "Yes," I say. "He's inside. I can go get him if you want."

He smiles slightly, not showing any teeth. "Thank you for the offer, but we will just knock."

"He might be, um, busy," I say, figuring he and my mother have a lot of catching up to do. "But if knocking is your choice of method, by all means, go ahead."

Kyle gives me a funny look and I know he finds my choice of vocabulary just as humorous as I found the man's. The man gives me a slight nod and knocks on the door.

"Do you two live here?" the oldest looking of the three asks.

"Yes," Kyle says. "Our parents are Jordan and Samantha Knowles."

He nods and turns back to the group just as the door opens. "Hi," a voice says. It belongs to my father. "I think I know what you're here for."

The youngest man holds up his briefcase as if in explanation and says, "I'm sure you do. We're here to investigate the crime scene and the possible murder of Chris Brown, the head of the Intergalactic Corps. Is he still inside?"

"Yes," my father answers. "Along with some of his henchmen. Feel free to come in and do whatever it is that you do."

So that's why they're here. Usually workers from the House don't stop by your home unless they have to investigate something, recruit members for the war, remind the people in the household that their supply of food is ready to be picked up, or if there has been a death in the family. Other than that, if something needs to be said, they will usually leave a message on the home cell saying that someone has to go down to the House to talk with a representative of the government.

The men enter the house and my father closes the door, giving us a tired smile before leaving. A sudden worry runs through me. Something I haven't felt in a while. What if Chris is still somehow alive? What if they try to revive him?

I don't think they would revive him, considering how big of a threat to the galaxy he is. I'm slightly comforted, but I won't be completely until I know for sure he's dead.

"Do you want to go inside and see what they're doing?" Kyle asks, interrupting my thoughts. I look over at him, worry clear on his face.

"Are you okay?" I ask him.

"Yeah, I'm fine," he says. "Are you?"

"I will be, when Chris is gone and we can put all of this behind us."

"Yeah," he says, nodding. "I understand." He hesitates a little bit before going inside the house, leaving me alone with my thoughts.

A slight breeze goes by, and to most people it probably would feel nice on a day like today. But I pull my light jacket tighter around me and decide to go inside. Maybe it'll make me feel better to see the men test Chris's body for a heartbeat and not find it.

When I enter the house, the three men with briefcases are spread out, looking over each body carefully, examining for anything unusual. Kyle stands next to my father, who's watching the men from the lowest step on the staircase. My mother is nowhere to be seen. I walk over to my father and Kyle, both of them looking worried.

"Is everything okay?" I ask them.

"Yes, but they're taking longer than usual," my father says, his eyes staring at the body of one of the guards.

"How do you know what usual is?" I ask.

"Well, when my brother was murdered in his own house because he didn't pay someone back for something, a House worker came to our home and asked if I wanted to go over there," he explains. "I said yes because I wanted to see what happened and maybe say a last goodbye to my brother. They worked much faster."

"But it was only your brother," I say. "One person. There are multiple bodies here."

"True," he says. "But there was only one House worker last time."

I don't feel like waiting around much, so I go upstairs and try to find Cody and Lila. I haven't been upstairs in this house yet, but it looks a lot like my other house. A bedroom off to the right of the staircase, where I would sleep if I lived here. I turn the corner and find a larger bedroom, most likely my father's. That's where I find my mother, huddled over something underneath the bed.

"Mother, are you okay?" I ask.

She sniffles a little before turning to look up at me. "I'll be alright," she says.

"What is that you're holding?"

"Oh this," she says, gesturing to a medium-sized box on her lap. "Nothing. Just mementos I kept from when your father and I were dating."

I sit on the floor next to her, and she shows me what's inside. A napkin with a note on it. A small round pendant hanging from a silver chain. A ticket stub from when they went into the Recreational part of the House together. A small Stoneard wrapped in a cloth for safekeeping.

Everything in the box has so much meaning, especially to her. When she picks up the Stoneard, she brings it near her heart and holds it there, closing her eyes. She looks peaceful and relaxed.

"Did he give you that Stoneard?" I ask.

She looks at me. "Yes, after he came back from one of his excursions. He said it wasn't very valuable, but it was all he could find. However, to me it was probably the most valuable thing I owned and it meant even more coming from him."

Chris took something very special from my parents: a love only heard of in fairy tales. That moment of reunion should have been memorable, monumental. But it wasn't. At least, not in the way it should have been. It's his fault my father left and it's his fault he didn't come back sooner. He took the person I love away too, multiple times. I've never been more glad to have someone out of my life.

Except he isn't. He will never completely leave me. There will always be that part of me that remembers him and everything he did. And the more I think about it, in a way he brought me and the people I love most closer together.

Daniel wouldn't have proposed to me if we didn't end up on Vulcona. We maybe could have got there someday, but it's not certain. My father wouldn't have left, but in a way I feel as though it brought my parents closer together. I haven't seen her this happy in a long time. And there's Kyle, who was a scared little child when this adventure began and is now a young man, ready to take on the world head first. And even Kelton, who helped me grow closer and stronger in my relationship with Daniel. Without him, I may never have realized how much I want, how much I need, Daniel in my life.

I didn't love Kelton, I love what he did for Daniel and me. All those weeks where I thought I loved Kelton, I really just loved Daniel and was too scared to admit it to myself. He brought us closer together without knowing it, without me knowing it. He didn't take anything from me, he supplied me with the materials I needed to realize it's Daniel I want to be with forever. It's Daniel I will choose every time.

Six months later…

"Are you ready to go?" I ask.

"Yes, give me one second," Daniel yells from upstairs.

I look over my dress again and can't believe this day is finally here. It seems like forever ago when he proposed to me for the first time. I was so excited, but other things got in the way and it almost tore us apart. But when he slipped the ring on my finger the second time, every single doubt I had escaped my mind and never returned. That was a few weeks ago.

It's hard for me to remember everything that Chris did to us, since I tried so hard to forget it. But if I focus enough, everything comes back, and I realize the memories never really left me. Some of the memories I'm thankful for, and others I try to lock away in a part of my brain and never let them out. Daniel helps me focus on the present and the future instead of the past, but he has his own problems that won't let him forget.

I walk around in my parents' house as I wait for him. I walk around the staircase and down the hall to my father's office. I stand in the spot where Damien became Daniel. That's a memory I like to visit often.

I walk back out of the room and stand in the area where Chris was shot. I get a chill up my spine just thinking about that afternoon—the way Daniel was able to get the perfect angle that got rid of the galaxy's problem once and for all, the way the men came into the house and hauled him and his henchmen's bodies away, and the way I collapsed into my father's arms because I was too tired to support myself anymore.

I shake my head and move into the kitchen, where the house cell rang. It was a House worker calling to tell us we needed to go downtown right away. Once we did, a representative came to get my parents, Kyle, and me and explained why we were there.

"We ran some tests just to be one hundred percent sure, and yes, Chris Brown is dead," the representative had said. "He was shot in the head and collapsed to the floor of your house, is that correct?"

"Yes, sir," my father responded.

"Because it was manslaughter, we have some paperwork for you to fill out since you are the homeowner of the house he was killed in," the representative said.

"Of course, sir," my father replied. The representative handed him some forms to take home and told him to return them to the Checks and Forms portion of the House when he was done.

Hearing that he was dead was a huge weight lifted off me. Even though I had to wait about a week for them to tell us the results, it was good to know that the galaxy would be rid of him and he wouldn't be tormenting us any longer. When my father turned in the forms, it was a statement of finality that he was gone forever.

I walk out of the kitchen, a full-length mirror greeting me from across the hall. The dress I'm wearing is the same one my mother wore but altered to fit me, complete with blue strands of silk coming down from my waist. My hair is pulled back into a sleek ponytail, blue strands of silk intertwined into the strands of my hair to match my dress.

I hold up my left hand, and my reflection holds up her right. This time, a ring is on both of our second from the left fingers, and she isn't giving me advice. I still remember the dream of me in the mirrored hallway, but now it actually seems like a dream instead of a supposed reality.

My mother comes down the stairs, wearing a light golden dress that reaches to her knees. Her hair is straightened and clipped back on one side. She slips on shoes that give her a little height and walks over to me.

"Oh darling," she says gasping. "You look so beautiful."

"Thank you Mother," I say beaming. She rests her hands on my arms and pulls me into a tight embrace. She smells like sweet spring air.

My father comes down the stairs a little later, wearing a black coat with an elegant white undershirt and bowtie. He puts on his shoes and walks over to us. "You both look amazing," he says, giving my mother a kiss on the cheek.

Kyle follows closely behind my father, wearing a similar ensemble to him. He embraces our mother and then me. "Daniel said he'll be down soon," Kyle reports. "Should we leave now?"

"That's probably a good idea," my father says. Then he turns to me. "You'll be with us shortly?"

"Yeah," I say. "When Daniel gets down here. Is the aircar waiting outside?"

"Yes," my father replies. "We'll take the first one and you guys come when he's ready."

My father helps my mother put on her coat and then grabs his own. Kyle slips on his shoes and coat and they all leave the house, bounding down the stairs. I watch them pull away from the house and toward downtown. The House permits only the immediate family of both the bride and groom for weddings since the marriage room isn't extremely big and most people don't live with extended family anyway. The House sends out notices to extended family so they know there was a marriage in the family, and then they can get together for reunions if desired.

I hear something crash from upstairs and run to find out what the source of the noise was. It leads me to the guest room to the left of the stairs, where Daniel is getting ready. I knock on the open door to let him know I'm there. He turns around, giving me a slight smile. "Hey," he says. His eyes wander to my dress and back to my face. "You look amazing."

"Thank you," I say blushing slightly. I look around the room and see that a small lamp sits sideways on the ground. He follows my gaze and then looks back at me.

"I'm sorry," he says sheepishly. "I was trying to open the closet door and-"

"It's okay," I say, moving into the room. "I never really liked that lamp anyway."

After everything that happened six months ago, my father decided we all should move into this house since our old one was falling apart. In the process of moving, I tried to get my parents to get rid of meaningless things. Or so I thought they were meaningless. My mother nearly scolded me one time after I mentioned getting rid of an old vase.

"That was your grandmother's," she said sternly. "How could you even think of getting rid of that?" It didn't seem special to me but I packed it up anyway as long as it kept her happy.

"Are you almost ready to go?" I ask now.

"Yeah," he says. "Could you help me put my jacket on?"

I walk over to him and grab his jacket that's hanging on the back of the closet door. I help him slip it over one arm and then the second. I grab his bowtie from on top of the dresser and help him tie it.

"Thank you," he says, taking my hand. The feel of metal against my flesh doesn't scare me as much as it used to, but it still brings back memories.

After the announcement of Chris's death to the public, I went to see Daniel in the emergency medical care office downtown. Everyone was still in a daze from hearing that Chris Brown was dead. That the galaxy could end the war and go back about business. A couple days after the announcement of Chris's death, the Corps' headquarters closed down and all of the guards and workers were left to their own devices.

I went to see Daniel to help take my mind off of things, but instead it just filled my head more. One of the nurses explained to me that he lost so much blood that they had to amputate his arm from the shoulder down. I was in such a shock that I didn't even cry until they let me see him. He was asleep, but I could still tell he was in pain. I went to hold his hand, but it wasn't there to hold. I touched his shoulder and moved my hand only slightly farther down before there wasn't anything left except the bed he was laying on.

The nurse touched my shoulder as a gesture of sympathy, and I broke down crying. I hovered over his body like he was gone, as if I would never see him again.

A couple days later, I went back to the medical center. They were in the process of attaching a metal arm to his shoulder. I cried again and the same nurse from before sat next to me and explained what was happening. He was awake at this point, but the nurse said they had given him some numbing shots so he wouldn't feel anything.

He was released a couple days later, and I took him back to my house to help him and let him rest. Once he got better, I properly introduced him to my family and they all seemed to like each other. He's been more limited with the metal arm than before.

It used to scare me that I couldn't feel his body heat when I held his hand. I'm more used to it now, but it's not the same. He still has his other arm, but it's his nondominant one, so he's had to reteach himself basic skills. His metal arm is also not very useful, which makes it harder on him. It doesn't grasp things well and is slow when he tries to move it.

I know he despises Chris even more now that he took something else away from him. But I also know if he had the chance to get one of them back, he would choose his mother every time. It hurts me to know how much pain he's been through, and it hurts me even more that there's really nothing I can do about any of it.

I put my hand on his face, moving my thumb back and forth slowly. He covers my hand with his good one and closes his eyes. I don't want this moment to end, but my family is waiting for us at the House along with a marriage representative. "We should probably go," I whisper.

He nods and removes his hand from mine. Then he sits on the bed and pulls his shoes out of their box. He slips them on, clumsily at first, but he masters it by the second one. He proceeds to stand up slowly, gripping the side of the bed with his good hand. It's hard to watch him struggle, but I know he's come a long way from six months ago.

He walks over to me and takes my hand in his good one, giving it a reassuring squeeze. We head down the hall and descend the stairs, taking it easy and slow. He stumbles a couple of times, but my arm around him gives him reassurance. We make it down to the first floor and I open the door for him. He moves with more ease this time and descends the patio stairs.

The air outside is cool, which feels nice against my skin. A gentle breeze blows through, brushing my hair around. Daniel opens the door of the aircar for me and I slip inside. I smooth my dress and push back the loose strands of hair that fell from my ponytail. After a couple of seconds, Daniel appears next to me. He takes my hand in his, and I can feel the warmth of his skin against mine. It's so comforting, and it's hard for me to imagine life without him.

"Did Lila and Cody go with your family?" Daniel asks me.

"Yeah, I'm pretty sure they did." After the whole fiasco with Chris, I wasn't sure what to do with them. They were so sweet, and I had grown close to both of them. Lila eventually opened up to me, and I've been happier ever since. I remember the day too, and the way it happened. She caught me off guard.

"How did you and Daniel meet?" she asked me. She never really talked to me, so I was taken aback.

But I gained enough composure to answer her. "He taught me how to fly a ship," I told her. She seemed intrigued, so I told her the whole story. By the end of it, she was sitting on the edge of her seat, leaning forward, eating up every word I said. And ever since, we've been close. There have been moments where she'll get sad at the mention of her parents. She asked me one time what Eli was like, and I told her what I knew about him. She seemed upset at the fact that she would never get to meet him, but I assured her that he loved her.

And I felt that I had grown to love both of them too. When I told Daniel this, he said he felt the same way. "It'll be a sad day when we have to give them up," he said.

Then a thought hit me. "Maybe we don't have to."

He gave me a confused look at first, but then things seemed to click into place and a smile slowly crept on his face. "Are you saying…"

I nodded happily. "After we get married, we can legally adopt them." The House's law on adoption is that the couple must be married first, to make it less confusing for the kids. And today is that day. By the end of today, I'll have a husband and two children. And my parents agreed that once Daniel and I got married, we could have the house everyone is currently staying in and my parents would buy the house next to us.

Thinking about all of this makes me so excited that I almost miss seeing the House as we pull into view. The driver pulls up to the curb and gets out of the aircar. He pulls open the door for me, helps me out of the aircar, and then walks around to the other side to help Daniel. I smooth my dress again and walk to the front of the aircar and wait for him. He slowly gets out and makes his way over to me.

"Thank you," I say to the driver. He nods and gets back in the aircar.

I take Daniel's hand in mine and we walk up the stairs that lead to the House.

It's a really big building, three stories high and three blocks long. The stairs are outlined by trees trimmed to perfect spheres. The trees are planted in a bed of small wood carvings, making the air smell of wood and dirt. I take in a deep breath, mostly because the air smells really good but also to calm my nerves.

Daniel can sense my nervousness and he moves his hand from being intertwined with mine to the small of my back. I don't know why I'm nervous, considering I've wanted this pretty much since I met him. But now that the day is here, I'm anxious.

Once we get to the top of the stairs and inside the building, my heart races even more. We walk over to the receptionist's desk. She's on the phone with someone and holds up her index finger to let us know she'll be a minute. I look at Daniel and he sighs, but not from annoyance.

"You know, the first time I proposed to you I was so nervous," he says. "I didn't know what you were going to say and it's not like we really dated or anything. And then after you said yes, I was relieved, until Kelton showed up."

I tense at his name. It's so weird, because I haven't thought about him for a while. I don't have many good memories associated with him, so I try my best to not focus on him.

He laughs a little. "Maybe I should've thanked him though."

"Why?" I ask.

"He made me realize how much I hated life without you in it," he says with a smile.

I smile back at him. "He helped me realize that too."

The receptionist sets the phone back on its holder and looks at us. "Sorry about that. What can I help you with?"

"Wedding for Daniel Thomas and Zandrea Knowles," Daniel replies. She looks at her computer, types something into the screen, and looks back at us.

"Right this way," she says. "My assistant will show you the room."

A young woman comes toward us from down the hall. She's wearing a blue pencil skirt and matching blouse with a pin on the left side. "Hi," she says in a bubbly tone. "Follow me."

She leads us down one of the many hallways leading away from the main lobby of the building. The ceilings are one story high and outlined in a translucent glass. The area is well lit from the natural light, but a huge chandelier hangs from the ceiling, the glass bulbs staggered at perfect intervals.

She leads us down to a room on the right side of the hallway and opens the door. "Everyone is inside," she says. "And, congratulations!"

"Thank you," Daniel says. She walks back the same way we came and disappears around the corner. I squeeze Daniel's real arm and we enter the room.

I'm amazed by how beautiful the room is. Trees decorated with small lights line the outside of the room. Chairs are set up in the middle of the room, with an aisle cutting through the center. A small stage sits at the opposite end of the room, a table across the length of the stage. A smaller chandelier hangs from the ceiling, giving the perfect amount of lighting to the room.

My parents, Kyle, Lila, and Cody sit in the front row of the room, closest to the stage. They turn around when they hear us enter. Soon, music fills the room and that's our cue to walk to the stage. A man appears on the stage, waiting for us. I squeeze Daniel's hand excitedly and walk toward the stage.

Time flies by, and before I know it, a wedding band is being slipped on my finger and Daniel kisses me. One hand is on my face, his thumb gently stroking my cheek. His metal hand is holding mine. I don't want the moment to end, but he pulls away all too fast, and the next thing I know, I'm being ambushed with hugs from my parents.

I'm floating on a cloud, this moment being one I've dreamed of for so long. It almost doesn't seem real, but I know it is. I know this is the happiest day of my life. It's hard for me to imagine everything that happened leading up to this moment since I've been trying to forget it. And despite all that went on, I wouldn't want to change any of it. It helped me realize who I truly love and need in my life.

Meeting Kelton changed my life. He helped me figure out who I loved by forcing me to be without him. I'd like to think that Kelton took Daniel away from me on purpose so I could figure out for myself that I needed him, that I wanted him.

I remember what Eli said about him marrying his best friend. It didn't work out for him. But he also worked for the Corps, an organization that died the day Chris did. No longer a threat to the galaxy. Vulcona has been pretty dead ever since the Corps fell. Everyone who worked for them is stuck trying to find a new job, and most places won't take an ex-Corps employee.

With Chris no longer a threat to Coreno, people have been coming back and reclaiming their homes. We've been getting new neighbors, old neighbors that my mother was friends with, even people from Vulcona looking for a new, safer place to live.

I don't think there will ever be a normal, but I'm okay with that. I'm content with the way things turned out, and even though everything isn't perfect, I've never felt safer than I do right now, in this room, with the people I love most.

The End